Italy
at the End of the
Fifteenth Century

© '05 jackie aher

LEONARDO'S SWANS

LEONARDO'S SWANS

A Novel

Karen Essex

DOUBLEDAY

New York London Toronto Sydney Auckland

PUBLISHED BY DOUBLEDAY
a division of Random House, Inc.

DOUBLEDAY and the portrayal of an anchor with a dolphin
are registered trademarks of Random House, Inc.

Book design by Nicola Ferguson
Endpaper map and illustration by Jackie Aher
Frontispiece: *Leda and the Swan*, School of Leonardo da Vinci (1452–1519);
courtesy of Réunion des Musées Nationaux / Art Resource, NY

Library of Congress Cataloging-in-Publication Data
Essex, Karen.
Leonardo's swans : a novel / by Karen Essex.—1st ed.
        p.   cm.
1. Leonardo, da Vinci, 1452–1519—Fiction. 2. Italy—History—1492–1559—
Fiction. 3. Artists' models—Fiction. 4. Sibling rivalry—Fiction. 5. Milan
(Italy)—Fiction. 6. Sisters—Fiction. 7. Artists—Fiction. I. Title.
PS3555.S682L46 2006
813'.54—dc22   2005048468

ISBN 0-385-51706-8

PRINTED IN THE UNITED STATES OF AMERICA

January 2006
First Edition

1   3   5   7   9   10   8   6   4   2

Leonardo's Swans

Prologue

*I*SABELLA spreads her arms like angels' wings over her sister's cold marble form, running her fingers down the exquisitely carved folds of her burial gown and tracing the delicate veins in her hands. Next to Beatrice, the exiled duke, Ludovico, lies as if in repose, though he is in fact still alive, breathing the dank air of a foul French prison. Isabella must be careful to lavish her grief only on the figure of Beatrice, face so serene upon the pillow of stone, and neglect that of the duke, now out of favor. Isabella knows that from the rear of the church eyes are pointed like daggers at her back, ready to report that her vow to be "a good Frenchwoman" is false. Kneeling, she presses hot, curled lips onto the cheeks of Beatrice's death mask and whispers.

So, my sister, it is true what we always joked—that once you had given birth to a few children, you would be as fat as mother. Only one and twenty at the time of your death, and yet they told me you had taken to wearing vertical stripes to disguise your weight. Still, I did not dream that you could have aged so much so quickly. And to think, for so long I considered you the lucky one.

Who could have predicted such a turn of events? Did you see from your crypt how the whores of the French soldiers made off with all four hundred of your spectacular gowns? The thousands of gems and pearls so delicately sewn and artfully placed have been torn off, I imagine, to buy a potion to end some slut's unwanted pregnancy, or to treat a nasty canker, or to put food in a whore's soon-to-be-toothless mouth. These few years later, the dresses I so coveted are cast aside, filthy and frayed, and you are dust.

Ah, but at least you were buried still clutching a tiny portion of your innocence. You did not live to see the things I have seen, or to make the impossible decisions I have had to make, or to turn your back on those you love to survive their foolish choices. Remember our parlor games? You were always the winner, so clever at Scartino, surprising everyone with your moves and taking the purse. I have been playing a similar game, though every move has to be made with great care. I have chilled my own blood with some of my decisions. Beatrice, I am a fig-ure on a chessboard of poison, where the players change from black to white and back without notice. Remember the elaborate system of trumps at which you were so adept? With which you, giggling hysteri-cally, won game after game of cards? There is a new dimension to the landscape now that neither you nor your duke anticipated, but I did: France trumps Italy, and that is that.

If Fortuna had not been so fickle, so remiss in the proper arranging of things, and our roles had been reversed—if I had had my way— would I be lying in your grave? Or would the course of history have been changed? How is it conceivable that your illustrious husband, whose attention I craved, wastes away in a French prison with only a copy of The Divine Comedy *and a pet dwarf to give him solace? Wouldn't you love to know whose face he tries to conjure as he falls asleep on his lice-ridden bed of straw—which sister? Which mistress? Poor Ludovico. He doesn't even have Magistro Leonardo's images of his lovers to console him now.*

My own match of wills with Leonardo has continued. I wonder if you haven't reached out from the grave, Beatrice, to meddle with my ambitions. Without your interference, and with the power I hold over his new patron, I should have concluded my business with Leonardo by now. I have pledges from the artist himself, but you know what a promise from Leonardo is worth. Sometimes I think he is the most adept player of us all. And yet, there are whispers that I might receive satisfaction from him on this very evening. Wouldn't that be lovely, my sister? Then, you and I might both rest.

The bell in the tower rings the five o'clock hour. I would love to stay with you past the twilight time. I remember that you do not like to be left alone in the dark. But I must go dress for yet another of King Louis's balls, where we shall all convene in the very rooms where you once lived, in the service of the new master, carefully avoiding any mention of the past—including yourself. Adieu, my love. Remember how we hated to speak the French language? One must speak it all the time now.

The bells have stopped chiming, and Isabella imagines that her attendants grow impatient with the visit. Still, she finds that she does not wish to leave. She stands, caressing Beatrice's peaceful visage one more time, touching her stony locks, and nestling a warm cheek against her sister's cold, chiseled one.

Beatrice, Beatrice, it's not that I didn't love you. You were like the swans in your pond—born awkward and ugly, maturing into beauty, bringing magic into the world, and singing at the hour of your death. You mythical creature, who on earth or above could not have loved you? It's just that for so long, I imagined that you had stolen my Destiny, when all the while, unbeknownst to us, you were preserving it for me.

Chapter One

X * FORTUNA (CHANCE)

FROM THE NOTEBOOK OF LEONARDO:
When Fortune comes, seize her firmly at the forelock, for I
tell you, she is bald at the back.

IN THE YEAR 1489; IN THE CITY OF FERRARA

SHE grew up in a land of fairy tales and miracles. That is what Isabella is explaining to Francesco as they ride through Ferrara's streets. It is Christmastime, and though there is no snow on the dry stone road, the horses shoot clouds of steam into the frigid air through their nostrils.

This is the first time she has been allowed to escort her fiancé through the city on one of his visits. Francesco Gonzaga, future Marquis of Mantua, has come to Ferrara to romance his soon-to-be bride and to enjoy the city's many Christmas pageants ordered by Isabella's father, Duke Ercole d'Este, a great patron of the theater. Isabella believes that the more she tells Francesco of

Ferrara's secrets and wonders, and the more she shows him of her father's spectacular building projects and improvements, the more he will realize her value.

In this very church, Isabella says, pointing to St. Mary's of the Ford, almost two hundred years ago on Easter Sunday, the priest broke the Eucharist in two, and flesh and blood came spraying forth, covering the walls of the church and splattering the entire flock.

"The parishioners watched in awe," Isabella says, eyes wide with drama. "The Bishop of Ferrara and the Archbishop of Ravenna came to see it. They instantly recognized it as the body and blood of Christ and declared it a true miracle of the Eucharist."

Francesco solemnly makes the sign of the cross as they ride past the church, but his eyebrows arch skeptically, making him look entirely out of step with the act.

Beatrice trots ahead of the pair of lovers, her long braid swinging in saucy rhythm with the horse's mane, as uninterested as her steed in their conversation.

"Isn't that right, Beatrice?" Isabella asks her sister for confirmation of her story, hoping that the odd girl does not say anything to contradict her. Beatrice is a puzzle to Isabella, a fact that the older sister blames on the girl's unsupervised upbringing in wild Naples. The girl is a feral, unformed thing, alternately shy, naïve, aloof, and bold—the latter especially apparent when riding or hunting. How such a small fourteen-year-old girl, who is not particularly courageous outside of these activities, excels at all manly sport is a mystery to Isabella, but the fact of Beatrice's prowess remains, no matter how enigmatic.

"I wouldn't know. I wasn't there!" Beatrice finally answers without turning around, but they can hear her laugh at her own joke.

The animal's swaying ass taunts Isabella, who knows that her sister is dying to break away from them to test the horse's speed.

Francesco has brought Drago, the pure white Spanish charger, from his family's stud farm on the island of Tejeto, as a gift for the girls' father. But Beatrice immediately took over the animal, talking to him in whispers that should be reserved for a lover, and hopping upon him and riding away, as if the painstakingly bred horse was meant to carry a little girl in a pink riding dress and not a fearsome knight in armor.

"I'll tell you a miracle that happened right here in Ferrara that is even better," Francesco says, sidling his horse right up to Isabella's so that their legs touch. She knows she should pull away, that her mother would rail against this sort of indiscriminate physical contact, even with leather riding boots providing a barrier to the couple's much-craved intimacy, but instead, she rides with slow care so that they might continue to brush against one another.

"What miracle is that?" she asks, suppressing a smile.

"That your father agreed that you should be my wife," he answers.

You have no idea just how miraculous, she thinks. If the timing had been slightly different, he would be marrying the jaunty girl riding ahead of them, but this, he does not know. When the marriage agreements were made nine years ago, Isabella was only six and Beatrice five. Who could have cared at that time which sister married what man, as long as both marriages were politically expedient for the city-state of Ferrara? Isabella wants to tell him the story but she would need him to say that if things had worked out differently, his life would have been a ruin. And he cannot possibly say that in front of Beatrice.

Duchess Leonora had long ago drummed into her daughters' heads that marriage between noble houses was no whimsical arrangement based on ephemeral qualities of preference or attraction. The peace of Italy depended on these unions, especially at this juncture. The Venetians had become doubly aggressive since the Turks pushed them out of Constantinople. They began to push farther and farther inland into Italy because they needed land for their farms and their citizens. They hired condottieri to take over towns—Verona, Padua, and Vincenza, all near Ferrara. The Venetians wanted complete control over the trade routes and the rivers, as well as the land. Ferrara was venerable and strong, but small. For her to remain independent, she must have strong alliances with the city-states of Mantua and Milan.

"You girls are ambassadors of Ferrara. Its welfare depends upon the success of your marriages. Therefore, you must do nothing, *nothing*, to endanger these alliances. You must do nothing prior to the marriages that may cause the families to renege on the commitments. Your behavior must be impeccable. You are as much the protectors of Ferrara's welfare as our army or our treasury. You are, in fact, its greatest treasures. And when you enter your husbands' houses, I expect you to act like it. Your bodies are the very bindings that will hold us all together and stave off conflicts and wars. Do not think that you can behave like the women in fairy tales and poetry. The duke and I will not tolerate it."

Looking at Francesco now, Isabella thinks that she must be the most fortunate of women. Her fiancé is not handsome, but has a rugged quality that gives an ugly man appeal. Already three and twenty, he will never be tall, and his eyes bulge, a condition that she knows will worsen over time, because she has seen old men with this affliction, and they look like reptiles. Yet he is as solidly built as any man alive, and his courtly manners contrast so thrillingly with the wicked look in his protruding brown eyes. Besides being from one of the oldest noble families in Italy, he already is considered a brilliant student of warfare, destined for an illustrious career in the military arts. Undoubtedly he will lead one of Italy's great armies to many victories. Isabella feels that Francesco is the perfect man to help her realize her destiny—which is to have a powerful husband and reign with him over a great and enlightened realm.

Beatrice, riding three lengths in front of them, begins to pick up speed. She turns her head to the side, giving the lovers a sprightly profile, before dashing off with the horse.

"We had better follow her," Francesco says, a look of grave concern coming over his face.

"That will not be easy," Isabella replies.

Isabella does not like to see any interest in her sister from her betrothed, though she cannot imagine why. With her exceptional qualities, she should not worry one bit. But worry she does. Francesco is from a family famous for breeding horses. Nothing arouses the passions of the Gonzagas of Mantua like a great horse, or a rider who can handle one. Beatrice looks back one more time before guiding Drago through one of the city's grand arched portals to a road where she can ride faster. Francesco takes up the challenge and speeds after her on his dark stallion, the jewels in his silver saddle catching just enough of the winter sun to sparkle.

Isabella follows, but at a slower pace. It would be extremely unladylike for her to compete with her boyish sister in this game for Francesco's attention. Besides, she does not want to sweat so badly under her new habit that she will be embarrassed later, when, helping her descend from the steed, Francesco will take her small hand and slyly raise it to his lips. Let Beatrice dismount in her typical disheveled state—damp, stringy hairs hanging about her face, and oozing sweat like the horses she rides into the ground. Isabella settles into a steady canter as the two race ahead of her, first Francesco taking the lead, then Beatrice gaining on him, so close that it looks from this distance as if she is trying to make her horse bite his stallion's rear end.

If one is to look upon the two sisters objectively, as Isabella prays Francesco does, one has to observe Isabella's advantages. Isabella has spent all her life at her distinguished mother's knee, while Beatrice, from the ages of two to ten, was left behind at the court of Naples all the way on the other side of Italy as a peace offering to their grandfather, King Ferrante, whom everyone feared and hated, but who had taken an instant liking to Beatrice.

Isabella reads Latin impeccably and can recite Virgil's *Eclogues* to the satisfaction of her tutors and her father's eminent guests. Beatrice, on the other hand, has spent the four years since her return to Ferrara being pushed to catch up with her sister in their studies. She can barely spell. She can recite a poem or two in Latin, but Isabella doubts that she has any idea of what she is saying. Isabella plays musical instruments and sings like an angel. Beatrice loves music, but must be sung to. Isabella has studied rhetoric and mathematics and can take either side in an argument over at least one Platonic dialogue. Beatrice enjoys poetry, but prefers that others read it to her. Isabella is the loveliest dancer in all of Ferrara, turning her head elegantly this way and that. Not only does she have the correct timing, style, and balance necessary for the art, she also knows just where to place her smile as she turns, dips, and lowers her head, eyes lingering on their specific target, until the lids fall modestly in time with the music. Beatrice manages at dance, but is no match for her graceful sibling. Isabella has read all of the books in her father's library and all of her mother's romance novels about the chivalric days of old. She has watched carefully as her parents commissioned and acquired paintings and other works of art from the most illustrious talents of the age.

In addition to her intellectual accomplishments, Isabella has tumbling blond curls, large, wide-set black eyes, and a slender body. Beatrice shows signs of stoutness, with thick thighs and ankles, though only her sister, her servants, and her husband—should the man to whom she is engaged actually honor their betrothal—will ever know this. She has a round face, a small, uninteresting nose, and dark hair that lacks luster, so much so that she must wear it in a long pigtail down her back. She prefers the outdoors to all pursuits. She is the kind of person Isabella would not find terribly interesting if she were not her sister.

Isabella consistently outperforms Beatrice in all pursuits but this, the equestrian. Now, and in the presence of her betrothed,

Isabella fears Beatrice is trying to make her pay for her crimes of superiority.

Suddenly Francesco stops, pulling in the animal, whipping him about so that he is facing Isabella. She realizes that he is looking for her, has stopped this competition with her sister because *she* has entered his mind, even in the midst of the wild ride.

Beatrice, who has bolted ahead, stops too. No longer enjoying the ride without the competitive aspect, she trots back to him. Isabella hears Francesco say, "I wanted you to show me the city's newest improvements, not race me to your death."

"You just don't want to lose to a woman," Beatrice retorts, flushed scarlet from her escapade, adjusting the velvet cap that she wears at a clever tilt.

"Do you fail to remember that I was not losing?" he answers.

"Settle down," Isabella says in Beatrice's direction, hoping that she does not sound too much like the admonishing older sister, the sour one who does not want to be a part of their game. "We are supposed to be showing him the city!"

"Be a good girl, or I'm going to take Drago back home with me," Francesco says to Beatrice in a tone that conspires with Isabella's parental attitude toward her sister.

Beatrice clutches the reins close to her chest. "He wouldn't go. He would run away with me first!"

"Don't be too sure, little princess," he replies, sounding like a father.

Thank God he considers her a child and Isabella a woman! Satisfied that she can recapture Francesco's attention with her more mature demeanor, Isabella leads them over the bridge and back inside the city walls.

"Now, Beatrice, do listen to what I am telling Francesco so that when your betrothed comes to visit Ferrara, you might show him these same things."

Beatrice groans. The subject is a sore one.

Mistress once more of the little expedition, Isabella explains how the city of Ferrara has changed in recent years; how her father, the duke, had gotten it into his mind to rebuild the city along the enlightened architectural guidelines set by Leon Battista Alberti, the Genoan. She explains (to demonstrate her knowledge of not only architecture, city planning, and mathematics but political subtleties as well) how Ercole had sent to his ally, Lorenzo the Magnificent in Florence, for the ten manuscripts of Alberti's *De re aedificatoria*, to set about modernizing his city and its buildings according to that great theorist's vision. Streets were widened into broad avenues. New structures were created with careful attention to classical values of proportion and harmony. Aesthetics were linked with and equal to the mathematical proportions of things.

While all this construction had flown up around her, Isabella had felt that, along with the old-fashioned city of pointed arches and endless spires, life itself was spreading out in broader directions. Narrow streets, dark halls with low ceilings, and cramped corridors were things of the past. Lamps and candles illuminated rooms once kept dark. People were reading and talking in these well-lit drawing rooms late into the night. Ancient manuscripts, once the property of the church and private collectors alone, were being translated from Greek and Latin into Italian right here at Ferrara's university, and Venetian and Milanese printers were making copies of them and selling them all over the country. In the years after her father had defeated and executed his rivals and made peace with the Venetian Republic, the old Castello d'Este with its famous four towers was quickly transformed from fortress to grand residential palazzo. The soldiers, along with their weapons and artillery, were moved to the older, colder, more stern quarters, while the family and members of the court occupied the newer and more spacious halls and apartments, decorated with the works of the greatest artists of the decades, all of whom had passed through Ferrara in the service of the Este family—Pisanello, Piero della Francesca, the Venetian Jacopo Bellini, Cosimo Tura.

Isabella points out to her beloved Francesco and her uninterested sister an example of the new architecture, the Palazzo dei Diamante, the residence named from her father's sobriquet, the Diamond. Twelve thousand diamond shapes jut into the air from the palazzo's ominous façade—not exactly a subtle reminder of Duke Ercole's omniscient power over Ferrara, but an effective one.

"Do they call him the Diamond because he is worth so much?" Francesco asks.

"It's because he's thin and sinewy and his body is cut in hard lines," Beatrice pipes in, suddenly part of the conversation.

"It's because in negotiations, he's as hard as the hardest rock," Isabella says. "Something your family undoubtedly found out when they negotiated our marriage contract."

"I think he made a terrible deal for himself," Francesco replies.

"Why?" Isabella asks, now wishing to defend her father.

"Because you are priceless, that's why. If you were my daughter, I would know that you were too good for any man."

Beatrice skewers her face at Francesco, in mock disgust over his syrupy lover's comment.

"You probably stole that from some bad poet," she says.

"Or a stable boy courting a kitchen maid," Isabella teases. It would not do to let Francesco know how deeply his every word affects her.

BEATRICE looks restless. Isabella watches her sister's eyes scan the city walls as if she is looking for an escape. Isabella gets jittery when she sees this mood descend over the younger girl. She can tell by the sudden, secretive smile and the darting eyes that Beatrice has a new surprise and is searching for just the right moment to reveal it. Beatrice is often predictable in her unpredictability.

Isabella tries to distract her sister by beginning a new conversation. "My father's latest project is to rebuild the city walls,"

she says, gesturing to the towering redbrick fortifications, decorated with hand-carved medallions of the city's symbols, and the
crests and portraits of the illustrious members of the ruling Este
family from days gone by.

"At the top are wide footpaths. You can see all the way out into
the countryside, beyond the Po River. If you like, you can circle
the entire city."

"Or anticipate an invader, which is more likely what your
father had in mind," Francesco adds.

"You men with your military minds!" Isabella says, flashing
him a smile that lets him know that she is saying it with admiration.

Before she can bring her lips back together, the thing that
Isabella has anticipated and feared begins. Beatrice breaks from
the other two, pulls back her horse's head, and eggs him on up the
brick stairs that lead to the top of the city walls. Isabella would
like to simply be annoyed at her attention-seeking sister, but the
problem is twofold. First, one is not allowed to take horses to the
top of the wall. Second, and perhaps more serious, the project is
not yet finished. Great gaping holes leave the brick walkways dis-
connected. But Beatrice is not one to think on these things. She is
not particularly observant, nor does she plan ahead.

Duke Ercole's sentries on the walls' top tier anticipate the
runaway rider, ready to apprehend the unruly person, until they
recognize the duke's daughter. Everyone knows that she spent too
many years with her indulgent grandfather in faraway Naples.
Without the watchful eye of her mother to restrain her, the girl
was allowed to run wild, much to the king's amusement. It was
said everywhere that the mean old man encouraged the girl in her
antics, much the way that little boys tease their dogs until they
bite. So that when the sentries realize it is just Beatrice, they
shake their heads and jump out of her way, one even bowing as
she rides by as if inviting her passage. Isabella knows that they
assume, as does Francesco, that Beatrice will give a little per-

formance for her companions below and then come down. Isabella knows her sister better.

Beatrice looks down at the astonished Francesco, taunting him by taking off her little cap and tossing it in his direction. "Remember me!" she cries. Then she cracks her leather whip on the horse's flank and is gone. When the sentries realize where she is headed and at what breakneck speed, they abandon their posts, futilely running after her on foot.

"Beatrice! Stop!" calls Isabella. The girl hears her, she is sure, but only looks down once with a fast and gloating glance to see that she is leaving the others behind. Isabella kicks her own beast, racing along the walls to catch up with Beatrice.

Isabella imagines her sister's big, round laugh freezing into a circle of panic when the girl sees what is ahead. The wall comes to an end, dropping off many feet below where a few bricklayers work lazily in the cold from wooden scaffolds. Perhaps ten feet of empty space separates the new path from the old. Isabella anticipates the calamity, and prays that her sister has seen the danger. She does not quite like or understand this untamed creature, spoiled by too many years of Neapolitan splendor, untempered by parental discipline, but she does not want to see her hurt.

Beatrice, long brown plait flying behind her like a kite, makes no motion to pull in the beast, but pushes him on, faster and faster, toward the crevasse. Francesco and Isabella both scream madly for her to stop, but the girl either no longer hears them over the sound of her horse's hooves on the uneven bricks, or she does hear but is out of her mind, possessed by some demon that causes mental disease—something Isabella has considered about her before. The desperate sentries chase after the duke's daughter, and the others keep yelling her name louder and with increasing horror.

Beatrice's elbows pump wildly as if she believes she can take flight over the great gap in the wall. Like a creature in a fairy tale suddenly transforming into a bird, she leaps into the air on her animal's back, and he, like Pegasus, flies beneath her. Her body is aloft, high above the seat, as the horse stretches its length, trying to please the will of its rider.

The animal's natural stride is impossibly short to gap the distance, and Isabella wants to turn her eyes away to avoid seeing Beatrice tumble down the wall, the horse falling upon her and crushing her to death. But something about the way that her sister seems to float above the animal, relieving it of her weight, forces her to keep watching.

Francesco is now making the sign of the cross with the heavy silver crucifix he wears at his neck in utter earnestness and is calling upon his God. But Beatrice does not need Divine intervention. The horse's front legs close the distance, hitting hard the bricks of the old pathway. Before Isabella can feel any relief, she sees that the animal's back legs are slipping down the gap. The horse scrambles to achieve balance, his hinds churning as if he is trying to turn them into wheels. It looks for a moment as if animal and girl might career backward down the wall and onto the bricklayers who, instead of leaping from the scaffolds to their own deaths, or at least to broken bones, hunch over, hands on heads, to try to protect themselves from the inevitable. But Beatrice, unfazed, yells, "Oh, come on!" and pushes the animal, against all laws of motion, up the craggy wall and onto the footpath. Triumphant, laughing, she looks back at her two companions, gives a little cock of the head, and rides away.

Isabella, breathless, heart pounding, turns to Francesco expecting him to share in her anger. Instead, he does not even try to hide an admiring smile.

"Fearless," he says, watching the girl gallop toward the palace.

"IF your father had waited a mere month to send his ambassadors to Ferrara, Beatrice would have been yours, and I would have been marrying Ludovico of Milan." Then Isabella adds co-quettishly, though not without trepidation: "Would you have liked that?"

Isabella and Francesco are standing in a small parlor in the Castello where two portraits of the sisters are displayed side by side, waiting for Francesco's servants to pack Isabella's image in layers and layers of cloth for safekeeping through the journey back to Mantua. Isabella is scrutinizing Beatrice's portrait to see if there is anything Francesco might find more pleasing to his eye than in hers.

"Only if I had a taste for plump little boys instead of exquisite beauties."

Isabella is certain that Francesco should not be saying these kinds of things to her before they are married, nor should she allow him to pass such an unflattering remark about her sister, but his words make a flutter in her stomach, erasing all feelings of impropriety. Besides, she had nothing to complain over. Her be-trothed—this manly figure who is to inherit the title of Marquis of Mantua from his father—is here in Ferrara courting her while Beatrice's affianced, Ludovico Sforza, who isn't even Duke of Milan, but regent to his young nephew, shows nothing but disin-terest in their pending marriage.

One of the purposes of Francesco's visit, besides enjoying the renowned Christmas pageants, was to bring to Isabella's mother a painting she craved by Andrea Mantegna, Mantua's court painter, and to collect the betrothal portrait by Cosimo Tura of the lovely Isabella. Cosimo had been commissioned to paint be-trothal portraits of both sisters, though Ludovico has been too busy with his latest mistress to send an emissary to pick up the one of Beatrice. This, after Messer Giacomo Trotti, Ferrara's am-bassador to Milan, had to embarrass him into commissioning the piece in the first place. Other gossip circulating Ferrara's court is that Ludovico had to be invoiced three times for the four florins owed the artist before he finally paid.

Isabella had loved being painted, loved how the maestro's brushstrokes replicated her very existence. She loved being frozen in time at this precious moment, when her maidenhood was rapidly coming to an end. What magic it was to be able to halt fleeting time! Forever she would be remembered at this age, with her face and body and countenance in this state. That a portraitist could reproduce not only a physical being but a singular moment—in this case, one in which she turned her face slightly to the left but cast her eyes directly at the artist as if answering a question—was miraculous to her. If she could, she would be painted every day of her life to record her progress.

She had prepared arduously for the sitting. Cosimo was an old man now, but famous for having painted the exquisite altarpiece at San Giorgio in which the serene Blessed Virgin holds a sleeping Christ on her lap. Her eyes gaze gently downward at the angelic musicians playing celestial music for her pleasure. For Isabella, the painting had mysterious powers. Every time she attended Mass at the church with her family, her eyes remained riveted not to Our Lady or to the winsome child, but to the color green that seemed to jump out of the painting and animate the wooden panel to life.

"The road to achieving all perfection in womanhood on earth, and eternal bliss in Heaven, is paved by meditation on the sweet face of Our Lady," her mother assured her time and again, pleased that her daughter could not remove her eyes from the religious scene. But it was the composition and color scheme of the piece that intrigued Isabella. When she looked at the panel, she felt as if her ears were miraculously filled with saintly music. She could hear the lutes, trumpets, and chorus of voices, and she attributed this phenomenon to the life-giving powers of that strange green, which had not the verdant color of nature but the radiance of jewels.

Convinced of the color's magical properties, she had asked her mother to have their favorite Venetian silk dyer replicate it in the dress she would wear to sit for Cosimo Tura's portrait. There is no need, Leonora had replied. The painter already knows how to produce the color. But Isabella argued until her mother went to her parsimonious father with the request, and their Venetian agent was sent a color sample, a small block of wood with a swash of the paint placed upon it by Cosimo himself, and the fabric was produced and procured. Isabella had sat for Cosimo wearing the gown, which she accented with a brocade vest in the pinkish color also found in the upper reaches of the altarpiece because she had so loved the contrast of the two colors. Her parents complained of her exacting tastes, but what did they expect? "It is because I have been raised by two connoisseurs," she countered.

The portraits further contrasted the sisters. Leonora had insisted that both girls wear their hair loose about the shoulders like Neapolitan princesses, a look that was most attractive to men of all ages. But the coif only suited Isabella, whose blond curls danced about her shoulders in springy coils. "Like little golden snakes," her father had said, curling one golden lock about his finger. "It is as if Our Lord, to make up for the sins and cruelty of the pagan gods, has re-created Medusa as an angel." Beatrice's dark hair, let loose from its plait, looked limp. She had sat for her portrait in a royal blue gown with tiny pearls sewn in crisscross patterns across the bodice. Her puffed sleeves were of an unusual scarlet, embroidered with blue roses that matched the body of the dress. Isabella had to admit that her sister, despite all her other oddities, did have nice taste in clothing, and was as meticulous about her dressmaking as Isabella herself. Yet the rest of her toilette lacked style, and her natural appearance was not the most impressive, at least not at this age. Luckily, the two sisters were not painted together, where their differences would be in sharp relief.

"I am going to take this beautiful picture back with me to Mantua," Francesco tells Isabella, reaching for her hand. "But I cannot decide whether to hang it in a place of great prominence, so that everyone can admire your beauty, or whether I will put it in a private place, where I alone might meditate upon it. It is only one year until our wedding, but for me, it will seem painfully long."

It is thrilling for Isabella to hear these words, which reflect her own thoughts, though she cannot resist interjecting her opinion: "If I were you, I would hang it where others can admire it as well. That should add to your meditations, not detract."

Why hide a thing of beauty?

To think that he can take a piece of her back with him to his Castello, which she will soon occupy. Isabella is grateful that in less than one year the portrait will soon be back in her possession. She adores collecting beautiful things, and would hate to have a portrait done by a master of painting lost to her. All that she has collected thus far she will be allowed to take with her into her marriage—the many cameos, the intaglios cut so delicately by Ferrara's jewelers, the trunks painted by famous artists that hold her wardrobe, and the necklaces and belts that she designed with the smiths. Of these she is most proud because they are expressions of herself.

"Of course," Francesco concedes to the request to display her portrait. "Why should I have all the pleasure of looking at you myself?"

Exactly.

He has been, thus far, the most delightful of potential husbands. Though he is twenty-three years to her fifteen, and possessed of superior maturity, over the years of their engagement, he has written her at least one letter per season, assuring her that he lives for the day when they will be husband and wife. If word reached him that she was ill, he always sent a fine gift in the form of a perfect pearl pendant, a foggy miniature landscape by a new Flemish painter, or once, when a high fever had held her too long in its grip, a tiny Spaniel puppy that licked the fever from her face, or so she believed.

"So one month might have changed our destinies?" Francesco asks. "Tell me the story of how I almost was made to live out my life in utter misery, without your companionship."

So she tells him how, many years ago, when Isabella was only six years old, Ludovico Sforza had sent an ambassador to Ferrara to ask for the hand of Duke Ercole's eldest daughter. Ludovico was a rising star in Italian politics. Already the Duke of Bari and the regent to his nephew, Gian Galeazzo, Duke of Milan, Ludovico was thought by many to be the most illustrious young ruler of his day. He did, however, have a reputation for a certain wickedness. But, as Fortuna had it, one month prior, the Gonzagas of Mantua, important because of its geographic location between the powerful city-state of Milan and the Most Serene Republic of Venice, had sent their own emissary to ask for the hand of Isabella. And because an alliance with Mantua was crucial for the welfare and safety of Ferrara, Duke Ercole happily concluded negotiations for Isabella to marry Francesco Gonzaga, who would become marquis upon the death of his father. The Milanese messenger had to return to Ludovico to ask if the second daughter of Ercole d'Este would do. And the answer came with great swiftness—yes. Later it was discovered that Ludovico did not mind that Beatrice was only five years old and would not be ready for marriage for at least ten years. He was a supreme ladies' man, and was in no hurry—and indeed, perhaps had no particular intention—to settle down.

"I shudder to think how Fortuna might have played her cards differently, and I could have been saddled with an old man like Ludovico, who—goodness!—is already almost forty," she says boldly to Francesco. He looks at Beatrice's portrait and Isabella's portrait and does the thing that he must know makes her whole body quiver, which is to kiss her hand, letting his lips linger two seconds or three past propriety. "I shudder too," he says.

Oh, he was perfect! At the Christmas pageants, for which people came from all over Italy, he sat next to the duke at each performance, complimenting him on his devotion to reviving the theater. To please the clergy, Ercole always staged a religious tableau or two so they wouldn't complain about his more pagan theatrical endeavors. This year, Ercole chose the Annunciation for the opening pageant, in which a bold player wearing angel wings flew onstage on ropes to announce the Virgin's fate. The following evening they witnessed a reenactment of the birth of Christ in a manger. The court artists had filled the stage with real barnyard animals, and at times the bleating goats drowned out the players' words. Still everyone agreed that this did not distract from the drama of the tableau, but added realism, since such animals were undoubtedly present at Our Lord's birth.

After Christmas, and to celebrate the New Year of 1490 as well as the beginning of a new decade, the duke let loose his passion for the sort of theatrical presentations he loved. In the old Palazzo della Ragione, remodeled into a theater, he presented ancient Latin comedies which he himself translated into Italian, hiring actors, dancers, and musicians from all over Italy. He collaborated with Niccolò da Correggio on a new version of Ovid's *Metamorphoses*, a lavish production with music, dance, and recitation. Francesco sat with the duke during the performance, gasping in awe at how convincing the actors were in both behavior and costume as the gods of old, thus proving himself a worthy son-in-law.

Isabella did see her betrothed making flirtatious conversation with some of the ladies of the court, which she did not like at all. She had thought that this enticing demeanor of his had been her private reserve. But her fiancé had charm to spare, and virility too, and someday, she reminded herself, she would be the happy recipient of all of that. In the meanwhile, her mother, Leonora, counseled her that a woman must always forgive her husband any indulgences before the marriage. For it was natural for an unmarried man to give in to these urges. And besides, it did not do for two innocents to tumble into bed together after a wedding and have to figure out the entire map of lovemaking. If he carried these proclivities into the marriage, well, a woman could choose to rebel and demand fidelity, or to adjust and remain silent. Either way, the outcome would probably be the same. The man would do whatever he wished, quietly or openly, for that was the nature of men. Some Italian women were getting just as bad, but thanks to Our Lord and her own good discipline, Leonora was certain her daughters would not join the ranks of the promiscuous. The women of the House of Este must be above these things.

"So if Ludovico Sforza had been less interested in making mischief in Milan and more interested in arranging a good marriage for himself, I would be taking home the portrait of Beatrice? Is that what you are telling me?" Francesco smiles naughtily as his valet shakes out the thick muslin he will use to wrap the painting of Isabella.

"That is correct," she says as she watches her image disappear behind the heavy white cloth. "The court records show that there were a mere thirty days between the arrival of the ambassador from Mantua and the arrival of the ambassador of Milan."

"Then your family concluded the business of our marriage rather quickly. Perhaps they were afraid you would receive no more offers," he teased.

"Sir!" she exclaims. Might he really believe that? "Have you so little regard for me?"

Francesco quickly takes her aside, away from the ears of his servants. "It was God Himself pushing your father to hurry because He ordained this union from Heaven. You are not meant for Ludovico of Milan or anyone else, but me. That is what our marriage is going to be, Isabella. Heaven."

How does he always know exactly what to say to please her? He is right; marriage with any other man is unthinkable. How grateful she is that she will spend her life with the man she loves while her sister must go live in the strange city of Milan in a huge fortress where her husband pleasures himself with the company of other women.

"What about you, my dear Isabella? Do you not wish the ambassador from Mantua had slipped from his horse, or had run into terrible weather or a band of thieves or something else to detain him so that you would be going to Ludovico? He intends to rule a great portion of the European continent, you know."

"Oh, how can you suggest that? Ludovico is old and terrible! He has no interest in marriage. Beatrice's portrait will probably be eaten by worms before he sends someone to collect it!" She leans as close to her fiancé as she dares to share her secret. "It is very bad, sir, what has happened. Please do not betray my confidence. My father had no higher wish than to marry his daughters in a double wedding, but Ludovico refused, making some excuse for why he could not marry next year. Messer Trotti, our ambassador to Milan, has pushed him as hard as he dares to set a firm date into the future, but Ludovico will not! They say he is in love with a woman named Cecilia, who is very beautiful, and that he holds her up as a wife in his court. But her family is of no use to him politically, and therefore he cannot marry her. My poor sister! Do you think I would trade places with her?"

Francesco does not seem at all surprised by this news, gossip in Italy being impossible to suppress. Perhaps the entire country knows of Ludovico's slight to Beatrice and to the Este family. Francesco does, however, take advantage of being this close to his beloved with no eyes upon them. He moves his lips to her neck. He doesn't kiss her exactly, but takes in a deep breath, as if he wishes to carry her scent with him back to Mantua. He runs his nose the length of her neck from the bottom of her ear to the nape, breathing her in. Then, he pulls away, whispering, "That will have to linger in our memories until our wedding day."

While she is still recovering, she realizes that he and his valet and her portrait are gone, and she will not see him again for three months.

To: Ludovico Sforza, Duke of Bari, Regent of Milan
From: Leonardo the Florentine, Master of Engineering,
Weaponry, and Painting

Most Illustrious Lord,

Having now seen the creations of all those who call themselves masters and inventors of the instruments of war, and finding that these inventions are no greater in any respect than those in common use, I am emboldened to write to you to acquaint you with my secrets, and offer to demonstrate at any convenient time all those assertions which are recorded below:

1. I have designs for bridges that are light, strong, and easily carried to pursue and defeat the enemy. I also have plans for destroying the enemy's bridges and siege equipment.
2. I know how to cut off water from trenches, and how to construct an infinite number of movable shelters, scaling ladders, and other instruments crucial to the enterprise of a siege.
3. I have plans for destroying every fortress or other stronghold unless it has been founded upon rock.
4. I have designs for making cannon, very convenient and easy to transport, with which to hurl small stones like a rain of hail, causing great terror, loss, and confusion to the enemy.
5. I can make armored vehicles, safe and unassailable, which will infiltrate the ranks of the enemy.
6. I can make cannon, mortars, and light ordnance of very beautiful and useful shapes, quite different from those already in use.
7. I can supply catapults and other engines of wonderful efficacy for slinging great stones and other instruments of destruction.
8. Also, in times of peace, I will prove myself as adept as anyone else in architecture and in the construction of buildings, and in conducting water from one place to another.

9. I can execute sculpture in marble, bronze, or clay, and also painting, in which my work will stand comparison with anyone else, whoever he may be.

10. Finally, I would undertake the work of making the bronze horse, which shall honor the memory of your father and the illustrious House of Sforza.

If any of the aforesaid claims seem impossible, I offer myself as ready to demonstrate them in whatever place shall please Your Excellency, to whom I humbly commend myself.

—*Leonardo the Florentine, 1483*

THE NEW YEAR, 1490; IN THE CITY OF FERRARA

BEATRICE'S portrait sits alone for weeks in Leonora's studiolo, and the family practically goes mad trying not to mention it. Isabella takes pity on Beatrice and asks Niccolò da Correggio to set some of his sonnets to song so that she might sing them for her sister and cheer her up. That the poet Niccolò is hopelessly in love with Isabella and carries out her every wish as if she were doing him the favor by asking is common knowledge. He has now set fifteen sonnets to the lute. Every evening after dinner, Isabella plays one or two for her sister, followed by a game of cards, at which Beatrice excels. Isabella either lets Beatrice win, or Beatrice wins fairly, and then Isabella rushes to her room, where she can enjoy in privacy the memory of Francesco's breath on her neck.

When she becomes bored with entertaining Beatrice, she sends her pet dwarf, Mathilda, to make Beatrice laugh by lifting up her skirts and chasing Beatrice's greyhound puppy around the room, shooting little squirts of pee in his direction. Mathilda reports that Beatrice has laughed at no jokes, but cannot stifle her delight at this routine. "I ran after that little dog 'til I was bone dry and out of breath. The princess finally passed out on her bed, and the servants had to come in and clean so she wouldn't have to wake up to the stink of piss, God bless her little soul."

Isabella has also become very devout in recent weeks, attending Mass daily, much to her mother's happy surprise. She does not reveal the reason, but it is this: she gives thanks to God for the celestial secretary who arranged the schedules of all parties so that Francesco Gonzaga's ambassador from Mantua arrived in the nick of time to save her from a betrothal to Ludovico, who would have humiliated her as he is doing to her sister.

Isabella knows that Beatrice inquires daily whether their father has received correspondence from Ambassador Trotti in Milan. Finally, on one of the frigid, last days of January, Trotti returns from Milan, and asks for an immediate audience with the duke and his family.

The family, minus the three little brothers, Alfonso, Ferrante, and Ippolito, who are already sent to bed, gather in the small drawing room that is easiest to warm to a crisp by its large fireplace. The ceiling is not so very high, and the room has an intimate feel, conducive for spilling gossip, for that was the main product that the Ferrarese ambassadors brought back from their missions.

Trotti is as puffed up as a pig's bladder with his news. Impatient to get through the small talk and the niceties, he turns to Duke Ercole. "Your Excellency, how I wish you had been there to see it! It was the most magnificent spectacle in the world. All of Italy is talking of it."

The family looks at him mutely.

"So, you have *not* heard?"

No one says a word. Ercole and Leonora, practiced at receiving the most devastating news without reaction, remain as inscrutable as ever while Isabella guesses that Trotti will announce some magnificent ceremony at which Ludovico has married his mistress after all. Beatrice anticipates his words like a poor starved dog waiting outside a tavern for scraps.

"The Masque of the Planets? The Feast of Paradise?" Trotti looks at them as if their very knowledge of the Italian language is in question. "Don't be surprised if you soon receive dozens of letters describing the wonders. It was the most magical, spectacular thing I have ever witnessed, and all designed by the painter and engineer Leonardo the Florentine. Picture this: a gigantic dome built under the ceiling of a great hall. All night long, there was music and dancing and processions of gigantic murals of Italy's most glorious battles, from the days of the Romans all the way to the days of Ludovico's father's great victories for Milan. The scenes were so detailed and so gloriously violent, I felt as if I was thrown into the midst of battle.

"Then, when the bells rang at midnight, Ludovico presented himself costumed as an Oriental pasha. I must say, he looked every bit the magician. He ordered the music stopped and the curtain to rise. Suddenly, all the foliage fell away from the dome, revealing it to be a replication of the sky itself. The entire sphere was gilded, a great golden universe, if you can fathom it. Live players representing all seven of the planets and the twelve signs of the zodiac began to orbit, exactly as they do in the sky! Everything was lit by dozens of torches. The players, each dressed according to character—Mars, Venus, Neptune, and the like—spun around the sky so many times it made us all dizzy. Then, one by one, they floated in front of the stage and delivered fine orations. They hung in the air, as if by magic! No one knows how it was done, but afterward, everyone crowded around the Florentine, who would not reveal any of his secret means."

Silence.

"They say that in ancient times, the sculptor Pheidias alone was given knowledge of the exact image of the gods, which he revealed to man. I believe that Leonardo has been thus gifted."

More silence. It must occur to Trotti that Beatrice and her

family have waited for weeks for news of her pending marriage, and here he is describing a theatrical presentation. Isabella, for her part, is no longer thinking on Beatrice's humiliation, but is caught up in the magnificence of the scenario and wants to hear more.

"Well everyone's talking about it," Trotti says with a defensive sniff.

"And to what purpose was this *festa* held?" Duke Ercole finally asks.

Isabella sees Beatrice hold her breath.

"It was to celebrate the anniversary of last year's marriage between Ludovico's twenty-year-old nephew, Gian Galeazzo, the young Duke of Milan, and his wife, your cousin Isabel of the House of Aragon. That was the intention, but of course it was held entirely to raise esteem for Ludovico. He holds these pageantries allegedly to glorify his nephew, but there is no question that he intends to keep the boy out of the business of government entirely and, as soon as possible, steal the title of duke for himself."

He looks at Beatrice. "By the way, he *likes* to be called Il Moro."

"Does he truly look like a Moor?" Beatrice asks.

"You will have to judge for yourself," Trotti says, and Isabella assumes that he is being the diplomat. Ludovico must be called Il Moro because he is dark and savage like the barbarians she's seen in paintings—those men who live in tents, cut the throats of their enemies, and eschew the teachings of Our Lord. Poor Beatrice! Imagine having to allow such a man entrance into your bed.

"And of the wedding?" asks the duchess.

"Il Moro expresses his deepest regrets that he is unable to gratify you on the date proposed early next year, but he pledges to send alternate dates by his own messenger in the coming months."

"There is still no hope, then, of the double wedding of my daughters?" asks the duchess.

"Il Moro repeats that his duties preclude the celebration of the marriage at that time. He asks for your patience."

"I am losing faith in this man's promises," says the duke.

"Your Excellency, it is my opinion at this time that this one may be worth waiting for."

Beatrice shrugs, curtsies, and asks to be allowed to go to bed.

But Isabella's curiosity has been piqued by the description of the spectacle at Milan. A thorough interrogation of Trotti is in order, though the hour is late. She has heard stories about the Florentine Leonardo, called Magistro throughout Italy for his innovations in painting. So now he is in the service of Ludovico, Beatrice's future husband. Beatrice's *possible* future husband. Pity that the opportunity to be painted by so great a master will be wasted on Beatrice, who cares nothing for posing.

"How is it that the Florentine came to serve the Regent of Milan?" Isabella asks.

"The story goes that Prince Lorenzo the Magnificent insulted the Magistro by giving the commission to do a mural of the execution of the Pazzi conspirators to Sandro Botticelli. Leonardo wanted the commission badly, and had submitted beautiful drawings—or so they say—of the hanging men, so lifelike that one felt as if one were present at the scene. Then, to add to the injury, Lorenzo sent Florence's 'best' painters—Botticelli, Signorelli, Ghirlandaio, and Perugino—to paint Pope Sixtus' chapel in Rome, but not Leonardo. Imagine!"

"Oh, Lorenzo doesn't always see what's right in front of him," says Ercole. "He's overly impressed with manners and formality and the reading of Greek. He is quite capable of treating a great genius like a laborer if the man has not studied classical literature. Bravo to the Magistro for going over to Ludovico. Milan—not *Florence*—is the new Athens, and Ludovico its Pericles. That is why we are putting up with the duke's procrastination over the marriage."

Isabella has noticed that though her father pays public tribute to Lorenzo, he is not so generous to him in private dialogue.

"True enough," Trotti says, building on Ercole's comment. "Leonardo must have known that he had to escape Lorenzo's service so that he could play Pheidias to Ludovico's Pericles. So he made a magnificent silver lute in the shape of a horse's head. And he convinced Lorenzo that he should present the thing to Ludovico at Milan as a gift from the city of Florence! Leonardo appeared at Il Moro's court with his exquisite lute and sang in his exquisite voice. All of that is true. Then he secretly slipped Il Moro a letter listing all of his qualifications. And so it was accomplished. Leonardo enchanted the duke with his beauty and his voice and the playing of his own compositions, and Leonardo never returned to Florence."

"He is beautiful as well, the Florentine?" Isabella's interest heightens.

"So beautiful that he cannot find a model as intriguing as himself. They say he has built an octagon of mirrors so that he might view himself from all angles and paint himself in profile."

"And have you seen the painting?"

"I have seen others," Trotti says, tantalizing both of the elder Estes and the young one, all of whom he knows have a mania for collecting.

"What have you seen? Anything we might procure? Or should we approach him with a commission?" asks the duchess.

Isabella realizes that in a few months, she will be Marchesa of Mantua, who, like her mother, will have her own allowance to purchase art. If she wants to commission a painting by a genius, she will have agents and ambassadors of her own to conduct the negotiations.

"Unfortunately, he is notorious for not completing commissions. The monks of San Donato in Florence are suing him over an incomplete *Adoration of the Magi*, though they display it with pride in their chapel. But most things, he leaves undone."

"So it goes," says Ercole. "Men of genius rarely behave conventionally."

But Isabella and Leonora have no intention of giving up.

"What have you seen that is completed?" Isabella asks. "Is it up for purchase?"

"I shudder to think, my daughter, that when you are Marchesa of Mantua, I will have to compete with you over these items," Leonora says with a mixture of pride and acceptance.

Trotti sits quietly, unusual for him. He looks at the duke, who merely looks back.

"It's rather indelicate," he says.

"Our daughter is about to become a bride and a marchesa. I believe you can speak openly in her presence," replies the duke.

"I have seen a magnificent portrait done by the Magistro of Cecilia Gallerani, Ludovico's mistress. It is completed. And it is not for sale." He lowers his eyes.

THE conversation is not pursued. Isabella is promptly dismissed to her chamber. She leaves the room humbly and without protestation, because long ago she discovered a wonderful secret. If she turns the corner discreetly, she can linger against the wall out of sight and hear everything her parents say inside their favorite room, in which they seem to hold their most intimate conversations.

"So Ludovico's attentions are still solidly affixed to this woman?" Ercole asks.

"She is regarded as a wife at court, Your Excellency."

"Do you think he will honor the betrothal with Beatrice?"

"He *must*. He has proposed the idea of marriage to the Gallerani woman many times to his advisers, and each time the proposal is rejected. She is a woman of beauty and brilliance, but her family brings nothing in terms of strengthening Milan either politically or militarily. There is danger from Rome and from Venice. There is great danger from Naples. There is danger from France. Losing your allegiance to any of the others would be deadly. He will honor the commitment, but at a time convenient for himself. That is how he does all things."

"Messer Trotti, speak candidly," says the duchess. "Are we sentencing our daughter to a lifetime of misery?"

"Your Excellency, Milan is a marvel. Ludovico has summoned the most brilliant artists and architects and engineers and craftsmen in Italy. The finest minds in Europe are now at the universities of Milan and Pavia, thanks to Ludovico's invitation of intellectual freedom and high salaries that are tax free. In many ways, he is an enlightened man. In others, he's a snake. But he is not unkind. Though he will probably not love Madonna Beatrice, he will treat her generously. At any rate, my eyes will constantly be upon his affairs."

The duchess looks at her husband. "I fear for Beatrice's happiness. She is not as stable as Isabella, and not entirely in control of her emotions."

"She will have to learn to be so," answers the Diamond in the icy tone that earned him his nickname. "Beatrice is not daft. She is smart and capable."

Trotti shakes his head. "Your Excellencies, I say this with all respect for every member of your family, and the high honor due you, but it is a pity that the marriage contracts cannot be switched."

"Do you believe that we should renege on the contract?" asks the duke. "That will leave us with only remote marital ties to Milan."

Isabella hears the impatience in her father's voice.

Trotti continues: "Il Moro *will* make himself the Duke of Milan. He will never be satisfied being the regent to the young duke, Gian Galeazzo, who is weak and incompetent. Il Moro feeds the boy's vices steadily, as one feeds one's favorite pets. Gian Galeazzo has weaknesses for wine and for boys with pretty faces. Il Moro sends him an endless stream of both. His wife, Isabel of Aragon, complains loudly of still being a virgin. Of course! Ludovico keeps the boy in a dissolute state, all the while ruling Milan, making alliances with foreign powers, building the army, consolidating his powers, and waiting for the day the boy will drop dead of decadence."

"What does any of this have to do with our daughter?" asks Ercole.

"Madonna Beatrice is a lovely girl, but—how shall we say?—somewhat flighty. Madonna Isabella has an accomplished and astute mind, and already at her young age, the judgment necessary to be duchess of a world power. Not to mention—the Moor loves blond hair and a womanly figure. Madonna Isabella would be a formidable rival for Cecilia Gallerani, who is also a very brilliant woman, and like Madonna Isabella, has the intellect of a man."

The duke is silent. Isabella wonders—fears—that he will begin to intrigue with Trotti to make her forsake Francesco and marry the horrible and cunning Moor.

The duchess sighs. "There is nothing to be done. Isabella's betrothal to Gonzaga was negotiated years ago. At this point, it is a love match as well as a consolidation of the powers of two ruling families."

Trotti sighs too. "It's just a pity that the brilliant daughter is going to the provincial, and the one who loves horses as much as the provincial is going to a true man of learning in a city like Milan."

ISABELLA has been listening to this conversation holding her breath. She tiptoes away, slowly opening the door to the colonnade and walking outside. The air is freezing cold, and she has no cloak to keep her warm. She leans her back against the wall, breathing in the frigid atmosphere. She would like to murder that gossipmonger Trotti for calling her beloved a provincial. Francesco is intelligent and masculine and worldly and courtly. She feels disloyal just having heard what was said about him.

At the same time, there is another conversation going on in her mind, battering her love for Francesco and her joy in anticipating her life with him. This conversation she cannot stifle. Her sister is going to preside over a kingdom in which its ruler might achieve the immortality of Pericles; where an artist the caliber of Pheidias is building monuments as spectacular and perhaps as eternal as the Parthenon. Is this not what she, Isabella, was born for? To reign over one of the most powerful realms in the world. To sit for the genius Leonardo. To supplant this beautiful Cecilia Gallerani in the famous Castello Sforzesco and in Il Moro's heart. To take her place among the immortals who are creating this kingdom of mythical proportions whose monuments and structures and artistic achievements and legends will live on and on long after their bodies have turned to dust.

These are challenges for Isabella, not the wild and naïve Beatrice.

Has Isabella been a fool all along, thinking that Fortuna has been on her side? What irony is this, to find out these things now? Now that she is in love with her betrothed. Now that nothing can be done.

What if Isabella has been cheated out of her true destiny by Chance? Can one challenge Fortuna? Would that be the same as trying to challenge God? Even if there was a way, would she dare?

But, she reminds herself, the Ferrarese have always believed in miracles. Wasn't that what she was saying to Francesco? If God made manifest the body and blood of His Son in St. Mary's Church, surely He would not allow anything so terrible as missing out on one's own destiny to happen to a princess of Ferrara. Surely.

She calls upon her sensibilities to save her. After all, Ludovico is old. He is twenty-three years older than Beatrice. By the time he marries her—if he ever decides to honor his contract—he will have an old man's musty smell. His skin will be hanging off his bones. His flesh will be decrepit, and his gait bent and crooked. He may even be too old to perform his marital duties, and Beatrice will die childless, whereas Francesco is virile and young and has eyes only for Isabella. The two of them will make gallant sons who will have the best qualities of the Gonzagas and of the Estes. There will be no scheming decadence in Mantua, no evil regent contributing to the ruin of the true ruler of the realm in order to steal his title.

Yes, surely Isabella will be better off after all. She and Francesco are noble people who will rule a noble society; Il Moro and the court of Milan are corrupt.

And if it comes to pass that Fortuna has played some clever trick on her, then she will take her destiny into her own hands. She will know what to do to remedy Fortuna's mistake. She has often wondered if Fortuna is in God's jurisdiction, or reigns over a realm of her own. Though she is certain that this thought is heresy, she cannot help but to ponder it. She has been taught that God is, was, and always shall be. But this singular idea of Fortuna has survived centuries of the church's doctrine. God's power is omniscient, but Fortuna is left over from the meddling Olympian gods so interested in worldly affairs. While Zeus and Hera and the like are only alive today in paintings, sculptures, myths, and the ruins of antiquities, Fortuna is still active in the daily intercourse of human events. Isabella is not alone in this belief, she knows. Doesn't every kitchen maid, every soldier, shout pleas and gratitude to Fortuna?

God, Fortuna—one or both will take care of her, or she will take care of herself. It's as her devout father has always advised: "Believe passionately in Our Lord. Pay tribute to His greatness day and night. Build cathedrals to His glory. Have faith in His will. But don't always rely on Him to do your bidding."

Chapter Two

0 * IL MATTO (THE FOOL)

FROM THE NOTEBOOK OF LEONARDO:
An old man, a few hours before his death, told me that he
had lived a hundred years and that he did not feel any
ailments other than weakness. Thus while sitting upon a
bed in the hospital, without any movement or sign of
anything amiss, I watched him pass from this life. I made
an autopsy to ascertain the cause of so peaceful a death,
and found that it was from weakness through failure of
blood and the artery that feeds the heart and the lower
members, which I found to be parched and shrunk and
withered.

The other autopsy was on a child of two years old, and
I found everything to be contrary to that which was in the
case of the old man.

On the contrast between old and young:

The veins in the young are straight and full of blood,
but in the decrepit they are twisted, flat, shriveled, and the
blood is blocked from its passages.

The liver, which in youth, is of deep red color and
strong consistency, in the old is pale, without the redness

from the healthy flow of blood, and the veins stay empty.
Moreover, in the old, the thin texture of the substance of
the liver may be likened to bran steeped in a small
quantity of water.

The colon in the old is thin, becoming as slender as the
middle finger of the hand, whereas in the young, it may
have the width of the larger part of the human arm.

In life, beauty perishes; not in art.

IN THE YEAR 1491; IN THE CITY OF PAVIA,
IN THE REGION OF MILAN

BEATRICE kicks the stomach of the fiery evil spirit who is pulling on her arm, trying to drag her through the gates of Hell. Her high-heeled boot passes right through the flames of his belly, and he laughs at her while his red eyes shoot yellow sparks into the air, momentarily blinding her. She is screaming, writhing, trying even to bite his flaming flesh. She is arguing that she is not *that* Beatrice, not the poet Dante's lover, not his inspiration or salvation or anyone's for that matter. "Leave me alone," she yells at the demon. She can see smoke and flames in the distance. She feels hot, but the heat is coming from her insides. She knows that if she cannot escape, she will implode even before the devil's fires engulf her. "I've done nothing," she says over and over again, trying to yank her arm from the devil's claws. The monster is stronger even than her big horse, Drago, and has no compunction to obey her. "I'm not the one," she cries. "I'm not the one that you want."

"Beatrice d'Este!"

Suddenly, the devil has the voice of a woman.

"Beatrice!"

The devil's claws sink deeper into her arm. With his other hand, he grips her face, shaking it violently until she opens her eyes.

Her mother's insistent face shocks her out of her dream state and into the bedroom, where she sweats beneath the thick blankets. Her face is hot, her brow damp, but her nose, sticking out into the air, is cold. She is not certain where she is, but she wonders how her mother knew that the devil had come for her, and that she needed to be yanked from his deathly grip.

"The ambassadors are coming, child. You must get up." Duchess Leonora rolls her daughter over on her side, pulling the blankets down and her nightgown up.

Beatrice is aware that heavy drapes are being pulled aside, allowing stark gray morning light to replace the devil's glittering flames.

"Not much, but it will have to do," Leonora says.

Before Beatrice can ask what she means—is she speaking of her daughter's behind?—two of her ladies are pulling Beatrice off the bed and slipping a heavy embroidered robe over her shoulders.

"You accommodated your husband, thank God!" Leonora exclaims, examining the messy sheets. "Or you know what would have happened. We would have had to write to your father. *He* would not have taken kindly to a daughter's skittishness on her wedding night. You know how he is about duty."

Officious footsteps marching in threes, echoing off stone floors, approach. Messer Trotti and two dour gentlemen Beatrice does not recognize enter the room. Ignoring her, their attention goes directly to the pink-stained, rumpled bedsheets.

"There is little blood," says one of the men to Leonora. "Either Il Moro was not allowed full access, or this is a well-traveled tunnel."

Messer Trotti is stone-faced, his thin eyebrows arched and indignant, but the other man snickers.

"The girl spends her days on the back of a horse," Leonora says. "I will not have you suggest such things about a princess of the House of Este. If you take that idea out of this bedroom, I assure you, it will cost you your position at this and any other court in the land."

The man is silent. No one would doubt Leonora's ability to carry forth the threat.

Beatrice marvels at her mother's ability to intimidate not one but three men with nothing but a pair of big brown eyes and a haughty voice. Not only that, but how is it that someone can be so alert so early in the morning? Would this be expected of her now that she is a wife?

"The child pleased her husband. There is the proof. Now take the sheet and carry out your duty. The marriage is officially consummated." The men start to back out of the room, like the servants from exotic eastern lands that Beatrice saw once in Venice. "Your every word will reflect nothing but happiness over the success of this event."

Beatrice is surprised that all of her insides have not spilled out onto the sheets. The smattering of blood staining the white cloth brings back last night's event. Avoiding the faces of the receding men, of her mother, and of the two ladies who are removing the evidence, she wraps the robe tightly around her frame and turns to look out the window. Snow has fallen overnight, weighing down the landscape. The trees seem burdened; the branches, ready to drop under the weight of the icy overlay. Beatrice's womb, jostled from its virgin's slumber the night before, also feels similarly heavy. She squints her eyes against the white vista, which reflects its brightness back to her, startling her memory. As images come rushing into her mind, the activity in the room falls away, and the memories of previous days flush her face with shame.

Could the weather have been more inauspicious for a wedding? It was so cold this winter that Beatrice's father had to hire ice cutters to chop great frozen blocks out of the Po River so that the wedding party could depart for Milan. Beatrice had watched the men hack away with their giant axes, hoping as the frozen splinters flew like sparks into the brittle air that the ice would prove too thick, and the wedding would have to be postponed. Perhaps in the interim, she would fall off of one of her horses and die.

But she had no such luck. After many cancellations and excuses, Ludovico had finally confirmed the date, but for the most frigid time of year, when traveling down icy rivers and through frozen paths was usually impossible. Beatrice and her family were certain that he was trying to buy himself yet more time.

On the twenty-ninth day of December, after the coldest Christmas in memory, Beatrice and her mother and the rest of the wedding party, wrapped in blankets of wool and ermine, were loaded into bucentaurs, finely decorated river barges. From Ferrara, they would sledge and trudge through the treacherous, glacial river all the way to Pavia in the duchy of Milan, where they were to be met by Ludovico for the official marriage celebration. The journey was full of disasters. The boat containing provisions for the wedding party got stuck miles behind them in the ice, leaving them without a morsel of food for two days. Their beds and blankets were stiff with spray from the river and water from the damp, freezing air. No one was in any mood to be cheery about Beatrice's great good fortune in marrying one of the most powerful men in Italy, least of all the bride.

Isabella, having married Francesco one year prior, had traveled from Mantua to meet up with the Ferrarese delegation before their departure. Isabella complained loudly that she felt like a living ice sculpture. She was doubly annoyed because Ludovico, by letter, had requested that she reduce her entourage to a mere fifty people and thirty horses. Every important personage in Italy was to attend the wedding, along with ambassadors from each allied or surrounding country and state. How was Ludovico supposed to house, entertain, and feed so many thousands of people and animals, first, at Pavia where the official ceremony was to take place, and then, in Milan, for the ensuing celebrations? Still, Isabella was incensed that she would have to enter that great city in a state of diminished grandeur. But once they were rocking in the river, the boat hitting massive blocks of ice, all passengers sick from the motion, Isabella stopped complaining and, with Beatrice and the rest of the women, merely prayed for a hot meal and a safe arrival.

Beatrice shivered in her berth, pulling her blanket over her eyes and her hat over her numb ears to muffle the sniffling of spoiled ladies-in-waiting, crying over the cold weather. She had two dogs under the covers with her, but worried that with the lack of food, she would soon have to throw their poor little corpses overboard. But at that moment one slept under each of her arms, giving her the only warmth she had felt in days. She had given up crying because the hot tears rapidly turned into little icy streams running down her face. Plus, with no food to eat, the tears and the heaving took too much of her stamina, keeping her in a more frigid state than if she contained her emotions. She had been told by the river navigator that within hours she and her party would be warming themselves by a blazing fire in a palazzo in Piacenza, and that the next day, fed and refreshed, they would continue the short journey to Pavia, where they would be greeted by Ludovico himself. She did not know whether to hope for this, or for death. She did know, however, that with the bone-chilling cold, and the humiliating circumstances of her marriage, she felt more that she was sailing toward her funeral than her wedding.

Everyone in Italy knew that Ludovico Sforza had a mistress, Cecilia Gallerani, a beautiful and accomplished woman whom he held up as a wife, and who was pregnant with his child. Cecilia presided over Ludovico's fabulous court of diplomats, philosophers, royals, intellectuals, and artists. They admired her without qualification. She owned palaces given to her by Il Moro. She wrote heart-wrenching poetry, which, when sung in her own lovely voice, brought tears to the eyes of knights and ladies alike. She was known for her fluent command of Latin, a language in which she read and sang to Ludovico's many visitors.

All of this was common knowledge, information on the tip of every Italian tongue. Everyone knew that Beatrice's betrothed prized this woman *so* dearly that he had cajoled Leonardo the Florentine, who *never* finished a painting, into completing a spectacular portrait of her. They say it was displayed in his apartments, and people came to pay homage to it as if it were an altarpiece in a church, and Cecilia, the Madonna herself. And yet she, Beatrice, a princess of the House of Este, favorite of the feared and terrible King Ferrante of Naples, was being forced to be a player in this colossal farce of a wedding.

Beatrice was aware that love was an accident in a marriage arranged for political purposes. But a man had an obligation to behave nobly and pay his betrothed some attention prior to the wedding. Her father had done this, and her parents had made a successful marriage because of it. Francesco had courted Isabella as if she were truly his beloved, and so she had become such. Ludovico, on the other hand, never made an appearance or wrote a kind letter. He had canceled two dates for their wedding, offering vague excuses about his schedule. Beatrice might have had a lovely wedding this past July, when travel through Italy's northern countryside would have been delightful. As summer approached, however, Ludovico sent his ambassador yet again to Ferrara, with the excuse that urgent business would preclude a summer wedding. Worse, Beatrice had to suffer this embarrassment in front of Isabella, who had come to Ferrara to visit her family flushed with marital bliss and the news that Francesco had been appointed captain general of the Venetian army, the youngest man in the Republic's history named to that post.

With the wedding date also came news of fresh corruption in Milan, which sounded like a complete mess to Beatrice, a snake pit of connivances. Young Gian Galeazzo, Duke of Milan in name only, remained a constant source of scandal. His wife, Duchess Isabel of Aragon, with whom Beatrice had played as a child in Naples, was forever writing to her family, begging to be taken back to their court. The young duke paraded his boy-lovers in front of Isabel, leaving her bed cold. Tongues wagged all over Europe that Ludovico kept the young duke busy with sodomites so that he, as regent, would not have to compete with any legitimate heirs. Only when King Ferrante informed Ludovico that he would not pay the final (and enormous) installation of Isabel of Aragon's dowry did Ludovico see to the consummation of the marriage. And then, if rumors were correct, all sorts of bribes, potions, and illusions in the dark had to be used in order to get Gian Galeazzo to impregnate poor, lonely Isabel. Now the rumor was that she was pregnant, and Ludovico had another legitimate heir to worry about.

Oh, there seemed to be more intrigue in the court of Milan than in a Venetian assassination plot. The cast of characters was sinister indeed. She had heard that Isabel of Aragon was terribly threatened by the idea of Beatrice's marriage to Ludovico. Already he had too much power. The last thing Isabel, the rightful Duchess of Milan, wished to see was Ludovico's legitimate sons competing with her husband and her own offspring, should she be fortunate enough to bear this one to fruition. In Isabel of Aragon was Beatrice to find not a long-lost childhood playmate but a formidable and dangerous rival?

At the same time, Beatrice had read a letter that Messer Trotti had sent to her father from Milan, expressing concern over Ludovico's ability to hold power, due to the amount of maneuvering he would have to continue to do against his enemies. "The Duke of Bari is already the great man that he fully intends to be. At the moment, he is everything. But who knows? In a short time, he may be nobody at all."

Duke Ercole had assured Beatrice that the ambassador was

merely trying to console them on the occasion of another of Ludovico's postponements of the marriage. That was possible. But she wished that she could remain in Ferrara forever, under her father's protection. Such as it was. She was fully aware that girls were often the sacrificial lambs to their father's political ambitions.

Lying on her back now under the covers as the barge jerked over rocky waters, with a wet-nosed puppy on either side, Beatrice contrasted her circumstances with those of her sister. Here she was, floating on this funereal barge toward the dreaded Ludovico, while a year earlier, Isabella had made a grand entrance into Mantua as its new marchesa on a gold-draped chariot, with Francesco on one side and the Duke of Urbino on the other. Royals and nobles had come from all over Italy, and Isabella had basked in their attentions.

The entire year prior to Isabella's wedding, the Duke and Duchess of Ferrara had employed hundreds of artists, jewelry and furniture makers, weavers, ceramicists, glassblowers, and goldsmiths and silversmiths to prepare for this great union. Leonora sent to Naples for exquisite tapestries that were part of the Neapolitan treasury, which, it was said, had taken Flemish weavers one hundred years to make. Wedding trunks decorated by Italian masters, a luxurious carved marital bed that looked most promising for beginning intimate relations, and a chariot draped with gold were all made in a frenzy of activity, with Isabella and her mother supervising and approving each singular detail. The two were entirely overbearing the year long, acting like generals preparing for the most important confrontation in history. Beatrice was made to observe Isabella's constant joy while she experienced only heartache and humiliation over her canceled marriage dates.

Why was it that Isabella was getting everything, especially a man who looked at her as if she were Eve before the fall? Who couldn't wait to see her, to give her the slightest little kiss or touch, which seemed to thrill the both of them? Just standing between Isabella and Francesco was to feel a current of intolerable heat, particularly if all that you were receiving from your own betrothed was one cold stab of disappointment after another. Beatrice had to admit, her sister was the essence of beauty and graciousness on her wedding day. She bore no jealousy toward Isabella. Except that she and not Beatrice would have constant access to those famous Gonzaga steeds. But gallant Francesco saw Beatrice's lust for the animals and promised her that he would make her a gift of one very special horse every year, if that were her pleasure.

No, Beatrice knew that she and Isabella had very different ambitions. Achievement and recognition were everything to Isabella. She wanted to rule a kingdom and have all the interesting and powerful and artistic men in Italy at her feet, whereas Beatrice was not fed by the good or bad opinion of others.

Beatrice thought it had everything to do with the difference in their childhood years. Isabella grew up in Ferrara having to perform and be perfect for her exacting parents. Beatrice grew up in Naples with a bunch of indifferent nurses looking after her with one eye closed while they took yet more lovers among the king's staff. The rules and standards of the Duke and Duchess of Ferrara were almost the death of Beatrice when she returned to their home. She longed powerfully for the days when she was set free to ride along the coast at Naples Bay, making picnics with the other unwatched children of the court, sneaking wine from the tables, and spying on the lascivious adults late into the night. Ferrara was a cold and damp prison of rigorous intellectual standards and artistic disciplines compared to wild and sunny Naples.

Isabella grew up behind the tall walls of that daunting castle and had prepared for a life of one public triumph after the next. Beatrice simply wanted to be happy, which did not include throwing her young life away on a man with a long reputation for dishonesty and intrigue, whose heart already belonged to another.

With every breath, she felt as if the air was freezing her heart into a solid, lifeless thing. Perhaps she could keep it this way through the long years to come in an undoubtedly loveless marriage.

FROM THE NOTEBOOK OF LEONARDO:
The heart: A marvelous instrument, invented by the
Supreme Creator.

"Il Moro! Il Moro!"

Hundreds of people shouted his name as Beatrice rode next to her fiancé on the wide Strada Nova at the head of the royal pageant. It seemed to her that the entire population of Pavia, this city of one hundred towers, this ancient home of the Lombard kings, had turned out to meet her. Even the busts of the great rulers of the past that lined the street and the characters in the frescoes on the walls of the palaces seemed to be looking in her direction, welcoming her to her new home. The muted winter light was soft on the grand palazzos on one side of the boulevard, and on the marble colonnades of Pavia University on the other, one of the oldest and best of all European institutions of learning. Today it was Isabella's turn to ride behind Beatrice, which she did graciously, while Beatrice rode proudly next to her powerful bridegroom. Looking at him now, she was embarrassed by the fears that had gripped her on the journey toward this remarkable city and this remarkable man.

"My ancestors, the Viscontis, moved the capital to Milan long ago, but I still have tremendous love for Pavia," Ludovico said to her as he waved to the multitude who had ventured from their homes wrapped in their warmest winter wools to get a glimpse of Il Moro and his bride.

Though it snowed lightly, it was warmer today, and the sun peeked out occasionally from the clouds, making a miraculous difference in the weather and in Beatrice's temperament. The snowflakes fell so slowly and delicately upon her face that she felt as if the Lord Himself was dropping each and every one of them into place just for her as a gift for arriving into her new life.

She had heard so much damaging information about her future husband that she imagined him disliked by the people of Lombardy. She was stunned at this enormous public display of approval. In fact, she wondered if all the information she had collected over the years was wrong. Ludovico was not old. Oh, he was almost forty, which sounded almost elderly compared to her fifteen, but he was tall and formidable. He had shiny, straight black hair, which showed no signs of thinning, like so many men his age who lost the little round patch on the back of their heads so that they could be mistaken for monks. Ludovico's thick mane hugged the outline of his face almost as if it was painted on. He had strong features that must bespeak of a sound personality. His nose was broad and straight, as the nose of a man should be. He had good, sharp cheekbones, whose peaks had been softened by love of food. His only physical defect, which Beatrice found ironic in that she believed she shared it, was a weak chin. Because he was older, she would be able to, if she cared to once they had gotten to know one another, and if he allowed it, playfully pinch a good bit of flab under his chin.

His manners were the finest. He had personally escorted herself, her mother, and Isabella off the royal bucentaur and courteously welcomed them to Pavia. He had paid particular attention to Beatrice, sizing her up with his eyes as he took her small, gloved hand. If he was displeased with the sight of her, he did not demonstrate it. He apologized for the cold as if he might have done something about it but did not have the time.

Her pessimism melted with each stride of this beautiful cinnamon-colored horse that Ludovico had presented to her as his first gift. She blushed, feeling foolish, indeed, when she reflected on the childish behavior she had exhibited yesterday, and as recently as this morning. The wedding party had stopped the day before at Piacenza at the palazzo of Count Scotti, where they ate roasted meats and plates of cooked vegetables at his long dining table, which sat between two fireplaces. The count laughed that the women attacked the food like a pack of starved chickens. Beatrice took advantage of the opportunity to bathe in a tub of warm water, in which she thawed inside and out, and then slept so soundly that she had to be threatened like a child with no breakfast by her mother to get out of bed. Her undergarments were dry, but cold and stiff from hanging before a fire that had long burned out. She did not want to leave, was determined, even, to find a way to remain behind. Clutching her mug of milk, she had taken the count aside and asked him if he wouldn't provide her with the last vestige of a father's protection by allowing her to remain with him and be his daughter. He called to her mother, asking if she had not done her maternal duty to dispel the little virgin's fear of marriage. Leonora pinched Beatrice by the ear. "You are marrying the most powerful prince in Italy in the very city where Charlemagne was crowned. Pull yourself together or I will pull this ear right out of your head," she whispered angrily, all the while yanking Beatrice toward her future.

Just a few hours later, all the lords and ladies of the land had lined up to welcome her to her new home, and Beatrice was marking the morning's embarrassing behavior as her last act of childhood.

Ludovico's entourage carried his flags and standards bearing his symbols, the head of a Moor and the mulberry tree, blooming in a remarkable shade of violet. As the horsemen turned the standards to the crowd, the shouts of approval for Il Moro amplified. What a great prince she was to marry, Beatrice thought. He looked at her so pleasantly as they rode side by side through this city of his ancestors, the great Viscontis, as if nothing could please him more than having her at his side; as if, had he known how lovely she was, he would have not postponed their rendezvous.

A convoy of knights wearing Ludovico's colors of scarlet and blue awaited the procession at the end of the street, in front of the old Certosa. One in particular, whose curls pranced as he trotted toward them, rode ahead of the others on his white steed. He was younger than Ludovico and, if possible, much more handsome. A great white smile cut across his olive skin. He radiated light, or so it seemed. If the rest of the city was in midwinter, he alone looked as if he was living in an eternal summer.

He descended from his horse, bowing to Beatrice. "Galeazz di Sanseverino, madam. At your service and your command. From this day until the end of my life, no favor, no courtesy, no feat is too great for you to ask of me. There is nothing I will not do for you."

He looked up at Beatrice, his golden eyes dancing. Galeazz di Sanseverino: son of a great knight; one of twelve brothers renowned for their mastery of the arts of war. But this one was the most famous of all, the finest jouster and equestrian in all of Italy. He was undefeated, or that was his reputation. She did not know how to respond, but respond she must. And yet nothing came from her mouth.

"Your reputation precedes you, sir," Isabella said, walking her horse to the front of the procession and diverting the knight from Beatrice.

As Galeazz switched his attention to her sister, Beatrice felt all the air go out of her body. Yet it relieved her of the burden of speaking to him.

"As does yours, Marchesa," he answered. "Though for once, the wagging tongues have been too modest in describing your beauty."

"I wonder if that is true of yourself," Isabella said, her voice suddenly sweet with honey and seduction. "Are you the master of the lance, as they say? Like the knights of old in the days of

Charlemagne, knocking all contenders to their deaths, thrilling the ladies with their jousts?"

Galeazz stood up straight. He was tall and cut a fine figure, broad at the shoulder, narrow at the waist, strong at the calf. "Madame, in those days jousts were held with rude bats and stubs. I will soon enough show you contest with a lance, the length and breadth of which you shall never forget."

His impertinent eyes made his meaning clear, and Beatrice expected a haughty retort from her sister. Instead, Isabella returned his suggestive tone.

"I am looking forward to that unforgettable moment," she laughed. "They say you are unrivaled."

"I am unrivaled at many things," he added.

Beatrice could not believe that her sister, a married woman, was inviting these implications from a courtier she had just met. She wondered if she had misunderstood the reference, or if this was simply the way that married women joked with men. Maybe the marriage bed changed a woman. But so quickly? She had never heard her mother utter such words, but then perhaps one hid these tendencies in front of one's children. She must learn quickly these subtleties of womanhood before she gave Ludovico, or this marvelous Galeazz who has offered her his service, a reason to think her childish. She must watch her sister for clues, and think on her as a mentor, not a competitor. That was the old model. Now she could observe Isabella quietly and steal her tricks.

"Captain general of my army. And my son-in-law," Ludovico said proudly and dryly, presenting the cavalier. Galeazz was betrothed to Ludovico's daughter, Bianca Giovanna, by one of his early mistresses, though Ludovico doted on the girl. She was only three years younger than Beatrice. Galeazz was waiting for her to come of age so they could marry, but in the meanwhile, he had adopted Ludovico's surnames, Visconti Sforza.

"But he is more like a son to me," Ludovico finished.

"No one believes that, Your Excellency," Galeazz retorted, and Ludovico assumed a hurtful look. "Because you are far too youthful to be the father of me."

"And now that I shall be married to one who is the essence of youth and all its charms, I will be even more mistaken for a young man." Ludovico addressed his words to Galeazz but directed them at Beatrice, as if thanking her for performing this miracle of reducing his age.

Beatrice laughed, but wondered if perhaps they had rehearsed these lines before. Still, she was grateful for the good nature that Il Moro showed with this handsome young man, not to mention the compliment to herself. She liked that he treated his captain general as a family member and an equal. Such a ruler was bound to inspire loyalty—something she had not expected her much-maligned husband to elicit. But between the shouts of the crowd, the assemblage of the nobility come to greet her, the affectionate glances her betrothed threw in her direction, this glorious man before her offering his service and protection, and the absence of anyone known as Cecilia Gallerani, Beatrice wondered if life as Ludovico's duchess was going to be far from the nightmare she had anticipated.

LATER that day, when the long procession was over, Beatrice looked through the blurry glass of the arched windows of the library, over the snow-veiled lakes, parks, and gardens of the Castello di Pavia, one of her many new homes. The sun was almost down, but she could just make out the iced-over prongs of Poseidon's trident, staking its claim in the middle of a frozen fountain. All shrubbery, lawns, trees, and intricate pathways were a seamless blanket of white, fading almost to purple with the dying sun. She could feel the temperature drop as she stood by the window. Tomorrow would be colder still. It was beautiful, though, and she could hardly believe that she would be back here in the spring, when instead of this mantle of white, all would be alive and green and blooming with life, and she, mistress of this castle, would be riding through the expansive parks and grounds on the lovely cinnamon mare.

The library was a series of rooms with tall vaulted ceilings, dark mahogany woodwork, and marble columns in the ornate, Corinthian style supporting great arches. Shelved were thousands of precious manuscripts that Il Moro had collected from all over the world, decorated with painstakingly beautiful miniature paintings. He was showing one of these to Isabella and Leonora, who looked with admiration at tiny renderings of the Viscontis of the past smiting horrific dragons and other mortal enemies. Ludovico had assembled, he boasted, as complete a collection of the great works in Greek and Latin as exist in Europe, certainly in a private home.

"Perhaps the Vatican has a few more," he said, trying, Beatrice thought, to sound modest. "But I spend many days sending letters to those who can make the collection more complete. So much has been carried off in the past, what with wars and the like. They've been scattered to convents, monasteries, and dilettantes and such who do not even know what they possess."

Leonora had already told the duke about her own library in Ferrara, and now was expounding on her husband's particular interest in translating the knowledge of ancient civilizations into the native tongue.

"A worthy pursuit," he agreed. "So you see that your daughter will not be deprived of knowledge, even though she is leaving the company of her learned parents. I assure you that I will continue the tradition in which you raised Madonna Beatrice. Her smallest desires will receive my greatest attentions."

"All that you have shown me here, as well as your assurances, give me great comfort," Leonora said to her son-in-law, whom Beatrice knew her mother had been prepared to dislike.

"Madonna Beatrice!" Ludovico's voice called Beatrice to turn around, though she had been enjoying listening to them converse as if she were not present. "I hope you will be able to spend many happy hours here, reading at your leisure and according to your interests, for I know they are many."

"My sister is the connoisseur of literature," Beatrice offered, wishing to be seen, if not as lettered, then as generous. She hoped to divert any questions Ludovico might throw at her about some ancient Latin text or another. Let Isabella show off if she must.

"*My* sister is too loose with her compliments," Isabella replied, appearing even more generous. "When you see her riding a fine horse in the open countryside, you will know that your wife is not only unique but superior among all women in the world."

"Madame, I am certain of that fact already. Her youthful loveliness overwhelms."

The three of them stared at her as if she were a pretty little babe in the cradle. Oh, she could understand her mother's wistful gaze, but Isabella was only one year older than Beatrice, a mere sixteen. Why did she seem so much more the woman? Was it her full breasts to Beatrice's small chest? Was it the intellect that gave her the confidence of a man in conversation? Whatever the cause, there could be no doubt that Isabella already had a distinguished, mature manner, whereas she, Beatrice, had the more anonymous face of a little girl.

"And now I imagine you ladies will want to rest," Ludovico said.

He had already announced that despite the rugged, half-starved, sleepless voyage they had just endured, they would only have one day before the marriage ceremony, which was to take place in the chapel at the Castello di Pavia. Then, days later, everyone would travel to Milan for the *feste* honoring the new couple. The duke's astrologer, Messer Ambrogio, thought by him to be infallible, had singled out the day after tomorrow as the most fortuitous for the wedding.

"Nothing is done here without his advice," Ludovico said. "Three years ago, I was near my death, and his medicine, administered at the most propitious astrological times, of course, saved my life. They had all given me up for dead. Some had hoped, I'm afraid. But here I am, and I never ignore his counsel."

The astrologer and medick was not present. He had already been sent to Milan to gauge the timing of all aspects of the marriage celebrations to take place in the capital. Along with him went Magistro Leonardo, who had been studying anatomy and architecture in this very library, but who was in charge of the theatrical decorations and other details of the days of *feste* to come.

"But we have just missed him?" Isabella looked forlorn at the mention that the Magistro was gone.

"He spent the summer and most of the fall here. I gave him access to this library, and also to my scholars at the university. A mistake," said the duke.

"But how could it be a mistake to allow such a man to study?"

"The man is in my employ as a painter and an engineer. But, oh, to get him to paint! He has a thousand other pursuits that come between himself and his brush."

"One must be understanding but persevering with the artists in one's employ," Leonora said, the voice of experience. "Duke Ercole and I have a game we play with them. He makes me out to be the most demanding of creatures in these matters. Then, feeling sorry for the duke that his wife is so troublesome, they produce the desired thing."

"Madame, that is a brilliant technique. Perhaps I will be able to engage my own wife in employing it here. Perhaps even on the Magistro, though he is an especially difficult case. I tell you, he would spend all of his time dissecting human and animal cadavers if I left him to his own pursuits."

"But why?" Beatrice asked. She and Isabella suddenly huddled together, as if it would give them protection from this grisly news.

"Why, to learn of organs and veins! That is what he says. He says that if he had been allowed, he would have devoted his life to learning the workings of the body's interior and not the glorification of its exterior. Thank God he was born a bastard not allowed to study either law or medicine. If his father had not been an indiscreet youth, this great artist would be lancing sores on the legs of plague victims!"

"He paints the exterior," Beatrice offered. "Why must he study the interior?"

"He is a medical man at heart, my dear. Oh, he is many things, but especially that. He has spent far too many hours drawing replications of organs, veins, limbs, and even one of a baby dead in the womb, when he should have been giving his mind to making the Castello at Milan a marvel for your eyes at our wedding." Ludovico smiled at his young bride, giving her a little nod. As he lowered his face, she felt his eyes roam the length of her from tip to toe. It was a suggestive glance, the first indication of romance to come, or so she hoped. "You must see some of these drawings, for they are as extraordinary as they are macabre."

"I do not think I would like to see such things, Your Excellency," Beatrice said. She cannot think of what else to call him. When in public and in letters, her parents used such titles with one another as well. "Death comes to too many babies in the womb. It cannot be good luck to look upon such a thing."

She wanted him to know that she would never jeopardize a child of his in her womb by looking at a dead fetus.

"Perhaps in exploring the interior of the body, he is searching for its essence, that ineffable thing that animates the eyes, the expression, the gestures. Perhaps he is looking for the soul," Isabella offered.

Ludovico paused, cocking his head to the side, giving Isabella's idea what seemed to Beatrice like a very long consideration. "Madame, when you meet him and speak with him, and when you see his paintings, I believe it will give confirmation to your theory. He is as much a philosopher as he is an artist or builder or man of anatomy. It would be just like him to open up a body in search of a soul."

Beatrice did not like the way that Ludovico kept looking at Isabella as if she had just forged some pathway in his mind, had illuminated a road of thought for him that he had been trying to find on his own. Beatrice could see by some uncomfortable change in her mother's face that Leonora had observed this too. How could this be? There was no Cecilia Gallerani in sight, but it was as if her own sister was trying to usurp her. Just a few hours ago, Beatrice believed that she had captured her husband's attention, and now it was seeping away, leaving her cold, as if the hot draft that had begun to warm her bones was suddenly redirected toward her sister.

FROM THE NOTEBOOK OF LEONARDO:
You have named painting among the mechanical arts!
Truly, if painters were as equipped as poets to praise their
own work with the written word, I doubt whether painting
would ever have to be so defiled with such a description.
You call it mechanical because it is by manual work that
the hands represent what the imagination creates. Aren't
you writers setting down your words with the pen? Is that
not mechanical? If you call it mechanical because it is
done for money, who is more guilty of this error—if indeed
it is an error—than you writers? If you lecture for the
schools or academies, do you not go to whoever pays you
the most? Do you do any work without monetary reward?
If you say that poetry is more everlasting than
painting, to this I would reply that the works of a smith

are more enduring still, since time preserves them longer
than either your words or paintings; nevertheless, they
show little imagination, and painting, if it be done upon
copper in enamel colors, can be made far more enduring.

We painters are the grandsons of God, the
grandchildren of Nature. For all visible things derive their
existence from Nature, and from these same things is born
painting. So therefore we may justly speak of it as the
grandchild of Nature and as related to God himself.

The next night, Beatrice lay in bed, head spinning from wine and dancing. She had not consumed so much wine since she was a child, thieving it with her gaggle of playmates at Naples as the adults passed out, and drinking it until they vomited all over the nursery. As the hands of her ladies had dressed her for the first night in her marriage bed, she had prayed that she would not give a repeat performance of her childish pranks for her husband.

With perfumed kisses and knowing smiles, the women had laid her upon the most sumptuous bed she had ever seen—so soft that when her small body sank into it, she wondered if she would drown in its feathers before Ludovico made his appearance. Lions and serpents carved into the canopy above stared at her, and to take away her fear, she stuck her tongue out at them, giggling. The reds and golds of the brocade fabrics draping the bed began to run together, making her dizzy, and she closed her eyes. Nestling deeper into the bed, she ran her hands up and down the white silk nightgown, feeling the small mounds of her breasts and the strength of her stomach muscles. The cold fabric titillated her skin, giving her gooseflesh.

The marriage ceremony, she reflected, had come off spectacularly well. Most of the decorous lords and ladies who had come to

Pavia to welcome her had returned to Milan, where the celebrations were to take place in the Castello. But Ludovico's intimates, as well as representatives of the Houses of Este and Gonzaga, had remained for the ceremony in the Visconti Chapel within the Castello di Pavia. Upon entering the chapel, she was greeted with a whirlwind of faces, almost none of which she recognized in her nervous state. Niccolò da Correggio was present, happy to take advantage of Francesco's absence so that he might have Isabella all to himself, though, since every man sought it, no man ever had her sole attention. Galeazz di Sanseverino had appeared with four of his brothers, who all had gleaming smiles despite their martial appearance, and were no less dashing than he. Other faces she could not associate with names, at least not at this moment.

Isabella and Leonora each took her by an elbow to lead her to the altar. She was sewn into a brilliant white robe, embedded with a thousand small pearls. Streams of sapphires and diamonds met in sharp angles in the tight bodice. She had insisted upon keeping her long plait, into which was woven white and silver ribbons lined with pearls. Beatrice was used to formal gowns, but she had never worn one as heavy as this, and she had to walk slowly, feeling weighted to the mosaic floor of the chapel. She was in no hurry to get to the altar. This was her moment, with the faces of all those who were important to her husband and to her family glued to her as she walked past them like a bejeweled angel.

The Mass seemed to pass very quickly, her mind whirling with thousands of thoughts and images, none of which she could remember after the ceremony was over. It was all a blur until Ludovico had taken her left hand and placed upon her finger a ring with a huge square diamond at its center, surrounded by the tiniest pearls she had ever seen, strung on wires. It was so heavy that, had he not been holding her hand, it would have dropped right to her side. Would she have to wear it all the day long, she wondered? Then he was walking her away from the altar and the rush of faces came at her again, and she just smiled and smiled.

After the ceremony in the chapel, dinner for the hundred or

so guests had been taken in the immense dining hall, with tall ceilings painted in glittering gold and ultramarine, the paint of which Ludovico told her had been made from thousands of crushed lapis lazuli. The walls were covered with frescoes of the Visconti men and women of the past who had built this royal house. Beatrice searched their faces for similarities to her husband; he explained, however, that alas, he resembled the Sforza side of the family. She believed him. Everything about him was *strong*, the literal meaning of Sforza.

Each of the arched windows high above were set in triangular marble shafts. Coats of arms from the Visconti, the Sforza, and the House of Savoy, into which Ludovico's family often married, decorated the empty spaces in the walls. Never had Beatrice seen such grandeur, not even in her grandfather's court at Naples. Perhaps the Pope lived in greater splendor, but she was certain that even those fabled Turkish sultans, or the doges of Venice, could not possibly live in more magnificent surroundings.

Beatrice did not remember eating anything from the platters of meats and delicacies that came in an endless parade from the kitchen. She tried to take a bite or two, but she had gone through the entire day without being able to feel her body. All she could manage was to keep picking up various goblets of gold and silver and drinking whatever was inside. It was always wine—sometimes red, sometimes white, sometimes sweet, sometimes dry. After a while, she could no longer taste it at all. She could feel the weight of her dress and her ring, and she could feel the cold air hit her face as they left the dining hall and entered the courtyard, but there was a strange absence of her corporeal self.

She had almost forgotten the strangest event of the day. When they had left the chapel, among all the faces was one in particular, wearing a black velvet mask and a long black cloak. She knew the man, she was sure, but could not decide exactly who it was until she saw Isabella turn utterly white. Then she realized, it was Francesco, come in disguise. Beatrice had been forewarned that her brother-in-law's employer, the Doge of the Venetian Republic, did not quite approve of this marriage between Ferrara and Milan. It would be if not unseemly and disloyal, then impolitic of Francesco to attend. The doge neither liked nor trusted Ludovico, and relations between Milan and Venice had been more than strained for some time. It was bizarre, indeed, then, to see Francesco standing in the courtyard, a part of and yet apart from the wedding party. She had wanted to welcome him, but her husband had taken her in a different direction to greet the Prince of Mirandola, and by the time she turned around again, he was gone. He did not come to dinner. She hadn't time to speak to Isabella about it either. Strange. What could it mean?

Soon, thoughts of Francesco left her. She shut her eyes tight, running her hands along her body, feeling again the cool silk of her nightgown, enjoying the strength in her arms and legs from long days on the horse, and thinking on all the riches in her future. Not even her future, because her future was now. She was *now* the Duchess of Bari. She was *now* the official mistress of this magnificent and ancient castle. She was *now* the wife of the handsome Moro, who had promised, in the presence of her mother and sister, to spoil her and indulge her every wish.

She was lost in reverie when she heard him enter the room, his footsteps approaching the bed. The sound of her husband's slippers on marble tile would become a familiar sound. Had he been watching her? She froze, hands at her sides, afraid to open her eyes.

"Your dreams appear to be giving you pleasure, my pet," he said. She couldn't tell if he was making fun of her. His voice sounded dreamy and distant, as if he were coming from some far-off place.

Before she could open her eyes, before she could take another breath, he was lying next to her, his hand upon hers, taking over its movements, and guiding it over her breast again. Torn between pleasure and mortification, her eyes popped open to see his swollen red lips inches from her face. His cheeks were flushed, not so much with wine, she thought, but with mirth.

"Will there be blood on the sheets for the official inspectors in the morning?" he asked.

"I have not done this before," she said, wishing he would be more serious.

"Of course you have not," he laughed. "You are a child."

"I am your wife," she countered.

She looked at him, waiting. She had no idea what was expected of her. He had stopped guiding her hand. They both lay still. What could possibly be next? He gave her a kiss on the lips, soft and slow. She tasted the wine on his hot breath and on hers, still sweet. She felt herself awakening inside, and she reached forward to kiss him harder. His hand moved to her breast, caressing it over the nightgown, teasing one nipple and then the other. Just as she began to roll to her side to push herself against him, he stopped kissing her and said, nonchalant, "Perhaps they will grow."

He must have heard her inaudible gasp because he quickly covered his blunder. "Oh, do not despair, little one. Whether they grow or not, it doesn't matter. Your life will be very good, indeed. You will have everything you ever dreamed of, my little princess, and so much more—more than your mother, more than your sister, more than anyone you have known."

She wanted to ask, *Will I have your love?* But she dared not. At least not yet.

"Maestro Ambrogio says that the stars are aligned for the conception of a son. That is why the ceremony had to happen today. I did not want to tell you this before. But it is the truth, and so we must be very serious."

He pulled up her gown, letting it bunch at her waist. He fumbled briefly with himself, revealing his member to her, as if offering her a cut of meat from the kitchen. It looked benign enough—fat, pink, blunt, and not so very long.

He took in the lower part of her body with his eyes in a way that embarrassed her, as if he was regarding the flank of a horse he was about to buy. Finally, he looked into her eyes.

"It seems almost a sin," he said with a small giggle that she did not find either kind or attractive. He should not be laughing at her now. Did he not just say that they had serious business to attend to? How did he expect her to give him a son? A strong son could not be born on the brunt of a joke.

Beatrice knew that if she could say to Ludovico what was burning inside her head, he would cease to be amused by her as if she was his little baby and not his wife. If he knew the woman she truly was inside, he would even begin to love her, she was sure. But something, some silly fear in her, some misplaced vestige of girlhood, prevented her from letting her true thoughts be known. She shut her eyes tight against the tears that welled up behind her eyes, and she got angrier still because she knew that he would think that she was crying because she was afraid.

"Ah, it is time," he whispered. Without another word, he mounted her, spreading her legs, letting the air hit the warm, private part of her. She wanted to snap those strong legs tight, denying him entrance, but if she did, he would have to report it to the Ferrarese ambassador as well as her mother, and they would send a letter to her father, and that would be intolerable because then all of Italy would think that the scared little virgin refused her husband his rights on the night of their wedding. Instead, she lay still as a corpse, waiting.

Slowly, he put the thing inside of her, and she wondered at the miraculous way it had turned itself into a hot poker, or some other feudal instrument of torture. She was about to scream at him to stop, but he anticipated it, and put his hand over her mouth as he moved in and out of her, scorching her. Tears formed, and he moved faster and faster, searing her with every motion. How long could this go on, she wondered? How could he bear to harm her in this way, after he promised her mother that he would take care of her?

She could hardly breathe. She smelled the scent he wore on

his fingers, and she wondered if she would suffocate before she passed out from the pain. Eyes shut like fortress doors, he gyrated on top of her, as if concentrating on some great mental problem. As his lids squeezed closer and closer together, he let out a loud whinny, like a horse in revolt, and suddenly, the horrible thrusting came to an abrupt end. Still, the pain didn't stop, and just when Beatrice had some hope that it would, he grunted, delivering one final insulting thrust. Then, slowly, torturously, he rolled over and onto his back.

Beatrice lay stunned. Was this what she must look forward to for the rest of her life? Surely there was something wrong with her physiology. She must have been born ill-formed in the vagina. Some women professed to enjoy this activity, her own sister among them, or so she claimed. It would be just like Isabella to tell her that intercourse was lovely when it was really horrible, if only to make Beatrice think that she was inadequate in yet one more way. She had just made up her mind to speak to her mother in the morning and demand to be sent to a convent, or to take that cinnamon mare and flee before anyone awakened, when he interrupted her indignant thoughts by brushing her sweaty cheek with the backs of his fingers.

"It gets easier with practice. The next time will be much nicer, and soon, the pain goes away entirely, and the woman begins to desire it, just like a man. Sometimes even more. But for you, that may take a little time."

"Are you displeased with me?" she asked, wiping her tears away.

"We are together, you and I, to make sons. If you give me sons, I will hold you up as the greatest woman on earth. I will come to you each time the maestro reads in the stars that it is fortuitous for conception. It will be your duty to receive me.

"Other than that, you may do as you please, spend as you like, and order whatever trinkets and delicacies you want. I will be attentive to you in company, and you will be the public recipient of my praise. I will spoil you with every jewel and bangle and pleasure that money can buy. You will have absolutely no cause to complain to your family. No cause. Do you understand, my little pet?"

I'm not a pet, she wanted to yell at him. But before she could gather the courage, he was gone, and she was lying alone in the great bed with his semen and her blood slipping out of her and onto the clean sheets.

BEATRICE hears the footsteps of the officials marching out of the bedroom, holding in their hands the triumphant evidence that the union of two great houses has been accomplished, and the Italy of their fathers is once again safe.

"Your bath is being prepared," she hears her mother say. "Ludovico has left for Milan to prepare for the celebrations there. Dress quickly. Messer Galeazz has agreed to take us on a tour of the hunting parks."

Duchess Leonora does not wait for her daughter's response. She is not a mother to coddle her children, not the daughters anyway. Beatrice knows that both her mother and her father expect her to rise to the occasion of being a wife with nary a stumble, though just days ago, they had still considered her a child.

She waits until she is certain that no one remains in the room before she turns away from the snowy scene outside the window. She falls upon the bed, blankets still warm where she had lain asleep. The tears that she has been holding back since last night— since Ludovico deflowered her out of duty and then cast her aside—begin to flow in a gratifying angry stream.

Oh, she is a fool, married to a man who thinks she is a child who can be tossed aside. What on earth awaits her in her new life in Milan? Will her children, if they come, be put aside for the children borne for him by Cecilia Gallerani? Surely, even in the corrupt court of Milan, it would be impossible for the illegitimate to usurp the legitimate. But in this strange world into which she has entered, the impossible might happen.

She feels like a fool, and she knows that to everyone who is aware of her situation, she looks like a fool. But how often does the fool turn out to be the wise one? How often does the fool get away with saying things that others must stifle? Ludovico, indeed all of Italy, might see her as a fool or a child, but both fools and children can be willful and cunning.

Beatrice wipes her face on the blankets. She must not succumb to these emotions that threaten to overtake her and drive her to ruin. After all, she is officially a duchess now—strangely, Duchess of Bari, a port city on the Adriatic that she has never seen—and the wife to Milan's powerful regent. She will be expected to play a part. All eyes will be on her, especially in Milan, where they will meet Ludovico in a few days and begin the celebrations for their marriage.

Beatrice makes up her mind. After her bath, she will ready herself, not just for the day but for the life ahead. She will behave impeccably, even if she has to ignore her every emotion and every injury caused by her husband's neglect; even if she has to imitate Isabella's every gesture to win the admiration and approval of those who have come to watch the farce of a marriage, like spectators at a blood sport. It may take some time and some learning, but soon she will show everyone just what this little fool is made of.

Chapter Three

XV * IL DIAVOLO (THE DEVIL)

FROM THE NOTEBOOK OF LEONARDO:
You can have neither a greater nor a lesser dominion than
that over yourself.

IN THE YEAR 1491;

IN THE CITIES OF MILAN AND MANTUA

HOUSANDS of celebrants come for the wedding *feste* assembled on horse at the gates to the city of Milan, meeting up with Beatrice, Isabella, and the rest of the party arriving from Pavia for the royal procession into the city. The wedding party and the assemblage of European royalty who had come as guests were greeted by the reigning duke and duchess: Isabel of Aragon, a beauty with dark circles under her eyes, either because of how early she had to rise to dress in her elaborate gown or because of her famed unhappiness in her marriage, and Duke Gian Galeazzo, so young, thin, and pale, eyes still beet red from whatever debaucheries he had engaged in the night before. The duchess seemed tender enough in her greeting of Beatrice, the little cousin she remembered from the court of Naples. In fact, she seemed relieved at the presence of another young woman at Milan, a potential ally or at least a compassionate ear. The young duke, to Isabella's eye, was more pitiable than despicable.

Isabella was grateful that she had spent so much time and money on her wardrobe, for the most important eyes in the world would be upon her this day. She had badgered Messer Brognolo, the Gonzagas' agent in Venice, to scour the shops for eighty of the finest sable skins to make a luscious mantle, which she had lined in eight yards of crimson satin. Isabella had wrapped herself so that the red fabric, so flattering to her skin, peeked out from the dark fur, highlighting the natural rose color in her cheeks. She had no intention of trying to show up her sister on this important day; neither did she intend to fade into the background.

Dozens of trumpeters heralded the royal procession as they entered the city, and from the moment she rode through its gates, Isabella was sure they were depositing Beatrice in a magical place. Il Moro had issued an edict before the wedding, summoning all the artists of Lombardy to adorn every inch of the city. Whichever artist or craftsman did not show up was fined, and so the attrition rate was not very great. The whole city teemed with newness and life, though they say it had been founded in Roman times. Even lovely Mantua seemed an austere old matron compared with this fresh place. Snowflakes lit on red bricks against an icy Italian sky. Every wall, balcony, and column of the city was draped in the Sforza colors of bright scarlet and blue. Ivy, now sprinkled with the morning snow, twined its way around each column and doorway in a never-ending bacchanalian pattern. Artists had painted bright crests and symbols of the Sforzas and the Viscontis—coiled vipers, helmeted lions, fierce-looking arms raising hatchets, giant torches, and many other inexplicable things—on every spare surface. Isabella was most enchanted by the armor-makers' tribute to the new bride on the Via degli Armorai, lined with displays of glimmering swords, shields, lances, breast-plates, and helmets. Full suits of armor stood at shimmering attention on both sides of the street as the procession rode by, a silent, metallic army.

Beatrice did look lovely, Isabella had to admit, though who would not look so, costumed in many thousands of ducats' worth of fabric and jewel? Her ceremonial dress hung well below her feet, making her look as if she were floating in a cloud of gold. The marriage belt their father had charged to the finest jewelers in Italy had cost a fortune, and it sat nicely on Beatrice's best feature, her small waist. The bodice was low, but lined with ermine, covering the fact that she had no bosom at all. Her sleeves, held to the dress with ribbons into which many pearls were sewn, left the arm at the elbow, draping in flowing triangles all the way to the floor. Pink-cheeked, eyes glowing, always her best on a good horse, she rode with great stature next to her husband.

Ludovico was down to the last thread of his garment every bit the prince in a blinding mantle of golden brocade. It was clear that the illustrious assembly who had come to help celebrate this union was there to honor Ludovico, and considered him the true ruler and power of the duchy of Milan. The young duke, to whom Ludovico extended every courtesy, let his eyes wander when greeting important personages, and at one point, almost tipped over backward on his horse. Gian Galeazzo might possess the official title, but what was that compared to the power that Ludovico commanded?

When Isabella first met Ludovico in Pavia, she felt a shock run through her body. Everything she had set in her mind turned out to be entirely wrong. She had so envisioned him to be elderly and miserly, especially after he had asked her to reduce the number in her entourage. She had been indignant; after all, she was the sister of the bride, and the marchesa of an extremely important city-state. But when he greeted them at Pavia, the sight of him destroyed all of her previously formed impressions. He was

tall, sensuous, and impressive; a great and rich prince in the full
bloom of his power, intellect, and sexuality. Isabella felt his attention upon her immediately, even before they had a chance to
discover that they were kindred spirits, interested in—no, passionate over—all the same things. He was able to send her signals
of his interest, all the while paying particular, polite attention
to Beatrice and Duchess Leonora. A polished player, Isabella
thought. His full features—were they Moorish after all?—thrilled
her. His plump red lips always looked ready to deliver a kiss. His
hands were manicured and graceful but manly. She could just
imagine them on her body from the moment she saw them un-
adorned by gloves. He had hundreds of people attending to him at
all times, and yet when he turned his attention on her, she felt as
if she and he were entirely alone, even though her sister, his wife,
was standing right there.

And now what was she to do, because this was Beatrice's husband, and Beatrice's city, and Beatrice's life, but Isabella could
not help but feel that though Beatrice would be delighted by all of
this wonder in her life, she did not have the depth to appreciate it
past the superficial. What was she to do now that she, the Marchesa of Mantua, in love with her own husband, was also aching
for the man her sister has just wed?

She was not alone in her aching.

She could have predicted the visit he had made to her room at
the Castello di Pavia the very night of his wedding ceremony, not
moments after he had consummated the marriage with her sister.
Isabella had already been suspicious of his intentions when he
put her in an apartment on the other side of the courtyard from
both her mother and her sister. Shouldn't a sister attend the
bride on the night of her wedding?

He had made a great fuss with her ladies-in-waiting at the
door. He had to speak with the marchesa. Isabella sent the girls
away and let him in, clutching a fur-lined wrap over her thin
nightgown. He made his intentions known immediately.

"I've covered for us with a story. I told your ladies that I've

come to discuss a delicate matter about Beatrice with her sister,
who will advise me."

"What advice do you seek, Your Excellency?" she asked.
"Surely you do not need my help in deflowering a maiden. I imagine you're quite practiced at the art."

"No, the deed is done, but it has left me unquenched."

"May I offer you some wine?"

"Marchesa, do not play games with me. I am not a stupid man,
nor do I lack perception in a woman's intentions. I am here because you summoned me."

She began to protest when he stopped her. "Not with words.
How could you, when we have had no time to be alone? But I've
been reading your thoughts, your gestures, and your eyes."

Before she could deliver a coy reply, he had his arm around
her waist. The wrap dropped to the ground, and he pressed up
against her. She could feel that indeed, though he had consummated the marriage, he was ready for more. She could smell the
wine on his breath, but had to turn her face away when it entered
her mind that this was the same breath that had mingled with
Beatrice not moments before.

"What is it, Marchesa? Do not tell me I have read this situation poorly?"

He knew what she had been thinking. She was not yet practiced in the womanly art of hiding her deepest emotions. But
there was no giving in to him, she knew. Here was a man who had
wife and mistress. If he bedded her now, he would cast her aside
and move on to the next—lady-in-waiting, kitchen maid, stable
boy, who knew? Men were forever trying to quench their insatiable lusts with some new thing.

She put her hand on his chest—affectionately, but also as a
shield, trying to give herself time to decide how to play this opportunity. "Your Excellency, I'm afraid that this is neither the
time nor the place to indulge in our desires."

He took her hand and kissed it, then wrapped it around his
waist as his lips made their way to her ear. She felt his wet tongue

caress the lobe and then bite it, sending a shudder through her body.

"Did you not see the mysterious man in the mask today at the ceremony?"

"I did not think anything of it. Many people wear the mask, either to hide the pox, or just as a matter of fashion, as the Venetians do."

"That was my husband."

"Why did he not make himself known?"

"Sir. You know that my husband is captain general of the Venetian army."

"Yes, and at such a young age. You must be very proud."

Oh, he was sarcastic. He was mocking her as he tried to seduce her. He did not know it, but with every drop of sarcasm, he only strengthened her resolve to restrain her desires. She knew that she was no match for him as a player, not yet. But with some practice, and with him as a mentor, what might she learn?

"And you also are aware, are you not, that the Venetians consider you their enemy?"

"Yes, I've heard. What does that have to do with us?"

"Why do you think Francesco was here? As a Venetian spy? No, he was spying on me! He is a very jealous man, and also a hot-tempered man."

"Where is he now? Under the bed?" Ludovico reached right into the top of her gown and put his hand over her breast. "Ah. Sizable. Much better."

She decided to let him feel her breast. It would be better if he whetted his appetite for her. She knew from her marital relations with Francesco that a plump, white breast with a full pink nipple held some kind of power. She wanted to have that power over the most powerful prince in Italy.

"I have no idea where my husband is. I had no idea he was going to make an appearance at your wedding. I tried to talk to him, but he signaled me not to approach him."

"He is a strange man, indeed. But if he is not here, then what is our obstacle?" Ludovico moved on to the other breast before trying to grasp both of them in one hand, which he could not do, and so he settled for kneading one breast and then the other.

"I'm afraid of him," she said. Then she put her arms around his neck and reached up and kissed him, kissed those full, red lips, opening her mouth so that he could slip his fat tongue inside. She sucked on his tongue while he felt her breasts. Then, she broke away.

"You have to leave."

"You have a strange way of saying goodbye," he said.

"Francesco could be anywhere. Do you have any idea what he would do if he caught me with another man? Do you have any idea how happy the doge would be if my husband had an excuse to kill you? It would be just like Francesco to look for a reason to have a lovers duel. He both loves and hates that other men pay attention to me. I tell you, he is a bit insane, and would not hesitate to murder you if he had the chance."

Ludovico sighed. "Always one complication or another."

"We will have time again," she said, kissing him lightly on the lips, taking his hand from inside her gown.

"I am a patient man," he said. "And I do not wish to die. Not tonight, when there is so much to look forward to tomorrow. Besides, the wait can make it so much more delicious."

FROM THE NOTEBOOK OF LEONARDO:
Moderation curbs all the vices.
The ermine would rather die than soil itself.

Days later, riding in the royal procession through the streets of Milan and crossing the drawbridge over the great, wide moat that surrounded the Castello Sforzesco, Isabella felt as if she were entering the kingdom of one of the fairy tales she and Beatrice had recited to each other as children. The façade, with its dramatic tower, faced an elegant city square. Archers stood sentry from what seemed like mountain-high ramparts. The bridges into the castle swarmed with activity. Indeed, as she discovered in coming days, messengers, pages, soldiers, merchants, ladies, ambassadors, and knights exited and entered at all hours. The frenetic movement never seemed to stop, not even at night, when riders and their torchbearers galloped across the bridge on some urgent mission.

Surrounding the other sides of the Castello were beautiful meadows and woods, thick and enchanted. There, Ludovico housed his stables and his fine collection of horses, where Isabella guessed that Beatrice would be spending most of her time. The rooms of the Castello were too numerous to count, and at this time were filled with Beatrice's magnificent trousseau, to be gazed upon and admired by the visiting guests. Walking through the winding rooms where thousands of gifts for the bride and groom were on display was like being on a tour of the world's great treasures. Plate of gold and silver, exquisite and delicate ceramics, mounds of spices in exotic bowls, weavings from many countries, lengths of shimmering brocades, and necklaces of gems and metals that Isabella could not even identify—lavish offerings to the great Italian prince and his bride on view for all to admire.

Isabella also knew that hidden somewhere in these magnificent apartments was Ludovico's mistress, Cecilia Gallerani. Isabella was dying to get a glimpse of the rival to Beatrice and herself. She roamed the halls, pretending to get lost, but made no progress in discovering this lady's whereabouts. She could not decide what she wished to see most, the lady or the famed painting of her by the Magistro. She decided that she would neither rest nor leave Milan until she had seen both. She sent her own servants to inquire discreetly, but all palace lips were sealed on the subjects of mistress and painting. She made up her mind to ask Ludovico himself to arrange a viewing of one or both, though it would require extraordinary gumption. But the opportunity to do this was not forthcoming.

She had not had a single moment alone with Ludovico since he tried to invade her bed in Pavia. He had departed the next day to attend to the details of the celebrations in Milan, leaving Beatrice and Isabella to be entertained by Galeazz, who spent two uninterrupted days in their company. Like wild children, ignoring the cold, they rode through the hunting parks of Pavia, where Galeazz let loose his best falcons for Beatrice's pleasure. Though he flirted with Isabella, he paid particular attention to Beatrice, indulging her desires to ride, to hunt, to explore the grounds, and to chatter, to the point of exhaustion. He made wordplay with both sisters, making a fierce debate about the higher qualities of the legendary knights Rinaldo and Orlando, until they were almost out of breath. But there was a particular quality to his demeanor with her sister. Isabella had the distinct impression that, despite the fact that Galeazz was to eventually marry Ludovico's daughter, Bianca, he was trying to make Beatrice fall in love with him. She could not tell whether Beatrice was profoundly glad to find a friend at court who could hunt and ride as well as she, or if she was succumbing to his more romantic efforts. An odd situation, she thought, and one to keep an eye on.

Private moments with Ludovico were further sabotaged when Francesco showed up *again* in Milan wearing his mask, trying to mingle anonymously in the crowd of thousands. Ludovico recognized him and sent a message for him to join them at their table for dinner. Francesco, of course, could not refuse. He joined the party, sitting beside her at table while hundreds of Milanese peasant girls dressed in Sforza scarlet and blue performed folk dances for their pleasure. He joined his wife in her bed, too, which she welcomed. Yes, she had taken quickly to the marriage bed, and who would not, with the way that he caressed her for long hours, whispering hot words of his desire for her into her ear. She had grown accustomed to his warm body beside her and his habit of rousing her out of her sleep and coaxing her into meeting his lusts. She certainly did not wish for this to change.

Francesco would not give a good reason why he appeared on the scene in disguise except that in light of his relations with the Most Serene Republic of Venice, he wished to act discreetly and diplomatically, while still not missing the monumental occasion of his beloved sister-in-law's wedding. Isabella had no choice but to accept his explanation, though when Francesco had ever acted diplomatically, or when he had formed this great love for Beatrice, she did not know. It was like Galeazz's courtly love for Beatrice, manifesting out of nowhere and, as far as Isabella could see, for no good reason. Would the captain general of Milan's army actually try to entertain himself with Ludovico's wife? Isabella had no answer to these questions, nor could she figure out the situations. But she was confident that with time, all would reveal itself.

FRANCESCO remained in Milan for the first day of the jousting contests. His brother Alfonso led the Mantuan contingency, twenty knights wearing green and gold, the colors of the House of Gonzaga. The tournaments would last for three days, attracting knights from all over Italy, festively dressed for the prince's wedding, and bearing the heralds and crests of their states. Even their horses were costumed, wearing horns to make them appear like deer and unicorns. Ludovico's riders were led by Galeazz's brother Gaspare, donning dramatic black-and-gold costumes in the style of the Moors, in honor of Ludovico. They looked most severe in their black armor, almost as if they had been sent from Hell.

Isabella watched for three days while Beatrice searched everywhere for Galeazz, but he did not make an appearance. Finally, on the last day, a swarm of masked men, costumed like ancient Scythian warriors, wearing breastplates and belts of blazing gold against jet-black clothes, arrived on ebony-colored chargers, carrying immense golden lances, the longest that Isabella had ever seen. How they maintained their balance on the horses while carrying these gigantic sticks she did not know. They galloped across the piazza, the silky cloth from their headdresses flying behind them, until they made a dead stop in front of the box where Ludovico and Beatrice sat with the young duke and duchess. Their leader stuck the giant golden lance into the ground and ripped off his headdress.

It was Galeazz. He bowed to the dukes and duchesses and glanced at Isabella, giving her a little smirk as if to say, *I told you I wielded the biggest lance.* He recited a poem of his own invention about Beatrice bringing the bud of youth's first bloom to the ancient land of Lombardy—all predictable stuff—and included a couple of lines about his own betrothed, twelve-year-old Bianca Giovanna, who sat next to Beatrice and received the compliments shyly. Isabella was not in love with Galeazz, but she wished that he had included a reference to her in his recitation. She had been the muse of many poems already in her young life, and nothing thrilled her more than moving a man to take up the pen in admiration of her—unless it was a man taking up the brush to render her likeness.

By the time the last tilt came to an end, Isabella was exhausted with Galeazz's victories. Of course he took the day, knocking dozens of men from their horses in disgrace. Beatrice presented him with his prize, a length of priceless gold brocade, and he was the guest of honor at the evening's festivities.

Isabella congratulated the knight on his victory and on the surprise of his arrival in disguise. "The costumes of the barbarians were magnificent," she said. "I had no idea that it was you. I was ready to run for my honor, what with the appearance of such fearsome men."

"Just between the two of us, I stole Magistro Leonardo away from his duties decorating the Castello for the wedding to have the costumes designed for us. I paid him very handsomely, I assure you, but I believe it was worth the expense."

"He does seem to be able to cast his genius in a myriad of directions."

"Yes, he is incomparable in all things. I preyed upon him to do me this favor, not for myself, of course, but because nothing is too extravagant to please and impress Madonna Beatrice."

"I sense that you have a special affection for my sister," Isabella says.

"Indeed I do, madame. My sole purpose is to serve her."

Did men think that because she was young and fair she could not see right through them? The perfunctory smile on his face might have been convincing to some, but to Isabella it was a mere clue that there was more to the story than he was telling.

"So you are a patron of the Magistro?" she asked.

"Indeed, as I have just said."

"Then you must know of the painting of Madonna Cecilia Gallerani."

"I do." Galeazz seemed relieved to be off the subject of Beatrice, but not happy with the new topic of Cecilia.

"If you are so fond of Madonna Beatrice, then surely you want to remain in her good graces by pleasing her sister."

"Nothing would please me more, except of course to please Madonna Beatrice, because I have made that my life's quest." This man was so practiced at playing the knight to ladies that his confidence exceeded that of a playactor.

"Sir, there is a way that you might please me in the extreme."

"I was hoping you would suggest it," he said, suddenly very alert, smile widening, anticipating her offer. Now she had him. If he were in love with her sister, would he stand so quickly at attention from the mere hint of flirtation from herself?

"I want you to arrange for me to see the portrait by the Magistro of Cecilia Gallerani."

He did not speak. She had caught him by surprise. He just looked at her.

"Well?"

He collected himself from the disappointment of her request, fidgeting with his vest, pulling it down again and again. "Your Excellency, that is a most bizarre request, and a most indiscreet one at that."

"I will tell you what is indiscreet. That would be the way that Ludovico has charged you, his future son-in-law, with distracting my sister with your gallantry so that she will not notice that he is still seeing his pregnant mistress. That, my dear Galeazz, is indiscreet. Arranging for me to see a painting need not be indiscreet."

It takes Galeazz less than forty-eight hours to arrange the request. Isabella knows that she should feel guilty for blackmailing this beautiful and gallant man, who is only doing his duty to his prince, by making him do her bidding in exchange for keeping his secret from her sister. Instead, she feels deliciously wicked as they sneak down the halls of the quarter of the Castello where Ludovico shares an apartment with his lover. The appropriate servant has been bribed and walks ahead of them with the large bronze key to the rooms. Everyone is having a nap after a morning of riding and eating. Madonna Gallerani is taking the noonday sun in her private courtyard, as is her habit in this late stage of her pregnancy. Isabella and Galeazz will not be noticed or missed.

Once in the salon, Isabella has to admit that the duke has had the decency to furnish his wife with more luxurious surroundings than his mistress. Cecilia's apartment is lavishly done, with antique tapestries of the Judgment of Paris and other events leading up to the Trojan War, but Beatrice's quarters have been decorated by the likes of the Magistro and are better still. That, Isabella thinks, is to Ludovico's credit. Still, he has provided well for his mistress. The quarters are large, filled with grand furniture appropriate to its proportions. The remains of a lazy fire burn to embers. Isabella places her backside to the flame, lifting her skirt discreetly, allowing a rush of heat to climb up the backs of her legs as her eyes search the room.

The painting sits on a tall gilded easel. A beautiful woman emerges from dark, spooky shadows like an angel floating into this realm from the fog of a dream. Her face is luminous, her skin, translucent. Her hands are pale, her fingers, long and elegant. A white, snouted creature sits on her lap, its ears round and delicate, its claws emphatically rendered, its gaze as attentive to some unseen thing outside the frame as that of its mistress. It is as if both creatures are listening to a distant, beckoning sound.

Isabella loves the way the Magistro works the dark upon the light; loves the muted colors, and the way that he managed to paint fragile netting upon her hair, tied ever so delicately under her chin. How does one paint translucence? How does one paint skin so lustrous that brushstrokes cannot be seen? And the hair! Like an alchemist in reverse, he spins gold paint into hair. She looks at Cecilia's long, fair hair, not nearly as lush and thick as her own, and she knows that she wants the Magistro to spin her own golden locks with his magic. He has made this woman look as if she has come from the ether, delicate, teetering between this world and the next.

Isabella realizes that she was correct about the Magistro: he is in search of the soul. The essence and mystery and beguiling qualities of not just this woman but of *woman* emerge from within, peek out just enough from the eyes and from the skin's tiny pores to reveal a touch of the ineffable. What is it that Isabella sees? The power of the feminine? The godliness of the female?

"It is as if he has stolen a glimpse of her soul," she says to Galeazz, who still stares though he has seen both the picture and the woman many times. "It is pouring from her eyes."

"That is what the Magistro says, that the eyes are the window of the soul," he replies quietly. "Knowing the lady, I must say that in this case, he has indeed captured her essence."

"He must have used layers upon layers upon layers of thin paint to achieve this luminescent quality of the facial skin and that of the long, graceful, bony hand."

"Madame, no one knows how he performs his miracles. After the initial sittings, he paints alone in secret."

"She is beautiful and girlish, yet serious. She looks studious, does she not?" Isabella asks, as she cannot help but realize that she has all of those qualities. And she would like to sit for the master who might capture them in a painting.

"Yes, as is the lady herself."

"And what is the small animal on her lap?"

"Why, you wear it next to your skin all the time. Do you not recognize the ermine in its living state?" he jokes with her.

"Does she have a pet ermine?"

Did anyone?

"No, it's just that the ermine is one of the many symbols of Il Moro. He wanted it in the painting. Or perhaps it was the Magistro who suggested it. The ermine is a favorite of his. The legend of the animal is that being chased by a hunter, it went to its death rather than run into a hole because it did not wish to get dirty. The Magistro is a fanatic about cleanliness."

"Perhaps he is also making the point that the duke is a bit of a weasel."

She can see that Galeazz wants to laugh but does not. "Is that what you think of your brother-in-law?"

"I think he is many, many things."

"The ermine is also a play upon Madonna Cecilia's name, which is why the Magistro allowed its inclusion in the picture. *Gale* means ermine in Greek."

"I love the cleverness of it all," Isabella says, "no matter what it means. But I think it might mean that Madonna Cecilia has Il Moro under her palm!"

Out of the unearthly shadows of the painting's background comes a door, leading to nothing but light. "Where do you think that door in the corner of the painting is leading? It's strange and mysterious, is it not?" Isabella asks.

"I never thought on it. Perhaps the Magistro wanted to give her a door through which she might escape if she chose to."

What a startling observation, she thinks. Would her sister have such an exit? That was both the joy and the sorrow of the life of a mistress. You could leave. But you could also easily be told to leave. Now that Galeazz has put the idea in her mind, she is certain that the Magistro inserted this irony into his painting. Finally, she says, "Sir, I believe you are even more brilliant than meets the eye."

"We must go now," he says. "She will be back at any moment for her afternoon rest."

"Ah, but there is the second part of our arrangement, the viewing of la Gallerani herself."

He sighs. "If we are lucky, she is in the garden below. She is in confinement, you know."

"Is that because my sister and everyone in Europe is here for the festivities?"

"No, that is because she is about to deliver a child, though I hardly think that Il Moro would be parading her around during the celebrations for his marriage."

Galeazz leads her by the arm to a window. They do not approach it directly so as not to be seen. He puts her behind him, and leans into the side of the window, gazing below. "We are in luck." He takes her by the elbows and places her in front of him, but still aside the window, holding her closer than she thinks is necessary, but it adds to the daring of the moment. He is bigger than her husband, bigger even than Ludovico. She feels that she could fall back into him and be in bliss. Does he know how he is making her feel? Taking a deep breath, she sticks to the task at hand.

"Be quick about it," he warns.

She leans forward so that she can see below into the yard. A woman with the same golden hair walks awkwardly, hands low on her hips, great belly jutting out, leaning slightly backward as if to balance herself. She is wrapped in a scarlet velvet cloak lined with fur and her elbows stick out like ungainly wings. She is enormous. She looks up, and Isabella almost darts away from the window, but the woman is merely trying to point her face to the sun to catch its weak January rays. Her face and neck are swollen, whether with childbirth or with age or with weight gain, Isabella cannot know. But even at this distance, in the stark midday light, she can see that bags have crept under Cecilia's eyes, and that her skin is no longer the quality that it was at the time she was painted. Or perhaps the Magistro was generous in his portrayal. He did, after all, have to please both the subject and the powerful patron who commissioned the piece. Cecilia blows all the air out of her puffy cheeks and into the heavens as if exasperated by some thought or condition. She does not look happy.

Isabella leans back into Galeazz, wishing to remove herself from the window before she gets caught in her spying, but also to feel his strong body once more within the boundaries of propriety.

"I have seen enough," she says.

Once they are safely down the hall, she asks if Cecilia was ever as lovely as she was in the painting. "Did the beautiful maiden transform into the cow with her pregnancy, like some mythological creature, or did the Magistro transform the cow into the beautiful maiden for the picture?"

Again, he wants to laugh, but his gallantry would not allow anything more than making a smile at her as if she is a mischievous and evil child. "I suppose it is a bit of both, though the painting was done some ten years ago when Cecilia was just your age. She was lovely, though the Magistro performs his magic well."

And yet she is immortalized as the beauty of ten years ago. No matter what she does from this time forward, she will always have that painting, rendered by a genius, that shows her at the pinnacle of her attractiveness.

Immortal. Was Cecilia aware at the time that the way to immortality was gotten not by being just another mistress of a powerful man but by being painted by the master of masters?

Isabella must have that prize, no matter what it takes. What if the same fate that has befallen Cecilia happens to her, only sooner? What if by this time next year, she is puffed up with Francesco's baby and has lost her figure forever? What if Francesco planted his seed last night and she is already with child? The idea that once would have made her happiest now makes her shiver with fear. Their mother had been slender and beautiful before the birth of her children too. Now she is still handsome, but portly. No, Isabella wants to be frozen in time now, right at this moment when all men stare at her with that same look of admiration and desire; that gaze of absolute longing to know her and to possess her. This is the very second in time that she wishes preserved, and not just by any court painter no matter how skilled. She must have Leonardo.

Perhaps Galeazz can make that happen for her, be her aide-de-camp in the mission.

Isabella stops walking, turns to Galeazz, and takes both of his hands. She looks up into his eyes, which seem to await her every desire. "I want to meet him."

LUDOVICO had given the Magistro elaborate quarters in the Corte Vecchio, the old ducal palace, for himself, his household, and his workshop. Il Moro set him up there so that he could use the immense courtyard to work on his colossal equestrian sculpture that was to be a tribute to Ludovico's father, Francesco Sforza, the great condottiere who won the duchy of Milan by the sword.

"Yet you will see, upon entering the courtyard, that there is no horse in sight!" Galeazz says. "Thus adding to the duke's great frustration with the Magistro's stubborn procrastination in all things."

Galeazz fills Isabella in on this and other odd details of the Magistro as he escorts her to the studio in his chariot. They include: The Magistro does not eat meat of any kind because he refuses to let his body be "a tomb for other animals." He is so empathetic toward all of God's creatures that when he passes caged birds for sale in the marketplace, he buys them and then sets them free. When he was a youth, a rustic from the hills of Tuscany—some tiny dot on the map called Vinci—he was apprenticed to the great Florentine sculptor Andrea del Verrocchio. It is said that after the first time Verrocchio allowed Leonardo to paint an entire figure, an angel in the master's version of *The Baptism of Christ*, Verrocchio took one look at it and quit painting. The apprentice had already exceeded the master to the extent that he put down the brush and would only sculpt thereafter. Further, Isabella must not expect for him to treat her like some courtier would do. "Though he is unrivaled for painting the female face, as you saw with the portrait of la Gallerani, he demonstrates no interest in the company of women. In Florence, as a young man, he was arrested and tried on sodomy charges for consorting with a male prostitute. That may be one reason why he chose to leave the city, for there is no better place for evil gossip than Florence, with the possible exception of Venice.

"Now, he is followed around by a twelve-year-old beauty of a youth who steals and makes trouble. He even stole from the purse of one of my own cavaliers as the man was being fitted for his costume. Leonardo treats the little demon like a son, though he calls him Salai, which I believe is the Tuscan expression for 'limb of the devil.' He dresses the scamp in the height of fashion and parades him around like a prize. Everyone suspects that the relationship is sexual. Everyone talks—and not in a positive fashion—about the fact that Leonardo has better-dressed servants than the nobility."

He is a mass of contradictions, Galeazz explains. "As gentle as a dove, but strong as an ox. He can bend a horseshoe with his left hand, the hand with which he paints and writes."

Isabella's head is swimming with facts about the man, so many that she cannot decide upon the attitude with which she will greet him. But it does not matter because when they arrive, an apprentice informs them that the Magistro is not to be found in his quarters.

"He may not return for some time," says the thin, stringy-haired boy. The boy is probably about Isabella's age, but his thinness and simple wool robe set against her grandeur make the gap between them seem more than a generation. He appears nervous, but at the same time eager to represent his master to these illustrious visitors, even to appear knowledgeable about him. "We never know when he is going to come or go."

"And where might he be?" asks Isabella.

"He could be anywhere, searching the city for models for his paintings, or visiting with metallurgists to discuss the nature of bronze, or perhaps he is wandering in the woods behind the Castello. He loves to lose himself in those woods, he says, communing with the very essence of things."

The apprentice invites them to come into the studio, apologizing for its chaotic condition. They have so many projects, and of such magnitude, that it is difficult to keep order. He tries to find Isabella an appropriate chair, but she assures him that she does not want to sit. Cats and chickens wander in and out of the large, open door, ignoring one another, or perhaps the cold weather makes them indifferent to their natures. Another boy, even younger, lazily plays a lute in the corner, fingertips cut out of his well-worn gloves. When he sees the visitors, he stops, but Isabella encourages him to continue. A younger apprentice stokes a furnace. "For baking pots and shaping metal," the chatty apprentice offers. "It also has the very practical use of keeping us warm."

Windows have been cut, the apprentice says, gesturing above, so that the light falls at the perfect forty-five-degree angle the Magistro insists is correct for capturing a subject. The loft above, she thinks, must be where the apprentices make their beds. Big clay molds of what appear to be horses' parts lie about in bizarre arrangements—a flank here, a head there. The walls are covered with drawings of every kind, some of which Isabella cannot identify the subject, but she is excited when she sees the renderings for the costumes that the Magistro designed for Galeazz's jousting match. The drawings look even more savage than the men had appeared. Otherwise, she is not certain of what she is looking at in his renderings—men with wings; sketches of dozens of types of legs and arms; a huge page of a variety of types of noses and another of ears; and many mechanical drawings for machines that she cannot identify. Mathematical equations cover the margins of every sketch.

"The Magistro is also a mathematician?" she asks the boy.

"Oh yes, Your Excellency, the Magistro believes that the artist must know all subjects, as well as every creature and phenomenon of nature firsthand, as if he is the very thing itself. An artist must be one with the very motion and rhythm of the universe. Mathematics is a great part of the knowledge. Without mathematics, there is no perspective, and the Magistro is a fiend on the subject of perspective. I am made to study mathematics late into the evenings after we have finished our work."

"Rigorous, indeed," says Isabella, strolling to the one large, coherent work in the studio, a painting on wood, which leans casually against a white wall, the light falling upon it, illuminating the faces and highlighting the Magistro's play of shadows upon radiance. The panel rests against the wall, almost as if someone had discarded it. It is the simplest of mother-and-child scenarios, but it happens to be a painting of the Blessed Virgin with the baby Jesus in her lap, holding a flower that the two of them examine. Isabella does not think she has ever seen the two portrayed in such a manner, so casual and uncomplicated. No marble thrones, elaborate columns, cherubs, angels on high, or soaring doves of peace clutter the scene. The identities of the subjects are given away only by delicate halos. The Madonna looks like a toothless Italian peasant girl, and the baby, her chubby son. Isabella wonders what the Magistro is trying to accomplish with this painting: Is the girl some Tuscan rustic he knew in his youth? His own mother, perhaps? It's an odd picture. The Madonna looks very young, as childlike in appearance as Beatrice, yet her hairline recedes like an old man's. Artists inevitably model the Madonna after the goddess Venus, or at least after the most beautiful, virtuous-looking women in Italy, or the pallid, ethereal women from the land of the Flemish.

"If this was a commissioned work," Isabella whispers to Galeazz, "I imagine it was rejected."

"It is almost sacrilege to portray the Blessed Virgin so pitifully," Galeazz says. "Like a coarse girl."

"I thought the same," Isabella says. "Though her dress is lovely enough, and she wears a nice jewel at the chest. And what attention the Magistro has given to the folds and drapes of her skirts. Look at this velvet; it is as if you can touch it and feel the soft texture."

"But there is a lack of elegance to the face, is there not? Why make the Blessed Virgin look like an ugly, toothless girl losing her hair."

Yet there is beauty to it, she wants to say, but she does not want to argue. Not the kind of beauty the Magistro had given to Cecilia Gallerani. This is just a mother and baby, in a simple setting, much as the Virgin Mary must have inhabited. Surely she and Joseph did not live with thrones in their houses and cherubs flying over their heads, as she is customarily portrayed. With all the magisterial symbols absent, it is as if the artist is saying that the act of a mother playing so gently with her child is in itself Divine. All the traditional signs of glory are replaced by the simple feeling between the two.

There is something Platonic about both of the paintings, Isabella thinks; some quest of Leonardo's to arrive at a kind of pure feeling, some absolute truth about feeling, rather than the sloppy and specific human emotions laid bare for all to see. It is as if he is attempting to surpass ordinary and commonplace feeling for the essence of Feeling. Is the expression of that essence a mortal attempt to evoke the Divine? All the religious painting in Italy represents the sacred as separate from humanity. Leonardo, it seems to Isabella, is expressing the impersonal sacredness within the mortal form.

There again, too, is the mysterious illuminated opening in the corner of the picture.

"Look, Galeazz, how as in Cecilia's portrait, there is the window in the background, which has no landscape behind it, but only light."

"Perhaps it is unfinished," Galeazz says. "Perhaps the teeth and the grounds outside the window and the rest of the Virgin's hair are yet to come."

"Let us not insult him by suggesting it," Isabella warns. She walks away from the panel both comforted and disquieted by it.

"What are those sketches on the table?" she asks the apprentice, pointing to a sheaf of pages strewn about a workbench. All she sees are wings, spreading, flapping, and jutting about, some wrapping themselves around nude female forms.

"These are the Magistro's swans," says the apprentice. He spreads out the pages so that Isabella can see the many renderings of the creature. There are black swans, white ones, swans large and tiny, swans with their wings spread as if in attack mode, swans sliding peacefully on the water, and several sketches of swans copulating with naked women.

"He is preparing for a painting of the legend of Leda and the swan," the boy says. So that explains the odd cracked eggs at the naked woman's feet. Isabella has always loved the story because of its bizarre elements. Zeus, god of gods, possessed of epic sexual urges, in his untamable desire for Leda, the mortal queen of Sparta, turned himself into a swan in order to appear less threatening to her, for he knew that young girls were enchanted by the creatures. The two coupled—thanks to the god's inimitable trickery. But instead of having children the normal way, poor Leda laid two eggs. All was put well again when the issue turned out to be two pairs of twins, Castor and Clytemnestra, and Pollux and Helen, of Trojan fame.

Isabella is riveted to these renderings, though she cannot rationally figure what is erotic in coupling with a swan. Perhaps the priests are right in their condemnation of the old myths as vulgar and perverse.

Still, there is something irresistible about these swans, particularly the way that Leonardo has drawn them. The god-bird copulating with the vulnerable Leda, who looked stunned to have this gigantic and seemingly gentle bird suddenly taking her from behind, draws Isabella into the picture, though she knows that she should look away. She is embarrassed to be so captivated by it in the presence of Galeazz, but it seems to have captured his attention as well.

"It must have been nice to have been one of the Olympian gods," he says. "Imagine the possibilities."

"Blasphemer," Isabella says lightly. "Besides, I think you are probably gifted enough in this arena. I loathe to see you with a god's edge."

"The Magistro tells us that the painter must create as if he were a god," the apprentice offers. He is an earnest boy, Isabella thinks, quoting his master frequently. She wonders if he has any talent of his own.

"Not as if he were being *inspired* by God?" she asks.

"No. He says that painting is an act of creation, and the painter must be God-like in his ability to imagine."

"No wonder he left Florence," Galeazz says. "Fra Girolamo Savonarola and his agents of condemnation would have his head on a stick for likening a painter to God."

"Sandro Botticelli is right now doing penance with the priest for painting his fantastical nude goddesses," says Isabella. "I believe he is saying twenty-five rosaries a day and submitting to the lash every evening because his paintings make one yearn for that time when beautiful gods walked the earth and mingled with the mortals."

"Oh, the Magistro does not admire Maestro Botticelli," the apprentice says, ever eager to share his knowledge of his master's mind. "He says he is a nice man, but he floats his subjects in space as if perspective did not exist. The Magistro attributes it to laziness. He doesn't condone any painting ignorant of the laws of mathematics. 'Perspective is the bridle and the rudder of painting,' he always says."

"Whom does he admire?" Isabella asks.

"Your Excellency, he does not care to look at the work of other painters. 'He who paints from others is creating something false.' That is another of his favorite sayings."

"I must admit that I am growing fearful of meeting a man who holds so many powerful opinions on such a variety of subjects," Isabella says. "It would be rather like an encounter with my father, who can seem daunting."

"No, Isabella, he is the essence of charm," replies Galeazz, taking the opportunity to put his arm about her shoulder as if he thought she truly was afraid. "You shall see."

"Your Excellency is too kind."

The voice is low in register, knowing in tone, and inscrutable.

His scent of lavender and poppies reaches her nose just as she turns around. How long has he been standing there? She sees a mature man of beauty and detached amusement. What strikes her first is his clothing, so elegant that he must design it himself. Despite the cold, he wears a short, rose-colored garment, probably to show off his fine calf, easily discernable beneath black hose. His vest is of gold brocade, trimmed with rosy stones, dusted at the collar by his long, curly hair, worn in the manner of a Greek youth.

As he stretches out his right hand in a formal bow, she sees that unlike every other artist she has met, his hands are pristine and show no sign of labor. His nails are as clean as a pampered princess's and look buffed to a shine. There is neither a splatter of paint nor a speck of dust about him. On one finger is a great intaglio of a ring that she thinks is a delicate carving of some naked god. Despite the immaculate appearance and the flowery scent, there is nothing of the feminine in him. He is muscled and looks as strong as a bull. At his side stands an overdressed adolescent boy, with shining black hair and eyes, ivory skin, and a little too much lace about his neck. He has a terrible, knowing look about him, and has the nerve to stare at Isabella as if she were some housemaid that he might lure into the loft above.

"We were just admiring your swans," Isabella offers, ignoring the brat and speaking to the Magistro. "We own many swans at Mantua."

"Your Excellency, is it possible to own a swan?"

"I do not mean that we possess God's creatures, but that we have many nesting in our ponds. They are very beautiful, lovely to observe."

"But like so many creatures of beauty, untrustworthy," he replies looking at the boy. "Bring our guests some wine," he tells him, and the boy takes leave, turning on his buckled shoe, and brushing his black locks away from his eyes, as if inconvenienced to do his master's bidding.

Strange arrangement, Isabella thinks. The master is the slave. Leonardo follows the boy with his eyes, which are large and russet-colored, a good match to his mane. Unlike the boy, he has a look that penetrates, but does not violate. His expression has a sweetness to it that one does not expect to find in a man of genius. He is beautiful and grand and retreating all at once. Isabella finds herself fascinated with his features—the aquiline nose and sensuous, symmetrical lips slicing his face like a mezzaluna. In fact, there is a perfect symmetry to his face as if he himself had painted it. He possesses the features of one who could play the role of the beloved in a love affair, if so he chose, but he is probably too remote and untouchable for that. Perhaps in his youth? But now strands of gray twist like ribbons through his curls. Lines that will undoubtedly deepen have made themselves at home on his face like scars interrupting his otherwise unblemished olive skin. He looks more model than artist, even at his advanced age, which must be approximately forty; more like a nobleman than any artist she has seen.

"Magistro Leonardo, I am fantastically interested in commissioning a portrait by you," Isabella says, getting down to business. "I am the Marchesa . . ."

He interrupts. "I have seen your star shine at the festivities in honor of your sister's marriage, and have heard many tongues sing of your love of all things of beauty, Marchesa."

She could not say that he did not sound sincere, but something in his tone puts him in command of the conversation. She cannot name the quality. She has grown up and holds her own in the most heated intellectual circles, among the most cultured men in society. But this man is of a different nature than the courtiers with whom she has sparred. Isabella is known in the courts of Ferrara and Mantua as one who can defend any argument, but here is a man who will never argue. Of this, she is sure. And yet she imagines he rarely does anything he does not want to do.

"I paint only at the pleasure of Il Moro," he continues. "I am his servant; he is my lord and master. I cannot take any commissions without his permission, and to be truthful, I am behind schedule on so many of his projects."

"But you have done commissioned work for Messer Galeazz."

"But with Il Moro's permission, no?" Leonardo raises his brows in question at Galeazz.

Isabella knows that Leonardo knows that the Moro was not consulted, but there is deep conviction in his questioning look.

Galeazz merely gives an apologetic shrug.

"I am pleased to have served you, sir, but we wronged my lord Ludovico, did we not?"

"No, the enterprise was for the honor and pleasure of his bride, and I am certain that her squeals of delight at seeing our costumes so skillfully designed by you compensate for any time lost on his own projects," Galeazz says.

"Magistro, a portrait of me by your own hand would bring the same pleasure to my sister, knowing as she does my love of fine painting." She hopes that she does not sound coy. It works so well with most men, but she knows it will do her no good with this one. Nor does she sense that, like all other artists, he would be swayed by praise. With this one, she is not even sure that money would motivate, though with his taste for fine costume for both himself and his liege, it might influence.

"It would be my privilege. But Your Excellency must take the subject up with the duke. I do his bidding. I am nothing more than his servant in these matters."

The boy never does return with the wine. Leonardo neither calls for him nor offers any more conversation. Their business, Isabella realizes to her dismay, is concluded.

THE journey to Milan: A success, a failure? Isabella cannot judge. She sits in her studiolo in Mantua taking stock of its contents. She has returned to nothing but incompletion: the decorations she wants for the walls of her office are not finished. She has just written to the artist to inform him that she will have to have him executed if he does not return to Mantua and finish the job. She hopes that her letter struck just the right note between teasing and threat. These artists! It is easier to coax small children to go to bed at night than to get these grown men to finish their commissions. Perhaps more women should take up the brush. They might be more easily coaxed to do one's bidding. Stacks of documents and letters sit on her desk waiting for her attention. The finance minister wishes to spend the afternoon reviewing the bills that must be paid and others that must be collected. Francesco is a good husband and a great soldier, but he is no administrator. He leaves the detail of running the government up to her while he brandishes his swords with his lieutenants or talks breeding with the trainers in the stables.

Francesco certainly would characterize her Milan trip as a success. She charmed all the people with whom he had wished to strengthen their political ties, and when she came home, she poured all of her pent-up desire for her brother-in-law into her marriage bed. She felt as if she was making love to two men at the same time, and the idea thrilled her. Francesco was amazed at her appetites, letting her stark desires swell up the pride he had in his ability as a lover of women. If he could have read her thoughts, he would have murdered her, or murdered someone. But as she kept them to herself, he took her sudden advances as evidence of his own power over her.

But thoughts of Milan gnaw at her, like so much unfinished business. Never before had she seen such an assemblage of royalty, presenting itself to honor Ludovico's marriage to her sister. Yes, the House of Este is an old and influential one. Ferrara is an important state. Her father holds powerful sway with Italy's strongest and richest princes. But she is under no illusion that the princes and kings and ambassadors from all corners of Europe who gathered at Beatrice's wedding were there to garner favor with the Este family. They were there to strengthen ties with Ludovico Sforza, Regent of Milan, controller of one of Italy's greatest treasuries; brother of a powerful cardinal in Rome; friend to the German King Maximilian of the Holy Roman Empire and a host of other royals; and now tied to the venerable House of Este by marriage. What a pity that her sister is to be the partner and mate of such a man; Beatrice, who would prefer to ride all day long rather than worry over matters of government. What a wife—what a duchess—Isabella would have made for him. How she could have aided him in his endeavors. Oh, the list of his interests and accomplishments goes on and on—planner of cities; patron of universities and of scholars of all subjects; collector of books, of priceless jewels, and of antiquities; benefactor of Italy's greatest artists; builder of churches and cathedrals and libraries. Conqueror of women. Yes, especially that. And in that arena, Isabella has shown herself to be if not his equal, then at least his match.

How much would he do for her favor? How far would he go? These are the questions that occupied her mind during her last days in Milan. She wanted to test his affection for her, but it was not simple to shake loose of her family to garner private moments with him. Her mother must have observed this special connection. On the morning after Francesco left Milan, Leonora took the apartment next to Isabella's, using the excuse that since she could not intrude upon Beatrice in the days after her wedding, the least she could do was comfort herself with proximity to her eldest before she had to take leave of both girls. It was not at all like Leonora to exhibit such a cloying display of motherly attachment. Isabella was certain that her mother was trying to act as a shield between herself and her brother-in-law.

Nighttime visits were not possible. One afternoon when Beatrice was getting fitted for some dresses to wear into her new life, Isabella boldly strutted into Ludovico's office, where he sat studying some long edict issued by the Pope.

"What has so captured your attention, brother?" she asked.

"A lot of papal nonsense, my dear. Our Holiness has decided to dictate to whom we must and must not give our allegiance. It is drivel." He cast the paper aside and sent his secretaries away.

When they were safely alone, she said, "I have wanted to see you, but my mother has been sticking to me like an eel upon the neck. We leave tomorrow."

"But I will make certain that you return to Milan without your saintly mother to guard you, and without your masked husband to keep us apart." He rose from his chair and took her arms. "We must be very careful. Every pair of eyes within these walls seeks idle gossip like a fishmonger's wife."

He kissed her very lightly on the lips and then invited her to sit down. "Do you think that, thus far, your sister is happy?"

It was not the question she had hoped he would ask.

"I suppose so. She is being fitted for magnificent gowns, given tours of the treasury and told to pick out her favorite jewels, brought delicacies and sweets from the moment she awakens until she tumbles into bed, and taken for endless rides through the countryside by the most handsome knight in Italy, who has pledged his very life to her every whim and desire. Besides all of that, my mother lectures to her day and night on her duty to be happy. The peace of all the world hangs on her delight, haven't you heard?"

Ludovico threw back his head and laughed. His laugh was deep and lusty, showing all of his big white teeth and his long red tongue. Isabella wanted to throw herself upon his lap, taking that fat snake of a tongue into her mouth, but she remained in her chair.

"By the way, my dear, I am on to your game with Messer Galeazz and my sister."

"What on earth do you mean?" he asked, still collecting himself from his great chuckle.

"Your little Bianca—adorable, by the way—is only twelve. Galeazz cannot marry her for at least another three years. In the meanwhile, you've commissioned him to distract and woo my sister so that she will not notice that your real wife in Milan is Cecilia Gallerani."

Ludovico stopped laughing. He slapped his hands on his thighs, and he stared at her, his normally open face suddenly unreadable.

"I hope I haven't made you angry."

"Actually, my dear Marchesa, I commissioned him to distract her attention from my infatuation with you."

"How clever you are, Your Excellency, to compliment me beyond my wildest dreams and divert our conversation from your mistress, all with the stroke of a sentence."

He jetted from his chair, landing on his knees at her feet, almost frightening her. She threw herself against the back of the chair, but he put his head in her lap, rubbing his cheek against her thigh. Then he looked up at her. "I never dreamed that I would find a woman as clever and intelligent as Cecilia, who would also exceed her beauty. But you are that woman. When I think that I had sent to Ferrara all those years ago to ask for the hand of the eldest Este daughter, and when she was already betrothed, I so quickly and without thought accepted the younger."

"And now, there is nothing to be done about it."

"Oh no, there is much to be done. You will see. I will send for you very soon. Your husband will not be able to turn me down. I am very persuasive when I wish to be. Ask anyone in Italy. To demonstrate the depth of my affection for you, I will do anything for you that you like. You have my word. It will be as if a magical genie from the land of the Turks has entered your life. There is a reason they call me Il Moro, you know."

"There is one feat of magic I would like you to perform," she said. "I have visited the workshop of Magistro Leonardo. I have spoken with the man. I wish to have my portrait done by him. He tells me that I must speak with you for he is merely your servant."

"Ha! If that were only true. He is his own master. But I will demand this of him, just to see your face preserved for all time as lovely as it is at this very moment."

"Thank you, Ludovico. It is all that I ask of you."

As the idea sank in, Ludovico's eyes darkened. He used Isabella's thighs to pull himself up to a standing position, and he began to pace, shaking his index finger in the air.

"This will not be easy, you realize. Sometimes, I want to send him away. I am certain that someone who is less than a genius might be more productive. You have no idea how frustrating this man can be, Isabella. If I ask for a portrait, for instance, he will not simply sit the subject in a lovely ray of light like other painters. No, he does not even pick up the brush, but spends years lost in the study of *light itself*. He could not proceed, he once told me, until he comprehended the nature of light as if he had created it himself. Only then could he paint the face properly. You see the problem in getting a simple likeness of yourself out of the man?"

Il Moro was working himself into a state. Isabella thought it best to say nothing, to let him work out his frustration. Then she would take up the practicalities of sitting for the Magistro.

"His greatest pleasure is to lose himself in himself. He would study the day long if he did not have to earn a living. He is so intent upon finding the mystery behind his process that he loses interest in the process. It's a pity that no one can enter his brain and paint the contents of his mind, for I am convinced that he keeps his genius locked up inside that head of his."

Exasperated, Ludovico fell back into the chair behind his desk. "And then there is the problem of Beatrice."

"Why is Beatrice a problem? She does not even care so much for painting."

"But she must be kept happy. She must not suspect a thing. We cannot have her running to your father, or—Our Lord Jesus forbid—your husband, with stories of how I have allowed you the privileges of a wife. I will simply tell the Magistro that he must do portraits of the both of you."

"Separately, of course?" Isabella asked. She didn't want to get into an ownership dispute with her sister.

"Of course. Because she is my wife, Beatrice will have to be painted first. Then, my dear, there will be no problem. That is, if I can force his hand. I cannot promise. He continues to frustrate me over the situation with the equestrian statue of my father.

Leonardo got himself a place in my court with promises of that statue. That was ten years ago! Do you see any giant bronze horses in Milan?"

"I understand your frustration, Ludovico, but one cannot treat these artists as one treats ordinary men. One must be very patient. They create in their own time. But if nothing is forthcoming, I highly recommend withholding their pay. It's the most expedient persuader of all. Even geniuses must eat."

Isabella was so happy to have conducted her business successfully that she almost forgot to give Ludovico the expected kisses and tenderness in this, their private goodbye.

True to his word, he hired a private courier to ride every other day to Mantua, allegedly so that she and Beatrice might stay in close touch, but in actuality to deliver to her long, secret letters in which he spoke his heart and his mind. In two weeks, she had received four of them, each one of which she answered at a length just slightly shorter than his. A woman, her mother had taught her, must always withhold just a little bit. What she thought at first would be a lover's correspondence was rapidly transforming into a sharing of minds. They wrote of political gossip, of family news, and of pieces of art they were trying to purchase, for they soon realized that they both shared a collector's particular mania. They vowed to read certain books at the same time and discuss them in their correspondence. Sometimes Isabella asked his advice on matters of state. Sometimes she forgot all about his hot kisses and felt as if she were corresponding with a twin soul. But she never forgot that this man was Beatrice's husband.

Now two weeks have passed, and still no word from him about sitting for Leonardo. She is surprised because before she left Milan, she took care of the matter of her sister sitting for the artist once and for all. On the evening before her departure, she mentioned to Beatrice that she had visited the workshop of the Magistro and was considering commissioning a portrait.

"Would you really want to sit for him?" Beatrice asked. "I

have seen him only once, but he frightens me. He is very grand. I don't like the intense way he gazes at things."

Isabella was very happy to hear that Beatrice was predisposed in this manner. She had already thought the situation through. If the Magistro were so reluctant to take up the brush, then it would be a miracle if he delivered a portrait of each sister. Isabella was determined that if only one portrait was to be done, it would be of her and not of Beatrice. Beatrice did not even like to sit for artists. Hearing this verdict on the Magistro from Beatrice's own lips was music, and just another indicator that it was Isabella's fate alone to be painted by Leonardo.

But Isabella was loath to trust anything to Fortuna. So she planted this thought in Beatrice's mind: "I do not blame you for not wanting to be painted by the Magistro. It would put you on par with your husband's mistress. Everyone in Italy knows of the painting of la Gallerani. You must not stoop to that level. You are the duchess and his lawful wife. You should hold yourself above that."

She could tell by the stricken look on Beatrice's face that the poison had taken hold. There was no way that her sister would agree to sit for Leonardo.

Now, back home in Mantua, she asks herself what she might do to put a seal to this deal. She wants to send Il Moro a gift, the perfect token of her affection, something that could be taken as impersonal, but was loaded with meaning. What can one give the man who already has everything? It should be small but significant. She looks over the treasures of her studiolo—paintings, sketches, statues from antiquity, even a bust of Caesar Augustus from his own time, cracked at the ear, but still beautiful.

But what to send a man whose collections and tastes outshine even hers? Her eyes scour the rooms, finally gazing out the window, where she sees the family of swans waddling along the half-frozen pond. The great white male with his huge wingspan is followed by a slightly smaller female and three fat white babies.

The male squawks loudly at the pond, annoyed that his winter bath has been interrupted by the big blocks of ice. The majestic creature acts as if his complaints will melt the waters. It is odd for the swans to appear in weather this cold. Perhaps it is a sign.

The next morning, Isabella sends Ludovico a pair of the young swans, a male and a female. Two days later, she receives a letter from him thanking her for these beautiful birds, who will remind him daily of her, the most graceful and beautiful creature he knows.

When she writes back, she suggests that it is not she but he who is the swan—the god in disguise, the seducer of women, a creature no one can resist. She even suggests that he is more powerful than Zeus because he does not need to transform himself to transfix women. In his mere mortal form, he already has her heart.

She knows that if nothing else, no man can resist the idea of himself as irresistible. She thinks upon which seal she will use for this letter, settling on a musical note cut in a wide, orange carnelian stone. She presses the cold imprint into the hot wax, hands the letter off to a secretary, and then settles back into her routine at Mantua, confidently waiting for him to summon her for her sitting in Milan with Leonardo.

Chapter Four

VI * GLI AMANTI (THE LOVERS)

*IN THE YEAR 1492; IN THE HUNTING PARKS AND
PLEASURE PALACE AT VIGEVANO,
IN THE REGION OF MILAN*

E look like unicorns," Beatrice says playfully, trying to think of some way to pull her cousin out of her gloom. It is a glorious spring day, with lords and ladies dressed for the hunt in matching green splendor, all of Beatrice's design, and she is tired of wasting this, her grand moment, on propping up the flagging spirits of the Duchess of Milan.

Surprisingly, Isabel of Aragon responds by bucking at Beatrice with the jewel-encrusted horn at the top of her forehead, and Beatrice nudges back with the identical crescent. Their horses, not entirely comfortable being so close while their riders play-joust, snort and shimmy to gain distance from each other.

Beatrice straightens her headdress, signaling for Isabel to do the same. It will not do, on the occasion of a royal hunt, with so many companions of noble birth—and nitpicking tongues—to have a crooked horn jutting out of one's forehead. Grateful for the moment of levity, Beatrice hopes that it lasts for the rest of the day; with the exception of the morose, anxious cousin who rides beside her, she cannot, in her beautiful clothes, riding in and out of cool shade and shimmering sun, think of one foul thing to spoil her own mood. The mere touch of her silk green veil grazing at her face and cascading down her shoulders all the way to the ground when she is standing, but now covering the rear of her horse like a tent, is enough to make her happy.

"They say that all the ladies of France are wearing such head-dresses," Beatrice replies. "But undoubtedly, they were invented here."

"Undoubtedly," replies Isabel, eyes glued straight ahead again, and mouth slouching back into its downturned grimace.

Beatrice has been noticing all day that Isabel of Aragon has tried her best to avoid looking at her husband. Gian Galeazzo, the young Duke of Milan, has spent the day falling off his white steed while trying to pick boughs and fruits and flowers to give to his swarthy young lover who rides beside him. Every time he sees some bauble from nature that he thinks will please the hulking youth, he reaches for it without caution, sliding unconsciously from the horse and into the dirt. Everyone smiles apologetically, with the exception of the young lover, who laughs without re-straint at the duke's antics.

His green satin doublet—identical to those worn by the twenty lords who are today accompanying them on this adven-ture—is disgraced with stains, standing out against the still-pristine satins and moirés of the other men. The belt sewn with diamonds and emeralds with which he started the day has long since been captured by a faithful page, after the duke threw it to the ground for constricting one of his many attempts at garnering a white blossom for his paramour. He has not stopped drinking since the previous evening, Isabel has confided to Beatrice, who, frankly, would prefer to concentrate on the great feats of hunting being performed by Ludovico's special dogs and falcons. Ludo-vico himself is very kind to his nephew, making excuses for him each time he makes a fool of himself, cajoling him to be more careful.

"How my nephew loves nature!" Ludovico says to the lords and ladies who try to hide their snickers as the young duke again nearly slips from his saddle in another comical inebriated lurch. "You must not let it be your demise, my lord. You must be more cautious in reaching for God's little presents."

Yet each of Ludovico's generous apologies for his nephew makes Isabel of Aragon's proud face sink deeper and deeper into an ugly frown.

Beatrice has her frustrations with Ludovico, but in comparison to his nephew—intoxicated with liquor and lusting for a crude country boy—she can hardly complain. Ludovico had allowed her to commission matching costumes for forty lords and ladies for this occasion, tearing the artisans and seamstresses away from his decorating projects throughout the many houses and castellos he occupies to satisfy Beatrice's desire for the clothing, which she had designed herself. Before they had departed from Milan, he had taken her through the Treasure Tower and selected a wardrobe of gems to adorn her riding habit. He picked out hundreds of pearls, emeralds, diamonds, and rubies, all of which were then sewn into her headdress, bodice, *camora*, and sleeves.

"You must outshine the Queen of France," he said.

"My lord, I do not think the queen is going to be present on the hunt," she replied.

"Ah, but if all goes according to plan, someday you and she may be the best of friends," he countered. He kissed her sweetly on the forehead and would say no more on the subject. Well. He had grand plans for her, indeed.

Now her jewels shimmer in the lazy May sun, making her look like an angel in a painting haloed with God's own light. She has asked to stop at every pond and stream so that she can admire her radiant reflection, and the lush landscape of Ludovico's hunting park at Vigevano is full of such opportunities. All day long, they have been riding along the perimeter of wide lakes and jumping across rushing brooks and streams, stopping often to let their horses partake of the sweet waters. Each time she catches a glimpse of her grand figure in the water's surface, she falls in love with her own image, and has to remind herself not to get so lost in the glowing, undulating likeness of herself that she tips, like Narcissus, into the water and drowns.

Surely Ludovico must notice that she cuts a striking figure in this magnificent dress, riding her white palfrey. How can his eyes avoid the dramatic effect of her long dark hair and olive complexion against the emerald green of her habit, the color of which makes her look as if she is rising directly out of the lush landscape like some nymph. He must have observed how the diamond-and-pearl choker elongates her neck, making her seem tall, and that her bodice is tight, demonstrating that she has the smallest waist of any woman present today, with the exception of his thirteen-year-old daughter, Bianca Giovanna. He must also have perceived how Beatrice has taken Bianca Giovanna into her confidence; how Beatrice allows the girl to have all the attention when they are in the presence of Galeazz, her fiancé. Surely, taking note of all of these things, Ludovico's heart must be opening up to her. Did he not spend hours of his time adorning her with jewels for this outing? That was a good sign of his growing affection.

He is polite, generous, and complimentary. Yet he treats her much the same as he treats his little Bianca Giovanna, as a charming child who amuses him but cannot hold his attention. He only comes to his wife after consulting with his astrologer on fortuitous nights for conception, rapidly completing his husbandly duties so that he can spend the evening with Cecilia, whose son by Ludovico is over one year old. After hours of prayers to the Blessed Virgin, however, the physical pain caused by Ludovico's visits has diminished, and only the loneliness lingers after he leaves Beatrice's bed.

Beatrice knows all too well what her husband likes, and she does not have it. She remembers the way he stared at her sister's glorious bosom, but he does not even touch her tiny buds when they make love—if one can give such a lofty description to the polite mechanics they practice in the dark. From all reports, Cecilia sounds as if she might be Isabella's twin. Isabella is womanly and has a fountain of golden blond hair and is a great lover of literature and learning. What justice is there in this horrible fact that one's husband is *naturally* drawn to the qualities one's sister *naturally* possesses? Between the time Il Moro spends in correspondence with Isabella and the time he spends with his mistress, he has no time at all for his wife, so he has thrown her at Galeazz who distracts and entertains her.

At this moment, with Beatrice riding at the rear of the party to keep her cousin, the Gloom of Aragon, from falling into despair, Galeazz is demonstrating to a delighted Bianca Giovanna how his finest falcon, Osiris, chases prey. Birds clamor and caw from inside a cluster of old oak trees, rustling the leaves as if someone has invaded a nest of hissing snakes. Galeazz gently removes the falcon's leather hood, dotted with a tiny V shape of dark sapphires that crest at the beak, revealing his intelligent feathered face. The animal remains perched on Galeazz's white leather glove, though Beatrice can sense that he is already alert to his surroundings. His eyes go immediately to the trees and do not move from them.

"Look, Isabel, Galeazz is releasing Osiris!" Beatrice says excitedly, trying to interest her cousin in the day's activities. But Isabel only glances in their direction, then returns her snarling sideward glare to her husband.

She would not put a damper on this, one of Beatrice's favorite sports. Even the sleek greyhounds and snapping spaniels stick their snouts into the air, aware that something exciting is about to begin. A flock of gray heron soars into the air at once from behind their camouflage, flying with long, deliberate strides on the way to their watery habitat in the lake ahead. Beatrice knows that they nest high in the trees, and she hopes that no little babies try to fly away with the adults, for there is no sport in killing an animal before it is grown. The long-necked, wide-winged birds flap lazily toward the lake, unaware of the danger below.

Galeazz need only raise his wrist ever so slightly, and Osiris shoots into the air after the birds. The pages, in their costumes of dark green on the heart side of their bodies and pale green on the right, race ahead with the dogs, and the entire party gallops to keep pace. Beatrice leaves her miserable cousin behind as she rhythmically whips her mount, passing Ludovico and his daughter, until she is at Galeazz's side. As Osiris soars straight into the skinny neck of the lead heron, four other lords receive their falcons from their attendants, remove their hoods, and send them shooting into the sky. Before the others reach the flock, Osiris has killed one bird, which spirals to the ground, and is on to his second victim. The others catch up with him, each attacking a prey. As the birds fall to the ground, the dogs are immediately upon them. Before they can tear them to pieces, making them unsuitable for dinner, dog trainers are pouring blood collected from slaughtered pigs into bowls from crusty leather sacs, distracting the hounds from the birds while the pages collect the prey. Beatrice does not particularly care for heron, but once the bird is braised with wine and garlic and onions, it is suitable enough to serve.

Beatrice's heart races as she slows her pace to survey the kill. Gray feathers fall from the sky, skimming her forehead, nose, and shoulders. The falcons have destroyed so many of the herons that for a moment it seems as if the sky is raining feathers. Their long, lifeless legs dangle like fringe as the boys collect them, holding them by their bleeding necks.

Osiris returns to his master, who invites his young betrothed to let the hero perch on her small, gloved wrist. Beatrice can tell that the girl is enchanted, but afraid. Osiris bleeds from the right wing, and he has lost many feathers in the fight. Bianca Giovanna lets the falcon rest upon her wrist, and she whispers sweet words to him while Galeazz prepares to hood him once again.

Beatrice adores Bianca Giovanna and is happy to see her fiancé treat her so sweetly, but it reminds her of the courtly and tender ways of Francesco when he and Isabella were in the betrothal stage. Why must Beatrice have a husband who is in love with another? Not just with one other woman, but if truth be known, two.

As if she doesn't see the way that Ludovico stares and stares the day long at that pair of swans that Isabella sent him as a present for his ponds. Beatrice is an extraordinary archer and would like to shoot those elegant white beasts. If only they were not so lovely, she would send two arrows straight through their hearts. Or at least, she would turn one of the fiercest falcons on them and watch the bird rip out their throats. Swans could be mean, however, and would protect each other with great bravery. At least it would be a fair fight, unlike what she was up against with Cecilia Gallerani and her own sister.

Francesco, too, seems aware of the infatuation. Ludovico keeps inviting Isabella to Milan for "Beatrice's sake" without even consulting Beatrice, and Francesco keeps coming up with reasons why his wife has to remain in Mantua. First he was away in Bologna for his brother Giovanni's wedding to Laura Bentivoglio, and demanded that Isabella stay at home and conduct all matters of business and government. Then he made a side trip to visit his sister Elisabetta in Urbino, Beatrice was certain, just to keep Isabella at home a little longer. When he came home, he was mysteriously ill, and insisted that Isabella remain at his side to nurse him. Lastly, and Beatrice only knows this through the gossip that flies from court to court, Francesco reminds his wife all the time that they "are not rich like the Sforzas," and with the way she likes to travel—with hundreds of attendants and an entire new wardrobe so that she won't feel inferior to her sister—she has to keep her trips to a minimum. The last report was that Isabella had threatened to come to Milan in her chemise if Francesco refused her a proper wardrobe.

Ludovico's disappointment over his spurned invitations to Isabella finally culminated in a shocking gesture. Morose, he canceled the games and jousts at Pavia to be held in honor of the birth of the duke and duchess's son, the little Count of Pavia. Isabel of Aragon was furious at the insult to her son. She fired off angry letters to her relations in Naples, demanding that they use whatever means necessary to remove Ludovico as her husband's regent. Beatrice knows this because all the court secretaries share information. Beatrice also knows that the royals of Naples would love to comply with Isabel's request, but for the fact that Gian Galeazzo is an imbecile and a drunkard; he is a disaster leading a horse to water, much less leading the most important city-state in Italy.

Look at him now, losing his seat in his saddle again in an attempt to grope at his beloved's stubbly face. At least Beatrice is in competition with two women of beauty and grace, and not some country bumpkin with long, gangly limbs who cannot read or write. As Duke Gian Galeazzo's attendant pulls him back into the saddle, Ludovico hands him a flask of wine. Beatrice watches Isabel's eyes land on Il Moro like the tongue of a venomous cobra on its victim. Color shoots into her cheeks, and her bosom, already pushed up high by her bodice, rises in a steady, belabored heave. Beatrice knows that Isabel blames Ludovico for Gian Galeazzo's degraded condition, but what else is Il Moro supposed to do? Turn power over to a man with half a brain, who has no interest in administering the government? Lose the duchy of Milan to whatever enemy first strikes after the foolish boy is put in charge?

Beatrice has no illusions about Ludovico's love of power; yet she thinks that he treats the feeble young duke with more respect than that idiot deserves. Another man might have had him quietly done away with. Italian politics were full of such stories. Even her own father had tried to poison his nephew Niccolò, who repeatedly conspired against him, until finally, after an attempted insurgency, the Diamond had him beheaded. No one thought the less of her father. Indeed, respect for him grew. He and Duchess Leonora and all of their children were alive and prospering, and not rotting in a tomb in Ferrara's Duomo like so many families of leaders who failed to eliminate their enemies. No, after Duke Ercole executed his nemesis, the streets of Ferrara rang out with cries of *Diamante! Diamante! Long live Ercole!* The people of Ferrara then gave him his second nickname, the North Wind, to acknowledge how his cold decision-making abilities had saved their land.

But the belle of Aragon has no such affection for Ludovico. She does not allow herself to consider that, by assuming power, Ludovico is saving Milan from ruin at the hands of the inept Gian Galeazzo. Whipping her horse around, Isabel rides to Beatrice, almost sideswiping her. "Come with me, cousin," she hisses. It is not a request, but a command. "I know an especial pond from which your horse would love to drink."

Beatrice, reluctant to hear one of Isabel's tirades against all the world on this lovely day, follows anyway, although something inside of her is telling her to make an excuse and remain with the party. Against her better judgment, she allows Isabel to lead them down a narrow path, where thistles snag at their veils and scrape their horses' flanks. Finally, they reach the promised pond, a puddle of stagnant scum.

"That's disgusting," Beatrice says. "I wouldn't let Drago drink from that."

"Strange that nature's formation disgusts you, but the actions of your husband do not."

"I don't know what you are talking about," Beatrice says, backing Drago up to maneuver him away from the poison on the ground and the poison coming from her cousin's mouth.

"Do you not see how Ludovico keeps my husband drunk so that he may continue to usurp his power?"

Beatrice says nothing, but she would like to fire back that the duke would have come into his full power when he came of age two years ago if he had shown any interest in or ability for running the kingdom.

"Ludovico is betraying us all," Isabel says. Beatrice waits for her to go on. Perhaps after she has delivered her speech, she will be spent.

"Are you pretending that you don't know how he promenades Cecilia Gallerani around at public functions as if she were his wife? Would you not like to be in attendance with your husband on these occasions and not locked up in your apartments in the Castello like a child in a nursery?"

Beatrice is aware of Ludovico's nightly visits to Cecilia; she has had no idea that they have been appearing together in public. She knows that she should stop listening, knows that she should dig her heels into Drago's sides and flee this news, but she cannot move.

"Do you think people wonder why Ludovico's lawful wife is kept hidden while he struts his mistress and his bastard all over the city?"

Beatrice whips Drago around. Her veil sticks on a thorn, pulling her headdress askew. Annoyed, she yanks the thing off. "You are no friend, cousin, if you insist on infecting my mind against my husband by spreading these rumors."

"Cousin, what rumors? This is but the truth: you and I are the most ill-treated, unfortunate women in the kingdom." Isabel grabs the jeweled horn at her forehead. "Let us not lock horns, Beatrice. There is so very much we might do together to affect our fates—and the fate of Italy."

Beatrice says nothing. Her father always told his children that the wise man listens while the fool gabs away.

"Have you any idea that your husband is conspiring with the

French King Charles against our own grandfather?" Isabel asks, her voice low and full of knowing. "The French want Naples; that's no secret. Ludovico believes that if he helps the French take Naples from King Ferrante, then Charles will invest him with the title of Duke of Milan. Do you know what will happen in that case to my husband and me? Ludovico either will have us exiled or will have us murdered in our sleep, whichever suits him. But imagine, Beatrice, your own husband joining the French to depose our grandfather Ferrante. Is that what you want?"

"That is ridiculous," Beatrice says. "There is no such intrigue." But she cannot forget the comment Ludovico had made about her someday being the best of friends with the Queen of France, *if all goes according to plan*. Now, in light of Isabel's accusations, it makes perfect sense.

"Join *with* me," Isabel says. "Ferrante loves us both. If he knew that not one of his granddaughters but two were suffering constant humiliation at the hands of our husbands, he would send an army here to rescue us. We are princesses of two of the greatest families in Europe—Aragon and Este. We are blood, Beatrice. Your mother is of the House of Aragon. Who is Ludovico but the son of a mercenary who stole power at an opportune time? You can pay him back for all that he is doing to sink our names into disgrace!"

"I must think on this, cousin." These are the only words Beatrice can say and she mumbles them, not meeting Isabel's angry eyes. She feels fear now, fear of her cousin and fear of her husband, and she does not know which is or should be the greater. Isabel's eyes are so wild and her voice so full of venom that Beatrice wonders, if she refuses to conspire with her, will Isabel try to kill her? On the other hand, could Ludovico's plans be so far-reaching and sinister?

As if answering Beatrice's unspoken question, Isabel says, "Ludovico Sforza would conspire with the devil himself to become Duke of Milan. He would happily betray you, your family,

my husband, our family, or his own family to satisfy his ambitions."

Beatrice starts to turn Drago around so that she does not have
to look at her cousin. "I said I would think on it."

"Think on this, while you are thinking." Isabel's words fly
like arrows past Beatrice's ears—whizzing, angry, dangerous, and
seeking a soft target. "If Ludovico joins with France against
Naples, Beatrice, what will be your lot? Have you thought of that?
I can tell you: you will be sent back to your father, and while your
bed is still warm, a French bride, taken to please King Charles,
will be sleeping in your quarters. That is, if Ludovico does not see
that you are mysteriously given some bad meat first."

Beatrice wants to answer that Ludovico would never do such a
thing, but she is not so certain that her cousin has not hit upon
some unfortunate truth. Not that she intends to allow the horrible
prediction to come to fruition. She says nothing. Her shoulders
rise and her arms and legs shoot out to the side to gain strength.
Stretched out like some awkward bird attempting to take flight,
and breathing in a little more warm air, she slaps her legs against
Drago and gallops away toward the sounds of the hunting party.

Thoughts pass through her mind like the wind, making her
heart pump faster as she races along the narrow path. She feels as
if her body is going to implode from the dozens of emotions rising within her and yet she cannot think. Does not want to think.
Despite all she feels, her head is empty.

She rides as fast as she can, but she can hear that the hunting
party has picked up speed and is riding away from her as quickly
as she tries to catch up with them. Arriving at the end of the
path, she comes to the clearing and sees in the distance that
Ludovico, Galeazz, and several of the men are giving chase to a
pack of brown wolves while the women hang behind, chattering
among themselves under little green tents, taking umbrage from
the sun.

Beatrice picks up speed, heading for the chase. The horses and hounds have pushed the wolves to the edge of a river, surrounding them. The hounds bark madly, and the wolves—Beatrice counts seven—ululate with ferocity in response. The men cry out to their pages for their bows and spears.

Ludovico smiles as he sees Beatrice approach at breakneck speed. He raises his hand, signaling her to slow down, but she gallops ahead, almost knocking over a page who is quickly trying to thread a dark wooden bow with a green arrow.

"Bow!" she demands, and the boy, startled, freezes. Beatrice circles him, and before he is aware of what she is doing, leans to her right, grabbing the weapon as she circles Drago around the page.

In a split second, she identifies her target, the largest of the animals, looking at her with eyes like icy moons. She thinks for a moment that she sees the landscape reflected in its eyes. It growls at her, frightening her horse, which backs up skittishly. Galeazz shoots, and one of the wolves drops to the ground, making the survivors howl yet more fiercely. Beatrice thinks she might go mad from this wailing chorus. If only to silence at least one of them, to stop this ear-splitting lamentation, she clutches her legs tight around Drago's superbly veined belly for balance, and releases the arrow into the wolf's side. She knows that she has missed her precise mark, instead piercing the animal through the upper chest. Perhaps in anger, perhaps from the pain that must be shooting through his front legs, the wolf leaps in the air at her, burying his teeth into Drago's chest. The horse rears back, hooves kicking into the air high above his head like an acrobat. Beatrice feels herself leave the saddle. Like a kite, she rises into the air as Drago bucks wildly, trying to release himself from the wolf's grip. She sees blood from the wounds spreading over the coats of both animals. She sees that the afternoon sky is lapis blue, and that lavender buds have already begun to hang like jewels in the wisteria trees. The last thing she sees is the look of horror on Ludovico's face, his eyes bulging and his hands frozen in the air like a statue of an ancient orator. She thinks, but cannot be sure, that he has just screamed "No." Then she feels her body hit hard earth, and all is black.

FROM THE NOTEBOOK OF LEONARDO:
Of the movement of birds: When birds wish to fly from one spot to another they will fly faster by making spontaneous headlong movements, and then rising up with reflex movement against the resistance in the air, and again making a fresh descent, and so on and so forth.

Dissect the bat, study it carefully, and on the model of this animal and his wings, design the machine.

A tiny chirp breaks the silence. Beatrice thinks it must be morning, though she is not ready to open her eyes. She feels a cool rag on her forehead and a blanket over her body. She thinks that she might be in Naples, and her governess has come in during the night to cover her from unexpected cool evening breezes. Why the cool cloth? Has she suffered with fevers? She hopes that Nanny won't scold her again for riding through a cold spring day without a cloak. Beatrice remembers riding along the windy coast of Naples Bay—yesterday, today, or many years ago?—calculating that a short illness is an easy price to pay for the ecstasy of dancing the day long with fresh ocean breezes. Now a large, strange, hot hand is on hers.

"Beatrice?" A man's voice rises above the warbling bird. "Can you hear me, darling wife?"

She opens her eyes. Her husband is inches away from her face, staring at her as if she has awakened from the dead. Startled by his large features and his concerned look, she pulls away, but has nowhere to go. Head glued to the pillow, she waits for her memory to catch up with her, and it does: the sickening conversation with Isabel by the stagnant pond; the wolf's bare teeth, screaming with pain, blood spurting everywhere; and Drago rearing up like some wild dancer and knocking her into the sky. Beatrice winces, remembering it all. They have taken her back to her room at the palace at Vigevano, where she wants to close her eyes again against feelings of anger and disgrace.

"Is there pain?" Ludovico asks. "The doctor says that no bones are broken, nor is the skull injured."

Beatrice manages a slight smile and then directs her gaze away from his face. Why is he looking so concerned if he intends to replace her with a Frenchwoman, or poison her in the interim? Even without Isabel of Aragon's insinuations, Ludovico's worry about one whom he so neglects seems misplaced. She cannot figure it unless, as she has been hoping, he loves her more than she thinks.

The drapes and shutters are still open, and she can see the dusky sun nearing the end of its day's journey. The sky is purple, leaving much of the room in shadow. Someone has lit a small lamp. Ludovico turns his face upward, thanking God in Latin—Our Lord's favorite language—for not taking his little wife, but returning her to "those of us who love her the most."

Galeazz shows himself, holding a small, gilded cage with a little red finch. He lowers the cage so that Beatrice can see its fluttering wings. "I told them that you would hear the song of the bird, and that it would bring you back to us." He is smiling, his teeth gleaming at her, the brightest thing in the room.

"Madonna Beatrice, please say something to us." The voice is officious and not at all pleasant to the ear. Messer Ambrogio, Ludovico's astrologer, steps out of Ludovico's shadow and looms over her bed. Beatrice does not like him. He is too thin. Not fit and sculpted like her father, but the kind of thin that results from a dislike of food or from a body full of worms that eat away anything he ingests. Either way, she has never understood why Ludovico has chosen this person upon whom to rely for the timing of so many crucial decisions.

"Step aside, sir, so that I can see the setting sun." There. That was exactly what she wanted to say to this man and she said it. Perhaps a fall from a horse, a knock on the head, is exactly what she has needed to shake up all the words that roll around in her brain and make them come out of her mouth. She almost giggles at her impertinence, but she sees that Ludovico and Galeazz are both snickering behind the astrologer's back.

"Look who is here," Ludovico says. He puts his arm around her neck and helps her to sit up. Mathilda springs forth with a devilish grin, then dives with her hands to the ground, turning over into a handstand. She wears no underwear. She kicks her legs into the air, spreading them apart, demonstrating her hairy crotch, before jumping back to her feet in triumph.

Beatrice gives her favorite dwarf a little round of applause.

"You're just fine, aren't you, Duchess?" Mathilda's anxious face, with her too-big nose and ears, is side by side with Ludovico's, both staring at her with the intensity of governesses searching a child's hair for lice.

"Yes, Mathilda, I am just fine. You may go now, and tell the steward that I have ordered him to give you a special bottle of red wine from the cellar. The finest vintage of what we have just brought up from Osteria."

To show her appreciation, Mathilda cartwheels her way out of the room, giving her bare behind to the royals, cackling all the way down the hall.

Galeazz has put the birdcage down on a dressing table and kneels by the bedside, taking her hand. "You are the bravest woman in all the world. You were magnificent today. We are having the wolf stuffed for you. He'll make a nice trophy."

"And Drago?"

"Superficial wounds," Ludovico says. "No wild creature will

take that animal down. He is resting in the stables with a fragrant ointment upon his chest, made especially for him by the stable master."

"I will mix Your Excellency a potion for sleep," declares Messer Ambrogio.

"No, now that I am awake, I intend to remain this way as long as I can," Beatrice says.

"But Your Excellency needs rest—"

Beatrice interrupts him. "Gentlemen, I would like to be alone with my husband, if you please."

Galeazz kisses her hand again and again, pressing it to his face. Without another word, he backs out of the door smiling. But the astrologer waits behind. Did he not hear her? Is her voice faint and inarticulate? Beatrice waits another polite second and then asks, "Sir, are you my husband?"

"Your Excellency is either not well or is joking."

"Then I really must ask you to leave."

He looks stunned by her command, turning to Ludovico who confirms with a nod that the astrologer and medicine man is no longer needed in the room. With emphatic clicking heels and no further discussion, he leaves them alone.

"You gave us quite the scare," Ludovico says, taking the cloth from her brow and kissing her forehead. "Thank God you are not harmed."

He says this not as if it is the beginning of a conversation but as if he is winding up his business with her so that he can leave the room. Beatrice feels fury rise up within her. Does he have Cecilia hidden somewhere at Vigevano?

"My lord," she says, "I wish to tell you about my terrible dream."

"What dream is that, child?"

Child. Soon he will no longer think upon her in this way.

"I dreamed—oh, it was frightening and ridiculous," she begins, trying to achieve just the right rhythm and tone for what she is about to say. "I dreamed that you were in secret conspiracy with the French King Charles against my grandfather Ferrante. You know that this arrangement would cause me terrible pain, because I grew up in his court. I know that he is not a well-liked man, but I sat on his lap and pulled on his beard all during my childhood, and he loves me very much. In my dream, you were going to war with Naples. This angered my cousin Isabel of Aragon, so she appealed to me to throw my lot in with her, and with the House of Aragon, and against you, my own husband!"

Beatrice gives Ludovico a little smile, as if to say, isn't that silly? She waits for him to speak. He looks at her gravely.

"And how does this go in your dream?"

"Not well, my lord, at least not for you. Because I did join with Isabel and the kingdom of Naples—which isn't so far-fetched because my mother is of the House of Aragon—so of course, Ferrara supported me, as it would support one of its princesses. And since Ferrara supported Naples, then Mantua was not far behind. And the worse part was that Mantua gave Venice a good reason to attack Milan, because Francesco is captain general of their army, and they would naturally support him. The Venetians would love to do you in, my lord, and that is not just a fiction of my dream!"

Ludovico seems keenly interested in what his child-bride is saying. She wonders if she has ever before so thoroughly captured his attention. He sits on the bed and speaks to her, slowly and deliberately. "Tell me, Beatrice, exactly how does this fantasy play out? You flee to Naples with Isabel of Aragon?"

"Oh no, my lord. We send for their army. My uncle Alfonso rides at its head, because, as you know, he deeply hates you. No, we do not leave Milan, but the army comes here and rescues us! Oh, it's very exciting. The Neapolitan army rides up from the south, and the Venetians, backed by Ferrara and Mantua, attack from the east, with Francesco commanding them. You wouldn't believe it, but he sits on his horse at the walls of the Castello screaming at you for trying to take his wife."

"Now why would Francesco engage in such nonsense, even in

a dream?" A little smile cuts across Ludovico's face, yet his eyes are very serious.

"He's terribly jealous, and if a man even talks to Isabella, much less corresponds with her regularly as you do, he takes great offense. At any rate, in my dream, the French do not come to your rescue, and the armies of Italy demolish Milan."

Beatrice waits quietly. Does he see through her ruse? She realizes that a better woman would have confronted him directly with Isabel of Aragon's accusations, and with his clandestine lust for her sister, but this is as direct as she can be. Her mother has a saying about attracting flies with honey, but at this moment, she cannot remember it, only its moral.

Ludovico does not jump to his own defense, but speaks with measure. "Surely you know that your sister depends on me for advice. The marquis leaves so many functions of government to her, and she is barely eighteen years of age."

"Oh I understand that, my lord, and I would die rather than deprive my sister of your good counsel. But there is no controlling the thoughts of a man like Francesco. He is not in possession of good reason when it comes to his wife."

"That is what they tell me," Ludovico sighs. The mocking she had expected in his voice is not there. "That is quite the terrible dream. Did I die?"

"I do not remember, exactly," she goes on, now more confident that her tactic is working; he is neither yelling at her, nor laughing at her, nor walking away from her in anger or disgust. "But after the armies captured the Castello, they took you away and left the city to Gian Galeazzo and Isabel of Aragon, with my uncle Alfonso as governor. It was what Isabel wanted all along, to get rid of you so that she could be the true duchess. She kept saying in the dream that you would collude with the devil himself to become the Duke of Milan."

"And you believe that, Beatrice? Either in your dream or in your waking state?"

She waits. She knows that when she is playing a good hand of cards—good, but not infallible—she must choose precisely the right moment to call the opponent's bluff. Because if he pulls a trump on her, she loses all. She wants no surprise from Ludovico laid on the table. She speaks slowly, trying her best to appear nonchalant. "No, my lord, I do not. Because I know that you are an intelligent man, and if you were truly intent upon becoming the official Duke of Milan, the first person you would enlist as your ally is your wife. Since you have not seen fit to make me your partner and ally in any real sense, then you could not possibly truly wish to become Milan's duke. I do not believe what they say; I believe you are perfectly satisfied being Gian Galeazzo's regent."

Beatrice cannot believe what has come out of her mouth, but she is quaking with excitement. Could her fall really have awakened a courageous and eloquent part of her brain that has lain dormant all her life? She keeps looking at Ludovico, trying to read his thoughts.

"Let us say, for the sake of argument, that this were true; that my ambition was to become Duke of Milan. Why, exactly, would I require my wife as my partner and ally?"

"Because, my lord, there is no one else in Italy who would not betray you for his own gain but me. Many people respect you; even more fear you. But the greatest number would like to see your ruin."

"And why are you not among that number?"

"I promised my father that with our marriage, the Houses of Sforza and Este would be forever united. That is my duty to my family."

"Are you such an obedient daughter?"

Her mask crumbles. She can no longer dissemble. She makes her hands into small fists and pounds on the bed. "No, my lord, I am not obedient at all! Why can't you see that I love you and want to be your wife?"

She puts her shamed face in her hands and begins to cry. Now he is free to laugh at her if he must. Instead, she feels his arms go around her. He holds her close, but as if he does not wish to hurt her with too much pressure.

"I see, I see," he says. "Little one, you must rest. The day's events have shaken your emotions. This dream seems to have confused you, Beatrice. You should sleep. Perhaps in the morning your good cheer will have returned."

She is about to protest that he is wrong, that it is her love for him that moves her, when he continues, "The astrologer says that in a fortnight, the stars will again be aligned for me to sire a son. That is how you can be my partner. Rest now, and get well so that you can give us children."

Is he just trying to get away from her again? She has not been successful. He does not fear her alliance with Isabel of Aragon or with Naples; he does not see her as woman, wife, and partner, but as a birthing machine. If she is not that to him, then she is nothing.

"My good cheer will not return, my lord, unless you begin to treat me as a wife."

"But you have everything you desire," he protests.

"I have everything I desire but my husband. I may as well return to my father's house. I think you would like that." She rubs the tears from her eyes and looks directly at her husband. She realizes that she has shifted from astute political player to whining child in these last moments, but she is no longer in control, so she hurls angry words at him. "I believe that would please you. I believe that I will have Messer Trotti go to my father tomorrow morning with the news that Ludovico Sforza does not care for Beatrice d'Este. Then you may fight all of Italy on your own, with your beloved French at your side, as if they will be loyal to you once they have finished with you. I hope everything in my dream comes to pass. Then you will see what you lost by not loving me!"

She tries to get up. She is sore from the fall, but she is also young and strong, and she wills herself to roll away from her husband. She stands up, staring across the bed at him, but she has risen too quickly, and she feels the blood rush to her head. Steadying her legs against the side of the bed, she uses all of her strength to stay lucid and erect.

"Your Excellency, I have seen you handle the bow, and I assure you that I do not wish you to be against me," he says.

"Are you back to mocking me, my lord?" she asks.

"Never." He is smiling at her now, beaming, actually. There is no mockery in his face. "You are wonderful, Beatrice. You are bold and brave. One moment, a courageous woman, the next, a pouting girl. You are—oh, I don't know—you are my tiny Amazon." He rises slowly and walks to the other side of the bed. He takes her in his arms. She feels unsteady, and she leans against him for support. She wishes that they might remain this way forever.

"What must we do to make certain that this terrible nightmare of yours never comes to pass?" he asks.

She has no idea if he is softening to her or if he is trying to protect himself politically, but she does not care. She thinks the outcome will be the same: he will learn to love her.

She grabs on to his brocade vest, clutching it, pulling him closer to her. "The fall from the horse has stirred my womb, Ludovico. We don't need an astrologer's calculations anymore. Make love to me *now*. You don't need another woman. I am your wife. And I am telling you that any other woman trying to usurp that office will have to leave the Castello immediately. Otherwise, I will go home to Ferrara, or to Naples, or to wherever I have to go to escape this humiliation."

"But my dear—"

"Say nothing about it, Ludovico, but act before it is too late. I understand that we must be generous to your child. God knows, my father was kind to his bastards. But I will not have another wife in my house. If she is in the Castello when we return, I will go first to my sister and brother-in-law in Mantua and explain my predicament, and then on to my father's home. Whether my father chooses to avenge the disgrace I've suffered is beyond my control."

FROM THE NOTEBOOK OF LEONARDO:
On the penis: It has some relations with human intelligence and sometimes shows an intelligence of its own. Where a man may desire it to be stimulated, it remains obstinate and follows its own path. Sometimes it moves on its own without permission from its owner, or by any thought or desire of that person. Whether the organ's owner is asleep or awake, it does what it pleases; often the man is asleep and his penis awake, or the man is awake and it is asleep. Or the man would like it to be in arousal but it refuses. Often it desires action and the man refuses. That is why it seems that this creature often has a life and an intelligence apart from the greater organism that carries it. Yet it seems that the man is wrong to be ashamed of giving it a name or showing it off. That which those would have him cover and hide he ought to expose with solemnity, with the demeanor of a priest at Mass.

SEPTEMBER 1492; IN THE CITY OF MILAN

BEATRICE trots along in her new chariot that Ludovico had specially made for her. Its wood is fine and heavy, but Il Moro had one of the many artisans in his employ gilt its edges. A soft tent, the fabric of which is changed every day to match her outfit, keeps the September sun off of her face as she navigates her way through Milan's streets.

When she thinks on how her life has changed over the course of one short summer, she wants to sing—not softly and harmonically as one does in churches and parlors, but loudly, bawdily, like the dwarves do late into the evening during their wine-soaked orgies. She would like to take off all her heavy clothes and do handstands naked like Mathilda, showing her dimpled behind to anyone who cares to look. Sometimes she thinks that her small body is not made to accommodate such rambunctious happiness.

She had taken a big risk, but it had paid off. She would never have made good on her threat to leave Ludovico, mostly because the Diamond's reaction to her running back home would have been to spank her and put her in a convent.

But Ludovico had no way of knowing that.

Instead of being angry at her outburst, Ludovico was moved. Men adore to be adored, her mother always said, and now she had proof that it was true. That night, tears still wet on her face, back so sore from her fall that she could barely stand, she grabbed him by the vest and pulled him onto the bed. She climbed on top of him, kissing him madly, sucking on his tongue so hard that she could feel a pull deep within her womb. She remembered one of Mathilda's little jokes that had always made her blush. *If you rode that husband the way you ride that steed, all your problems would be solved.* She had always been too embarrassed by the joke to ponder its wisdom. But at that moment on top of her husband, feeling his arousal pressing against her, she decided to test the theory, for no one knows quite as much about sexual matters—or enjoys the activity with as much glee—as the little people.

Finally she understood what all the fuss was about. Men and women talked about, wrote about, sang about, dreamed about sexual passion all the time, and yet this was the first inkling Beatrice had of its power. She had undressed in front of him without modesty and asked him to do the same. Then she climbed on top of him and found that his hard penis slid with eager ease right into her slick wetness. *Velvet*, he had sighed, which had made her even more aroused. She thought of Mathilda, she thought of

Drago, she thought of a warm spring day in open countryside, and she began to canter—smoothly and easily until she was sure of the terrain. Then she let go of all control and launched into a spirited gallop, which she continued until she felt her whole body tense. She rode faster and faster, unaware now of the creature beneath her—man, animal, who knew or cared? Finally her womb felt as if it was exploding, but instead of fearing it, she rocked more frantically to quicken her demise. In a burst of sweat and cries, it happened, and Beatrice thought that this must be the kind of ecstasy that devout nuns talk about when speaking of the passions of prayer. But this is not how the nuns advocate achieving it.

For the next months, Beatrice and Ludovico were never apart, hunting and riding every day to exhaustion, exploring every inch of the parks of Vigevano. Game seemed to spring from every corner—hare, deer, and roebucks on the ground, and heron and other river fowl in the skies. Some days they would take a canoe and fish, netting big mackerel and delicate speckled trout from the river. Ludovico took a new delight in everything Beatrice did, whether she made Drago or one of her dogs perform a little trick, or whether she slew a buck with a single well-placed arrow. He laughed without control at her jokes and antics. He bought her surprises—pearl earrings, a rosary with a giant diamond cross, and a young white mare handpicked by Francesco from the Gonzaga stables to eventually mate with Drago. When Galeazz tried to whisk Beatrice away for a day of falconry, Ludovico advised him to start paying more attention to his fiancée and less to Il Moro's wife. Ludovico said it in good humor, making young Bianca Giovanna blush so hard that she had to hide her face in her hands, but Beatrice sensed that he was serious. Galeazz's days of distracting Beatrice were officially over.

Beatrice did get anxious when Ludovico returned to Milan a few weeks ahead of her to "take care of some pressing business," but when she arrived at the Castello, she was told in furtive, excited tones by the servants that Cecilia Gallerani and her son, Cesare, had been moved to a palazzo by the Duomo, and that

Ludovico had arranged her engagement to Count Bergamini, one of Il Moro's most loyal and chivalrous courtiers. The wedding was set for next month.

Now Beatrice is driving to the workshop of the Florentine, Magistro Leonardo. Ludovico wishes her to sit for the master. Beatrice has said that she does not want to be painted by Leonardo. Oh, not so much because of what Isabella said—that it would put her on a parallel with Cecilia, for that painting was done more than ten years ago, when Beatrice was but a little brat in the nursery—but because the man always leaves her with a feeling of disquiet. She has no idea why he has this effect on her, but it is almost to the point of superstition in her mind. If the Magistro paints her, the lovely world in which she has lived the summer long will somehow be altered. She knows it makes no sense, and she does not want to insult Ludovico, who is willing to take the Magistro from his colossal equestrian statue just to immortalize her "at this point of blissful youth and perfection," as her husband liked to say. So she has agreed to visit the Magistro to see if she can make herself comfortable with the idea of sitting for him.

Upon entering the Corte Vecchia, she sees that the Magistro has made some progress on the statue of the horse, but the gigantic thing is being cast in pieces, and Beatrice is disturbed at the way the head lies on its side on the ground, apart from the legs, which are upright and waiting to be joined with the rest of the body. The body parts lying on the ground remind her that Leonardo is known for acquiring human bodies and dissecting them before audiences. What is one supposed to think of a man who exposes the insides of bodies? She leaves her chariot with the courtyard page and slips quietly through the open door and into his workshop. Boys are silently at work on various projects. Two are finishing the details on portraits commissioned by the nobles of Milan, whose features were undoubtedly sketched in by the Magistro and then turned over to his apprentices for completion. Beatrice knows that if she agrees to be painted by Leonardo, the master will probably complete much of the work himself, as a tribute to her position as the wife of his lord and master. But if one were merely a rich merchant or an insignificant courtier who wished for a flattering engagement portrait of one of his daughters, or a picture of his wife in her best jewelry, then the Magistro would do the main sketch, turn the details over to his apprentice, and perhaps perform a little of his own magic in the finishing touches.

Beatrice stands quietly, looking at the Magistro's many drawings hanging on the walls, mostly of ugly, deformed people. Why would such a genius have a fascination with freaks when he is capable of making the beautiful even more so? Cripples, blind men, old men whose faces have been eaten by some horrible disease— could they be drawings of the dead? These are the things that line his walls. Intricate drawings of old, wrinkled, wizened men sit in pairs with heads of young men at the pinnacle of their beauty. The contrast almost disgusts her. The way he has placed these pictures seems to say: What is the use of such beauty? For soon it fades into the decrepit state of the elderly. It is as if he has shared some private joke with God over the arrangement of things. Beatrice does not like this; she thinks he is taking issue with the way that Our Lord has planned and executed man's fate.

The Magistro sits on a stool, hunched over a drawing that Beatrice cannot see. His focus seems intense. A motto in fancy calligraphy is placed above his working space: OBSTINATE RIGOR.

The others work in this manner too—focused, silent, intentional. It is so quiet that she thinks that she can hear their breathing above charcoal scratching on paper and brushes hitting wells of color. In front of Leonardo is a statue of Leda and the swan, which Ludovico has recently spent great effort to purchase from some dead cardinal's estate in Rome. Ever since Isabella sent him those two creatures for his pond, he has been obsessed with swans. Beatrice recalls that Ludovico had sent the statue, which was supposed to have dated from antiquity, to be cleaned and refurbished by the Magistro's workshop. Leonardo does not appear to have done anything to the statue, which is mottled with years of dirt and the droppings of birds, but is now staring at it, and then looking down to his paper.

"Sir!" She finally announces herself. Leonardo turns around, startled. Immediately, he stands, bowing to her.

"Your Excellency. A privilege."

"What is your drawing?" she asks. She knows that her husband will not be happy to hear that the Magistro is spending the day working on something other than the horse.

The drawing startles her. It is much more suggestive than the statue. Leda of Leonardo's invention is curvaceous and naked. The swan is huge, almost as tall as Leda, and he cups her body in lavish white feathery protection in a manner as proprietary as any man has ever claimed a woman. Her round hip fits neatly and perfectly into the curve of his wing, which drapes languidly down her thigh and leg. Beatrice cannot imagine how anyone has found eroticism in coupling with this animal, but the Magistro has done it. Leda shyly turns away from the swan as if she is embarrassed to be enthralled with such a creature. Yet enthralled she is. Beatrice feels her cheeks flush as she looks at the picture; she herself has recently been awakened to the look of pleasure and satisfaction that the Magistro has drawn into Leda's face.

"Ah, the swan," she says, groping for some innocuous comment. "My husband has a new fascination with the creatures. I am sure that your study will please him, should you ever choose to make a painting."

"Your Excellency, he has already commissioned it," answers the master.

He puts down his charcoal and raises his hand into the air ceremoniously. A young apprentice knows this signal and rushes to him with a bowl of water and a slice of lemon so that he may clean the carbon from his long fingers.

"Has he?" Beatrice feels the first pangs of jealousy she has felt in months. Could the obsession with swans signal his ongoing fascination with her sister?

"Do you think it will please him?" the master asks.

"It is beautiful. The swan, I mean."

"Oh yes. Zeus used the disguise to seduce, of course. The swan is the clever one, the one that cannot be resisted because of its beauty. No one imagines its purpose because it looks so pure." He adds in a low whisper, "I do not trust it."

"And the woman?"

"Look at her," he says. "What does she know? She is lost in her own pleasure."

Beatrice does not like to hear this judgment upon Leda. Nor is she willing to accept Leonardo's condemnation of the swan, because that would mean that those two creatures swimming in the pond inside the Castello walls have power over Ludovico, which is perhaps what Isabella had intended when she sent them.

"Can a swan not be pure?" she asks. "What of the tale of the swan maiden whose robe of feathers was stolen by a hunter so that she would remain in female form and be his wife? The swan is blameless for her beauty."

"And she left the one who loved her at the first opportunity. Besides, that is a tale suitable for children, nothing more. There are many others. I watch the creatures myself, you know. I see how they transfix those who observe their grace. And yet, if they are threatened in any way, they can be brutal attackers. What is one to make of beasts of this dual nature?"

"What of the story of the swan who sees its reflection in the pond and knows that it is dying and so begins to sing to its fellow creatures to console them for mourning his passing?"

"Do you suppose that creatures of nature may be as foolish as we human beings?" he asks gently, a tiny, woeful smile appearing on his face. "The swan knows when it is his time, knows that all things of this world are but an ephemeral gift. This inescapable fact evades only the human. No sooner is the poor mortal secure in his power and success than he is destroyed by forces larger than he."

"Do you mean that Our Lord destroys us just as he creates us?" Beatrice asks. She hopes that she does not sound huffy. She wishes Isabella were here to help her engage in this sort of dialogue. Isabella would know just the correct profound retort to such a pronouncement.

"I do not, Your Excellency. I mean merely that nothing is permanent. All is as fleeting as our emotions. Only man's delusional state of mind prevents him from seeing this inevitability."

Beatrice would like to get off of the subject of swans and mortality because it is adding to the anxiousness of being in this workshop. She, who is so sure-footed and grounded, is feeling a whirling vertigo. She does not want to look either up or down for fear that she will faint.

"That is a very sorrowful observation, sir," Beatrice replies, gathering her wits. "How might one retain one's good humor if one contemplates such thoughts? Man may soon turn to dust, but does he not leave greatness in his stead? The tales of Homer or the treasures of ancient Greece and Rome attest to this fact."

"Your Excellency, forgive me for saying this, but only the rare and extraordinary man leaves something behind on this earth other than his excrement."

He must have been startled by the shocked look on her face, because he adds quickly, "Your Excellency and the duke, of course, being the most notable exceptions, what with your generous patronage of great works."

"But you will leave behind many beautiful things," she counters quietly.

"Paint flakes from the canvas, much as skin falls from the flesh. Man destroys his own creations. Nature takes care of the rest. What survives does so by accident."

Beatrice turns her face away from the Magistro, but finds no comfort in the face of Leda, or in Leonardo's drawings, or in the motion of the apprentices as they go about their chores.

"I understand we are to have a sitting, Your Excellency," Leonardo says, interrupting Beatrice's search for a soothing place for her focus to fall.

"Yes," she answers in a low voice. She wants to get out of this room in the worst way. She will agree to anything and then change her mind later. If his reputation is correct, he will never make the time to paint her anyway.

"First yourself, and then your sister, the illustrious marchesa. Please explain to her that I know that I am not worthy to receive the commission to paint her likeness, and I am greatly flattered by her letters. But I have awaited the instruction of His Excellency, your husband. And he has finally granted her wish, with the caveat that I make your portrait first, as is only proper."

The room begins to spin as the information makes its way into her head. So that is the game. Isabella and Ludovico have not seen fit to play their cards for Beatrice, but the Magistro has revealed all. Ludovico has no desire to have Leonardo make a painting of Beatrice, but he cannot, in good conscience, have the master paint the sister without first doing homage to the wife. Oh, they are good players, but even the best eventually become transparent.

Anger and determination set in. Beatrice feels the vertigo leave her head. She looks down, surprised to see such elegant, buckled velvet slippers on the feet of an artist. She almost wants to giggle. Suddenly, she feels the power that comes with knowledge.

"Thank you for showing me your drawing," she says, looking back at the Magistro's intense face. "We shall be in touch, you and I."

Leonardo seems surprised that she is taking leave so quickly, before any arrangements or artistic considerations for her portrait have been discussed. She does not know why she is afraid of him; he has such kind eyes. But she does know that she has no intention of ever entering this studio again.

.   .   .

LUDOVICO is waiting for her to have a light supper in their apartments. He gives her a great innocent smile as she enters the room and sits opposite him.

"What, no kisses for your lord and master?" he asks, his dark eyes lit bright by the candles.

She gets up and gives him a perfunctory kiss upon the cheek.

"Did you have a nice visit with the Magistro? Did you make a time to sit for him?"

Beatrice affects her most earnest face. "No, my lord, I did not. The man gives me a feeling of disquiet. I am not comfortable sitting for him. I feel that he will steal my soul. That is what they say he did when he painted Cecilia."

"My dear, I observed Cecilia for ten years after she was painted by the Magistro, and I assure you that she was still in possession of her soul."

"Still, my lord, I do not think it wise for me to put myself on parallel with one who was your mistress. It would be unseemly."

Beatrice wishes with all her heart that Isabella could hear the words she used to manipulate Beatrice turned back against her.

Ludovico looks slightly anguished by her decision. "If that is how you feel. But you should consider that he is in our service and is the greatest master of our day. Do you not wish to be painted by such a man? Even your most illustrious sister has said that she would like to be immortalized by such genius."

"Oh no, my lord," Beatrice says, hoping that her face projects a sincere look of horror. "We cannot allow my sister to be put on the same level as one of your former mistresses. We can't let her risk her reputation that way. You know how people talk. Already your innocent kindness toward Isabella has been interpreted wickedly in certain quarters."

"You make too much of it, my dear," he replies. "Isabella has a mania for good painting. That is all there is to the wish to sit for Magistro Leonardo."

"I would love to see my sister happy," she says, cocking her head to the side wistfully, pretending that she is forming these thoughts as they come out of her mouth. "But we cannot allow it to happen. Having the Magistro paint another woman so close to you—about whom rumors have already spread—would fuel those wagging tongues. It would reek of adultery."

"What do we care what the gossips say? We are certain of our affection for each other."

"But my lord, we must be more careful in our actions. Oh, not on my behalf. But I believe that we might be expecting an addition to our family sometime early next year."

Ludovico stands, fingers white and tense on the table. He appears to be balancing himself. His lips slowly spread into a smile.

Beatrice raises a finger, signaling him to listen to what she has to say. She continues: "This would be the time to present ourselves in the best possible light, as an entirely devoted family, impenetrable and unable to be breached from the outside. This news will certainly strengthen your position with the people of Milan. I mean, what with a legitimate heir on the way."

Ludovico shakes his head. "You are a wonder," he says, rushing around the table to embrace his wife. She loves this feeling of being engulfed by him; loves smelling the scent he uses imported from eastern lands that makes her think of incense and spices; and loves crushing her face against the soft velvet of his robe. She feels that, for the first time, he is hugging not just her but the life that is stirring deep inside her.

"Let us wait a few more weeks before making an official announcement, my love, just to be certain that it's true."

"Very well," Ludovico says, "though suppressing such news will be difficult." He raises his hands as if issuing a proclamation. "Well then, the matter of sitting for the Magistro is closed."

Beatrice wonders, however, if beneath the surety, he is already trying to invent the excuses he will have to give to the persistent Isabella. "Perhaps," he begins ponderously, as if he is making an agreeable argument for himself, "if we do not distract him with portraiture, he will set his mind to completing the horse."

Chapter Five

III * L'IMPERATRICE
(THE EMPRESS)

*A*SABELLA sits in the June heat gently rocking in the bucentaur at the intersection of the Po and Mincio rivers, wondering what reversal of fortune has brought her to the point where her sister has risen so far above her that she cannot deign to stop for a few days to visit Isabella's home, but insists on dragging her out into the river in order to get a glimpse of her and catch up on the latest news.

> I would most willingly visit you at Mantua on my way home from Venice, but my husband is extremely anxious for me to return to him. I must beg you to let me enjoy the sight of you in the bucentaur. You must not insist that I take the time to land.

The ostensibly innocent words might as well have been sent with one hundred arrows straight to Isabella's heart. It seems that, these days, Beatrice cannot deliver enough slights to her sister. Whether or not it is intentional, each triumph in Isabella's life is immediately overshadowed by Beatrice's latest victory. Isabella does not want to be disagreeable toward her sister. Perhaps her sensitivity is a result of her pregnancy, for Isabella is finally expecting a child. But it is only the second month, and she wakes each morning with a queasy stomach and the absence of desire to leave her bed. She should have insisted that Beatrice come to Mantua instead of agreeing to this damned river meeting. Though the Po is calm, every ripple of the gentle waters threatens to make her sick. But Beatrice was adamant that the sisters had to meet and talk, and that it had to be in this inconvenient and hurried way.

Isabella's woes with her sister had started a year ago when Ludovico had seemed to fall in love with—of all people—his own wife. The first sign had arrived in the form of a letter from him at the summer's end, giving Isabella all manner of reasons why he could not arrange for Magistro Leonardo to paint her.

> You know how I live to please you, my dear, but I am having tremendous difficulty moving the Florentine to work on the horse commission, much less interest him in portraiture. I broached the subject of making your portrait with him, and he replied that he was in the midst of a study on the human eye and would return to painting faces once he has finally understood the mechanics of sight! You know how difficult he is . . .

This nonsense was preceded by a summer of letters from Beatrice, describing in great detail how close she and her husband had grown in recent times; they were despondent when absent from each other's company, even for an hour. She wrote on and on, ad infinitum and ad nauseam, about how they spent day after day in the pursuit of the various pleasures that Ludovico had designed for them—hunting, fishing, riding, falconry, *and buying extravagant things just to make me smile*, Beatrice had written most cloyingly. It seemed that Ludovico could not fulfill just one of Isabella's small requests anymore, so busy was he showering his wife with affection and finery. Isabella wrote to Ludovico asking him to send the sculptor Cristoforo Romano to Mantua to make a bust of her. He had done a lovely bust of Beatrice a few years ago, making her much more beautiful than she had ever appeared. Isabella did not say that she wished for Cristoforo to be her consolation prize for having to delay being painted by Leonardo for God knew how long, but she hoped Il Moro would have seen it that way and would send the sculptor to her immediately. But suddenly, Beatrice decided that she wished to make a short trip to Genoa, and she could not do so without the company of her favorite singers, Cristoforo being the most treasured member of her choir.

Finally, after this supposed summer of bliss that the two love-birds spent together, Beatrice delivered the *coup de grâce*, writing to announce that she was pregnant and wishing for the company of her sister—as if Isabella, who had yet to become pregnant, wanted to see Beatrice in the exalted condition of carrying Ludovico's first legitimate child.

It was all very puzzling to Isabella, with whom Ludovico had been conniving for the better part of a year to arrange a visit so that the two of them could be together. She wondered if this new-found affection between husband and wife was a figment of Beatrice's hopeful imagination. She would have to find out for herself. After a hundred delays—most of them curiously furnished by Francesco—Isabella left Mantua with her extravagant new wardrobe. She'd spent the previous year pestering Francesco into spending the money for its construction, and watching it being packed into trunks, felt the enormous sense of satisfaction one feels in persevering to achieve one's goals. She kissed Francesco goodbye and, days later, was all the way to Cremona when she realized that she'd forgotten her most fetching plumed hat. She promptly sent a sulky messenger back to Mantua to retrieve it. She was not about to ruin the effect of a fine, bejeweled costume by wearing a mismatched headpiece. "You'd better sneak it out of my rooms," she had told him. "I do not want the marquis to think I am frivolous." But what she really did not want her husband to know was that she paid a man several days' wages so that she could have the right hat, at the right time, on her head.

Isabella knew that she was going to Milan with fiendish thoughts on her mind, but she couldn't help it. One couldn't stop thoughts from arriving in one's brain. She hoped to find Beatrice big and fat in her pregnancy so that she, Isabella, could look more beautiful in Ludovico's eyes—that is, if he was not already beside himself with the wanting of her. Oh, she had no intention of succumbing to his advances. She had already worked out in her mind the scenario by which she would refuse intercourse with him. She would tell him that the Gonzagas were expert breeders, known throughout the world for their fastidiousness and genius in breeding perfect horses and dogs. Did Ludovico not think that Francesco would not see the signs of another man's features in his own child's face, should their affair lead to pregnancy? But she had no opportunity to play the rehearsed scene.

She arrived to the news that the duke and duchess were in conference with the Magistro. What luck, she thought. She would use the opportunity to directly schedule a sitting with Leonardo, avoiding the intermediaries. This time, he could not use Ludovico's demands upon him if Ludovico were there to release him to her. And surely Ludovico would do that for her. Beatrice, pregnant and secure with her husband, would surely support the idea.

Over the protestations of the duke's secretary—"They will cherish the surprise of my arrival," she assured the man—Isabella outpaced Ludovico's staff and entered the parlor unannounced.

Isabella perceived the inhabitants of the room as if players in a tableau. Ludovico's hands were in midair in the universal gesture of frustration. In one hand, he held a piece of parchment that fell limp over his fingers like a handkerchief. The Magistro had his weight on his back foot as if in a reluctant bow, his chin slightly tucked and eyes downcast like a proud Spanish don who had just suffered a slight to his dignity. Beatrice's hands were pressed together at the chest, as if she were making a silent prayer for conciliation between the two men. A skinny boy, presumably the Magistro's servant, cowered by the hearth. The conversation was hushed now, but the tension from whatever was last said hung in the air. All faces turned toward Isabella, each registering the surprise of her intrusion. No one moved but remained frozen. Finally, Ludovico spoke.

"What a charming surprise," he said, placing the parchment on a table with what appeared to be a series of drawings, which Isabella hoped were renderings and plans for one of the Magistro's great works. She so loved to see works of art in the planning stages.

Beatrice, plump, robust, and glowing, moved quickly toward her sister, embracing her. The Magistro, Isabella saw over Beatrice's shoulder, was making great circles with his arms as he bowed low and formal, showing her the top of his head. She noticed that his lush suede shoe, toe pointed directly at her, was decorated with jewels.

"How dreadful of me to interrupt your conference," Isabella said.

"Nonsense," Ludovico said. "It is wonderful to see you safely arrived. In fact, being a renowned patron of many artists, perhaps you can assist me in this discussion with our great master."

Ludovico took his sister-in-law from his wife's arms and kissed both her cheeks. Beatrice was uncharacteristically quiet, perhaps grateful that Isabella had arrived to mediate. She withdrew behind Ludovico and Isabella, sitting on a chair with a small sigh, relieved of carrying the weight of the baby in her belly. Isabella registered this fact, hoping that Beatrice's pregnancy would be keeping her more sedentary than usual and unable to interfere with any of her sister's schemes.

Ludovico spread the drawings on the desk for Isabella to see—dozens and dozens of sketches of every conceivable element of a horse's body from snout to tail. Flaring nostrils, open mouths revealing fierce teeth, prancing legs, sturdy flanks, even muscular rear ends with long flouncing tails jumped at her from the page.

"Ah, studies for the great equestrian monument," Isabella exclaimed.

The most startling of the sketches was of a horse rearing up on its hind legs, front legs scrambling violently in the air, with a rider clinging fiercely to its back.

"Why, it looks as if this creature might come to life, throw its rider, and gallop off the page," Isabella said. She scrutinized the Magistro's face for a reaction to the compliment and was happy to see a modest smile break across his face, as if she had scored a point for a team on which both of them might be playing.

"Yes, true enough," said Ludovico. "Lovely drawings, all. But our maestro will not begin sculpting the horse in earnest unless he can figure out how to accomplish the impossible, which is to make a colossal bronze of the animal rearing on its hind legs. I am told by everyone that this cannot be achieved!"

"Everything might be achieved with time and inquiry," Leonardo said.

Ludovico riffled through the drawings for a particular one, and finding it, waved it in Leonardo's face.

"And what does this have to do with your interminable goal of making the horse stand on its rear legs while synchronizing its front legs in perfect motion and harmony?"

The Magistro stiffened against the anger hurled at him. He stood slightly taller, Isabella noticed, rather than cowering before his benefactor.

Isabella took the drawing from Ludovico. It appeared to be an architectural plan for equestrian stables.

"With your permission, Your Excellency?" the Magistro said, taking the drawing from Isabella and placing it on the table. He pointed to what appeared to be a system of chutes. "This is a design for what I believe would be the perfect stable. Here, the hay would flow automatically from the lofts above, freeing up the stable attendants for other labors. Never again would one have to worry over feeding times. The troughs are replenished with pumps, a system of plumbing that would rival the finest of baths in castles and palaces. Clean water would flow freely and upon need." The Magistro stepped back from his creation so that he could see Isabella's response. But Ludovico interrupted before she could speak.

"But how does this get us any closer to the monument?" Ludovico asked, his shaky voice rising with each word.

"You are a forward-thinking man, Your Excellency," the Magistro countered. "I assumed that you would like to be the owner of the most advanced and modern stables in Italy."

Isabella was about to invite Leonardo to Mantua to show his designs to her husband, the most famous breeder of horses in Italy, who would surely appreciate his labors, when Ludovico spoke again.

"Magistro Leonardo," Ludovico began, his efforts to control himself visible in the tightening of his jaw, "we have been more than a dozen years in discussion, you and I, over the matter of the horse. If you do not soon present me with a monument, something with hooves, a tail, and a mane, I will be forced to cancel the commission and put a living horse on a pedestal, to be changed whenever it dies from thirst, inactivity, or heatstroke!"

Leonardo stood silently, amazed, perhaps, along with Isabella, at Ludovico's outburst.

"It would be less costly!" Ludovico added as if bolstering his argument. "Even if the horses were of fine quality!"

"Ah, Your Excellency, I see that you believe I have wasted my hours, when it has been my highest intent to create something not commonly seen, something extraordinary and new with which to honor the memory of your illustrious father." Leonardo's voice was silky and even. "I shall quicken my efforts, not because I believe that speed will contribute to quality, but because it is my fondest wish to serve you."

With that, the Magistro's nostrils flared, not unlike those of the horses in his drawings. He did not appear insulted or angry, but rather puffed himself up like a rooster who was about to leave a satisfied henhouse.

Before Ludovico could reply, the Magistro performed perfunctory bows in the directions of Beatrice and Isabella, snapping his finger at his mute servant before turning away from them and hurrying from the room. The boy scooped Leonardo's drawings off the table and, without meeting anyone's eyes, ran after his master. Isabella wanted to fly after the Magistro and invite him to Mantua, but she dared not. She wanted to assure him that neither she nor the marquis would ever hurry his genius; that they understood that such labors evolved in their own time. She looked to her sister, expecting Beatrice to admonish her husband for his impatience, but Beatrice was in the act of standing and offering her chair to him instead.

"My dear, you mustn't allow yourself to get so distraught over these dealings with the Magistro. It isn't good for your health. He does not mean to be a frustration to you."

Rather than sit, Ludovico took his wife into his arms, kissing her forehead. "Imagine, Isabella! My wife is heavy with child, and it's my health that concerns her." He raised Beatrice's face so that he could look into her eyes. "How did I ever live without you, my darling? Isabella, does she not look positively beatific?"

Indeed, she did. Beatrice's cheeks were cherub pink and, like her belly, rounded. She must have been staying off her steeds as a precaution because her skin was soft and pale like the petal of a white rose. Beatrice's brown doll's eyes were wider than ever, but in Isabella's mind, there was a new strength to her sister that belied her ever-softening features. Yet Ludovico was doting over her as if she were a newly acquired piece of precious porcelain.

"A rose in full bloom," Isabella muttered, aware that she had not only just lost an opportunity to arrange a sitting with Leonardo but was also losing whatever secret power she had formerly held over her brother-in-law. She even wondered if Ludovico had his outburst in front of her so that she would see his difficulties with the Magistro and stop requesting a sitting. Her brother-in-law was capable of such subtle intrigue, though mistaken if he thought his sister-in-law would be so easily deterred.

"The man acquired his position at this court after convincing me that it was his great passion to make the equestrian statue in honor of my father, but in the last twelve years, he has spent his time on everything but that."

"You don't know the half of it, Isabella," Beatrice said. "The Magistro tells us that he spends all his time working toward sculpting the horse, but we have heard that he is devoting secret time to inventing a machine that would enable a man to take flight as if he were a bird! Imagine!"

"Can you not withhold his household allowance?" Isabella inquired. "He should soon be hungry enough to do your bidding."

"Oh, I am soft when it comes to genius," Ludovico exclaimed, putting his head in his hands as if he was never sorrier for another soul than he was for himself for having this all-too-mortal foible.

Ludovico went on to explain how Leonardo spent all his days at the stables, admiring four particular stallions, as well as the magnificent frescoes of different-colored horses, and drawing them from every possible angle. "He has spent more time looking at a horse's rear end than any man in history," Ludovico complained, throwing Beatrice into peals of giggles. "I believe he is trying to make a horse's ass out of me!"

"One cannot hurry genius," Isabella said, aware that Ludovico was, with every utterance, also preparing her for the disappointment of hearing that Leonardo making a portrait of her on this visit was out of the question.

"I am beside myself," Ludovico complained. "A few months ago, I sent a request to Lorenzo the Magnificent to send me another Florentine sculptor who would execute the equestrian monument. But then Lorenzo—God rest his discriminating and shrewd soul—passed away. I'll never be able to replace Leonardo now. Damn the man!"

"You must rest, Ludovico," Beatrice said. "These things always have a way of working out for the best." She took Isabella's arm, leading her out of the room.

"Would Ludovico really send the Magistro away?" Isabella asked, wondering if she could use this opportunity to steal the Magistro away to Mantua without incurring her brother-in-law's wrath.

"Oh, Ludovico will calm down. Those two are like an old married couple, Isabella. At the end of the day, they always make up. They would no more part company than would Mother and Father."

ISABELLA had her first opportunity to be alone with Ludovico when he offered to take her on a tour of the Treasure Tower. Ludovico took the key from the steward and dismissed him, opening the door for Isabella and allowing her to walk in. Armed guards, replaced every eight hours, Ludovico explained, stood at attention as the marchesa passed by and into the vaults. She heard the door close behind her.

Light streamed from triangular windows set high in the walls, falling on bushels and bushels of silver ducats sitting in painted barrels and organized according to weight and worth. Long tables held jewels of every kind, the stones and gems too numerous in variety for Isabella to identify. Great silver crosses laden with diamonds were arranged from small to large covering the length of a dining table. Collars and belts glittering with variegated gems lay waiting to be placed about the neck or hip of the fortunate. Tapestries and paintings lined the walls from ceiling to floor. Trunks of silver sat upon handwoven carpets, and tall candelabra of gold and silver, perhaps two hundred pairs, crowded the corner of the great room like some strange army frozen in motion. In the far reaches of the vault sat heaps of coins of every kind, piled so high that Isabella guessed that Beatrice, on her best horse, could not have jumped it.

Isabella felt light-headed surrounded by so much wealth, realizing that she was visiting her sister's personal jewelry box. "Dazzling," she finally said to Ludovico, who had awaited her response.

"This is nothing," he said, producing another dark iron key

from the pocket of his robe. He then began to open the doors of the cabinets lining the walls. Isabella hardly knew how to take in the contents—crowns and other bejeweled headpieces; rings of every size, shape, and stone; ropes of pearls both black and white; and reams of golden cloth and heavy brocade.

"It is too much to take in," Isabella said. "Two eyes are inadequate to the task."

"The wealth of a small kingdom inside every cabinet," Ludovico said.

"The cabinets alone are beautiful," Isabella said, noting the intricate ivy pattern painted delicately on every door. She tried to trace the snaking design with her eyes, getting dizzy in the process.

"Designed and decorated by the Magistro himself," Ludovico said.

Ah, Isabella thought, an opening. "Having him make my portrait would be worth everything in this room to me," Isabella said, as if to the air.

"And yet I can give you anything in this room but that," she heard him say. She turned around to look at him. Gone was the dancing flirtation in his eyes that had been there the last time she saw him. He seemed older now, treating her as if she were the younger, and Beatrice the more mature. Could pregnancy accomplish so much?

"I must be very direct with you, Your Excellency." He had never sounded so formal when addressing her. Isabella knew it signaled the end of a certain intimacy between them. "I have already approached the subject with my wife. She will not brook such a thing. She fears that it would signal to the world that I have had another affair."

"But if the Magistro painted her first?" Isabella offered, feeling the hollow of her stomach sink, remembering how she, herself, had already sabotaged that possibility.

"She won't have it. She will not be placed on par with one of my mistresses."

Isabella leaned on one of the tables for support. She thought she would faint. How could she have been so stupid? So intentionally cruel? And now God was punishing her for the sin. She deserved to suffer.

At the same time, she knew that she was not about to give up. This would not be like giving up on a pearl ring or an antique vase or some other trifle. This would be like giving up on immortality itself. But at this moment, she was caught in the middle of a web that she herself had spun and unsure of what to do.

"You look unwell, Isabella," Ludovico said, taking her hand without a trace of the sensuality that used to pass between them. He looked at her like a concerned father.

"What can we do?" she asked him with tears forming in her upturned eyes.

"At the moment, nothing. As you know, there have been rumors enough about the two of us. The situation is delicate for many reasons. I have tried to make friends everywhere, but I am discovering that I have many enemies. I cannot afford to make one of my wife."

LUDOVICO palliated the pain he caused in the Treasure Tower by giving Isabella a lengthy bolt of gold brocade. "Have something lovely made up," he told her, kissing her on the forehead. The *forehead*! Then he took her hand, and with the old music back in his voice, confided that things were more complex than she imagined and she must be patient. He invited no further discussion as to what he meant by that cryptic statement, but left her to attend to other business.

The next day, Isabella's world was further shaken when she came to lunch, only to see a lovely blond woman—sweet of face, curvaceous of body, with sharp, intelligent sea-green eyes—laughing as Beatrice played with a hearty brown-haired little boy. Though she had filled out since she sat for the Magistro more than ten years ago, Isabella recognized the woman instantly from the portrait, and the boy, from the dark hair and full, pouting lips he inherited from his father.

Isabella had no idea how to react to the introduction to Cecilia Gallerani, Ludovico's former mistress, who now sat at table with Ludovico's wife, who was bouncing Ludovico's bastard on her knee. Beatrice could not have been more gracious, even hand-feeding little Cesare sweets and remarking on his resemblance to the Sforza clan. "He will have Ludovico's height," she said, as if nothing in the world could have delighted her more than that her husband's bastard son would not have to suffer being short.

Isabella was unusually quiet during the meal. She gulped three glasses of white wine from Ludovico's vineyards in the south, politely answering questions posed by Cecilia, while pondering how strange everything had become in the short time since she had last seen the Sforzas. After the meal, Beatrice announced that she was going to take a rest, and Isabella used the opportunity to ask Cecilia to take a walk with her through Il Moro's recently landscaped park west of the Castello. He had expanded the castle grounds to include fully three miles of forest and garden, and was in the process of having much of it planted in intricate patterns with flowering trees and bushes lining stone pathways.

Walking arm in arm with Cecilia through the grounds, Isabella was just drunk enough to ask her if she had perceived any recent changes in the relations between Ludovico and his wife.

"Oh yes," Cecilia said in a low tone laden with girlish mischief. "He confessed to me some months ago that he had suddenly and unexpectedly fallen in love with her."

"Madonna Cecilia, please do not think me indiscreet, but I must ask: Is Il Moro still in love with you?"

"Your Excellency, I understand your sisterly concern and I assure you that you may put your mind at ease. We have not been romantic in a very long time. I am quite content with my husband, and I adore your sister, whose kindness to me has been exceptional. I will always be indebted to Ludovico for arranging a marriage to such a lovely gentleman as Count Bergamini. I have become to Ludovico what an old lover should be, a friend and confidante." Cecilia tightened her squeeze on Isabella's arm and whispered in her ear as if they had been friends for years and not hours. "Anyway, after the excitement of the first bloom of romance, what is the difference between one man or another?"

Isabella did not have the experience to support or argue with Cecilia's assertion. After all, Cecilia was almost thirty. Isabella had experienced two men in her lifetime, one of whom was her husband, whom she did not think she would be ready to trade away in a few years, and the other, Ludovico, who had removed his attention as quickly as he had bestowed it. Isabella, just nineteen, was still trying to sort out her loyalty and duty to her husband, whose power she shared by day and whose lust she shared in the dark of the night, and her longing for her brother-in-law, with whom she had not only experienced an intense attraction but had shared the contents of her mind by letter for the better part of a year.

But Cecilia had no such conflicts; she allowed that she was devoted to her son now, and to decorating her palace, which she intended to compete with the finest private houses anywhere in the world. She was interested in the comforts of home, writing poetry, and acquiring beautiful things.

"Ludovico showers us with treasures for our quarters," Cecilia said. "I suppose he wants his son to live in the splendor worthy of his family line."

"I am certain that it is because you gave him many happy years," Isabella said. She meant it; Cecilia was kind, gracious, and level-headed, and Isabella found herself wishing that this older woman lived near her and could serve as a mentor in womanly matters. If only she knew her better, she could ask her advice about Ludovico's sudden attachment to Beatrice and what she should do about the ensuing quelling of his feelings for her after a year of courting her by letter.

But these were topics for a more intimate friend. Isabella gathered her wits about her, shook off the laziness in her body from the food and wine, and decided that she could not let the afternoon end without bringing up the subject of the Magistro.

"Oh, it was lovely to sit for him," Cecilia said. "Musicians played soothing music while he sketched, and food was served. He wanted the atmosphere to be bright and calming for me. I was very young, and nervous to sit for this great genius whom Ludovico had just stolen from the Prince of Florence's service. I sat for Leonardo several times, three perhaps. Then he took the painting away and finished it in secret. I am still not certain why it has created such a stir among lovers of art."

Isabella would love to tell her all the reasons why, but she can hardly confess that she had already sneaked into Cecilia's quarters just to get a look at it.

"It would be a privilege to receive a visit from Your Excellency, should you desire to see it. Though I must warn you that I have practically doubled in age and size, and it does not resemble me at all."

"I am sure that you are being unduly modest," Isabella said. True, Cecilia was no longer the thin, ethereal maiden captured by the Magistro, but she was softer now, more a creature of the earth, and in Isabella's eyes, no less beautiful. "Were you not asked to sit for the Magistro again?"

"No, but they say he used my face again. Have you seen the altarpiece at the chapel of the Confraternity of the Immaculate Conception?" Cecilia asked. She explained that the chapel was in the church of San Francesco Grande, not far from the Castello. "It is an image of Mary and Jesus on their flight from Herod."

"I have not, my lady. Did the Magistro use you as the model for the Blessed Virgin?"

"No. Oddly, though, the angel Uriel who sits aside the Virgin looks exactly like me when I was a young girl."

"I must see the picture, then."

"The monks hate it. In fact, they are suing Leonardo for it. They say that the whole point was to emphasize that the Virgin was born without original sin, but there is no evidence of that fact in the painting. They made a detailed contract with the Magistro, but he honored none of their demands in the painting itself. They wanted everything done with heaps of gold and ultramarine, but the Magistro eschews those qualities of religious painting. He considers them antique. He bases everything on the observation of nature, as you know, and he says he has yet to find bright gold and ultramarine blue in nature. Not to mention the seraphim floating about everywhere."

"What will happen to him? Will he be taken off to prison, or made to redo the painting?" Isabella asked. At this rate, she would never get to sit for the great master.

"Ludovico will probably have to intervene. There is talk that he will purchase the painting from the monks for his private collection. Then the monks will have to pay the Magistro to begin again. It's a terrible mess and has inspired much scurrilous dialogue between the monks and the Magistro."

"And yet, the monks display the painting, though it does not suit their purposes?"

"They display it with pride. After all, it is by the great Leonardo. It draws men with deep pockets into their chapel."

FROM THE PERSONAL FILES OF LEONARDO:
Appendix to contract between Leonardo the Florentine and the Brothers de Predis, and the Franciscan Confraternity of the Immaculate Conception:
  Herewith is the list of the decorations to be applied to the altarpiece of the Conception of the Glorious Virgin Mary placed in the church of San Francesco Grande in Milan:

• *First, we, the monks of San Francesco, the commissioners of said triptych, desire that everything except the faces of the figures is to be done in fine gold.*

- The cloak of Our Lady in the center must be of gold brocade and ultramarine blue. Her gown must be of gold brocade and crimson lake.
- The lining of the cloak is to be gold brocade and green. Also, the seraphim are to be done in graffito work. The angels above are to be decorated and their garments fashioned after the Greek style.
- God the Father is to have a cloak of the finest gold brocade and ultramarine blue.
- In the empty panels there are to be four additional angels, each differing from one picture to the other, namely one picture where they sing and one where they play an instrument.
- In all other sections, Our Lady shall be decorated like the one in the middle, and the other figures are in the Greek style, all of which shall be done to perfection. Any defective carving is to be rectified. No exceptions.
- The sibyls are to be richly decorated, and the background is to be made into a vault for housing the sibyls.
- The cornices, pilasters, capitals and all their carving— everything must be done solely in gold to the specifications above. No expenses spared.
- All faces, hands, and legs are to be painted to perfection, that is, without flaw.
- In the place where the infant is, let the gold be worked especially ornately.

Please execute this copy below in the presence of a notary of law and return to its originators.

The Monks of San Francesco

Isabella lay down for her afternoon nap, head spinning with wine and information. She slept fitfully, dreaming that she was chasing Francesco across a field, but he was running away from her as if he did not know her. She woke with the late-afternoon sun streaming into the window of her room. The women had forgotten to shut the drapes; no wonder she could not sleep. She turned away from the light and closed her eyes. She fell back asleep for either several minutes or an hour and then woke with a fresh idea and a renewed sense of purpose.

In the morning, Isabella proposed an outing with her sister to visit San Francesco Grande to see the altarpiece by Leonardo. "Though he is difficult, he is the most important artist in Milan, Beatrice, if not all of Italy, and you will undoubtedly be commissioning him to do many things for your family over the years. You said yourself that he and Ludovico are not ever going to part company. You may as well get to know his work all the more so that you may use him properly. It is your duty, my dear. You are duchess to the duke who is known for his love of art!"

Isabella could see that she had used just the right combination of sisterly concern and intimidation; Beatrice readily agreed to the trip.

The Gothic church of red brick and triple arches crowning its façade welcomed the sisters. Isabella had encouraged most of their attendants to remain behind, telling them that she desired private, sacred time with her sister in a house of worship. The chapel of the Immaculate Conception was small, an invention of the Confraternity formed to bolster the idea that the Blessed Virgin not only conceived the Christ child without human intercourse but was herself the first mortal born without the stain of original sin. The idea had come under some scrutiny and question from renegade quarters of the church, and these clergy had organized to protect the reputation, purity, and divinity of Our Lady.

Isabella was instantly struck by the clarity and simplicity of the triptych presiding over the altar. Perhaps seven feet tall, it was painted on wood and encased in a gilded frame, a little out of sorts, she felt, with the painting inside. It was as if the golden frame was made from materials of this world, intending to suggest the celestial, while the painting itself had arrived from out of the ether.

Outside of a gaping hole in the mountains—that, according to the biblical story, had miraculously opened to shelter the Virgin and her Son when they fled Herod's decree that all the infant boys of Israel be murdered—sat a simple picnic: the Virgin, a sweet-faced young girl with fair skin, ringlets, and downcast eyes that rested on the baby John the Baptist, who offered his hands in prayer to the infant Christ. The Christ returned the gesture of the future saint, pointing at him with two fingers, while sitting in the shelter of the angel Uriel, who was dressed in sumptuous robes of crimson and green, and looking every inch the female—as female as the Virgin herself, and pointing a long, bony white finger at John the Baptist, while glancing nonchalantly into the foreground at . . . what? Isabella could see the face of Cecilia in the angel—the long, triangular features, the sharp but kind eyes, the pert nose. It was as if the Magistro went back in time to Cecilia's coming-of-age to make this angel's fair visage. The party sat in desertlike foliage at the edges of Mary's lush blue velvet cloak. Why Uriel pointed at John and not the Christ, Isabella could not figure. It was as if he were anointing John. The odd fingers pointing every which way made Isabella wonder what these strange hand signals meant, if anything. John, Jesus, and Uriel seemed to be in dispute, pointing their fingers as if to say: *You—you are the one. No, you. No, you.*

The setting was the most disturbing part of the painting. The Magistro had put these holy personages not in any recognizable earthly place, ignoring the Italian craze for portraying the Holy Land as the Tuscan landscape; nor did he try to depict them in a heavenly setting. No, these figures sat before great tall rocks that jutted into the expanse of the cave. Light came from the fore and from behind. Why were these peaceful figures placed against this stark, desolate background? Perhaps the Magistro was trying to evoke the danger of a family fleeing the kidnapping and slaughter of its Holy Child. Stepping back, she also noticed that the four figures formed the shape of a cross and wondered if that was intentional. Isabella pondered all these facts and could not help but think that the Magistro might be a heretic and was not afraid to insinuate it in his art. He seemed to care nothing for the traditional ways in which biblical narratives were portrayed in paintings. No wonder the monks were suing him over the commission. Where were the magisterial symbols used in all religious painting to glorify Christ and his mother? This painting had the same quiet simplicity—with the addition of the disquieting finger-pointing—that she had observed in the painting of the toothless Madonna that she had seen in Leonardo's studio.

But she also understood why the monks displayed the painting in the chapel; it was unlike anything she had seen by another artist. Looking at Leonardo's paintings was like dreaming. Isabella knew that Leonardo had collaborated with two other artists on the altarpiece, the de Predis brothers: Ambrogio, an artist in his own right, and Evangelista, responsible for the woodcraft and the gilding. Now she saw those men's contributions, or so she thought. The painting was flanked by portraits of two long-haired angels playing musical instruments, more conventional representatives of Divinity, and entirely out of character with the unearthly scenario at the center.

Isabella did not think it wise to point out to Beatrice that Uriel bore the face of Cecilia. Not at this time, when she did not want to enforce any connection in her sister's mind between her husband's former mistress and the Magistro. She had come to suggest another connection and she was waiting for the right time. But truly, there was Cecilia—ethereal and angelic, the most divine part of herself revealed by the great man once again. Isabella was almost sick with wanting the same honor. Did the most glorious, highest part of her—her very soul—not cry out for expression? Was Leonardo not the only artist on earth who could accomplish such a thing? Only Leonardo could capture that part of Isabella that she wanted to announce to generations to come that she had been on this earth; she had lived, she had reigned, she had loved, she had *mattered*.

Beatrice was on her knees in prayer. Isabella waited for her to look up. She did not want to disturb her sister's communion with God. Finally Beatrice raised her face and stared straight ahead at the painting. She cocked her head to the side as if to ask a question. Isabella knelt quietly by her sister and touched her arm. Her sister looked positively saintly, skin gleaming in the cold light of the chapel.

"The Virgin looks as if she is still a child. A beautiful child," Isabella said. But Beatrice was not about to make conversation in the house of the Lord.

Beatrice made the sign of the cross and stood. Isabella followed her sister's cue, but got the distinct feeling that Beatrice was saying goodbye to God, while Isabella was saying goodbye to Leonardo's work. Beatrice dug several silver coins out of her purse and presented them to the monk waiting for them at the church's entrance. He took his craggy fingers out of his coarse wool pockets and accepted the money silently, bowing to the royal ladies, opening the door, and letting them out into the autumn sunlight. Beatrice raised her face up to the sun. Isabella stretched her arms out in front of her as if to embrace the fresh air; the church had been very cold, and she was happy to once again be outside.

Beatrice took Isabella's arm as they walked to their carriage. "The Virgin is exquisite, is she not? They say the Magistro used the face of Lucrezia Crivelli when she was only thirteen. Have you seen her? She is one of the ladies in my service. She's twenty-two now, and an awesome beauty. She is not warm, though. She keeps her distance from me as if she fears me. Though why would anyone fear me?" Beatrice asked.

"I don't know," Isabella answered. "You are too sweet to be feared, Beatrice. Perhaps she is shy."

"I don't think so. She is newly married. Perhaps she is preoccupied with her husband, though he is old and, I fear, unsuited for her. He is rich, though."

"Can you not dismiss her?"

"No, that would insult her family, and Ludovico says that they are of some consequence or another. I told Ludovico that she made me uncomfortable, and he said, 'Oh, think of her as ornament.' "

"It doesn't seem fair that she, a lady in your service, and not you, has had the honor of her beauty being celebrated in a painting by the Magistro." Isabella let her statement hang in the air between them.

Beatrice unlinked her arm from her sister's. "Why do you think that it is necessary for me to be celebrated by the Magistro?" she asked. An uncharacteristic tone of sarcasm tinged her pleasant way of speaking.

"Beatrice, I said something to you that I regret. I told you that being painted by him would put you on par with Ludovico's mistress, but I was wrong. It was a cruel thing to say. The Magistro paints all manner of women, including, as we have just seen, the Blessed Virgin. My words were foolish. I want to retract them, so that if you wished to be immortalized by the brush of the Magistro, you should not be denied the honor."

Beatrice stepped into her chariot, taking the reins from the attendant who would ride behind the royal sisters on his horse. She waited for the man to help Isabella onto the seat beside her. She clicked the reins, slowly guiding the horse into the street.

"Isabella, there is something you do not understand about

me. For you, immortality is at the end of a paintbrush. For me, it
is at the end of my husband's cock."

Isabella was stunned to hear such words coming from her
sister.

"I will achieve immortality through the births of my sons."
She flicked her whip at her horse, signaling to Isabella that the
conversation was over.

FROM THE NOTEBOOK OF LEONARDO:
*Drawn by great curiosity and eager desire, wishing to see
the various and strange shapes made by nature, I
wandered some distance among gloomy, overhanging
rocks, coming to the entrance of a large cave. I stood in
front if it for some time, kneeling and shading my eyes,
stupefied and amazed, for I did not have prior knowledge
of its existence. Suddenly, two things arose in me—fear
and desire. Fear of the menacing darkness of the cave, and
desire to see if there was any marvelous thing inside it.*

JUNE 1493; IN THE TERRITORY OF MANTUA

ISABELLA wakes from her nap on the boat, soft summer light
warming her cheek. She must have been asleep for some time.
The sun has moved enough so that the canvas tent over her head
is no longer keeping her shaded. The afternoon sun is high in the
air, the breeze is still, and she has been waiting for Beatrice, she
estimates, for several hours. The nap has taken the edge off of her
moodiness and her stomach has settled. When Beatrice arrives,

Isabella will not be tempted to be belligerent about having to take a boat into the river in the middle of a summer day just to see her illustrious sister.

The sketch of her nephew, which she promised to return to Beatrice, sits on her lap. She picks it up and holds it in the sunshine to take in for one last time its extraordinary details. The hand of the Magistro is unmistakable. Though Beatrice's letters had assured her that the baby boy, named Ercole after their father, had been sketched quickly, the details were remarkable. A thousand strokes of shading highlight the child's features. Wisps of dark hair crown his high brow like a Roman Caesar. His round, open mouth and bright eyes give the impression that he is surprised to have been born; to have found himself on this earth, framed in a golden cradle adorned with the Sforza and Visconti and Este crests, and wearing an embroidered robe and a tiny pearl-studded cap. Isabella has seen several renderings of the Christ child by the Magistro, who emphasized his mortality, whereas the son of Ludovico and Beatrice he rendered as positively heavenly.

A beautiful boy, though he probably no longer looks like the sketch, which was done five months ago. Isabella thinks she could reach through the painting and cover him with kisses. Her whole body yearns when she looks at the picture of the child. She feels doubly envious—both the boy and the drawing done by the Magistro belong to her sister. She knows that she has to return the sketch to Beatrice. It will be hard to give it up, but she does not want to bring a curse upon her own pregnancy by coveting either the son or the sketch of the son of her sister.

Beatrice is on her way back from a diplomatic mission to Venice, the city Isabella has herself just visited. Isabella had been thrilled when the elderly doge, Agostino Barbarigo, had personally invited her to visit the city during the festival of the Marriage with the Sea—a great honor to both herself and Francesco. Every year, in a solemn ceremony, the doge would mount a grand ship and throw a ring into the sea, to give thanks for the primary source of Venice's prosperity. Some version of this rite had been going on since ancient times. The ritual was always followed by an enormous banquet. To be feted by the doge at this event was an honor of the highest sort.

Isabella's joy was instantly thwarted when she received word that Beatrice was planning to be in Venice at the same time. Isabella almost canceled her trip; she was mortified at the prospect of appearing in Venice with her sister. Since her marriage, Beatrice had had more than three hundred gowns made—an amount that had disgusted Duchess Leonora, who complained to Isabella that Beatrice could stock the town's shops with her personal wardrobe. Her jewels, selected from Milan's Treasure Tower at will, were beyond compare. Isabel of Aragon had been grousing to anyone who would listen that she was sick of Il Moro going into Milan's treasury and decorating his wife "like a shrine." When Beatrice traveled now, it was with a retinue of hundreds. She went nowhere without her choir of singers, her Milanese courtiers, her poets and musicians, her dressmakers, her dozens of ladies-in-waiting all costumed and bejeweled like royalty, and her finest horses, the saddlery alone of which was studded with more gems than the crowns of the kings and queens of most small nations. No—Isabella was not about to appear in Venice at what should be her finest hour, looking shabby in comparison to her sister. Isabella's dress and retinue rivaled all but the great queens of the world. It's just that now, her sister was fitting into that category.

Francesco had counseled Isabella to proceed with her plans; he had correspondence from Ludovico indicating that Beatrice would postpone her trip for a few weeks while Ludovico finessed some finer points of negotiations he was making with France. Luckily, his information turned out to be accurate, and Isabella had a splendid trip to Venice, during which every honor was bestowed upon her. The doge himself received her into the city at

Santa Croce, along with the entire signory, and ambassadors from Naples, Milan, and Ferrara. After kissing the hand of His Most Serene Highness, Isabella was invited onto his barge, where one hundred of Venice's dignitaries—eyes, smiles, and jewels glittering—awaited her. The prince insisted that she sit next to him as they wandered up the Canal Grande. Bells chimed from every major church and cathedral, and an arsenal of guns and trumpets announced her arrival. It seemed that the whole city had come out to see the marchesa, wife of the army's captain general. Isabella felt as if the very stones of Venice were rejoicing over her presence. She spent a week being liberally entertained at the expense of the signory, and endured countless ceremonies with a cheery smile, even when the heat was extreme and the food lousy, thinking all the while of the honor she was bringing to Francesco and to the state of Mantua.

Everyone who was anyone seemed to have a palazzo on one of the canals, and Isabella visited queens, dukes, and other royalty from around the world. She learned astonishing things: that the Genoan explorer Columbus had found new trade routes in the west, returning with gold, spices, sandalwood, exotic birds, and a dozen copper-colored natives who were said to be strange but very beautiful. The Venetians were terribly worried over this new discovery because they controlled all the trade routes to the east. This Columbus had sailed west to reach India. The Venetians wondered if the astronomer Paolo Toscanelli had been right after all. Was the earth really round? At any rate, in true covert Venetian style, they had sent secret agents to Columbus to purchase a copy of his report to his benefactors, the King and Queen of Spain. Isabella adored hearing this kind of information that she could repeat all over the courts of Italy. She ended her stay with a tour of the city's great art, and made the acquaintance of the Bellini brothers, Gentile and Giovanni, who were painting frescoes in the Council Hall. She spent an afternoon with them—their sister was the wife of Mantua's court painter, Andrea Mantegna—

and left with a promise from Gentile of a portrait of the doge by
the year's end for her studiolo.

After leaving Venice, Isabella went to Padua, where she
prayed with all her heart at the Basilica of Il Santo that she was
carrying a boy, and then on to Vicenza and Verona, where the signory had arranged for her to be entertained by the local nobility.
Finally, at the end of May, since Francesco was traveling, she
went to visit her dearest friend, her sister-in-law Elisabetta
Gonzaga, Duchess of Urbino. The two of them spent glorious
weeks together, reading poems and singing, and enjoying the
fresh air. As a surprise, Ludovico sent her the viol player Jacopo
di San Second, who serenaded her with a special song about a
swan whose mate has gone. He misses her so much that he wants
to die. Isabella could see the suspicious look on Elisabetta's face
as the viol player sang this mournful love song sent from her
brother-in-law. It shocked Isabella too. Could it be that she still
had Ludovico's heart? Was that what he meant when he said that
they had to be patient? She reveled in the idea—not that Ludovico's affection carried the weight it had in the past. Now, outside
of the flattery, it hardly mattered. She was carrying her husband's
child. She had brought glory to Francesco by the impression she
had made in Venice. His letters to her reflected the heaps of
praise he heard about her from every important personage she
encountered on her trip, and he made no secret of how grateful
he was to have a wife who could enhance not only his position
with the Most Serene Republic, but the position of the city-state
he governed as well. Ludovico's affection at this point was like the
diamond clasp on a pearl necklace—nice, but not so essential.

Isabella returned in triumph to Mantua, until she heard that
almost as soon as she left Venice, Beatrice had arrived in un-
precedented splendor with a retinue of twelve hundred. She gave
not one but two diplomatic speeches to the signory and was received as a princess and ambassador. To honor her, the doge
commanded a boat race down the Canal Grande with female row-
ers for the first time in Venice's history—all for the pleasure of

Beatrice. Everyone was taken with her eloquence, her elegance, and her charm. From Beatrice's letters and all the other letters she received on the matter, Isabella discerned that everything about Beatrice's trip was slightly more wonderful than her own. Some sycophant even wrote that Beatrice's jewels "reflected the very wonder of the Universe, but none was so precious as the duchess herself."

The sun has already begun its descent to the west when that lauded duchess's bucentaur finally appears from the east, followed by a flotilla, undoubtedly loaded with Beatrice's attendants, gowns, jewels, loot from Venice, and whatever and whomever she travels with these days. Isabella decides that she will not leave her boat, but wait for Beatrice to come to her. It's the least she can do for refusing Isabella's hospitality, drawing her pregnant sister out of her comfortable chambers on a summer day.

It takes some time for Beatrice to understand that she must go to Isabella. After some confusion, she appears, flush, excited, and hurried. The sisters' hot cheeks meet in double kisses.

"What pressing business keeps you from allowing us your company for a few days, Your Excellency?" Isabella asks, smiling. "Francesco is beside himself with grief. He has a new Barbary steed—huge, with a neck like a tree trunk. He wanted to see you tame the beast."

"Oh, please tell him that I will make good on his challenge at another time. At the moment, there is no time to waste, and many things which I must discuss with you."

"I have received so many reports of your triumphs in Venice that I require no further details," Isabella says.

Beatrice spends not another moment on the niceties. "As you know, Ludovico has never had good relations with Venice."

Yes, Isabella thinks. They neither like nor trust your husband because he tries to play all sides against one another, or that is the common wisdom in Venice.

"I was given two audiences with the signory. Ludovico sent me there to inform them of his growing alliances with both

France and Germany. He is bringing these two factions together, Isabella. Imagine!"

"How is he maneuvering this?" Isabella asks. "They have long been enemies." But the question she is asking herself is, who will be sacrificed in the negotiations?

"You will hear this soon enough, but at present, please keep the matter secret. Ludovico has betrothed his niece Bianca Maria to Emperor Maximilian, King of Germany and Emperor of the Holy Roman Empire."

"Not the little beauty who is engaged to our Galeazz?"

"No, Ludovico would never do that to his own daughter. She adores Galeazz. You do not know this girl. She is Duke Gian Galeazzo's sister—sweet, but rather feeble in the head, just like her brother."

And she will come with an astounding dowry that will pad the Frankish coffers, Isabella speculates to herself. Why is Ludovico bribing the emperor? "Sounds like a very wise move," she says. "And who is he marrying off to France?"

Beatrice takes no notice of the sarcasm, but pulls Isabella closer to her, lowering her voice. "He has given his blessing for France to invade Naples."

"Interesting," Isabella says slowly while she works out the political puzzle in her mind. With France, Milan, and Germany against Naples, who is left to stand for them? The Pope, of course, who won't like the French so close to his borders. And possibly Venice, which would not align with Naples, but might be tempted to interfere with Ludovico's grand plans. "And you are going to stand with Ludovico against our maternal grandfather Ferrante?"

"Grandfather is near death, and he more than anyone is an example of the necessity of making pitiless decisions. If he hadn't done that himself, he would have died long ago, and not of old age. We are left with no choice, Isabella." Beatrice sounds more like one of the seasoned, cold diplomats in their father's service than the excitable girl she has always been. In fact, she sounds more and more like the Diamond himself.

"How is it that the invasion of Naples is the business of Milan?" Isabella asks.

Beatrice sits back a little, and Isabella is grateful to have the space from her sister, whose emotions are so heated at this moment that they are suffocating her, like some kind of turbulent, pressing wind.

"Ludovico has decided to take the title of Duke of Milan. France and Germany are supporting it in exchange for his alliance. Emperor Max has the power to invest Ludovico with the title. There is some ancient agreement that at the end of the Visconti line, the Holy Roman emperor may reinvest the duchy to whomever he pleases. The last male Visconti is long dead. It is that simple."

"And what of Gian Galeazzo and Isabel of Aragon? How will they be deposed?"

Isabella watches carefully for Beatrice's reaction to the name of their cousin, because she has neglected to mention her own rise in fortune, status, and title, should Ludovico's scheme come to pass.

"Gian Galeazzo is puerile and has sickening sexual habits. He has no interest in fulfilling even the simplest of his duties, and frankly, God help us if he did. He is the worst dissolute in the kingdom. He beats his wife!" Beatrice's indignation rises. "I feel sorry for Isabel of Aragon. I tried to be her friend, but she would have none of it if I didn't join her in asking her father to take Ludovico down. Now she has roused Uncle Alfonso to the point where he is ready to attack us. What should we do, Isabella? The moment grandfather dies, Alfonso will be upon us. Should we wait for that day?"

Isabella knows that much of what Beatrice says is true. She received a languid letter last month from the Duchess of Montferrat, who wrote, *There is nothing fresh to report from Milan but that*

Duke Gian Galeazzo has taken to beating his wife. She knows that Aragon's humiliation is unbearable, and that she complains to everyone how Ludovico and Beatrice have all the money, power, and glory, and she and her husband are treated like beggars. Yet Ludovico *did* already have all the power. Did he have to go to these lengths—intrigue, betrothals, invasions on Italian soil—to grab the title? As far as Isabella could see, Gian Galeazzo was pathetic, but in the scheme of politics, harmless. And she doubted that Alfonso would make such a drastic move just to appease his unhappy daughter.

"Beatrice, is it wise to *invite* the French into Italy?" This is precisely what Francesco has been asking since rumors of Ludovico's intrigue with France has been spreading about.

"We have the protection of Emperor Max, who is very dear to us, and will keep the French contained to Naples, and the word of King Charles that he will go no farther north once Naples is his."

Isabella sees that Beatrice and Ludovico have worked this scenario out in their minds and are committed to its fruition. Beatrice is not here to ask for advice. Her eyes shine and flicker with life as she speaks about the plan. Her cheeks are flushed with color and her hands wave about like some beautiful Fury. Isabella cannot tell whether the nausea in her own stomach is acting as some kind of warning about the folly of all this, or if the little creature growing inside her is raging again. She sits back in the wooden chair, leaning her head against its high back. "I don't feel well," she finally says.

Beatrice calls for something cool for Isabella to drink. She takes a cold cloth from the hands of Isabella's servant and wipes her sister's brow. Isabella thinks that Beatrice's hand might be shaking, or is that an illusion caused by the motion in her stomach or the rocking of the boat?

"You must go home and rest," Beatrice says. "But I must trouble you with one thing before I leave you. It is a message from Ludovico, a request."

Here is precisely what Isabella has not wanted to hear: what is to be her part in this plan that Ludovico and Beatrice and half the world, it seems, have been devising. Here is what she had hoped to escape because of her condition. But unless she feigns passing out, there is no escape.

"Ludovico has heard all about your conquest of the doge and everyone else in Venice. Oh, it's the talk of Italy, don't you worry. Everyone is aware of the powers of your charm and your intellect, Isabella. My husband merely hopes that, if given the chance, you will use those powers in his favor."

"I would do anything for my sister and my brother-in-law." She prays that Beatrice will leave the matter thus.

"Will you use your influence with Francesco to convince him to fight with the French in Naples? He is a great soldier and commander, and we would feel secure if he were leading the invasion."

Isabella wonders if her sister has gone mad. Does she really think that Francesco can just go command any army he pleases? Does she think he can convince the Venetians to support the hated French? "I cannot make commitments for my husband, as you cannot make commitments for yours. But I do not see how he can fight for the French when he is captain general of the Venetian army. Venice will not allow their army to be pulled into this conflict."

"It would not be as captain general of the Venetian army, Isabella. It would be a separate contract, as a mercenary soldier, a condottiere. It would be for money, and I can assure you that the price we are talking about would be worth it, indeed."

"Beatrice, I do not know what Francesco would say to such an offer, but I am afraid for you. These actions that you and Ludovico are taking are dangerous and come with great risk. Ludovico already has everything. Will adding the title increase his power so very much?"

"Isabella, I am surprised at you. If you were in my position, what would you not do to ensure that someday your son would have the title of Duke of Milan?"

So that is it: Beatrice is on fire with the dragonlike flames of a mother's ambition for her son. The kind girl who wanted nothing more than a long day on a good pony has transformed into Olympias intriguing for the rise of Alexander, or poisonous Livia promoting Tiberius. It does not even seem real. Yet is it not a pattern between mother and son that has played out over the centuries? Is history not littered with the corpses of those who crossed a mother's ambitions for her firstborn male child?

Isabella uses the excuse of nausea and dizziness to end this meeting as abruptly as possible. She has to get away from Beatrice's pressing ambitions. She wants to go back to this morning, when these plans for turning the world upside down were not yet known to her. When did everything change? When did the wild and distracted girl who had to be dragged by the ear by their mother to marry Il Moro turn into this frightening political force?

Isabella waves and blows kisses to Beatrice's entourage as they sail past her toward Milan. When the last bucentaur passes, she drops her smile, feeling as if the corners of her mouth are filled with lead. She sinks to her chair, head spiraling with unhappy thoughts. An attendant rushes to her side, but she shoos the woman away. She cannot wait to get home, to the safety of austere and strong Mantua, whose ancient fortressed walls will protect her from the turmoil that she fears is coming. She is so very tired; she feels as if the boat must sail through thick molasses to get back to the quiet comfort of her dark bedchamber. Her body is heavy and her slim arms and fingers feel swollen and droopy, hanging off the arms of the chair.

As she floats back up the river to her home—to Francesco, who will have some perspective on all this madness—the thoughts that she has wanted to avoid finally come barreling into her mind. How long has Ludovico been planning all of this? For surely one does not get the idea to make such drastic moves overnight. She cannot help but wonder how much of Ludovico's flirtation with and attention to her has been in anticipation of the day he would ask her to use her influence to convince her husband to lead an army to fight for his ambitions.

Is it possible that they are all, Beatrice included, pawns in Ludovico's elaborate game?

FROM THE NOTEBOOK OF LEONARDO:
In Ethiopia, the black races are not the product of the sun. For if black gets black with child, the offspring is black. If black gets white with child, the offspring is gray.

And thus is Aristotle proved wrong. The womb is far from passive, a mere feeding ground for the sperm of the male. The seed of the mother has equal power in the embryo as the seed of the father.

Chapter Six

IV * L'IMPERATORE
(THE EMPEROR)

IN THE WINTER SEASON, 1495;
IN THE CITY OF MILAN

*I*SABELLA kneels at the wooden pew set in front of her as a courtesy by the friar in the Duomo of Milan. She does not like this cavernous, dark cathedral with its frigid air, dwarfing marble columns, and eerie echo that seems to come from nowhere and whirls about her like a taunting demon. She had come to pay her respects to the poor dead Gian Galeazzo, late Duke of Milan, now locked up in the family crypt like so many Viscontis and Sforzas before him. Shivering in the dank air, clutching her rosary, she tries to imagine the cathedral as it was described to her on the occasion of the duke's funeral, with thousands of wax candles lighting its dark expanse, and the celestial-sounding requiem of Milan's finest choir chanting for the duke's soul as it ascended to Heaven, or to wherever it was going. Did all that ceremony matter to Our Lord when He considered the fate of one's soul? Was He swayed by the heavenly voices, the glowing cathedral, the prayers for the dead, or the wailing relatives cloaked in black?

Besides being even colder inside than it is out of doors on this January day, the Duomo makes Isabella uncomfortable. Surely this grand building, with its thorny Gothic spires, stacked tombs, and altars under which fabled treasures of silver and gold are buried, was built to appease God's darker nature. The loving, forgiving Father who sent His Son to redeem mankind does not make His home here; only the vengeful God, angered by the sins of the flock which squanders His many gifts. Isabella wonders which man has angered God more in recent times—the duke, who wasted his young life away in drink and perversion, or the one who all of Milan whispers is responsible for his death. She wonders if having put large amounts of one's fortune into the building and embellishment of this cathedral, as Ludovico and every royal in Milan have done for more than one hundred years, will slake God's thirst for vengeance when the time comes to answer for one's deeds.

She finishes her prayers for the duke's eternal respite—a full rosary of Our Fathers and Hail Marys and Glory Be to Gods—lingering on the last of the crystal beads. How has Our Lord greeted such a sad dissolute come early to His bosom? Did Gian Galeazzo meet the God of Forgiveness or the Avenger? She supposes that it is none of her concern, but she often wonders how God conducts His business. She has already said a rosary for her mother—God rest her loving soul—who passed away the year before. For an entire winter, both Beatrice and Isabella—distraught that distance had not allowed either to be with the duchess when she died—wore black moiré robes with long black sleeves and heavy black velvet mantles, their faces covered in delicate white lawn veils that draped from tall black caps.

Isabella presses her palms together to send up a prayer for which she has little hope of receiving an answer. She begs God that in time her heart will open up to her little daughter, named Leonora after Isabella's mother, because she was born so soon after the great duchess had died. Would not her mother want Isabella to love the little girl? Isabella knows that she is doing her mother's memory a great disservice by withholding maternal love from the child, but she has not been able to change the fact that she had wanted a boy so badly that she cannot muster any feelings for the girl.

"What is wrong with girls?" Francesco is fond of asking. "You are a girl, Isabella! The child is beautiful like you, and healthy. Why are you disappointed?"

Francesco, who could have been disappointed that Isabella had failed to provide him with a little marquis to inherit the kingdom, is utterly delighted with his daughter. But Isabella put away the golden cradle that Duke Ercole had Ferrara's best artists carve for his first grandchild in Mantua, and with that cradle, put away her heart. She would take it out when she gave birth to a boy. She did not want to feel this way. She instructed all the nursery attendants to shower love and attention upon the child; no discipline is allowed or necessary. Leonora is always clothed in elaborate dresses and bonnets of pearls and lace, given tiny sweets to suck on, and picked up and cuddled at the first sign of discontent. All this spoiling is meant to make up for the fact that Isabella has no room for little Leonora in her deepest heart of hearts. Not in the same way that Beatrice has taken her son to her bosom. No, Isabella knows the difference. She knows her own deficiency, and she prays to God that in time she will be able to make up for this coldness.

Holy Queen, Mother of Mercy, our life, our sweetness, and our hope. To thee do we cry, poor banished children of Eve. To thee do we send up our sighs, mourning and weeping in this valley of tears.

At the last of her prayers, Isabella looks up from her folded hands to the towering stained-glass windows above her, noticing that each is laced with the Visconti family symbol, a serpent swallowing a man. The windows are probably as old as the cathedral, put in place by the first Prince Gian Galeazzo Visconti, who broke ground on this monolithic structure one hundred years ago, but the same message holds true today—man is a hapless creature in the hands of the Viscontis. Even when it concerns their own blood, these creatures will swallow any who obstruct their ambitions. And now her sister is a part of this family of serpents—perhaps has become one of the very vipers.

Isabella can hardly believe what they are saying about Ludovico, and yet she can hardly deny it. It is all too convenient, the way Gian Galeazzo exited this world at the very point in time that Ludovico had rallied enough support to usurp the title of Duke of Milan. Now the shifting swirl of political alliances and betrayals that Isabella had foreseen from her conversation with Beatrice on the river is coming to fruition.

From the moment that Duchess Leonora died, it seemed that all of Italy was in a fever to bring in the French. With no one in Ferrara left to plead for Naples, the Diamond quickly gave his sanction for the French to attack his late wife's former kingdom. Duke Ercole had no love for the French—or for anyone else, for that matter—but along with much of Italy, he hated and feared Naples's ally, Alexander VI, the corrupt Borgia pope whose son Cesare wanted to reconquer all the independent Italian states in the name of the papacy. This, the Diamond could not bear.

"I am not trying to make an enemy of Naples. I am saving Ferrara from the Borgias' ambitions," he explained to Isabella. "If it takes the French to put the Borgias in their place, so be it. If your grandfather wants to align with the devil—and I assure you that Borgia is the devil—he will have to pay the price of his wicked bargain. Your mother—God rest her soul—would understand. We must wrestle the papacy back from this Satan. The French can help us unseat the abomination Alexander and restore a holy man to the throne in the Vatican."

At the same time, Ludovico and Beatrice were entertaining kings and emperors who would support Ludovico's ascent to Duke of Milan. They started to call their son, Ercole, "Max," to honor the German emperor. Last fall, Ludovico and Duke Ercole, who thus far voiced no objection to his grandson's name change, met the French King Charles VIII at Asti, near Turin, where Beatrice hosted a fabulous reception at the castle at Annona, with her choir of singers and musicians and eighty beautiful, well-turned-out ladies. She had bothered to write Isabella *every single detail* in a letter explaining how Charles—short, hunchbacked, big-nosed, pockmarked, and ugly as a frog, but a king nonetheless—adores ladies to the extent that he travels with a court artist who paints each lady the king beds in whatever sexual positions they enjoyed for his personal book of memories. Beatrice, once so pure, regarded this as a minor scandal in one who could do so much to promote her husband.

According to Beatrice, despite the fact that she found the French tiresome—they complained incessantly about the heat, and about Italian wine, which they found sour—she had charmed the king. She had enchanted him with her wardrobe—a green satin robe, the bodice of which was adorned by endless paths of diamonds, pearls, and other jewels, and a cap which sprouted feathers, held together by a clasp made of the largest rubies in the treasury. He was astonished that "with all of that on her head," she sat as tall and straight on her horse as any man. She danced for him in the French style, allowing him a single kiss with each of her ladies-in-waiting, including Ludovico's daughter, Bianca Giovanna, now fifteen and recently wedded to her longtime betrothed, Galeazz di Sanseverino. Beatrice did say that she had kept a close eye on the girl, however, turning the king's lascivious eye away from the dew-eyed newlywed and toward ever more compliant and experienced ladies. She is protective of Bianca Giovanna, who is lithe and delicate, and whose elongated white face sits above her neck like a lily on a stalk. Beatrice so dazzled King Charles that he had a portrait of her done by the painter Jean Perreal for his sister, Anne of Bourbon, who wanted to see what the most fashionable lady in Italy was wearing. "He is as generous and warm in conversation as any man alive, but would you believe it, sister, the king and the French barons are practically illiterate? They can barely make their letters and were astonished to hear our youth recite poetry and oration in the Latin!"

Isabella wondered how much of this letter was meant to inform, and how much was meant to rankle, for Beatrice had been rankling her for more than a season. Isabella had always been considered the superior dancer of the two; she was certain that this reference was intended to put her in her place. As for the most fashionable, well, even Beatrice would have to admit that if Isabella had been gifted with Ludovico's money, she would have a wardrobe greater than Beatrice's in style and ingenuity. Just this fall, Beatrice had asked Isabella for permission to use a design that Niccolò da Correggio had created explicitly for Isabella. She had been saving it for some special occasion, but Beatrice pleaded that she required something stunning for Emperor Max's wedding to Ludovico's niece, "where ambassadors will come from as far away as Russia, and all will be gold and silver brocade as far as the eye can see. The very worst-dressed people will be wearing lush velvet sateen!"

Isabella wrote back a short note saying, "Suit yourself," which she thought generous enough, considering that Beatrice had scores of designers in her employ. Why did she have to take this one special thing from Isabella? Isabella was further irked when Beatrice wrote at length about what a success the pattern had been, "perfect for the massive gold gown I had envisioned for this imperial wedding." Leonardo himself had designed Beatrice's sleeves for this brocade opus, using an intricate pattern of circular motifs that Beatrice called Fantasia di Leonardo. The Magistro had carried the pattern over to a magnificent, priceless ring, "outlining the largest green aquamarine stone known to the world in heavy gold with the circular pattern at each corner, all embedded with diamonds. It is so large that I cannot bend my middle finger when I wear it." All of this was made worse when Isabella could not attend the wedding in Milan due to a strange fever she had caught from Francesco. Would that man never stop devising ways to make his wife absent from important events?

Isabella knows she should not allow these grievances to pass through her mind, especially in the house of the Lord. *O my Jesus, forgive us our sins, save us from the fires of hell, lead all souls to Heaven, especially those who have most need of your mercy.* It would be doubly insulting to have to suffer envy for her sister on this earth, and then have to burn in the fires of hell for the sin.

Isabella soon found out that it was Francesco who was Ludovico's present object of pursuit. Not long after the imperial wedding, Il Moro had sent Monsieur d'Aubigny and three French ambassadors to Mantua to offer Francesco more than forty thousand ducats to command the French army. D'Aubigny kept speaking to them in that horrible French language, as if everyone should know it, while Isabella continued to answer him in Latin. When the delegation left, Isabella and Francesco discussed the matter. The amount of money was astonishing, but the position would surely offend the Venetians. Finally Francesco said, "Ludovico Sforza is the man of the hour, but Venice is eternal." He abruptly sent a messenger after d'Aubigny, turning him down.

Word—in the form of Donato de Preti, Mantua's envoy to Milan—arrived from that city informing them of Ludovico's fury at Francesco's rejection of the offer. De Preti arrived in a short velvet cloak, voluminous striped sleeves, and tight beige cuffs clasped together at the forearm with bright gold buttons. He removed his broad hat from his head in a great sweeping motion, simultaneously flinging it to a servant and bowing, trying, as Isabella saw it, to get all the niceties out of the way quickly. Apparently, he could hardly contain the flow of news itching to be released from his tongue.

"Oh, the duke was quite upset with the marquis," de Preti said. "He doesn't like his desires being thwarted by loyalty to Venice. But not to worry. He had very little time to consider the matter because King Charles arrived in Milan along with the marquis's rejection of the offer."

"How convenient. I suppose His Excellency did not enjoy breaking the news to the king," Isabella said.

"No, he did not. To reduce His Majesty's disappointment and to impress his extraordinary wealth upon the king's imagination, the duke took Charles on a tour of his Treasure Tower. The king could hardly keep the saliva in his mouth as he strolled through those rooms, I assure you."

"If I had such wealth, I would not be showing it to a man with a larger army than mine," Francesco said, reading Isabella's mind.

"It would require a perfect saint to gaze upon those sumptuous riches without envy," said Isabella. Both she and Francesco had previously discussed the dubious wisdom Ludovico displayed in showing Milan's treasures to visitors.

"I imagine the French king taking mental inventory of all that he was shown," Isabella continued. "Perhaps he even had his court artist sketch it for his book so that he could salivate over it at night when he reviews his salacious pictures of women."

De Preti smiled, impressed that Isabella had such knowledge of the French king. "Though he has quite an insatiable appetite for ladies, I assure you, Your Excellency, that his appetite for the duke's wealth is far greater."

De Preti explained that a few days later, Ludovico entertained Charles at Pavia, where Duke Gian Galeazzo had taken ill "after a good long drunk." Charles paid a visit to the languishing duke, who was his cousin, and also to the duchess, who it was said was on the verge of madness about Ludovico's support of the invasion of Naples. "It was the most wretched thing, Your Excellencies," de Preti said. "Isabel of Aragon threw herself at Charles's knees, making a pitiful plea for the safety of her family. Charles assured her that he would protect her and her children, but Ludovico turned a deaf ear toward her, advising her to pray. Imagine."

Two days after Charles left Pavia, the duke passed away.

"No one could ignore the convenience of this event to Ludovico Sforza's plans," de Preti explained. "One day he was entertaining the French king, who promised to support his bid for Duke of Milan; the next day, the man who holds the title of Duke of Milan died at the rather premature age of twenty-five."

"What precisely was the cause of the duke's death?" Francesco asked.

"The official word was that he caught a fever, but rumors of poison abound everywhere. The duke's doctor said that contrary to his orders, the duke ate pears and drank wine, which made him take a turn for the worse." Isabella could tell by de Preti's contemptible look that he did not believe the explanation.

"Whoever in this world has died of pears and wine?" she asked.

"I spoke with the Pavian doctor on the case, Theodore Guainiero." De Preti leaned as close to the marchesa as he dared. The marquis tucked his head into their sphere so that he might hear the secret. "He says that everyone believes that Ludovico Sforza had his astrologer—that incubus Ambrogio, who is also a doctor—slowly administer poison to the poor unsuspecting duke."

Deliver us from evil, oh Lord, deliver us from temptation now and at the hour of our death.

It was unthinkable. Yet, before Gian Galeazzo had been dead twenty-four hours, while his freshly washed and handsomely dressed corpse was on its way to the cathedral for display, Ludovico had assembled all the magistrates and clergy and nobility in the Rocchetta in Milan, where they quickly cast aside Gian Galeazzo's four-year-old son as the successor and named Ludovico Duke of Milan, pending investiture from the Germans, to whom Ludovico immediately sent for the official diploma. As a gesture of respect toward his dead nephew, Ludovico asked to be called only duke, and not Duke of Milan, until Gian Galeazzo was buried.

God rest Gian Galeazzo's weary and drunken soul, and the soul of Ludovico, if he has taken part in a sinister plot against him, Isabella prays now, shuddering in one of the cathedral's many frigid drafts, kneeling before the vault where the duke's body lay, and remembering the conversation with de Preti. She prays for them all—the dead, the living who may have expedited death, and all those who will have to live with the consequences—for surely all of them will need every prayer they can get. She prays for Francesco, who had no trouble believing Ludovico's complicity. She prays for herself to cease speculation of his guilt.

Glory be to the Father and to the Son and to the Holy Spirit. As it was in the beginning, is now, and ever shall be, world without end.

Isabella pockets her rosary and stands, knees sore and joints aching from kneeling in this glacial place, large and gloomy enough to be a tomb for all of mankind, sweeping aside the thought that she has been avoiding since the news had reached her months ago: Surely Beatrice would not have been involved? Yet Isabella had seen with her own eyes the newly stoked fires of ambition burning in her sister. Oh, she cannot even entertain that idea, not now when she is on her way to see Beatrice, pregnant once again. All the astrologers and midwives and card-readers and little people—anyone with the supposed ability to see into the future—are predicting that Beatrice will deliver another son. She and Ludovico had been insistent that Isabella be present for the birth. Why? So that she could relive again her own disappointment at delivering a daughter? *Thou shalt not covet thy neighbor's goods.* Nor thy sister's children. But she is not here for these reasons. She has come at the insistence of her husband, who had angered Ludovico when he turned down the commission to join the French. Isabella, caught between the two men, has come to smooth over the relations.

Isabella knows that her entourage, shivering outside in the windy piazza, is weary from the journey from Mantua and long for the comforts of the Castello Sforzesca. As much as she wishes to escape the heavy murk of this place, she would like to delay crossing the great moat that will lead her into the Sforzas' world. But she has lingered enough. Beatrice has surely been informed of their arrival in the city and would be worried that they had yet to appear at the Castello. It is only when the friars open the big bronze doors to the cathedral letting in Milan's cold white afternoon light that Isabella realizes that she has neglected to make the prayer she had most intended—for the safety of Italy, where voices everywhere were crying out to a foreign power to swoop down upon them and deliver them from themselves. Italy would have to wait; she was stiff and exhausted.

ISABELLA'S train parades up the wide avenue that will pour into the great brick piazza fronting the Castello. The pace of her party is slow. Though the weather is bitter, shopkeepers, workers, and children race into the street to catch a glimpse of the royals, or more likely, to catch whatever the gentry might be throwing their way. Coins, trinkets, tiny dolls, tops, bright baubles, buns, hunks of cheese, and other tokens of goodwill, all brought from Mantua to appease the poor, the greedy, and the curious, make their way from the pockets and purses of the nobles to the cold hands— young and old, mottled, stained with cow's blood, dyes, dirt, metal, grease—reaching out to them as they pass by.

Isabella is grateful to be under thick blankets riding in a carriage. She slips her hand out of her rabbit-fur muff to pass a toy soldier—nicely painted for a cheap toy, she cannot help but notice—to a green-eyed boy who has rushed out of the butcher's shop and snatches it from her like a hungry dog grabbing a bone.

As the boy runs away with his treasure, she looks up to see a conical helmet that seems to float in the air. The nose guard is up, exposing a face with strong features and a hawklike countenance. As the train approaches the piazza, she sees that the helmeted head is not floating at all but belongs to a colossal statue standing alone in the square. The figure, a soldier, sits on a strutting horse, supported by a marble plinth. The monument must be twenty feet tall, but the sinking afternoon sun casts a shadow across the piazza twice the length, making it appear that the entire square exists to house the beast and his master.

Isabella asks her driver to circle the statue so that she can see it from all angles. The horse is a wonder, as if the sculptor caught the animal in the act of prancing. Two hooves dance jauntily in the air, while the other two are firmly planted, and the tail swinging as if whipping the air around it. The nostrils flare and the mouth is agape, revealing big square teeth and a long, curling tongue. Though it appears that the rider has pushed the animal to the point of fatigue, there is an air of infallibility about the beast.

The Horse, the gigantic clay sculpture that the Magistro had promised for years, had finally been completed and displayed in honor of the marriage between Emperor Max and Bianca Maria Sforza to great accolades for the statue, its creator, and of course, Il Moro, who had commissioned it. One of the many reasons Isabella had regretted her illness at the time of that event was that she had missed the unveiling. She had only heard the descriptions in letters from those who were present—and who was not?—and the poems written in honor of Leonardo and his accomplishment. She could not remember the words now, but they were oft repeated— *Victory to the victor, and you, Leonardo, have the victory*, or some such. Then there was the commemoration from Taccone that had made her wince, comparing Leonardo to Pheidias and Praxiteles, and placing him above the both of them. Never had Greece or Rome seen such a magnificent work, or so said the poet. Long ago she herself had believed that, in Ludovico's modern-day Athens, Leonardo would rise to such heights. She had only regretted that she would not be the duchess of the land that would give the genius the opportunity to exploit his talents to the fullest. Such things required money—piles and piles of money, such as Ludovico kept in his Treasure Tower. Oh, they were able to create miracles in Mantua on what they had, but to truly give an artist's genius full rein required the mentality of a visionary, which Isabella could provide, and the fortune of a king, which she could not.

Isabella knows that the statue is meant to be a monument to the rider, Francesco Sforza, father of Ludovico and one of Italy's greatest soldiers and conquerors. But as far as she can tell, the statue is a monument to the beauty of the horse; not to this horse in particular but to all horses, or perhaps to the greatness of God who created these wondrous creatures. If Ludovico asks her what she thinks, she will say that the stamina and preternatural endurance and strength of the horse is evident, and symbolizes and reflects those same qualities possessed by his father—and by all the other Sforzas, including the one who commissioned the work. But this is not what she thinks. She thinks that the horse is a glory unto itself and to the genius who took so many years to apprehend the essence of the animal.

But there is nothing to explain to Ludovico, Isabella is told upon her arrival; he is away, visiting his French ally King Charles at his military encampment at the Castello di Sarzana in Tuscany.

Beatrice, who cheerily delivers this news, is large with child.

"My dear sister, you are tremendous! Should you not have already started your confinement?" Isabella really wants to ask Beatrice how she can manage to balance herself with her stomach swollen into such a great balloon.

"With Ludovico gone, and the kingdom in mourning over the duke, and the anticipation of my husband being invested by Germany with the duchy, I must remain as active and visible as possible."

Isabella would like to avoid any discussion of the dead duke. She scours Beatrice's face for any sign of guilt, or suppression of knowledge, or complicity in the crime, for surely participation in something so heinous would demonstrate itself somewhere on the face, perhaps in an inability to meet the eye of another. Or in the contours of a forced smile.

But Beatrice's face is bright and open. She glows and crows over the sketch that Andrea Mantegna has made of little Leonora. "It's as if the tiny creature extracted the finest features from both parents," she exclaims. Isabella cannot help but feel that her sister is trying to compensate for the fact that the child is a female. She wishes she could join in the ploy, but nothing can induce her to feign enthusiasm in the face of this disappointment, especially not with one who has one son, and undoubtedly another on the way. Either Beatrice is carrying another strapping boy or a baby calf, Isabella thinks, for surely no girl could make the womb stretch to such proportions.

A fat nurse brings in the boy Ercole, holding him by the hand, restraining his eager strut. He is two years old, with shining dark eyes and golden-brown curls. He has inherited Ludovico's sensuous mouth, already apparent on his little-boy face. Isabella picks him up and covers his head and face with kisses, most of which he accepts on the hair as he ducks his face into her shoulder. He squirms in her arms as she tries to take him in with her eyes.

Beatrice calls him Max, which makes Isabella wince. "Max, sing your new song for Auntie Isabella," Beatrice says. The boy refuses, shaking his head back and forth resolutely. "Max, where is your little brother?"

The boy's arm shoots out like an arrow, pointing a finger at his mother's stomach.

"Tell Auntie Isabella his name."

"Francesco!" The child sings out the name.

"After his grandfather *and* his uncle, two great soldiers," Beatrice says.

Isabella knows that after her husband has declined Ludovico's request for him to serve King Charles, he would hardly allow his second son to be named after *him*. She knows that the boy—if the baby is, indeed, a boy—is being named solely after the late condottiere sitting in the piazza on Leonardo's magnificent horse. Isabella decides to steer the conversation toward the more benign subject of the monument and away from the difficult topic of soldiering.

"After all of Ludovico's frustration with the Magistro, the result seems to have been worth the wait," she offers.

"Oh yes, Emperor Max was so impressed with it!" Beatrice replies. "The Magistro brought great honor to us all."

"It's a masterpiece," Isabella says.

"Ludovico will be so pleased that you like it. You must accompany me tomorrow on a mission," Beatrice says mysteriously. "I believe you will find the experience gratifying."

The next morning, Beatrice drives them to the western outskirts of town to the Santa Maria delle Grazie, the home of the Milanese Dominican friars, where Ludovico is investing huge sums of money in improvements. Beatrice elaborates on Ludovico's fervor for commissioning Milan's greatest artists to glorify Our Lord, but Isabella is certain that she reads a deeper motivation into the endeavor: the Dominicans are a mighty political force. With Lorenzo the Magnificent dead, Fra Girolamo Savonarola in Florence has escalated his hysteria against moral laxity and his campaign against the Pope. The more Ludovico honors the Dominicans, the less he will have to hear from the moralizing Dominican monk.

Upon entering the church, Isabella is immediately struck with the contrast between the Duomo, which seems to her to dwarf the human spirit, and this building, intimate by comparison, that celebrates it. Beatrice leads them to the center of the apse, where they stand in a cube surrounded by four huge arches. The sisters look up to the top of the dome, where small, round windows let in gentle circles of cold winter rays that illuminate the frescoes on its ceiling. A series of circular motifs line the arches, in harmony with their perfect hemispheric lines.

"It took Maestro Bramante three years to enlarge the apse," Beatrice says. "We think it was worth the time and money spent."

"It's magnificent," Isabella replies. "It is grand and soothing all at once, a difficult marriage of qualities."

"I did hope you would like it," Beatrice says. "Ludovico and I will make our final home here. That is why we are sparing no expense in the decorations. See how lovely the choir is. I often think of how happy I will be when I am lying here being serenaded by Milan's most beautiful voices."

"Please do not speak that way, Beatrice. You are too young for such thoughts!" Isabella touches her sister's stomach. "You are getting so big, I am sure that the little one already has sprouted ears and is listening to every word we say."

"Ludovico always says that he is much closer than I to making the church his permanent home. That is why he is pushing to have it completed. Of course, he is joking, but he did promise the Dominicans that all will be finished within the year—church, rectory, and refectory."

"Will he meet his promise?"

"I doubt it," Beatrice says, smiling. "One of the larger projects is in the hands of none other than the Magistro."

Beatrice guides Isabella from the church, through the courtyard, and into the refectory, a large rectangular room with plain wooden dining tables and benches in the center. A lone young monk sweeps the floor, the scratching of the broom against pavement echoing through the room. A vast mural of a Crucifixion scene is painted on one of the room's walls; the others are blank.

"Even with so large a mural, the room seems cold and empty," Isabella says.

Beatrice whispers, "They say that the Inquisition trials were held in this very room. I must say, I do not like it very much in here. It is cold and creepy, and I feel sorry for the monks who have to take their meals here."

"Oh, but what do monks want with cheer anyway?" Isabella jokes. "The gloom probably brings them closer to God."

"I wanted you to see the site of the Magistro's next great work," Beatrice says. "I also wanted to spy a bit on him to see if he had begun it. He promised Ludovico, but Leonardo is nowhere in sight, is he? No tools have appeared; no sketches yet drawn on the wall. The duke will go mad."

"What is this grand project?" Isabella asks, curiosity piqued as it always is concerning the Magistro and his schedule.

"We have commissioned a mural on the wall opposite the Crucifixion scene of Our Lord Jesus having his last meal with the Apostles."

"Why did you have another artist paint the Crucifixion?

Would it not have been better and more consistent to have the entire room decorated by one artist?"

"Oh, you are too clever," Beatrice says. "You can tell that the Crucifixion scene is not the work of the Magistro."

Isabella eyes the figure of Christ on the cross, flanked by the two thieves. "It is grand and large and dramatic, Beatrice, but the composition is poor for my tastes, and it is overcrowded with elements. It tells a story, but has little drama and no discipline of perspective. It could not be the work of Leonardo."

"And yet the artist finished it on time and without asking for a single ducat beyond what was contractually agreed upon. Imagine our delight. We had hoped to have the Magistro paint both murals, but Ludovico said that getting one mural out of Leonardo would be a great accomplishment. Another Lombard, Giovanni Montorfano, painted the Crucifixion. He's not quite the artist Leonardo is, but he began on time and did not quit until he was finished. Ludovico has asked the Magistro to insert portraits of us with our children into Montorfano's finished mural. That was the compromise."

"And when will the Magistro begin the Last Supper?"

"Oh, you know the Magistro. He says he has begun preparations, but his concentration lies elsewhere. We are hoping that he does not have to make a study of prayer itself in order to insert portraits of Ludovico and me with our hands folded into Montorfano's mural."

Isabella stares at the Crucifixion scene so that she does not have to look at her sister. "So, I take it that you have conquered your aversion to sitting for the Magistro?" She hears her voice rise as she asks the question. She knows that it is impossible to hide her agenda, but she cannot help but inquire anyway.

"No, not entirely. I do not like to sit for artists. I am too fidgety. I particularly do not want to spend hours under *his* scrutiny. Though I revere his work, and though he shows only charm in my presence, he makes me uncomfortable. There is something dark and intense about the man."

"I do not believe I have ever met the lighthearted genius, Beatrice. At least he is handsome and mannered, and not sickly and sour all the time like Mantegna."

"Ludovico says that the portrait by the great painter of our day will bring honor to the family, and so I must do it. He has convinced me that asking the Magistro to make my likeness is an act of love on his part. 'I must move mountains to get the man to paint!' " Beatrice says, throwing her arms in the air, imitating Ludovico. " 'I would only make these efforts and go through this frustration for those whom I love!' "

Isabella decides to say nothing. It is not her place to encourage or discourage. Beatrice will do as she pleases, and now it seems that she is pleased to sit for the Magistro, not because it will please herself but because it will please Ludovico. Or aid his ambitions. Or send the message to the clergy of Milan about their powerful benefactor. Or appease Savonarola. Or indelibly link in the minds of generations to come artistic genius with the mighty and powerful family. Or accomplish whatever it is that Ludovico wishes such things to accomplish. It is clear that Beatrice's motives are selfless.

"After all," she says to Isabella, placing her small hands atop her big belly, "Ludovico was in love with Cecilia when he commissioned her portrait. He is in love with me now. He tells me so all the time. I have seen how much effort and patience it takes to coax the Magistro to finish any of his works. I am sure that Ludovico would not take up this challenge unless it was in the name of love for me and for his children."

Leaving the refectory, entering the courtyard, Isabella and Beatrice see the broad back of a man sitting cross-legged on the walkway like an eastern potentate, staring at a courtyard wall as if in a trance. His shaggy curls hang incongruently on the shoulders of his rich blue velvet cape. The late-morning sun highlights the deep brown hues of his hair, as well as casts an elaborate shadow on the wall. A moldy water stain mingles with the shadows on the stucco.

"Sir!" Beatrice says.

The Magistro, startled from his meditation, turns around. Upon seeing the Duchess of Milan and the Marchesa of Mantua, he stands abruptly—and adeptly, Isabella notices—rising to a full stance without uncrossing his feet.

"What on earth are you doing, Magistro?" Beatrice asks.

He points to the stain on the wall. "I am looking at a great landscape of human drama, Your Excellencies. Do you not see it?"

"I see a rather mildewed wall," Isabella says. "If the duke is so intent upon renovating the church and monastery, surely he should order a fresh coat of paint for the exterior."

"Marchesa, if you will permit me." Leonardo steps toward the wall, bending slightly and pointing. "Everything in creation might be seen in these shapes and shadows and qualities if one looks with fresh eyes. I have seen, in these humble discolorations, great battles in progress, tableaux of life and death, jousting matches, babies being born, old women dying, goddesses rising out of the sea, boats crashing against the quay during a storm. It is all there, if one looks long enough and with enough concentration."

Isabella stares at the wall, unable to see what the Magistro is talking about. She has seen shapes and faces in cloud formations, but she cannot make a scenario out of these stains. Beatrice, on the other hand, is nodding politely, as if she has begun to delineate the Magistro's imaginings.

"Your Excellency," he addresses Beatrice with what Isabella discerns is either a sense of anticipation or anxiety in his voice, as if he is almost afraid to ask the question. "Have we word yet on the bronze?"

"The bronze?" Isabella asks.

"The Magistro wants to cast his horse in bronze so that it will last for all time, or for as long as bronze lasts—and I do not think the world is old enough as of yet to know the life of a good piece of bronze."

"It is mere clay, Marchesa, and will destruct with time and the elements," Leonardo says, making a funereal face. "I have been spending my days at the foundries, discussing methods of casting with the engineers and metallurgists in preparation for the project."

"The Magistro has become an expert in the study of metals, a veritable alchemist," Beatrice says.

"Your Excellency flatters me."

"Not at all. I had hoped to find you here so that I might tell you the news. The bronze for the horse has been located, and you will have access to it immediately."

Beatrice smiles, raising her eyebrows at Isabella. So this was her mission. Was she flaunting her power over the Magistro in front of her sister?

"My eternal gratitude to you, Duchess," he says, tilting his chin toward what Isabella thinks is the direction of his heart. His face flushes with color, leaving him looking relieved, touched, and slightly embarrassed that he is blushing.

"Congratulations, Maestro, your monument will last for a hundred generations," Isabella says, but she is thinking that this colossal new work will put her own sitting with the Magistro out of reach for God knows how many more years.

"The Magistro has devised the most fascinating method for casting the horse. Will you indulge my sister in an explanation?" Beatrice asks. What woman does not know when she has a man's pride in her grip?

Leonardo stoops down and reaches into a large leather satchel resting on the ground, pulling out a wide expanse of paper and unfolding it for Isabella to see. Two drawings of the monument sit side by side: one, the sculpture in its entirety replete with its rider; the other, the horse alone drawn upside down and quartered into pieces. Complex mathematical formulas and measurements, all in an impossible handwriting, cover the paper with other bits of unreadable scrawl.

"I have begun to supervise the digging of an enormous hole in the empty fields to the rear of the Castello. The purpose of this enterprise is so that the mold for the horse might be placed inside of it in an upside-down position so that when the bronze is poured, it will run through the animal's body."

"Astonishing," Isabella says. "Has this procedure been accomplished before?"

"No, Your Excellency, no such thing has ever been attempted. This will be the first equestrian statue of its size to be cast in the metal. Naturally, the endeavor demanded a new technique. The old methods are inadequate to the task, which is the reason for the delay." He looked pointedly at Beatrice. "Invention cannot be rushed. When one desires, as does our illustrious Lord Ludovico, to create memorials of a size and scope heretofore unseen upon this earth, one must tolerate the process of inquiry and experimentation."

Isabella has never heard the Magistro speak so excitedly. The news of the arrival of the bronze seems to have infused his body with a new vigor. For a moment, he has lost his perpetual look of detachment, and she believes that he even takes on the appearance of a younger man, what with his rosy cheeks and hurried speech.

"Speaking of my husband, he did wish me to add this caveat: you shall have your bronze immediately, sir, but on the condition that you begin the mural. The duke has promised the monks delivery of all improvements and decorations to the church and monastery by the end of the year. Please do not put him in difficult stead with the prior."

Admonished perhaps, but undiminished, Leonardo says, "Madame, I have already spent weeks in the study of numerous types of faces in order to do justice to Our Lord and the Twelve. The scenario I have in mind will be a great religious drama."

The church bells begin to ring the noon hour, and the white-and-black-clad Dominican friars file out of doorways and toward the refectory for their meal. Beatrice links arms with Isabella and excuses them, perhaps because she does not wish to be caught in conversation with the prior, who has a reputation for being long-winded and difficult. As they leave the company of the Magistro, Isabella says, "How marvelous of Ludovico to allow these grandiose experiments!" She wonders if her father, her husband, even herself would have the patience, money, and vision to finance such an experimental endeavor—and one of undoubtedly great cost.

"Ludovico was astonished at the breadth of his research and his labors and his passion, and so gave him permission to begin the dig. Did you see Leonardo's excitement, Isabella? He's worked so long on the horse and waited so long for the bronze that he looked like a bride who had been betrothed for years and was finally called to the altar," Beatrice giggles.

Isabella is not surprised that Beatrice would create the metaphor, since she also had lived that situation. But she has come so far from that humiliated girl who was not certain that her betrothed would honor the engagement that she doesn't even seem to make the correlation.

THAT night, as Isabella blows out the candle at her bedside and closes her eyes, her mind is as jumpy as a cat. When Beatrice speaks of her husband, she glows with the fervor of a novitiate at the feet of a saint. If Ludovico had been complicit in the duke's demise, Beatrice shows no trace of carrying the burden of that knowledge. Perhaps her adoration of Ludovico precludes believing the rumors. Or perhaps she condones what he has done—if indeed he has done it.

Isabella would like to soothe herself with the notion that she is now one step closer to being painted by the Magistro, since Beatrice has agreed to sit for him, even though he will undoubt-edly be years in the making of the bronze horse, much less the great mural. But nothing makes sense anymore; logic does not necessarily apply. She feels as if she has suddenly been dropped inside a play where she does not know any of the other characters, but is expected to perform as usual. She is watching the shifts in alliances—personal, political, artistic—in the same way that she observes the currents of a great body of water, which move swiftly and are beyond her control. Survival will surely depend upon staying dry.

Sleep is a gift; dreams are light and forgettable. She can't remember where she is or what she is doing when she hears dozens of horses' hooves pounding against the brick courtyard of the Rocchetta just outside her window. She is torn, wanting to remain where she is, wherever she is, because it is so pleasant, like the color pink or soft summer air. That is all she can hold on to of her reverie as her eyes pop open in the dark against her will and she is ripped out of her dream state. She pulls the blanket high up around her chin as a defense against the clamor. She had gone to bed past midnight and has been asleep for hours, she is sure. Could some army have invaded the Castello in the early-morning hours? The walls are high, the moat is wide, and Ludovico's forces eternally vigilant. The Rocchetta is the private sanctuary of the family. Many a soldier would have to meet his death—or be bribed—before an intruder could enter this part of the Castello.

Just the same, Isabella finds her wrap in the dark. Her eyes begin to adjust, identifying forms—the tall fat posts of the bed, the long table on which her hats sit in a row like ladies at cards, and the outlines of the vaulted windows high in the walls. She hears men in the hall, low, desperate voices coming toward her. She throws her arms around her chest, pressing her back against the bedpost. She has to struggle for a breath.

Isabella's earliest memory is this: rebels bursting into the palace quarters of the Este family in the dark hours while Duke Ercole was far away from Ferrara. Her mother, long, wavy hair and nightgown flying behind her, plucked the children from their nursery beds and took refuge in the fortress. The would-be kidnappers were on their heels as they fled capture, killing all who were helping the duchess and her children escape. Mother and children spent three terrifying days protected by a small guard until Ercole reached Ferrara with his soldiers and put the rebels down. Isabella still remembers running along the dark hall, her tiny sweaty hand clutching her mother's silky gown, trying to keep up with Leonora, who held little Beatrice in one arm and her infant son in the other. The sounds and images are never far from her conscious thoughts; the shrieks of the servants, the clash of armor as their guards tried to hold back the rebels while the royals escaped, the cries of people dying as she ran away, and the terror of letting go the piece of silk in her little hand, her only lifeline in that black tunnel of a hall.

Gasping now for a breath, she forces herself to stretch one hand before her like a blind man. With the other clutching her shawl to her chest she makes her way to the door, cracking it open. The shadow of a torch dances along the wall, undulating toward her like a snake on its belly. Above the din and clatter, she recognizes the voice of Ludovico, shouting orders. Relieved, she rushes into the hallway to intercept him.

He looks like a giant in his riding clothes. Black feathers plume from his broad-brimmed hat; a cloak of wool trimmed in thick fur hangs on his wide shoulders, swishing about him as he strides forward. The men surrounding him are cloaked too, but their garments are flung back around their necks and their hands are on their swords, slung low at the waist. Are they under attack?

Isabella stops running when she sees Beatrice, arms held by two servant girls, step into the hall from her chamber. Beatrice is bloated and awkward and falls like a rag doll into Ludovico's arms. One of the girls explains that the duchess has taken a potion for sleep.

"I was so worried," she mutters, looking up at her husband. "No letter from you yesterday."

"Go back to bed, my darling. All is well." Ludovico looks down the hall, spotting Isabella as he pets his wife. "Look who is awake! Isabella will share a cup of wine with us and hear our gossip." Ludovico kisses Beatrice tenderly all over her face as he speaks to her. "You must rest. Your time is near." When he lets her go, he leaves an imprint of the dust of the road on her pale blue shawl. Beatrice looks relieved, falling back into the arms of her attendants.

Ludovico motions for Isabella to follow the men down the hall and into his study. She walks in the wake of their scent—the sour sweat of men and horses clinging to their heavy clothes. They must have ridden long and hard, she thinks, to have mustered this odor.

The silent machinery that runs the Castello has sprung to motion. Everyone but Isabella is dismissed at the door. Valets hold out their arms to catch Ludovico's heavy coat and hat before rushing the garments to the laundry staff. Inside, wine has arrived, and with it, tubs of water and fresh towels to cleanse the grime and dust from his face and hands. Lamps are already lit, along with a great fire, softening the hard edges of Ludovico's heavy furnishings, and illuminating his face, glowing with sweat and what looks like fury.

Isabella keeps her distance. Ludovico's foul smell and foreboding arrival invite no outstretched arms, no tender, familiar kisses. She stays on the other side of the room, arms folded about her chest.

"Damn that pock-faced lying hunchback shit-sack of a French king."

Ludovico wipes the back of his neck with a towel and throws it on the floor.

"And that pale, quivering Florentine eunuch. A disgrace to his father. May they both keep Satan company for eternity."

Isabella waits for him to elaborate.

"Betrayed, manipulated, lied to, deceived. Done in by an idiot and a conniver." Ludovico takes a long drink of wine. A tiny stream of red liquid trickles from the corner of his mouth into his long hair. He freezes, back arched, dropping his goblet, crying out in pain. "Oh, my back, my legs!" His throws his hand into the curve of his lower back. "I cannot ride the way I used to, Isabella. Help me to my chair."

Isabella allows Ludovico to lean on her shoulder as she guides him to the big leather chair into which he sinks.

"Are you ill?" she asks.

"No, just pinched in the back and bowed and stiff in the legs. We have ridden day and night all the way from the Tuscan hills."

Isabella notices that Ludovico has grown heavier. His belly spreads out about him as he leans back, stretching his feet in front of him. She sits directly opposite, looking into his face for clues of what has happened. He narrows his eyes and licks his lips, and she thinks for a moment that he looks like a great black snake.

"We have been at the camp of the King of France. He lied to us to get what he needed. And we have been betrayed by Piero de' Medici, son of the late Lorenzo, who is a blight on his family's name." Ludovico leans forward, wincing with pain as he signals with his hand for Isabella to come closer. "None of this must reach your sister's ears. Not yet. Not until she has delivered the child. She is hearty and healthy, but also delicate in her way. She is very excitable."

"Brother, as of yet you have told me nothing, so that there is nothing to share but some name-calling."

"That craven idiot Piero de' Medici, who is unworthy of the title of Prince of Florence, literally threw himself at Charles's feet, offering him control of Florence, Siena, and Pisa, in exchange for—for nothing! To avoid invasion! Can you imagine? Lorenzo the Magnificent must be vomiting in his tomb.

"I was a witness to it all, Isabella. I could not disguise my horror. You should have seen the looks on the faces of the French. They were stunned. This fool simply handed them a substantial part of Italy, three of its strongholds. Even the arrogant French were hard-pressed for a response."

"They did not refuse him, certainly."

"No, they certainly did not. I saw de' Medici afterward. He came groveling to me, saying that he had tried to meet me on the road to welcome me but had missed me. I was with some French officers, so I could not tell him exactly what I thought of him. I made some excuses to Charles and left Sarzana immediately."

"But you yourself have sided with the French against Naples. Now Piero is siding with the French against Naples as well. Without Lorenzo to counsel him, perhaps Piero thought he was following your example." Isabella knows that these incriminating words should not have escaped her tongue, but she could hardly take them back. *Who invited the French into Italy in the first place?* That is what she wants to ask. Why is he so upset that others are simply doing as he did? And yet, he looks confused and vulnerable, like a man whose mind has made too many calculations and cannot believe the numbers he has ended up with.

"I sided with the French to contain Naples's aggression. King Ferrante was in deep conspiracy with the Borgia pope to trample over the whole of Italy and turn us all into papal states. Surely you understand that. Your own father sides with us. But now Charles has gone too far. It is worse than you know. His nephew, Louis, Duke of Orleans, is sitting near my borders, reminding everyone that his grandmother was a Visconti. *He* is claiming to be the legitimate Duke of Milan. Charles is not agreeing with him—not yet. Nor is he silencing him."

"What are we to do, Ludovico? Are we to become French?" Isabella is wondering how quickly she can get this information to Francesco; if there is a pair of hands in Milan that she can trust to carry the letter. It seems to her that this is the end of them all.

"From the road, I sent letters in secret to Venice, to your husband and your father, to the King and Queen of Spain, to Emperor Max, and yes, even to the damned Pope, though all of us despise him and pray daily for his demise. I have informed them of the French menace and the latest developments and have proposed that we form an Italian League to protect ourselves. I am under no

illusion that these can be permanent alliances, but we must stop
Charles. And Louis. And we are going to need our combined
armies to do it."

"But the French are marching on Naples and they believe that
you are their ally."

"We shall let them believe that for the moment. We cannot
stop them from attempting to take Naples. I sent letters to
Charles and all the French ambassadors congratulating them on
their various conquests around the world and assuring them of
my loyalty. I wished them good fortune. Charles has no reason to
doubt me. At his request, I left Galeazz in his service. He rides
everywhere alongside the French king. For show, I suppose."

"For show?" Isabella knows that Galeazz is loyal to Ludovico,
and would pretend loyalty to the French if his prince demanded.

"As you know, they couldn't have Francesco," Ludovico says,
a little too venomously for Isabella's taste. "For some reason, a
dashing Italian soldier at his side is essential to Charles's plans."

Isabella is trying to decide whether a mind capable of these
plots is also capable of murder. She knows that she had been
taken in by Ludovico; that he had cultivated her affection—she,
just sixteen when they had first met—in anticipation of requiring
her loyalty, not to mention the loyalty of her husband and her
father, at a later date. Oh, she has no doubt that he was attracted
to her, as she was drawn to him. They have shared—still share—a
love of all things beautiful. She has glimpsed into his soul. It is
not black, but full—of ambition, to be sure, but also of the desire
to improve and achieve and to make the world more pleasing to
live in. Ludovico is a forward-thinking man, as the Magistro once
said, a man who believes in the future. How far he is willing to go,
or has gone, to ensure that the future belongs to him, Isabella is
not certain.

"I have also proposed that Francesco be named captain general of the Italian League's army. Could you bear it if your husband commanded all the armies of Italy?"

Oh yes, she could bear it, if it served the greater good of all the city-states and not just the ambitions of Ludovico Sforza.

"If the Doge of Venice sanctions the appointment, how could he refuse?" Isabella does not want to get into a discussion of Francesco's various loyalties. At times, he could be as convoluted as Ludovico in his thinking.

Ludovico tosses back the rest of his wine, gulping greedily. For the first time this evening, he takes a deep breath, relaxing his features. His pinched eyebrows settle back into their perennially amused arched position. He wipes the wine from his lips with his sleeve, revealing a slight grin. It is as if he has suddenly decided to enjoy it all.

"My dear, with the French practically encamped on the doge's lawn, I seriously doubt he will question my wisdom."

FROM THE NOTEBOOK OF LEONARDO:
On the cruelty of men: A prophecy

There will be seen on earth creatures fighting each other incessantly, and there will be very heavy losses on both sides. The malice will know no bounds. And by reason of their boundless pride and arrogance, they shall wish to rise toward heaven, but the excessive weight of their limbs shall hold them down. There is nothing on earth or under the earth that they will not have chased, molested, or destroyed. That which is made in one country shall be taken away to another.

O Earth! What delays you in opening and hurling these attackers headlong into your huge abysses and caverns? Would that the savage and the ruthless were no longer displayed in the sight of heaven.

Isabella has been trying to get out of Milan for weeks, but her efforts have been daily sabotaged by the astrologer Messer Ambrogio, who can't seem to find an auspicious day for the marchesa to return to Mantua. Every day she grows more desperate to leave and is increasingly angry at being held hostage by the stars. She has neglected her own family long enough for the Sforzas, and recent developments have confirmed the need for her to hurry home.

Three weeks ago, she received a letter from one of her ladies-in-waiting, a devoted friend whom Isabella has known from childhood. The letter was written in a light tone, but the message the woman chose to convey has shaken Isabella.

> The marquis is out of sorts with you being away for so long. He's so desperate that he actually said he wanted to go to bed with me, but I saw the request for what it was—the plea of a lonely husband for the return of his beloved. Do hurry home. All of Mantua misses you and wishes to see you.

Isabella has paid no attention in the years of her marriage as to whether Francesco has been faithful. He has performed with vigor his duties as a husband. He acts as if he is mad for her, in bed and out. He is charming and flirtatious with all women, but she is willing to pay the price of jealousy to have a desirable husband. But the letter felt all too much like a warning.

Besides, she has done her business here in Milan and is anxious to leave. She attended the birth of Beatrice's second son, a beautiful dark infant who looked like a copy of Il Moro. She held the child at the baptismal altar in the Duomo as he was christened, wiping his little royal eyes with a muslin-and-lace handkerchief when the nearsighted priest dribbled the holy water down his forehead. She waited upon Beatrice for as long as Beatrice had agreed to remain confined. She helped to host the many parties and ceremonies around the birth of the boy, whom Beatrice did not want to short-change just because he was the second son.

To celebrate the birth, the entire city and its environs had been decorated beyond the splendor put forth for Beatrice's wedding. Every building and balcony was decorated in the Sforza colors of scarlet and blue; every column ribboned and wrapped with ivy and boughs; every statue polished and painted. Streets were repaved, sidewalks repaired. Even in the weak winter sun, the entire city glimmered. The greenery brought in from the countryside gave the impression that it was already spring and not the dead of winter.

Theatrical performances were given nightly, with parties afterward—feasting, drinking, and dancing until three or four o'clock in the morning. Beatrice had recovered quickly from the labor, and twenty days after her son was born, was in attendance of a splendid performance of the fable of Hippolytus and Theseus given at the home of Niccolò da Correggio. At the after-party, she danced every dance, including the last one. The next day, she was on her horse, racing through the park with Isabella, ignoring the cold weather, jumping fences, and threatening to arrange a hunt, though it had not been one month since she had given birth.

Isabella was enjoying herself through all these activities, but she wondered if the mad schedule of entertainment was meant to block out the trouble that was brewing just outside Milan's walls. It seemed to her that there was a new desperation to Beatrice's activities. Her sister had never been one to sit still; now it appeared to Isabella that Beatrice was unable to relax at all. Nights were spent in festivities; days were spent holding Ludovico's hand as he received responses to his secret plan to form an Italian League. Everyone contacted had agreed to participate. As Ludovico pointed out as he received word from solicitous ambassadors, what choice did they have, what with France closing in from every direction?

Then an omen appeared in the midst of the *feste*, or so Isabella regarded it. The widow Isabel of Aragon, bitter, veiled, draped in reams of coarse black cloth, left the castle at Pavia and moved back into the Castello in Milan with her three sorrowful-looking children. Like a specter, she silently wandered the halls, occasionally letting a lengthy sigh escape from her downturned mouth.

"They could not stand her another moment in Pavia so they've shipped her up here for us to cope with!" Ludovico complained one evening at a party. Beatrice had been tired that evening and had retired to her bedroom after supper. Isabella guessed that the presence of Isabel of Aragon, haunting the halls of the Castello where she had once presided as duchess—as if she, and not her husband, had died—was embarrassing to Beatrice, and was wearing her out. Suddenly, with Isabel's appearance, Beatrice's wild activities ceased.

"That witch has covered her apartments in black as if she expects the devil for dinner. She has the audacity to play the bereaved widow. Is that a joke? I had to promise her husband every bottle of wine and every choirboy in the duchy of Milan just to get him to fuck her!"

Isabella noticed that Ludovico directed his mock frustration at one of Beatrice's ladies-in-waiting. She also noticed that he was pleased when the lady laughed a little too loudly at what he had said, then covered her gorgeous mouth with her hand. She was perhaps in her early twenties, with dark hair that, in the candle glow, had the same hue as a rich red wine. Her eyes were green or blue, Isabella could not tell, and her skin creamy white beneath the rouged cheeks. She wore a robe of crimson satin with great gold cords at the sleeves and a very low bosom that revealed ample white mounds. Isabella knew the face, but could not place it; Beatrice had hundreds of ladies who served her on a rotating basis. Isabella did not like the way that Ludovico was eyeing this one as if she were pork on a platter and he, days from his last meal.

"We all well remember the poor boy's proclivities," Ludovico said. "Alas. I did my best to provide her with heirs, and I was successful."

"Despite your complaints, my lord, you have certainly done

your duty by poor Duchess Isabel," Isabella interjected. "My sister is so grateful that you relieved her of welcoming the duchess back into Milan while she has been recovering from the birth. But then, you are relentless in looking for ways to make my sister happy, are you not?"

Ludovico forced a smile. Perhaps he was unhappy to be reminded that he had a wife. Isabella wanted him to know that she was watching. She had once been the object of his sneaky attentions; did he think that he could get away with his flirtations under her nose? She looked to the lady in crimson to see her reaction to Beatrice's name. The woman smiled politely and turned her face away, as if suddenly bewitched by a tall candlestick on the table behind her.

It was true, however, what Isabella had said. Ludovico had met the bereaved duchess at the gates of Milan; he had held her hand, consoling her as they rode through the streets. He was seen crying with her in the Duomo as they visited Gian Galeazzo's tomb and he escorted her to her old quarters in the Castello, where, exhausted with a day's worth of tears, they fell upon each other's shoulders and cried a little more. All this was given in a verbal report to Isabella by Barone the Jester, a Mantuan in Ludovico's service who could not decipher whether the new Duke of Milan was chivalrous or hypocritical, or both. "Or perhaps he is trying to overcome his dark deed with a round of sympathy for the widow," Barone whispered. Only a jester could get away with such an utterance.

Isabella made it a point to visit poor Duchess Isabel in the Castello. Her rooms were hung with black curtains and the windows were draped. Her children—once meant to inherit the kingdom, but now mere orphans dependent upon Ludovico—appeared in and out of the gloom, showing their faces in the light of the few candles their mother lit, complaining that they could not see, and that the mourning clothes they were forced to wear itched their skin. They longed to play out of doors but were not allowed. Isabella stayed in the dark room as long as she could bear the proximity to the overwhelming misery. As she was leaving, the dethroned duchess hissed in her ear, *"You do know who has brought this misery upon us."*

Isabella did not answer. Aragon continued: "When my little boy rides through the streets, the people shout *Ducha! Ducha!* They are sick of your brother-in-law levying taxes to pay for his grandeur. You will see, Marchesa. Mark the words of a disgraced woman."

To which Isabella curtsied respectfully and fled down the hall.

Soon thereafter, they received news that Naples had fallen to the French. The elderly King Ferrante had recently died—thank God, agreed Isabella and Beatrice—so he did not live to see the downfall of his kingdom. His son Alfonso—father of Isabel of Aragon—who had pretended for so many years to be as fierce as his father, panicked, abdicated, and fled to Sicily, leaving his young son, Prince Ferrante, to face the French. Fearing the violence, the people of Naples opened the city gates to King Charles and his army.

Isabella began to plan her escape from Milan. The tragic sight of poor Aragon and her children, and the fate of Naples, reminded Isabella of the price of all the parties and feasts. Aragon had looked at Isabella with frantic eyes and asked, "What would your poor mother, a princess of the House of Aragon and the kingdom of Naples, think of the betrayal of her family?" Isabella had asked herself that very question many times and had never arrived at a comfortable answer.

With apologies to Ludovico and Beatrice, she made it known that she was to leave immediately and sent her envoys and stewards to prepare for their departure. But Ludovico would not let her leave. He had consulted with his astrologer, as he did on all matters, who said it was not safe for the marchesa to depart. Every night the astrologer gazed at the stars, and each time it was reported to Isabella that she had to wait for an auspicious time before the duke would allow her to go. She could not imagine what Ludovico was up to. Surely there was no reason to keep her in Milan. She had her own family and her own duties to attend to. She was tired of the feasts and nervous about the future—of Italy, of her marriage. If Ludovico was correct, Italy would soon be at war with France, and her husband would be at the head of the army. She imagined that if Francesco was trying to seduce the ladies of the castle, fear of what was to come was at least partially responsible. Didn't men always try to drown their fear in lust? Her absence all these months could not be helping. Finally, after ten days of inauspicious cosmic alignment, she was informed that Messer Ambrogio figured the day of March the fifth for her departure.

Though the weather was still cold, the ice on the river had melted, and Isabella decided to take a bucentaur back to Mantua. Ludovico insisted upon escorting her to the dock at Pavia, where he had other business to attend to. Though she would have preferred to travel alone, she allowed it—for who could say no to Ludovico these days?

They traveled to Pavia in a caravan of sorts, with Ludovico and Isabella on horseback and a train of enclosed carriages accompanying them, full of items that Ludovico said were to be used to further decorate the castle at Pavia. When Isabella tried to get a peek at his treasures, he stopped her. "You will only try to negotiate me out of the finest pieces," he said. Once they arrived at the castle, the items were stashed away, and Ludovico left Isabella after an early supper. The next morning, as she waited for him in the grand reception room, she saw from the window a woman walking alone in the courtyard—the giggling lady-in-waiting in crimson robes she had seen before. Now, without rouge on her face, in a simple cornflower-blue morning gown with a pale shawl over her shoulders, and her hair falling in lush ringlets, Isabella recognized her face. It was that of the Madonna sitting among the strange rocks in the Magistro's altarpiece in the chapel at San Francesco Grande. Beatrice had said that the model was one of the ladies in her service. Lucrezia Crivelli. Isabella did not have to ask herself what the woman was doing in Pavia. It was all too obvious; she was one of the "treasures" that Ludovico had transported to decorate his castle in the old city.

Isabella's stomach fell. Her heart ached for her sister. Beatrice would commit every drop of her blood to her husband's ambitions, based on her faith that she was forever to be Ludovico's young darling. But here was one who was ever the more darling. Lucrezia was sleek and curvaceous all at once. Her skin glistened in the pale morning light. She looked well rested, not kept awake as Beatrice had been for many a night, with worries over the health of two children, or listening to her husband's grand plans for his political ascent, or comforting him as his friends became enemies.

Or soothing him over his possible culpability in the death of Gian Galeazzo.

Beatrice had given everything, and this was to be her reward: infidelity with one of her own ladies-in-waiting, under the noses of the staffs of two royal palaces and God knows who else. Beatrice had betrayed her beloved grandfather, turned her back on the House of Aragon, borne two beautiful sons, befriended the duke's former mistress, presided over his court using all her charm, impressed the Doge of Venice, the Emperor of Germany, and the King of France, and supported her husband's ambitions to become Duke of Milan no matter what the cost. What more did he require?

Isabella can hardly look at her brother-in-law as they ride together in a chariot toward the dock. Yes, it is true that she had her own flirtation with Ludovico, but that was when Beatrice was a silly and skittish girl, not the devoted wife and fine duchess she has become. Isabella wants to race back to Milan and warn her sister, or put her arms around her, or somehow protect her from what is surely to come. Beatrice is not built for disappointment of this kind.

"You are aware of what must happen, Isabella," Ludovico says, breaking the silence.

He has interrupted her angry thoughts, and she has no idea what he is talking about. "No, what must happen?"

"The Italian League must be solid and strong. Venice has been a rival state for many years, but in order to preserve our independence from the French, Venice and Milan must stand together."

"Yes, of course," she says, realizing that Ludovico has kept her in Milan until he heard from every potential ally, including Venice. But the Venetians are known to be inscrutable and crafty. And this is why he insisted on accompanying her to the dock—to make a last-minute impression of the job she was to do for him with Francesco, to ensure that he would promote the cause of the Italian League with the Venetians. She says no more; she is not in the mood to be either supportive or solicitous of him.

The river is flat and gray at this time of year, a perfect match to the skies. When they arrive, servants are already loading her belongings onto the bucentaur. Open horse-drawn carts have been parked on the dock, their contents being loaded onto the boat next to hers, a long, flat river barge. The restless horses make great clopping noises against the wooden planks of the docks as they dance impatiently in place, while a crew of six men maneuver pulleys laden with heavy metal squares. A tall man wearing a royal blue cloak richly embroidered with metallic threads directs them as they guide and stack the bricks with great effort. Each package makes a loud thud as it falls upon the other.

"Is there anything you wish to send to your father in Ferrara?" Ludovico asks. "The barge is going directly to him."

"And what are you sending to him?" she asks.

"Bronze. To make a great cannon. The French have very strong artillery. We must equal or best them."

The man in the blue cloak turns around, and Isabella recognizes the face of the Magistro. Though it has been but two months since she saw him at the refectory, he has aged. The lines on his face have deepened into great crevasses, and his hairline has begun to recede. His curly mane and his beard are unruly and uncombed. His dress is impeccable and he is still grand, but something essential in him has changed.

"Why is the Magistro directing the shipping of goods on the river? Do you need a genius to do the least of your bidding?" she asks.

"That is the bronze that we had collected to cast the statue of the horse. I told Leonardo that conditions being what they are, we have to forgo the project for the time being. Everything is for the war now. He insisted on supervising the shipping of the material himself. He said it was an opportunity to test a system of hoists and pulleys that he devised."

"But he has already worked for years, my lord. The statue is a masterpiece, but the clay will decompose over time. It will be lost if he cannot cast it in bronze!" Isabella feels as if she is losing something in this transaction; as if something precious is being wrested from her. "What is a cannon compared to an immortal work of art?"

This is horrible, she wants to scream at Ludovico. But she can tell by his face that he would only accuse her of thinking like a woman, of valuing beauty over power, when all rational beings know that with the acquisition of more power comes the ability to acquire and produce more beauty.

"It is a temporary situation. He understands, believe me. He is a great military engineer and has already come to me with marvelous designs for new weapons. I believe he is excited about the possibilities of war. In the meanwhile, I have advanced him money to paint a mural of great scope and drama. It's better if he devotes his energy to that one thing. *The Horse* is an extraneous obsession that he does not need at this time."

Isabella does not believe Ludovico's justifications; she can read sorrow into every gesture as Leonardo watches his precious bronze floating away from him to create something that will end life rather than celebrate it.

"What was going to be a monument to a great warrior must now become a weapon," Isabella says. "It is ironic, isn't it?"

"Yes, but fitting, somehow," Ludovico says. "My father was a soldier first and foremost. He would not have objected."

"Still, is there no way?" Isabella can only imagine the Magistro's pain. Why should his work suffer for Ludovico's ambitions? She wants to run to the artist, to comfort him for his loss, to tell him that she will find him some bronze—in Mantua, or somewhere. She will talk her father into sending it back. But she knows that when men set their minds to war, the pleading of a woman will not alter the course.

"Perhaps it is better this way," Ludovico offers. "Casting the statue in bronze would have taken him years. He does not need another distraction. Can you believe that he still spends hours and hours in secret trying to make wings? I am told that he is making plans to soon attempt a leap from an undisclosed building of great height. I pray to God that he finishes the mural of Our Lord's Last Supper and the portrait of my family before he goes crashing to his death."

"Will he really attempt such a thing? He does not look insane." Isabella does not want to envision this broad-shouldered, middle-aged man trying to alight from a roof as if he were a bird. "Do you not think that all this nonsense about flying like a bird is gossip?"

"No, I do not. I have spoken with him of this obsession. It is real. His motto is that the painter must possess all forms of knowledge useful to his art, but what does taking flight have to do with painting? Must one actually be a bird to paint fowl?"

"We will never understand an artist's obsessions, will we? We must trust that they are following some mysterious path, known only to themselves."

The last of Isabella's trunks are loaded into the bucentaur. Ludovico kisses both of her cheeks, and then her forehead. He holds her close. "When we meet again, Francesco will have run the French out of Italy."

"Take care of my sister," Isabella says. "She needs a husband as much as a prince." She turns away from him, giving her hand to the river captain who will help her on board. Before she steps onto the boat, she looks upriver to see that the Magistro is watching her. He makes a small obeisance, never unlocking his mournful brown eyes from hers. He is beginning to look like the sketches of old men that she has seen in his workshop. She wonders if he has always been haunted by the inevitable specter of his aged self, aware that lurking in the shadows of his beauty was the ever-present ghost of his old age. Was that why the lovely adolescent boys he drew were always side by side with ancient men with craggy faces?

She nods her head to acknowledge him. She would like to bow to him in return, but it would be unseemly, so she puts her hand over her heart like a courtier would do for his king. It is a small gesture, but Isabella hopes that he receives it with the respect—and the sympathy—that she intends.

Chapter Seven

I * IL BAGOTTO
(THE MAGICIAN)

FROM THE NOTEBOOK OF LEONARDO:
On the arrangement of the figures of the Apostles in
relation to Christ:

One drinks, leaving the cup in its place and turns
his head toward the speaker.

Another twists his fingers together and turns with
stern brows to his companion.

The next opens his hands, showing their palms, and,
raising his shoulders toward his ears, he gapes in
amazement.

Another speaks into his neighbor's ear, and the
listener turns toward him and gives him his ear as he
holds a knife in one hand and in the other a loaf of
bread cut in half by this knife.

The next, holding a knife in one hand, turns over his
glass with the other hand.

Another rests his hands upon the table and
stares, while yet another breathes heavily with an open
mouth.

> *Another leans forward to look at Our Lord and shades his eyes with his hand.*
>
> *Another draws himself back behind the one who is leaning forward and watches the Christ between the wall and the one who is leaning.*
>
> *Perhaps Alessandro Carissimo of Parma for the hand of Christ?*

IN THE YEARS 1495 AND 1496;
IN THE CITY OF MILAN

EATRICE watches Ludovico lower his head to receive the tall ducal cap, allowing the emperor's ambassadors to drape the official mantle around his broad shoulders. She almost giggles when the same smile with which he receives a delicious platter of food or a good goblet of wine or the promise of sex breaks across his face as he accepts the golden scepter and sword of the kingdom.

If only Isabella could be here to see the height to which her sister has risen. That is all Beatrice can think as she sits on the great tribunal erected for this occasion in front of the Duomo, in the shadow of the Magistro's equestrian monument, watching as her husband is proclaimed Duke of Milan and Count of Pavia by order of Emperor Maximilian of Germany and the Holy Roman Empire. But Isabella is pregnant again, and Francesco alone represents the Gonzagas of Mantua at the ceremony.

Beatrice has participated in every detail leading to this moment, from acting as her husband's ambassador and adviser, to supervising the making of the enormous scarlet cloth draping the podium on which they presently stand. She visited the embroiderers every day to make sure that the mulberry leaves and berries—symbol of Il Moro—were woven into the fabric with the finest gold thread and in the most intricate detail.

When it is time for her to do her part, she cannot focus on the rush of words that whirl past her as every noble and patriarch who preside over the houses and great families of Lombardy pledge their allegiance and fealty to Ludovico, and then to his duchess. She recognizes every face, but she is nervous, gripped by fear and thrills alike. She has not eaten in days. Her mind is such a muddle that it would be difficult for her to call any of these individuals by name. Thank God her only duty at this moment is to stand and solemnly receive the honors being bestowed upon her as Duchess of Milan.

Ludovico had surprised her days earlier by announcing that he was appointing her Regent of the Duchy of Milan and guardian of their two sons. If anything were to happen to him, she would preside over the kingdom until their oldest boy came of age. It is not an unusual honor for a husband to bestow upon his wife, but Beatrice has just passed her twentieth birthday. In the event of Ludovico's demise, no elderly chancellor or body of governors would have sovereignty over her. She would inherit Ludovico's power in its entirety and would safeguard it until little Max could assume the title and the responsibilities.

After the ceremony, as the entire party rides in procession to Sant'Ambrogio Cathedral to give thanks, Beatrice is composing a mental letter to Isabella. *This is the grandest and most noble solemnity that has ever been beheld by our young eyes.* She does not want to sound as if she is boasting. She has missed Isabella terribly since her departure in March. Little Max, who had taken such a liking to his aunt, would run up and down the halls of the Castello calling her name. And Ludovico would look wistfully at his swans whenever they crossed the moat into the palace and proclaim Isabella "a woman whose every gesture proclaims her noble character." Beatrice is no longer jealous of her sister; Isabella no longer flirts with Ludovico, at least not in Beatrice's presence. Her sister even seemed to go out of her way to avoid Ludovico when she was last in Milan, reluctant, or at least it seemed to Beatrice, to spend any time alone with him at all. Years of marriage, duty, and mother-hood may have worked its sedulous, steadying effect on Isabella, as it has on Beatrice. The two are no longer girls competing for at-tention, but women, brought together by blood and by experience.

Events have been happening with such rapidity in Beatrice's life that she would love to have had her sister's cool-headed counsel these last few months. Now that their mother is dead, Isabella is the mentor and female protector in Beatrice's world. With no mother to turn to, when confronting a challenge or a sit-uation that threatened to overwhelm her, Beatrice has found her-self asking: What would Isabella do in this situation? Then she would act according to how she believed her sister would act. Even when Isabella was nowhere in sight, thinking of her gave Beatrice an invisible model of strength and courage to emulate. Sometimes she looks into a crowd and imagines that she sees Isa-bella coming toward her, only to discover that she has fabricated her sister's presence.

Later that evening, at the candle-bright *festa* for two thou-sand guests to commemorate the occasion, Beatrice finds herself drawn only to Francesco. Ludovico has asked her in advance to "chat with Francesco and try to read his pulse on the matter of fighting the French," but Beatrice finds that she wishes only for some firsthand news about her sister.

"Speak to me not of our usual obsession of horses, Marquis," she says to Francesco, ignoring the long line of dignitaries and well-wishers who want a word with her. "I only want to hear of my sister's health and her goings-on. You must tell me everything in great detail because I find that letters are inadequate and leave me wanting for more information."

"Well, she is about this big," he says, putting his hands out a few inches from his stomach. "And she is evermore the Arab horse trader when it comes to procuring beautiful things to decorate her studiolo. She bargains with tremendous conviction. Many a merchant along the trade routes would love to have her talents. I swear to you, she is so cagey and clever that sometimes I think she must be a Venetian." Beatrice can see his pride lighting up his wide, watery brown eyes. Of course, he should appreciate his wife. Beatrice has heard that Isabella—proud, beautiful Isabella—has pawned her most precious jewels to help Francesco pay for armor and supplies for the Italian League army.

"She asked Andrea Mantegna for a painting of such-and-such dimensions to cover a certain space on a certain wall in the studiolo, and requested that he make it of some classical theme. Well, what do you think the old man came up with? He is making a painting of the Nine Muses on Mount Parnassus, and who do you think is the golden-haired Muse in the dead center of the painting? It's our own Isabella, in her pregnant state, dancing among the others. She is more beautiful than Venus, who presides over the painting."

"She *is* more beautiful than Venus," Beatrice says. "Finally someone has painted her as what she is, a Muse."

"Oh yes, she inspires everyone," he says. "If I were a jealous man, I would already have killed dozens of poets and painters and courtiers."

Beatrice does not even attempt to stifle her laugh. "But, Marquis, you are a jealous man."

"So I am. Perhaps we should take a moment to reflect upon my self-restraint."

After all the guests have departed and the duke and his duchess are alone, Ludovico wants to know what Beatrice and Francesco had been discussing with such liveliness. She tells him about Isabella being painted as a Muse.

"Good. Then she will stop pestering us over Magistro Leonardo. At least for a while," he answers. "Mantegna is a genius too. I hope he can slake her thirst."

Beatrice has never known Ludovico to make any comment

about her sister in less than glowing terms and wonders why he is speaking of her in a snide tone now.

"Did you speak to your brother-in-law on any matters of importance?" he asks.

"I thought my sister's health and state of mind *were* important," she answers.

"The marquis is a short little prig, and I wish to God that we did not require his services," Ludovico exclaims. "He would not even speak to me of the confrontation with the French. I suppose he thinks he is employed solely by the Venetians, and not by me. Does he know whose money is filling his pockets?"

Beatrice is fairly certain that all of Italy knows whose money is filling the Italian League's pockets, not to mention the pockets of the kings of France and Germany. Though Ludovico is making the secret alliance against France, publicly he still sides with the French, and has just loaned Charles a large sum of money. When Beatrice had questioned him, he said, "It's important to make your enemies think that you are going to do one thing when you are really going to do another."

"Well, you certainly have accomplished that," she replied. Ludovico had publicly denied his involvement in forming the Italian League all the way through the celebrations of the coalition at Venice, where the French ambassador had demanded to know why all the bells of the city were ringing, and why all the houses were alive with parties and talk of throwing the French out of Italy. "We know nothing about it," Ludovico's ambassadors had been instructed to say. "And whatever it is, we assure you that our duke has no part in it."

Beatrice decides to ignore Ludovico's question about whose money is going into what pockets. "What do you mean, Francesco wouldn't speak with you about it? He was altogether charming all evening. I cannot believe that he would have slighted you on the celebration of your ascendance. If nothing else, he is no fool."

A dark, jagged vein appears across Ludovico's forehead.

Beatrice is not sure she has ever seen it before, but it makes him look meaner, older, and more malevolent. "Apparently he had already spent all charm and civility on you and on whatever women were in proximity. When I asked him how the plans for marching south to confront the French were progressing, he stiffened. In that arrogant way of his, he said, 'I am not going to fight the French. I am going to exterminate them.' Then he had the audacity to walk away, as if I had insulted him."

"Perhaps you did. Perhaps he thought you were questioning his ability or his judgment in military matters. You are a great prince, Ludovico, but no soldier, after all. Or perhaps because he hears one thing about your allegiance to the French, and then another about your new alliance with Venice, he is reluctant to speak openly with you."

"Why are you taking his side against me?" Ludovico yells. "Have you no good opinion of me?"

Beatrice cannot remember when he has raised his voice against her. Perhaps never. "I do not like this sniping at my sister and brother-in-law, who have only been loyal to you." What does he want from them? From anyone? "My lord, I do not understand why your mood is sour these days, when you are at the pinnacle of your success. You have assembled the most powerful alliance in Italy's history, backed by the greatest army we have ever seen."

Ludovico does not answer her. Instead, he glares for a moment or two, throws up his hands, and leaves her rooms.

She does not see him for two days.

She finds out from the servants that Ludovico has gone to Vigevano to recuperate from the festivities. She pretends to know this information, to stop whatever gossip is already circulating through the Castello. Beatrice cannot imagine what she has done to him to cause this retreat. For years now, he has looked to her for soothing and for companionship. Why has she become someone from whom he must flee?

When he returns, he is at the brink of death.

A terrified messenger drags Beatrice out of the bath where

she has gone to escape the heat of the afternoon. *The duke is sick and calling for the duchess. He is on his way home, accompanied by Messer Ambrogio the astrologer. Prepare the rooms.*

"Is it the plague?" she asks, feeling her breakfast rise to the level of her throbbing heart.

"No, it is something else," the man replies, turning his head away, she imagines, from the sight of the unkempt duchess, wrapped hastily in a linen robe, watery hair springing out of its braid. "Some strange fit brought on by bad news. I am not privy as to whatever that news is."

Beatrice is so impatient to finish dressing that she kicks her leg backward, slapping her heel against the shin of the girl trying to tie her bodice. She hears Ludovico's party and flies into the hall, half dressed, wet hair raining little streams of water down her back and into her bodice. Ludovico comes toward her, Messer Ambrogio and his assistant supporting him on either side. The duke's garment is loose at the neck; huge sweat stains mar the silky fabric beneath the arms. Spittle covers his chin and chest. His eyes roll wildly in his head. She notices that the left side of his body seems immobile as if being dragged reluctantly behind the right. Indeed, the left side of his mouth appears frozen, making his mouth look like a half-moon being pulled apart. Beatrice throws open the door to his quarters, and the doctor places him on his bed. Ludovico moans. He does not speak to Beatrice, but tries to catch her attention with his eyes. He seems confused, as if struggling against something he does not understand.

The doctor's assistant holds the duke's head in his hands and pours a potion down his throat. Ludovico gags, trying to spit it out, but it appears that he cannot control his own tongue. Finally he relaxes and lets the remaining liquid slide down his throat.

"I've given him something to calm him," Messer Ambrogio tells Beatrice.

"What is wrong?" she asks. "Has he eaten something foul?" She is frightened to see her husband and lord in this condition, but some overarching pride does not allow her to reveal her emotions in front of this man whom she does not trust. There is something miserly of spirit about the doctor that manifests in his paltry physique.

"He is having a fit, one brought on by adverse news. I have seen this before in men of his age. He must rest." The doctor guides her away from the duke's bed while the assistant tries to soothe Ludovico with cool cloths to his face.

"What is this news?" she asks.

The doctor waits, perhaps assessing whether it is appropriate to entrust the Duchess of Milan with whatever secret he is guarding. Ludovico's moans provide a backdrop to the conversation. Beatrice feels herself getting more upset.

"I must remind you that I am my husband's regent," she says.

"Word reached us this morning that Louis, Duke of Orleans, has captured the city of Novara."

"But that is *our* city. That is not twenty miles from Milan."

"That is precisely correct. Louis staged a rather aggressive surprise offensive from Asti. He arrived at the gates with a huge army and gave the town council a choice. They could open the gates and accept him as the true Duke of Milan, since his grandmother was Valentina Visconti, or they could risk a full-scale assault on the city."

Beatrice waits for him to finish the story.

"Naturally, they opened the gates."

LUDOVICO seems to be slipping ever more deeply into unconsciousness. He waves his right hand at Beatrice, while his left lies limp at his side. He tries to speak to her, but the words come out like the offerings of the deaf beggars who perch in the city's corners. Her mind tries to process all this information at once: her husband's illness; his desertion of her; Louis's claim over Milan. Louis's proximity to Milan. By now, the French King Charles must have gotten wind of the Italian League. The Italian army has already amassed and is preparing to march south. Surely Charles is aware that Ludovico—no matter how much he denies his involvement—is no longer France's ally. Perhaps Louis even acted on Charles's suggestion.

In any case, Charles would no longer stand in the way of Louis invading Milan. And God help us if either man learns of Ludovico's weakened condition, she thinks. The French would be at the gates of the Castello in due haste.

Beatrice remembers the story told by her mother and her sister of the night that the rebels broke in the Castello d'Este in Ferrara, trying to kidnap the royal family to take down Duke Ercole. She was just one year old and has no memory of this horror. By the time she was old enough to hear the story, all had long been made well. Her mother had acted wisely, ferrying her children to safety, and the brave duke had arrived at home just in time to quash the rebellion and save his family. There is no mother or father or big sister now for Beatrice to turn to. She is the mother. Isabella is far away. And the duke, who is supposed to rush in and save the day, lies grasping for words in his bed. Beatrice remembers how her mother's restrained dignity seemed to wrestle with her maternal pride whenever that story was told. She remembers the praise her father heaped on her mother for the courage she displayed in a time of crisis. Now it is up to Beatrice to make certain that when her children tell *this* story, they will not remember the terror, but will live to relate a happy ending to their children and their children's children. She wants to see the same admiration and gratitude in Ludovico's eyes when he, recovered, tells the story to others.

She grabs Ludovico's right hand as it waves in the air, squeezing it. It is surprisingly cool to the touch. "I'll take care of it, my dear," she says to his frantic eyes, forcing herself to offer him a calm smile.

She has her family locked inside the Rocchetta, that great sanctuary within the sanctuary of the Castello, with armed men to ensure that no one gets in or out. She sends messengers to each of the nobles, who just a week ago had publicly pledged their loyalty, asking them to assemble at the Castello without delay. She meets with them, delivering the news about Louis's aggression and sending them off to secure their areas of the city. When she is asked about Ludovico's whereabouts, she makes up a story on the spot: the duke is meeting in secret with his generals to plan a counteroffensive.

She summons Bernardino del Corte, one of Ludovico's oldest friends, who this winter was appointed warden of the treasury of the Castello. In Beatrice's own apartments in the Rocchetta, del Corte had sworn his lifelong fealty to the duke and duchess, and vowed with his very life to protect their assets. Now he repeats that pledge to her, and rushes off to fortify the Treasure Tower in case of attack. She holds a meeting with the commander of the guard in charge of the five hundred soldiers who protect the Castello around the clock, putting him on alert.

She sends word to Galeazz, who is already on the move to Novara with a good-size army. She calls for Bianca Giovanna, whom she keeps by her side so that the girl does not fall into panic, with her father ill and her husband heading a dangerous mission. She sends letters to their allies across Italy, and one to Emperor Max, explaining the treachery and asking for reinforcements to come to Galeazz's aid. If Galeazz is not able to contain Louis and his army, they will appear at the gates of Milan. What could hold back Louis's ambitions now? At night, she sleeps with an arm around each of her sons, reminding her of how, as a girl, she used to sleep with two puppies to keep warm and to feel safe. Now, she is taking precautions should she have to reenact Leonora's midnight flight from invaders.

Bianca Giovanna, whose groom has been wrested by war from the marriage bed, insists on sitting by her father's bed late into the night, holding his hand and talking sweetly to him when he rouses from his slumber or his fits. The girl has begun to look fatigued, her preternaturally white and flawless skin taking on a pearlescent glow. After Ludovico falls asleep, some nights Bianca Giovanna goes to the family's private chapel at the Castello, praying until dawn for her husband. One morning Beatrice comes in at daybreak to say her prayers, finding the girl on her knees at the altar. She has not been to sleep. The tall tapers in front of which she kneels in prayer have burned to the wick. Beatrice sees heavy circles resting like dark, sinister smiles under the girl's bleary eyes.

"You must sleep, Bianca," Beatrice says. "What good will you be to your father or your husband or to me and the children if you wear yourself out?"

"But I often spend the night in prayer," the girl confesses. "God has been so good to me. I was born illegitimate, but yet treated so tenderly and generously by my father after my mother passed away. He married me to the most gallant man in Italy. If I spent my life on my knees, could it be enough acknowledgment of Our Lord's goodness?"

The girl's earnestness is palpable. Not wishing to discourage her devotion, Beatrice holds out her hands to her, lifting her, and sending her off to her room to sleep an hour or two, promising to wake her if there is a change in Ludovico's condition.

A week passes. Every day Ludovico improves slightly; he can almost squeeze his left fist again. Words come easier. General Bernard Contrarini of the Venetian forces arrives in Milan with a mercenary army of two thousand Greeks to help safeguard the city. Beatrice receives daily reports from Galeazz, who is skirmishing with the French at Novara's walls. Beatrice hides from Ludovico the contents of the letters.

Though we are able to hold Louis of Orleans inside the city of Novara, I am spending far too much time convincing my troops to refrain from deserting. Madame, they have not been paid in recent weeks, and it is getting increasingly difficult to rouse them to fight. The quartermaster himself has empty pockets and is threatening to join the other side.

Beatrice speaks in secret with Ludovico's treasurer, Messer Gualtieri, only to be told that all the coin in the realm has gone to the Italian League army. As soon as they are victorious, the soldiers will be paid out of the bounty. She realizes that defeating the French now depends not only on the military ability of men like Francesco and Galeazz but on their diplomacy in coaxing their armies to fight without salary, but for the promise of pay. A delicate situation.

Beatrice tracks Francesco's progress in the march south to confront the French army, which marches north. She receives a letter from Isabella saying that she is spending her days with the clergy at Mantua in prayer for Francesco's success in battle. The confrontation is imminent. The people of Naples have quickly tired of their new French occupiers—pleasure-loving Charles, who is perceived by the Neapolitans to be as dumb as a plank, caring only about bedding beautiful women; and his army, who lie about drunk in the streets, raiding houses and women's bedrooms at will, taking whatever suits them.

Charles apparently has read the writing on the wall. The Neapolitans began rioting against the French, so Charles gathered the bulk of his army and left town, leaving in charge an officer, the Duke of Montpensier, who is Francesco Gonzaga's brother-in-law. Meanwhile, the duke's wife, Chiara, is being sheltered in Mantua by Isabella, who tells everyone that family is family, French and Italians be damned, and she will protect any member of her family if she chooses. Beatrice wonders if war will ever stop making strange bedfellows. Her sister shelters Chiara while Francesco marches on his brother-in-law's king. Francesco heads an army bought and paid for by his other brother-in-law, and supported by the Venetians, who are now in Milan protecting Ludovico, who for decades had been their declared enemy. How will it all end? *Will* it all end?

· · ·

IN the middle of the morning, Beatrice sits in her office wondering if and how she will govern the duchy of Milan when the Italian
and French armies clash, while the duke who envisioned and
funded the war lies in bed, an infirm man. Ludovico has continued
to slowly improve, dressing daily and sitting for a time in the sun,
but he is hardly in shape to command through a war. She is but
twenty years old. She tries reminding herself that she is also the
daughter of Ercole d'Este and the granddaughter of King Ferrante.
If she must, she will be a wartime ruler. It is not impossible. History is littered with the names of such women, but would Beatrice
d'Este actually join the ranks of Semiramis and Artemisia? Why
not? Ludovico's cousin Caterina Sforza of Forli is always waging
war upon one kingdom or another. At only nineteen, she took up
the sword and led an army into the Castel Sant'Angelo in Rome.
Still, the idea of ruling in Ludovico's stead at such a precarious
time is making her ill. What if the Italian League army is not successful, and the French are soon bursting through Milan's gates?

She pushes her untouched breakfast tray aside and looks up
to see Leonardo the Florentine at the door of her office holding a
satchel, an expression of calm concern on his face. He looks as if
he needs a good night's rest. Who let him in?

"How may I help you, sir?" she asks. Undoubtedly, he is here
to request another advance on the mural.

"Your Excellency, I received a note from the duke requesting
a meeting on matters of weaponry and fortification. But when I
arrived this morning, I was told that he was ill and not receiving
visitors."

"The duke sent you a letter?" she asks incredulously. So it is a
ploy to get more money, she thinks. Why else would he invent
such a story?

"A note. Written in his own hand, expressing concern over
the safety of the Castello in the event of an attack. I entered his
service originally as a military engineer and weapons expert. He
is calling upon those skills, these many years later."

Why would Ludovico send for Leonardo when he will hardly see anyone at all? But Leonardo produces the letter, which is written in her husband's hand.

"I am told it came through channels that would lead to his daughter, Madonna Bianca."

Ah, that would make sense. Bianca Giovanna could be coerced into doing her father's bidding.

"Your Excellency, may I speak frankly?" Leonardo asks.

"If you think it will be productive," Beatrice answers, dreading, as usual, what the Magistro will have to say.

"I have personally dissected the tongue, and while I have found no muscles therewith intended specifically for gossip, that seems to be the primary exercise for that organ—at least at court."

"I see," Beatrice replies. "Then you know of the duke's condition?"

"I do."

"You know that he is convalescing. Why, in this weakened condition, do you suppose he sent for you?"

"He must have many thoughts locked inside his mind that he wishes to release."

"Magistro Leonardo, allow me to speak plainly. Of all people, you are aware of how conversations between yourself and the duke can become rather heated. If something happened to disturb him, throwing him into another fit, we might lose him."

"That will not be the result of our meeting. Quite the opposite." Leonardo never looked more confident, at least in her presence.

"Have you taken to fortune-telling too?" she asks, smiling.

He looks for a moment as if he is trying to formulate an honest answer to her question before he acknowledges its humor with an appreciative smile. Then he speaks. "Your Excellency, I have made an extensive study of the inside of the cranium for my book on human anatomy. I have seen the brain and how it is fed by arteries. I have witnessed the point of intersection of all the senses. I have seen the locus of thought. God's genius is as evident in the alleys of this marvelous organ of the brain as in the rising of the sun or the birth of a child. You really should see for yourself its marvels. If I arouse the duke's passion, whether positively or not, his heart will pump more blood, which will flood the brain and reawaken and revive it. The swift flow of blood through healthy veins is the key to longevity!"

None of this makes any sense to Beatrice. Her mind had seized upon the image of Leonardo dissecting a cranium, which then shut down her ears to anything else he had to say. But his methods could not be any worse than Messer Ambrogio's, who lorded over his patient, switching the role between servant and master, and trying, in Beatrice's opinion, to drive a wedge between husband and wife. Besides, Leonardo frightened Beatrice, but she trusted him. She was not afraid of Ambrogio in the same way that she was afraid of the Magistro—in that mysterious way in which one might be afraid of an angel or a ghost, though the ethereal creature would mean no harm—but she trusts the astrologer far, far less.

So that at about the same time that she estimates that Francesco Gonzaga and his army of thirty thousand are colliding with King Charles on the banks of the Taro River near Fornovo, Beatrice takes the Magistro to meet with Ludovico in his private drawing room. The duke is dressed, albeit rather simply, his lap covered with a wool blanket. He looks older since his episode. His skin seems to have slackened, especially at the eyes and throat. To his young wife, he looks more the father than the husband, but his vulnerability only strengthens her tenderness.

The duke shows no surprise when the Magistro enters the room. In fact, he smiles broadly and thanks Beatrice for bringing the great man to him. The Magistro asks nothing about the duke's condition, but covers Ludovico's tables with sketches and architectural drawings of various kinds of walls and fortresses. The two put their heads together over the display, forming a barrier that excludes Beatrice from their communion.

Beatrice leaves them alone to whatever games they are going

to play. Perhaps a morning of Ludovico pretending that he is healthy and in control of the kingdom will bring about those very results. When she returns after one hour, Ludovico has yet more color in his cheeks.

"You must show the duchess your invention," Ludovico says, pronouncing the words more slowly than before he had his fit, but with regained clarity.

Beatrice steps over to the table, and Leonardo brings a wide drawing of the front of the Castello and its moat to the fore. He points to a series of windows that appear to float just above the water.

"It is a secret, underwater bunker!" Ludovico exclaims.

"The moat must be drained, of course," Leonardo says. "But the chamber can be built rather quickly, and out of materials that will resist the water. An underground passage, from the Castello to the bunker, will be built here," he points with his long finger. "Manning the bunker will not be a problem. Only these windows will be visible above the water. Shooters can fire their weapons at eye level before the opposition will be aware of where the volley comes from. Needless to say, the men inside the bunker will be impervious to enemy fire."

Beatrice finds that she is speechless. Leonardo and Ludovico look at her like two pups waiting for their treats after performing a series of tricks. It occurs to her that the two of them, with all their differences, are most often of one mind.

"The element of surprise is that which so often takes the day," Leonardo adds with complete confidence.

Still, she cannot think of what to say. Perhaps this is a woman's folly, this inability to recognize what men of vision routinely see. Perhaps she knows even less of military matters than she previously assumed. She wishes Isabella were here to pass judgment upon this fanciful thing the Magistro has presented. Beatrice can only think to ask how much it will cost, what kinds of materials repel water, and whether it is wise, in times of war, to drain the moat.

"That is dazzling, indeed," she says, the only response she can muster. Yet the new animation in Ludovico's face is undeniable.

"And that is not all," Ludovico says, looking conspiratorially at the painter—cum—weaponry wizard. "The Magistro has alternative plans for defeating the French."

"Your Excellency, I have demonstrated to the duke how we might burn the enemy en masse, flood them out, besiege them, or, in a last resort, repel their scaling ladders with fire and oil as they attempt to take the Castello, sending their scalding bodies plummeting one on top of the other to the ground."

The men's faces are luminous, scenarios of destruction igniting fire in their eyes. Beatrice wonders how someone like Leonardo—who is known to be so sympathetic that he buys tiny sparrows in the marketplace only to set them free, who will not partake of the flesh of animals of any kind, and who has put creations of unmatched beauty into the world—can experience such joy in the destruction of whole battalions of human beings.

"I am surprised to find you so gleeful over these gruesome inventions," Beatrice says to both men. "How is it that an artist may so easily turn his creative nature toward destruction?"

"Your Excellency, warfare is one of the greatest arts. What nobler pursuit than devising ways to preserve the lives of one's countrymen?"

Ludovico looks extremely satisfied with the Magistro's answer. "Do come back to see me tomorrow. We will conspire the more, you and I."

Beatrice walks with the Magistro to the door. "Thank you for reviving my husband's spirits," she says quietly.

"It was not I, Your Excellency, but the magic that occurs when the blood is stimulated."

When the Magistro leaves, Beatrice asks her husband if he needs to rest.

"Oh not at all," he says. "I am myself again."

Ludovico reaches up to Beatrice, guiding her face toward his.

To her disappointment, he kisses her forehead rather than her lips. "Thank you for acting when I could not. Few men are blessed with such a wife."

That is all the intimacy she receives, and she leaves his rooms feeling more puzzled and lost than before.

For days and days, Beatrice looks out of the window of the Rocchetta first thing in the morning to make sure that no one is yet draining the moat. What if Ludovico has lost his mind and starts to approve the Magistro's wilder schemes? What if the Magistro is indeed a conjurer who can take advantage of a man not entirely in control of his faculties? What if Leonardo has been waiting for such an opportunity all along? What would be next? Beatrice imagines great heaps of coin being barreled out of the Treasure Tower to finance the building of giant wings for each foot soldier in the army. Would she have to sell her own jewelry to finance the efforts?

Fortunately, news soon arrives that renders the aquatic bunker unnecessary.

On July the seventh, a stifling day of hot sun and still air, Count Caiazzo, extraordinary knight and brother of Galeazz di Sanseverino, comes riding like the devil into Milan with a report from the battlefield. He tells Ludovico and Beatrice that the armies clashed, with the two generals, Charles and Francesco, transformed into fierce warriors, each setting astonishing examples of valor and conviction for his troops. Francesco fought relentlessly, while three horses were killed beneath him. Charles's men were exhausted and suffering from heatstroke, their numbers diminished by constant desertion on the forced march from Naples up through the mountainous body of Italy. But the king rallied them with reminders of French honor, leading the charge time and again to inspire his troops.

"He kept crying out, 'Die with me!' while he brandished his sword above his head, riding like a wild creature into enemy lines," the count says. "You should have seen him on his white charger, with great purple-and-white plumes rising out of his helmet. I tell you, the king was transformed from a freakish little toad into a hero." Caiazzo went on to explain that by sunset, it was difficult to declare who had taken the day. But Francesco managed to capture the French baggage train, replete with ammunition, weaponry, and a good deal of the French king's booty from Naples.

"The marquis walked the battlefield in tears, looking at the bodies of his brave knights, some cousins, some friends from childhood, declaring a victory that was had at a tremendous price. I have never seen a man fight so well, or shed so many tears over fallen comrades. Charles and his army were horribly battered and reduced, but they escaped, and are headed for Asti as we speak. I am sure they have reached the city by now."

Beatrice collapses in relief. "Then my sister's husband is not wounded?"

"A few superficial scrapes, Your Excellency. It's a miracle. He said to tell you that he is sending some special trinkets from King Charles's tent to you for inspection. He thinks you will like them, though he is sure that you and your sister will fight over the best of it." Caiazzo's eyes glimmer as he reaches into his pocket, producing a small, bejeweled cross, which he places in Beatrice's hand. He folds her fingers over it, and then kisses her fist. "This is just a hint of beautiful things to come."

Where do these di Sanseverino men get their charm? Count Caiazzo looks so much like his brother, with the same insouciant wit and gallant manners, even after a long battle and a two-day ride. "If you see the marquis, please tell him that the only loot I require from this war is his safety. I am sure that is true as well of my sister."

"Ah, but I believe that the very sword and helmet of Charlemagne are among his prizes!"

"But why did he let the French escape?" Ludovico asks impatiently. "Charles could be on his way to Milan for all we know!"

Count Caiazzo does not like the implicit accusation against a man who has risked his life from a man who has not, Beatrice can tell. She knows all of Galeazz's facial expressions and what they mean. She is familiar with this very one now replicated on Caiazzo's face—surprise, indignation, and a flash of anger. "The marquis cost the French army a river of blood. He decimated their ranks and captured their supplies. It was a starving band of stragglers and their king that escaped. The marquis would have annihilated them altogether but for a large company of Albanian mercenaries who disobeyed his orders and, instead of attacking, left the battle to plunder the French camp. This betrayal cost him much grief, but was not his fault. I cannot imagine a man acting with greater courage on your behalf, Your Excellency."

Not to mention rallying soldiers who have not been paid, Beatrice wishes to add, but does not.

Still, Ludovico paces, mumbling that the French remain in Italy, and it was Francesco's mission to force them out. Beatrice is grateful when Bianca Giovanna flies into the room, flinging her arms around the count. Beatrice knows that Bianca is doing this because she longs to embrace her husband, who is still holding back the Duke of Orleans at Novara. Caiazzo is a reasonable substitute, looking enough like Galeazz to fill the girl with the idea that her husband is just as safe at this moment as his brother.

"If only I could bring him a portrait of you just as you are at this moment, he would vanquish the French immediately, just to get back to you," Caiazzo says to Bianca Giovanna. She wears a dusky pink dress that makes her seem to float on a soft cloud.

"Will you see him?" the girl asks, intertwining her delicately veined white arm with the count's muscular, burnished one.

"I am going to join my brother at the walls of Novara. I've only stopped here to feed the men and let them rest a day or two, and then we will be off."

"Will you give him this?" She slips a thick letter into Caiazzo's big hand. "There is so much I want you to tell him for me."

"Words are not everything, my dear," Caiazzo says to Bianca Giovanna. "He knows the longing you are feeling, and believe me, he feels the same."

"I'm happy to hear that you're not lingering in Milan," Ludovico says. "We cannot afford to let the French be so close to our border."

"I know my duty, Your Excellency," he replies solemnly. Solemn, but without the devotion that Beatrice would like to hear. "After a very brief visit with his wife in Mantua, and a ceremony in Venice to honor his extraordinary courage, the marquis will be joining us at the siege of Novara, though he will barely have had time to catch his breath."

Caiazzo bows formally—a little too formally for Beatrice's taste—taking his leave. She does not like the look on his face as he departs. She cannot help but think that it is some kind of warning.

BEATRICE has seen the pageantry and glory of a great army, and now she is a witness to its devastation. She puts her handkerchief over her nose against the stench of sickness and death. The cost of war is this: the dead and dying who lie rotting by the side of the road as she and Ludovico ride away from the city of Novara. The sight and sound of young soldiers retching and wailing make her ashamed of the victorious feelings she had basked in last month when the very army responsible for this wreckage had paid tribute to her.

In August, she had accompanied a rejuvenated Ludovico to Novara, where Galeazz had been laying siege since mid-June. Reinforced by Caiazzo and his cavalry, Francesco Gonzaga and the Italian League army, and a company of Swiss mercenaries sent by Emperor Max, put on a grand display for the Duke and Duchess of Milan. Italy's great condottiere donned glimmering armor for the occasion, carrying their flags and colors. Musicians played the music of battle; drums pounded and trumpets blared as the men paraded, brandishing their weapons in the air. Beatrice had never seen such a show of swords, jousting lances, crossbows as tall as a man, shining daggers, and guns dragged by horses on wheels. The procession stopped long enough for the guns to be fired, demonstrating their power. Beatrice put her hands over her ears and shut her eyes as balls of fire and smoke shot out of the long barrels, landing with great thuds. Galeazz and his men carried all of Ludovico's banners, which seemed to Beatrice more magnificent than the colors of either Venice or the Holy Roman Empire. She was so proud as both Galeazz and Francesco paid her special tribute. Everyone whispered that not since the days of the Roman emperors had Italy raised such an army. Beatrice let that glory wash over her. She knew the part she had played in the or- chestration of this crowning moment. Ludovico was the prince who had financed and assembled this great force, the result of his efforts to forge the former rivals into the alliances of the Italian League, and she was the wife who kept the kingdom alive while Ludovico lay incapacitated during his illness. She felt that both she and Ludovico deserved the honor bestowed. If not for them, King Charles would have marched the length of the country. In- stead, while he was fighting the league forces at Fornovo, her cousin, Prince Ferrante, slipped back into Naples and restored order. Now the French army was in tatters, trying to make its way out of Italy, and Louis's forces were starving inside the very walls of Novara upon which her eyes were resting.

She imagined that Louis and the French were cowering inside those walls, getting reports from their spies about the strength and grandeur of the Italians, and making plans to surrender. It was a perfectly wonderful day, except that at the end of the pro- cession, as Ludovico rode through the ranks inspecting the troops, his horse tripped, throwing him to the ground and all his lovely clothes were spoiled. Beatrice worried over this setback, especially because of his recent health crisis, but he did not let the incident spoil his spirits, despite the fact that some snide Venetians started to spread the rumor that his fall was a bad omen.

The next day, satisfied that the situation in Novara was under control, Beatrice and Ludovico rode to Vigevano, rather than endure the summer heat in Milan. Though it was warm, the country air was fresh and clear. The spectacle at Novara seemed to revive Ludovico's spirits—and his desire for his wife. Beatrice was not sure exactly what had triggered the return of his affection, but she quickly remembered the bliss his attention could bring her. For one long week, they relived the earlier days of their marriage, when he had discovered her charms. They indulged in the pleasures of country life, riding, hunting, fishing, and taking big meals out to the riverbanks where they ate slowly, drank white wines cooled by blocks of ice brought down from the Alps, and one day even read the sweet love poetry of Petrarch to each other. While taking their naps in the tent set up for them after lunch, Ludovico had made love to her as the fabric fluttered around them.

At the end of September, word reached them that Charles was weary of war and had sent Philippe de Commines, the French ambassador to Venice, to negotiate a truce with the marquis. Ludovico and Beatrice rushed back to Novara, where King Charles had already arrived. They settled into a castle at Cameriano, a very short distance from Novara, where ambassadors arrived from all the allies of the Italian League to discuss the terms of the truce. Beatrice was especially proud that Ludovico spoke with the French on behalf of all parties, including her father, who came late in the week from Ferrara. She herself spoke several times in the meetings, reinforcing whatever point Ludovico was trying to make, particularly that he was anxious only to recover Novara and to escort the French out of Italy, and, of course, for Charles to force his trouble-making cousin Louis to drop his claims to be Duke of Milan.

But Louis, starving yet unflinching inside Novara's walls, was begging Charles to break off negotiations with Ludovico and the Italians. As the week progressed, all the other ambassadors wanted to separately discuss Charles's terms with their governments, which Ludovico allowed would take months. So he met privately with Charles and negotiated his own settlement.

"Louis of Orleans has no claim to my title," Ludovico said.

"May I remind you that his grandmother was a Visconti," Charles replied in his cousin's defense.

"And may I remind you that there are thousands of bastards all over Europe with Visconti blood, but we do not seem to be investing them with the duchy of Milan."

Beatrice interrupted before Charles could reply. "Your Majesty, let us remember that it is peace we seek. Louis's claims over the duchy of Milan are an impediment to peace, which is simple to negotiate once it is truly desired. We desire peace, as does Your Majesty. In the interest of peace, Louis must be dissuaded from making his claim."

Charles responded at once, not only to her words, Beatrice was sure, but to her charms. "I am weary of it all, Your Excellency," he replied, smiling at her. "My wife informs me that there are no French reinforcements left, only widows mourning the whitening bones of their husbands that cover the Italian countryside."

He concluded the negotiations at once, urging that all papers of agreement be drawn up immediately, both in French and Italian, before he had cause to change his mind.

Beatrice's triumph was not even spoiled when, later, she overheard the French king asking one of the ambassadors from Ferrara about Isabella. Was it true, he asked, that there was another Este sister who might resemble the lovely Beatrice in looks and charm and grace?

"Is it even possible that there are two such creatures on earth?" the king asked, to Beatrice's delight.

The ambassador replied that in truth, the marchesa was even more beautiful than the duchess, surpassing all ladies in education, wit, and charm. He went on for a very long time describing Isabella in great detail, down to her figure, and the dresses, jewels, and sleeves that adorned it. Then he extolled her intellect. "She has governed Mantua through this war, and with wisdom and compassion, they say, all the while learning new languages and beautifying her city. She is the inspiration of artists and poets throughout Italy. She speaks perfect Latin, and plays the lute as well as the finest musician. She sings angelically, I might add."

"She is not too tall?" asked the diminutive Charles.

"No, she is taller than her sister, but of normal height for a woman," the ambassador replied.

"Thank God for that," the king said.

"The courtiers of Italy call her the first lady in all the world."

"She sounds like a vision of perfection."

"Why, Your Majesty, I do believe you are in love with her very description."

It was true, Beatrice thought. Isabella was more beautiful and more brilliant than she. But those facts—and the French king's possession of them—could not alter her present happiness. Not only had peace been achieved but her husband would be known as the prince who ran the French out of Italy. And that prince was once again in love with his wife. She sloughed off his rough demeanor of months before as a result of his illness. He was kind and attentive again. As a reward for her strength when he lay ill, Ludovico had commissioned Magistro Leonardo and Donato Bramante to refurbish her apartments in the Castello. Both she and the duke were anxious to return to Milan to see the results of this collaboration between the two brilliant talents, to cover their little boys with kisses, and to proclaim the peace they had achieved on behalf of their people.

In addition to all of this, Beatrice was pregnant again. Her time with Ludovico at Vigevano had been more fruitful than she'd imagined. She tells him on the night before they leave, and he is thrilled.

"What is your best guess, my darling? Boy or girl?" he asks.

"You do not even have to consult the astrologer, my dear. I know it in my bones. Our two sons will have another brother."

Ludovico does not look as pleased as Beatrice would like. "Boys grow up to be envious of their father's power. Girls love their father forever," he says.

"But you already have one perfect daughter in Bianca Giovanna," Beatrice replies.

"Yes, but her handsome husband has supplanted me in her heart, as it should be. It would be nice to have another daughter to love me into my old age."

"That is what I am here for, my lord," Beatrice replies.

With the peace signed, Francesco and Galeazz and their troops open the gates of Novara to escort the French out of the city. Beatrice and Ludovico ride in their wake, slowly becoming cognizant of the horror they are to witness as they overtake the fallen army. The French soldiers have no horses. "All were eaten during the siege," Galeazz tells Beatrice when she asks him why they are being made to walk to the border. She estimates that few will actually live to see their homeland. A band of fifty or so, dressed in rags, lingers by the road, leaning on one another to sit upright. Beatrice is astonished to see the ambassador Commines helping his staff to feed a clear broth to the soldiers. She sees that most of them are too weak to swallow, broth trickling down their slack mouths, and she turns away. But the view ahead is not pleasant. Dozens, finally in possession of some food given them by Charles's staff, simultaneously gorge and retch. Starved for so long, Beatrice imagines their bellies are rebelling against the nourishment. Young men drop as they walk, their companions too weak to look back at them much less help them along. Finally Beatrice's party passes the entirety of the French army. As they ride away, she can hear the sounds of the men—crying, sobbing, heaving, gagging—linger in her wake.

. . .

BEATRICE'S eyes trace the whirring path of looping golden rope twined through boughs and boughs of branches that make a painted canopy of jungle on the ceiling of her drawing room. A bower for my bower, she thinks, smiling at her own cleverness, then realizing that the Magistro had probably conceived and executed the little joke for her pleasure. Massive tree trunks shoot up from the arched curves of the walls, roots upending the layers of rocks that try to confine them, as if to say that the outbursts of nature cannot be contained. The greenery spreads like an eternal summer, sheltering the entire room in one endless grove. Each leaf, indeed, each vein in each leaf, is painstakingly delineated with precise, delicate lines. The branches, like the gold ribbon that winds through them, writhe together in an everlasting pattern like an orgy of snakes. Bits of sky—blue, violet, pink, white, gray—made with swirling brushstrokes that mimic the movement of clouds gleam through the tangle. But it's the plaited gold ribbon that puzzles. Unending, unbroken, elusive, it slips through the vividly painted leaves, around thick bark, and then loops and loops around itself in eternal, tortuous twists. Just when Beatrice thinks that the meaning of the mural is eternity itself, the entire landscape comes to a conclusion where, it appears, the painter put down his brush.

"It is spectacular," Beatrice says. "Monumental. Overwhelming. But it is unfinished."

"Ah yes, the specialty of the Magistro," replies Ludovico. "Another unfinished spectacle."

Messer Gualtieri, the treasurer, comes with the letter and the bad news. Like the boisterous roots in his mural, the Magistro has had an outburst.

"He was standing on the scaffold," Gualtieri begins, "touching up a portion of sky, when someone from his household arrived. I believe the boy asked for money. The Magistro threw his brush into the air and started screaming that he was not a bank, that he had creditors chasing him, and that the boy should get used to wearing woolen breeches instead of leather because they were all going to have to start economizing."

Gualtieri pauses. "Well. He called for some paper and wrote this."

Gualtieri hands Ludovico a letter on folded parchment. "He struggled over the words, Your Excellency. He wrote slowly, as if in great pain."

Ludovico mumbles as he reads the Magistro's words. Beatrice leans over to read the contents for herself.

To Your Lordship,

I regret being in need at this time because it prevents me from obeying your every whim and desire, which has always been my greatest pleasure. I regret very much that, having called upon my skills, you find me in need of the funds of which you have promised me. And I regret, further, that because these funds have not been delivered, I must leave your service and find other means of feeding myself and my household, which at this time numbers six mouths. In the last fifty-six months, I have received from your treasury only fifty ducats. Some creditors may be put off with the usual excuses, but I had to advance the money to the priest and the processioners and the gravediggers to see my dear mother put to eternal rest in hallowed ground and with the proper rituals and holy sacraments.

Therefore I must leave Your Lordship's service for a time—a very sad time for me, I assure you, to be separated from my greatest desire, which is to serve you—so that I might commence to raise the money necessary to keep my household fed and in breeches. I hope and trust that this period will soon come to an end so that we might finish the projects we began in earnest. I especially look forward to executing the murals I designed of you portrayed as Fortune's Son, driving out the decrepit hag, Poverty, with your golden wand; of your personage representing Wisdom, wearing magical spectacles that enable you to see through all lies and deceit; and of Your Excellency

*wearing judicial robes and pronouncing sentence on Envy. I be-
lieve that this series will present Your Lordship to his people in
the manner in which his benevolence toward them and his desire for naught but their happiness and prosperity should already convey. Your Excellency is familiar with my sorrow over
the fact that Bramante has been given the time and funds to
complete his series of frescoes of you administering justice,
whereas I have yet to have the tools of time and money delivered
to me. Further, I am anxious to test the designs for the canal
locks. As you know I have devoted many years to the study of the
flow of water and I am completely certain of this new system of
control. As for the mural of the Last Supper, I would like to finish it, but as you know, I have not been able to find an appropriate model for the face of Judas, nor have I received the
compensation to resume work. I will finish this, and the portrait of your illustrious family, when the finances I raise from
other commissions enable me to return to your service. At that
time, I pray that the duchess will sit for me, as I wish only to
work from the subject and not from another artist's rendering.*

*Of the casting of the horse, I will say nothing, knowing
what circumstances are at this time. One does wish, however,
to someday complete one's grand opus.*

*Forgive me for removing myself from my greatest happi-
ness, which is to serve and obey you.*

—Leonardo

Ludovico throws the letter into the air. "Does he think he's
the only artist in Italy?" he screams at Gualtieri. "Where is Pietro
Perugino working? Send him a letter immediately. Write to my
sister-in-law and have her send old Mantegna at once. Send to all
the states and find out who is available. I will not have my ambitions held hostage by the Magistro!"

"But my Lord, why can we not simply give him the money he
requires to return to our service?" Beatrice asks. It seems a simple enough request—the money to feed and clothe oneself and

one's dependents. "Why wait for another artist to travel to Milan when, for just a little money, we can persuade the Magistro to finish my rooms?"

Ludovico's cheeks puff wide as if he is about to blow some huge thing from his mouth. The vein, which Beatrice has seen before, jagged as a lightning bolt, appears abruptly across his brow. Beatrice wonders if he, like angry Zeus, will pull it right out of his head and throw it at her. "What? And play into his hands? This is exactly what he wants. More money so that he can procrastinate until Judgment Day and not have to finish a single thing!"

She prays that her husband does not fall into another fit over this, but she feels she must remind him of certain realities. "I do not understand how paying the man is playing into his hands. You sound as if you are talking about a conniving lover and not a man in your service!" She has long likened the two of them to a married pair. Would the analogy never wear itself out?

His fury is undeterred. "Do not think that you are innocent, madame," he says. "If you had not been playing silly games with your sister over the Magistro's attention, you might have sat for the family portrait long ago, and we would have at least one finished work for all our money. One that would bring glory to the family at that."

"If it pleases Your Excellency, I will sit for the Magistro immediately. I am sure that he can hide my condition. It is not yet so pronounced." Whatever will calm her husband Beatrice will agree to at this moment, when she fears he is aggravated enough to evoke a fit, and she, pregnant, will have to govern the kingdom at a time when peace with France is fresh and tenuous.

"How convenient. Now that you are willing, he is unavailable."

Was she wrong to have tried to beat Isabella at her own game? "My sister wanted the attention of my husband. If it had merely been a question of being painted by the Magistro, of course, I would never have stopped her. But my husband reserves the talents of the Magistro for painting the women he loves. I could not allow my sister to join those ranks. Not when court gossip and my own intuition whispered to me to prevent it. A strong family silences the tongues of its detractors. Don't you see, my lord? Everything I have done since coming to this court, I have done for you."

She says it tenderly, waiting for the simple truth to wash over him. She would like to add *and to make you love me*. But she is glad that she refrained because her words do not soothe him at all. Rather, he looks at her strangely before turning away and continuing his tirade.

"Oh, he is maddening," Ludovico says, as if talking to the trees Leonardo painted on the walls. "Who has fed him and kept him in his fancy brocades and velvets all these years? Am I to receive no gratitude? From anyone?"

Ludovico seems angered that Leonardo's tangle of leaves offers him no answer. Frustrated, he walks out of the chamber, leaving his wife behind as if he had forgotten altogether that she had been with him.

FROM THE NOTEBOOK OF LEONARDO:

1. Apply to Commissioners of Works at Piacenza Cathedral to make bronze doors.

2. Design sets for production of The Danae *at the home of Count Caiazzo. Ask for money to rebuild theatrical machinery from Feast of Paradise currently in storage. Test flame-resistant bodysuit for players to emerge from clouds of fire.*

3. Present brothel design to Messer Jacomo Alfeo. Convince him that a proper House of Pleasure, one based on discretion, with secret entrances to the female of one's choice, would cause profits to soar.

4. *Test flying machine. Make new leather strap for wings.*
   Present design to generals. (Uses: Outfit cavalry with
   wings to surprise the enemy in battle. Flying cavalry
   much more effective than one on horse. Wing all
   messengers, like Hermes, to deliver urgent news to
   princes and kings.)
5. *Present plans for weaving machine to Messer Soderini*
   the cloth merchant.
6. *Collect remainder of money from the foundry for the*
   system of hoists and pulleys built to lift quantities of
   metal.
7. *Finish masks for Count Bergamini's ball.*
8. *Make set of gold plate and eating utensils for la*
   Contessa Bergamini that she craves for entertaining the
   Venetians next month.
9. *Finish bath with hot-water pipes for Duchess Isabel of*
   Aragon.

   O human misery! Of how many things do you make
yourself the slave for money?

From: Milanese Envoy to Florence
To: Ludovico Maria Sforza, Duke of Milan
Re: Available Artists

   In accordance with Your Excellency's request, I have in-
vestigated the availability of several artists of the caliber you
require. Sandro de Botticelli, the most excellent master, is accomplished in panel and wall painting. His figures have a
manly air that Your Highness might admire. Filippino di Frati
Filippi is a disciple of Botticelli and a son of one of the great

and rare masters of our time. His figures, heads in particular,
are gentler and suave. Perugino, rare and singular, excels in
wall painting. His faces are angelic and sweet beyond com-
pare. I know you prefer him, but I believe the monks of the Cer-
tosa at Pavia are occupying his time. You might use your sway
over them and convince them to relinquish him so that the
duchess will not have to spend her confinement in unfinished
rooms. Ghirlandaio is a good master in panels but even better
at wall painting. He is industrious, which should provide a
much-needed contrast with Magistro Leonardo. All of these
masters with the exception of Filippino have proven their
talents at Pope Sixtus' chapel in Rome. Please let me know
your thoughts. One must be swift in procuring the services of
such men.

"Messer Gualtieri, I'd like you to take me into the Treasure
Tower," Beatrice says, sweeping into the man's office.

Beatrice has made up her mind to take matters into her own
hands. She does not want Botticelli or Perugino or even her sister's beloved Andrea Mantegna to come to Milan. Which among
those great men would even consider completing a project begun
by the one whom they consider their master? Besides, it's been
weeks since Ludovico sent his messengers with offers to the
artists and there have been thus far no replies. Beatrice wants the
Magistro to finish his extraordinary canopy of leaves in her
rooms, and she wants to sit for him and have him make the family portrait in the Crucifixion scene opposite the mural of Our
Lord's Last Supper. Oh, she does not want to sit for him, exactly,
but she thinks that if she can get the Magistro back to work, Ludovico can no longer blame her for interfering with his ambitions.
It should be simple enough, and once done, Ludovico will not be
angry with her but grateful.

She has not been to the Treasure Tower in more than a year.
What with the war, there have been no occasions to collect a
bucket full of jewels to adorn a gown for one ceremony or

another. There have been few reasons to celebrate lately. The defeat of the French came at such a high cost that relief and not jubilation had followed. All of Italy had made great sacrifices. In fact, Beatrice has a secondary mission today. She plans to pick out a small jewel for Isabella, who selflessly allowed Francesco to pawn her entire collection of gems to outfit his soldiers for the campaign against France. Isabella has given birth to another girl, Margherita, and has seemed even more disappointed with the gender of her child this time than the last. In correspondence, she does not even mention the child at all, despite Beatrice's sincere offerings of congratulations and the gifts she has sent. Beatrice thinks she will find something lovely for Isabella, and perhaps a tiny pearl necklace for the baby too. If Isabella thinks that others are pleased with her for producing another daughter, maybe she will begin to warm to the girl herself.

But Gualtieri does not move. "I wish to select a small gift for my sister," Beatrice says, wondering why the man does not leap to fulfill her request, as he would normally do, but stares at her as if she has caught him in an unseemly act.

"And then there is the matter of the Magistro," she adds. "My husband is being rather foolish. I thought we might, just the two of us, arrange to forward a few ducats to the Florentine so that he will come straight back to work. I thought we might not trouble the duke with the matter. Leonardo frustrates my husband. I am trying to relieve him of the pressure of dealing with a temperamental artist. We do not wish to see the duke ill again, I am sure."

Gualtieri's expression changes to one of sadness, if Beatrice reads him correctly. "Your Excellency, as you know, I cannot refuse any request made by you."

"That is correct, sir, so let us be on our mission."

Gualtieri turns his somber eyes to his secretary, a thin man seated at a small desk, eyes glued to a ledger book. "Send for the keys," he says, waving the man out of the room. "Your Excellency, has the duke discussed his finances with you of late?"

"No, he has not. The duke is fond of complaining that he is not made of money, but then continues to act as if he is. He has had nothing fresh to say upon the subject in recent times."

"Then perhaps it is in everyone's best interest for you to tour the tower," Gualtieri says, sighing as if he is suddenly very, very tired.

The first thing she sees as Gualtieri opens the door is the faint mist of dust floating in the last of the afternoon sunshine wafting through the high windows. The particles, dancing and twinkling like tiny stars in the shafts of sunlight, seem unfazed by that force which draws all objects to fall to the ground. She steps into the room, eyes drawn to the corner where she knows that from one of the tall wooden barrels of silver she will be able to fill a purse for Leonardo that will easily draw the artist back to his projects.

But the barrels are gone. A single wooden tub lay on its side, empty. The tables, once covered in gems of every type and color, are bare, collecting dust. Beatrice gasps, rushing into the second room of the great vault, where she finds the cabinets of treasure—designed by the Magistro—open and empty. The rooms are desolate, like ancient quarters abandoned and locked up for years upon end.

"Where is everything?" she asks Gualtieri, who has slowly followed her.

"Spent. Gone."

"But where?"

"Everything costs money. The wars were paid for by the loot that the Marquis Gonzaga took from the French, but that, too, is gone, mostly to pay a mercenary army. If you don't pay them, they turn against you. The duke is aware of that. The rest of the money was to defeat Louis of Orleans at Novara."

"But that's impossible. There was simply too much for it all to be gone!"

"Your Excellency, you must discuss this with the duke. All I can tell you is that much money was borrowed from the nobility of

Milan to pay for the many improvements the duke initiated in this city—the renovation of the canal system, the cathedral, the church and refectory at Santa Maria delle Grazie, the monuments, the celebrations, and most of all, the loans to the French, which will never be repaid now that they are defeated and in tatters. Let us also not forget the money that went to Bianca Maria's dowry when she married Emperor Max. That was considerable. After that, the Treasure Tower was all but bare. Recently the patriarchs of Milan demanded to be repaid for the loans the duke forced them to make to him. There was not much left, but since the duke wished to avert a revolt, he divvied up the rest of what was in the coffers to appease them."

"What are we to do now?"

"It isn't a very popular idea, but the duke is raising taxes. Oh, there will be complaints, but it's too bad. It's impossible to run a kingdom—especially this one—without money."

"But at the moment, you are telling me that we are . . ."

Gualtieri finishes her sentence. "Broke."

BEATRICE runs through the halls of the Castello, uncertain of her destination. She is looking for Ludovico, but is afraid to find him. She must confront him, she knows, but what, exactly, she will say, she cannot imagine. Anything she blurts out in this state of mind will sound recriminating and will push him farther away. *The point is to help*, she thinks as the puzzled members of the Castello staff watch the duchess hurtle past, ignoring their salutations. *The point is to band together and create solutions.*

One of Beatrice's secretaries links his arm through hers, yanking her backward. She pulls her arm away and squares off against the man, who bows.

"Your Excellency did not appear to hear me when I called out to her."

"No, I did not." Beatrice's heart is pumping hard against her chest and her lungs hurt. How long was she running?

"The Countess Bergamini waits in your quarters."

"Oh, I cannot see her today," Beatrice replies, trying to control her breathing. "Tell her I am not feeling well."

As if to illustrate that point, Beatrice engulfs her belly with her arms, hoping this attack of nerves has not harmed her baby.

"The countess begs me to tell you that her visit is urgent."

Beatrice takes a deep breath, silently instructing her heart to pump slower. She must calm herself. Cecilia is a friend and confidante—not malicious like so many visitors to court—and one who often has a soothing influence on both the duchess and the duke. Perhaps it will be good to sit with Cecilia and collect oneself.

Sometimes, when Beatrice sees Cecilia, she is amazed that she was able to wrestle Ludovico's heart away from this beauty. Though Cecilia is older and, truth be told, on the brink of stoutness, her creamy skin glows like a woman half her age. The weight has softened her angular aspects, and her sweet smile belongs on the face of an angel—a fact of which the Magistro must have been aware when he used her as his model for the angel in his strange painting of the Blessed Virgin with baby Jesus and John the Baptist sitting among the craggy rocks. For erudition and intellect, Cecilia is second only to Isabella. Cecilia writes beautiful poems and sonnets that are sung in all the courts of Italy. How could Beatrice's victory over her—over the two of them—have been so complete?

"It's good of you to see me on such short notice, Your Excellency," Cecilia says, standing and embracing the younger, smaller woman and kissing her cheek.

"I was told that your business was urgent," Beatrice says, signaling for her guest to sit, and for the parlor attendant to pour them some wine.

"Urgent and confidential," the countess replies, and Beatrice waves everyone out of the room.

The two women lean forward. "As you know, two ambassadors from Venice are staying at my home. It was kind of the duke to place them with us."

Ludovico had financed a lavish redecoration of Cecilia's

palace near the Duomo, now one of the finest residences in Italy. Beatrice was never jealous over this; Cecilia had given ten years of her life to Ludovico, not to mention one adorable son, Cesare. But now with the coffers empty, she winces at the mention of the extravagant home.

"Ludovico considers the Venetians his allies now, but I have overheard these ambassadors and their guests saying the most unkind and frightening things about him."

"For instance?"

"For instance, that he honors no agreements. That he says one thing and does another."

Both women let this pass without comment. Beatrice knows that, like herself, Cecilia is well acquainted with Ludovico's tendency to say one thing and do another.

"Ludovico has been boasting publicly that Pope Alexander is his chaplain, the Emperor Max his condottiere, the Signory of Venice his chamberlain—since they spend their money to attain his ends—and the King of France his courier. Ludovico was successful against the French, but with the assistance of his allies. Allies do not like to be regarded as servants. You know how proud the Venetians are. They find these statements to be most arrogant. I heard one of them say that either God or Venice or both shall find a way to bring the duke down."

"But why come to me with this information when you should be addressing this to Ludovico? Surely you are not afraid to speak with him. Not after the history that has passed between you."

Beatrice feels burdened with what Cecilia is telling her. She has heard Ludovico utter these same remarks. She has heard him boast that he will be known throughout time as the man who chased the French out of Italy. She has watched him employ artist after artist in a campaign of self-aggrandizement—one he could not afford. All these things have made her uncomfortable, especially when contrasted with her father's understated approach to both money and power. But her first aim has always been to preserve the love and intimacy between her and her husband, and she has not known how to approach these subjects with him without alienating his affections.

"My dear, I've tried to talk to Ludovico, but he won't take any of this seriously," Cecilia replies. "I told him what I've just told you, and he replied that he is now Fortune's Son, and no one has to worry over him. I reminded him of the old Venetian adage that one must always remember the inconstancy of human fame. But it didn't seem to affect him in the least. You have such influence with him. Indeed, the two of you are practically one. I hate to burden you with this, but if you can use your famous discretion and charm to coax the duke to act more modestly, at least publicly, and at least in the presence of the Venetians, it would put my mind at ease. Though the Venetians accuse the duke of duplicity, they are even the more so. Who knows what malice they are plotting behind his back."

Beatrice promises that she will speak to Ludovico and then sends Cecilia on her way before the older woman can discover the extent of the duchess's fear. How can this be? After all their success, how can they be without money? Loathed by their allies, who may be conspiring for their demise. Cecilia was right about one thing; there was no separating the fortunes of Beatrice and Ludovico. They may as well be one being. If a woman's star rises with her husband's, so does it decline.

Beatrice walks slowly down the halls now in search of Ludovico, eyes trying not to wander to the marvelous columns held high by great marble plinths, or the walls decorated by Leonardo and Bramante, or the paintings by the masters of Lombardy, because every spectacular inch of the Castello now appears a tomb for their money.

She finds him in a new quarter of the Castello, designed and executed last year. He is standing in front of a huge fresco recently painted by the de Predis brothers and their apprentices. Ludovico had held a contest challenging the artists of the region to enter ideas that would cast the duke in the most illustrious light. Ambrogio de Predis easily won, with the idea to represent the country of Italy as a beautiful and benevolent queen wearing sumptuous robes embroidered with the names of all the important cities. Il Moro gallantly stands at her side—attending Italy!— brushing the dust from her skirts; in other words, cleansing Italy of all that is not wanted.

Beatrice enters the room as Ludovico explains the meaning of the allegorical mural to Lucrezia Crivelli, who stares at it as if it is more miraculous than the Virgin Birth. Beatrice has heard all the talk about her husband's attentions to Lucrezia, but she has ignored it. Ludovico's bout of fits has left him paler, older, and frailer. He simply had not looked, at least to his wife, like a man who could entertain a mistress. And yet he had been erratic at best with his affections toward Beatrice. When they had their lovely interlude at Vigevano and she had conceived for a third time, she put all thoughts of his previous coldness and elusiveness out of her mind.

Now her husband wears on his face the same sort of surprised look she had encountered on Messer Gualtieri. Is it that she considers all men suspect of something or another, or is it that today they are all being caught in the act? Lucrezia is conforming to protocol, curtseying low to the duchess, eyes riveted to the floor, awaiting instructions, and Beatrice gives them immediately: "Leave us." Lucrezia looks up to make certain that the directive is for her. She rises quickly, not meeting Beatrice's eyes, and rushes out of the room, leaving nothing behind but the sound of her swishing velvet skirt.

"Lucrezia Crivelli is supposed to be a lady-in-waiting to me and not you. Why is it, sir, that you occupy your time with her, to the extent that it causes gossip in my court?"

"Madame, I regret that idle chatter has reached your ears. You know how malicious the courtiers are, and not just in Milan but all over the land."

"Is there more that I can do for you, Ludovico, besides bearing you sons, acting as your diplomat with foreign kings, administering the kingdom when you are unwell, and being your companion and lover? Because if there is something I have yet to do in your service, I would like to be informed."

She did not get Cecilia Gallerani kicked out of the palace by being meek. The voice that rose within her then—the one to which she can only find access when she is threatened most severely—arises now to stake her claim upon her husband.

"Dear Beatrice," he says, taking her hand, "you have to expect these things to happen. I am the man who drove the French out of Italy. Such an image makes an impression upon a romantic young woman like Lucrezia. She's bored with her husband. I mean to say, the man is little more than a *merchant*. But the family threw her at him for his money. What can she do? The conversation at home is lacking, to say the least. She seeks my attention, but that is all."

Oh, he looks so proud of himself! Beatrice would like to tell him that the gobble under his neck is hanging nigh down to his breastbone; that the paunch around his belt grows ever thicker; that the veins around his ankles form a grotesque network; and that she has a difficult time looking at this last reminder of how much older he is than she every time he removes his hose. She wishes to tell him that he *is* Fortune's Son, but that is because he has a young wife who not only loves him but is his fierce political ally and defender. That is the truth, but she knows by the pompous look on his face that such information would only deflate his grand opinion of himself and chase him back into the arms of the woman who just ran from the room.

Instead, she squares off with him, looking up into his eyes. She cannot help but notice that the bags beneath them are thicker and heavier. "My lord, I have just visited the Treasure Tower and have found it bare. What say you? Am I, a princess of the House of Este, to live like a pauper? Are my sons to be sent out to learn a trade?"

"My dear, you must come to me when you have questions or concerns, rather than snooping about and discovering things which look worse than they are." His calm voice is like fine silk slipping over her, soothing her ruffled emotions. What kind of snake is he, to be so serene under attack?

"I wasn't snooping," she protests weakly. "I wanted to send poor Isabella a small jewel since she let Francesco sell hers to outfit his army. I thought it was the least I could do, until I found out that we had no money."

"Beatrice, since when have you lost all faith in me?" he asks, a hurt look clouding his face. "I sent most of the treasure to the vaults of our other castles for safekeeping. With the French a mere twenty miles from us at Novara, I thought it would be prudent. Coin and jewels have been hidden with relatives and allies all over Italy."

"But Messer Gualtieri said that we had to repay the loans made by the nobles, and that is where the money went. And now, you must raise taxes, which will anger the citizenry even more."

"The Milanese will have to understand about the taxes. They want beauty, they want progress, they want comfort, they want modernity, they want God to be honored in the highest ways with gilded, art-drenched cathedrals reaching up toward the heavens, but they don't want to pay for any of it. Ah, but that is the way with human beings. And by the way, Messer Gualtieri only knows what I tell him, my dear."

And that is also true for me, she thinks. Yet his words have soothed her.

"Now come to me," he says, opening his arms to her. "If you are not careful, you'll produce a nervous baby."

Beatrice walks straight into her husband's arms, letting her body go limp against his. She closes her eyes, rubbing her face against the brocade of his vest, allowing him to put his arms around her. She does not care, in this moment, to examine her thoughts any further, but lets herself sink into the tranquility his body seems to offer.

Chapter Eight

XIII * LA MORTE (DEATH)

To: Ludovico Sforza, Duke of Milan
From: Leonardo the Florentine

Your Excellency,

It has come to my attention that the Dominican friar, prior of Santa Maria delle Grazie, has come to you with complaints about the supposed lack of progress on the mural of Our Lord's Last Supper in the refectory. Your Excellency should be aware that all is virtually completed but for the head of Judas. He was, as everyone is aware, an egregious villain. Therefore, he should be given an appearance befitting his wicked nature. To this end, for about one year, if not more, night and day, I roam the streets of the Borghetto, where Your Excellency knows that many of the ruffians of the city live. But I have not yet been able to find the face of evil suited to what I have in mind. Once I find that face, I will finish the mural in a day. But if my quest for the appropriate model continues on its fruitless path, I will use the face of the prior, who came to you to complain about me, as he would suit my *requirements perfectly. But I am still undecided as to whether or not I will make him a figure of ridicule in his own rectory.*

As for my alleged inactivity at the convent, you should know that I work on the mural at least two hours a day, and moreover, that higher minds achieve the most when they appear to be doing the least. That is when one completes his search of what he has been looking for.

JANUARY 2, 1497; IN THE CITY OF MILAN

UNDER the grand arch supported by four imposing pillars, Beatrice stands in what will be her final resting place. Since Bramante has finished his work in the church of Santa Maria delle Grazie, she and Ludovico have visited often to admire the work of the master, to pray, and to direct the completion of the sixteen-vault marble crypt Ludovico is building to eventually entomb himself, his wife, and the members of their family. Beatrice often wonders if Ludovico wants to be as far away as possible from his brother and all the other wicked Viscontis buried in the Duomo, but still remain in Milan. Surely, he does not want to be buried near Gian Galeazzo, the late Duke of Milan, as rumors of Ludovico's responsibility for his death still fly around the kingdom like stealthy buzzards. Though Ludovico has always denied that he had any complicity in the young duke's death, Beatrice imagines that he would not wish to spend eternity in a place where the duke's spirit might take vengeance upon him even if it is undeserved. The Santa Maria delle Grazie is all the way across town near the Porta Vercellina and well out of reach of any angry spirits entombed in the Duomo, or so Beatrice imagines.

She has had no idea that she would be spending so much time in this church while she is still living; no idea that one of the vaults would be filled so soon. But she has visited the church every day in the weeks since Bianca Giovanna has died. It happened suddenly, at Vigevano, in late November, right after the weather turned cold. The girl ate something that did not agree with her and took herself to bed. No one worried excessively over this; Bianca Giovanna was delicate of stomach, but the bouts she experienced had always been of little duration. But this time, her pains became increasingly difficult, and before a doctor could diagnose her condition, the life passed right out of her.

Galeazz, a groom for little more than a year, retreated. Ludovico was inconsolable and shut himself up alone in his quarters, closing his heart and his doors to his wife. Nor could Beatrice reach out to Isabella, for just a few weeks before the passing of Bianca Giovanna, Isabella's second daughter, Margherita, had died in her crib. Beatrice could not go to Isabella, nor could Isabella come to Milan. Francesco had fallen dangerously ill with a fever in Calabria, where he was stationed with his army, and Isabella was bringing him back to Mantua, slowly, and in small increments.

Seven months pregnant, Beatrice has been left alone to grieve. She has longed for her husband, sending him notes and messages, asking him to let her console him, and asking him to try to console her, since she has also suffered the loss of the girl. But Ludovico has ignored her pleas, finally sending a brief note in return: *Forgive me, Beatrice. You only remind me of her.*

The only place Beatrice could find solace was with Bianca Giovanna herself. Every morning, she would drive her chariot to the Santa Maria delle Grazie and sit by the girl's tomb, talking to her, asking her if she, from the spirit world, could inspire her father to open his doors, his arms, his bed again to Beatrice. The

talk was that Ludovico was not grieving alone, as he had led Beatrice to believe. Supposedly, he cried late into the night in the
arms of the beautiful Lucrezia Crivelli. Everyone whispered about
it, in low tones, of course, if Beatrice was present. But she could
not help but believe that these *sotto voce* mumblings were meant
to be heard by her ears. It seemed that no one approved of Ludovico's liaison, not even the pet dwarves. Mathilda let it slip while
drunk that she refused to be funny in the duke's presence, no
matter how much he begged her for a little joke, in protest of his
treatment of the duchess. Beatrice did not know which was more
humiliating: the fact that Ludovico was consoling himself with
the charms of Lucrezia while his wife was left to grieve on her
own, or the kingdom's pity of Beatrice over the duke's treatment
of her. Despite all of this, she has missed him. She wants him to
return to her confidence and her bed. Together they can solve any
problem, overcome any obstacle, even the obstacle of another
woman's clutches on his heart.

Beatrice has tried to take solace in the child growing in her
womb, as women are supposed to do when their husband's attention wanders, but the little baby has not comforted her. Children
were one of God's great rewards, but they did not take the place of
a husband at one's side. Beatrice's only moments of succor were
accompanied by great pain. Kneeling by the tomb of Bianca Giovanna, whispering her problems to the dead girl and making
pleas to Our Lord to improve her situation, she found the only
company agreeable to her.

Then, after passing a miserable Christmas, with no warning,
Ludovico came out of his room on the first day of the year. He
came to her apartments, not with arms outstretched to comfort
her but with a plan for completing his grand improvements to the
city. "I have been inspired," he said. "We must go on, Beatrice.
My little girl would have wanted us to stop our grief and return to
our earthly occupations."

It was not precisely what Beatrice had wanted to hear, but she interpreted his enthusiasm, after more than a month of his self-imposed exile from her, as a sign that things were about to improve.

"What have you in mind?" she asked.

"We shall use the Magistro's desperate financial situation to our advantage!" he said, his eyes displaying the stirrings of life that had been absent since putting Bianca Giovanna in the vault.

Ludovico explained that there was fresh coin in the coffers, thanks to his raising taxes. They would forward the Magistro enough money to entice him back to their service, withholding the lion's share until the mural of Our Lord's Last Supper and the addition of the portraits of the family on the wall opposite were complete. Perhaps they might even tempt him to finish Beatrice's apartments in time for the birth of the child. In any case, the two projects in the refectory of the Santa Maria delle Grazie had to be completed first because Ludovico was exhausted with the complaints from the prior about the Magistro's procrastination. Ludovico promised that he would use whatever means necessary to coerce the Magistro into finishing the projects, but he also capitalized on the prior's frustration by demanding that the Order of the Dominicans absorb some of the cost of the great mural, which made the prior grouse even more.

"Why can the Magistro not act in the ordinary manner of an artist, say, as Montorfano did? We agree on the contents of the mural, in this case, a painting of the Crucifixion. We forward him half of the money. He painted for a month or two. The oils dried. We approved his work. He is paid and out of our hair!" Beatrice noticed that the special frustration Ludovico reserved for the Magistro was often more intense than the ire manifested against his political enemies.

"And yet, Your Excellency, may I remind you that Montorfano's mural is rather ordinary, or at least all the experts in your court say so. Isabella remarked on it as well. It is large and grand, and it honors the order of the Dominicans. But there is nothing of the genius on the wall." Beatrice was thinking that both she and

Leonardo had given Ludovico so much above the ordinary, and he still considered them tools to further his own ambitions. Nothing more. Ludovico regarded himself the sun and the rest of them, lesser planets.

"That is further to my point, Beatrice," he said. "The painting of the Lord's Last Supper is turning out to be a masterpiece. People will come from thousands of miles just to see it, to study it, to praise it." Ludovico seemed to be bringing himself back to life with each word he said, suddenly aglow with his own thoughts. His cheeks, grown hollow in recent weeks, puffed up as they had in the past. "On the wall opposite, incorporated into the mural by Montorfano, they will see the portraits of the family under whose patronage the Magistro fulfilled his genius. At last, the world will have one of his grand works in a completed form to admire. And we will be eternally recognized as those who made it possible for this unparalleled talent to flourish. Think of it, Beatrice, we and the Magistro shall all be linked together in immortality!"

You should have married my sister, she wanted to say. For Isabella was always seeking fame and immortality. Beatrice was more concerned with the quality of their lives in the here and now.

"I will have him incorporate our heralds and coats of arms—not just mine, but yours, and those of our sons—in his mural so that forever more, all will know that it was the Sforza family who brought about, by their considerable efforts and funds, this great work!"

"Surely you do not wish for me to sit for the Magistro in this bloated condition," she said, putting her hands on her belly.

"But Isabella sat for Mantegna when she was pregnant, and look at the result. The painting of Mount Parnassus is a masterpiece, talked about all over Italy. They are saying that Isabella looks more the goddess than Venus herself. And so shall you."

"I doubt it," she said. "I am already stouter than I was the last pregnancy. Let me wait until the baby has come. I'll exercise my horse daily until I am trim again."

"Who knows what strange inventions will be occupying the

mind of the Magistro by that time? He needs money now. He is willing to work now. Let us strike. I tell you, this is our chance. They say he is making secret plans to test his flying machine. I insist that you sit for him before he throws himself off a roof and plummets to his death."

"But I do not care so much to be around him, Ludovico, especially while I am pregnant. He is charming, to be sure, but to me, he is also frightening, even foreboding. I do not like that he draws babies in the womb, or that he cuts open the dead to uncover the secrets of the body. Those are God's own mysteries. They are not for men to know, otherwise, Our Lord would have made us all transparent."

"Ah, Beatrice. You easily tame horses that turn great warriors white with fear, but you are afraid of an artist. You make no sense, my wife."

He smiled at her in the old way, the way that bespoke of an intimacy between them, that bespoke of his knowing her better than others did and admiring her for her uniqueness. That comment, that smile, encouraged her to agree to sit for the Magistro the very next day.

Thus, this morning she is on her way to sit for Leonardo in the refectory. Before meeting with him, Beatrice has stopped in the church to thank Bianca Giovanna for interceding with her father. Beatrice would have preferred a return to their old days of enthrallment with each other—nights of lovemaking and laughter—rather than conspiring to complete a work of art. But perhaps this bout of enthusiasm was all Bianca could instigate from the grave. Perhaps a return to the way things were would be a gradual one. With the birth of another child, Beatrice might be able to oust Lucrezia from Ludovico's heart just as she had with Cecilia. Yes, perhaps it would all turn out well in the end.

Despite that it is a sunny day, the temperature inside the church is frigid, and Beatrice feels the chill this morning all the way inside her bones. She thinks she feels the little one inside her shiver, so her talk with Bianca is hurried. "I wish I could wrap my arms around you and save you from this awful cold, my darling girl. Remember how we used to sit close together by the fire and talk? Little saintly girl, ask Our Lord if He will allow us such moments when I join you in His heaven, for that is the only place you could possibly be."

She always hates to leave Bianca Giovanna alone in this chilly place, with fifteen empty crypts surrounding her, but she forces herself to imagine that the girl's spirit is not lonely, but seated near the foot of God, for that is where such a sweet soul belongs. Beatrice has the fleeting thought—or rather, hope—that she is pregnant with a girl; another beautiful little girl to replace Ludovico's perfect daughter. A little girl would open his heart, both to the child and to the woman who gave him the child. She hesitates, wishing to turn to the altar and make a prayer that her child be a female. But if the child is not—and she has spent months thinking it is not—she does not want to insult either the baby or God, who makes such decisions. What if she angers God, questioning His judgment in sending her a child the sex of which He has chosen? Isabella had prayed for a boy, and God had taken the child from her sister when the little baby was only two months old.

"I'm sorry," she whispers to the baby, warming her cold hands on the velvet covering her stomach. "I didn't mean to wish you away. I love you no matter what you are. Whoever you are, boy or girl, I cannot wait to see your sweet face and touch your little tiny hands and hear your angel cries."

It occurs to her that it cannot be good for a nascent life to have spent all this time in the company of the dead, and she hurries out of the church and into the courtyard of the rectory, where she sees the Magistro finishing the last of his loaf of bread. He quickly chews, bowing to her, she thinks, to cover up the fact that he is swallowing.

"Good morning, Magistro," she says. "Is the sky not an extraordinary blue for this cold winter's day?"

"Your Excellency," he says, wiping the crumbs from his beard, "the sky is not really blue. Did you know that? I have made a study of it. The blue is an illusion. The color is merely a result of the way that the sun's rays reflect upon the water contained in the skies."

"But if it is not really blue, then what color is it?"

"This great blue ceiling is merely covering an eternal and un-fathomable darkness. As with so many things, a façade of beauty hides the dark and the unknown."

Leonardo takes her arm, leading her toward the refectory, unaware, she thinks, of the effect his statement has had upon her. She does not think it wise for a man to make such investigations of the wonders of nature. If God wants us to see blue, then we ought to just see blue, she wants to say. The Lord would have His reasons. What good can come from revealing His secrets?

Beatrice stops Leonardo outside the double doors leading to the dining hall of the friars. "Magistro, I must ask you. Is it true that you have built a machine with wings and that you intend to fly?"

"Yes, Your Excellency. It is true."

"But if you fail, or if the flying machine fails, will that not put an end to you? I ask you this out of concern. The duke and I have the highest regard for you. I would be remiss in my duty if I allowed a man of your talents to undo himself while in our service."

But he only smiles at her. "I have made some preliminary tests which have left me quite optimistic. As you can see, I remain uninjured."

"Are you not afraid that in trying to fly, you are defying God, who made the birds with wings and man earthbound?"

"Why no, Your Excellency. I believe that God Himself inspired me to create the flying machine. Even if I were trying to defy God by flying, I believe He would forgive me. Men are always acting in defiance of Our Lord, and I cannot see where He has struck too many of them down."

They pass into the refectory, bringing a gust of cold air into the room with them. Much of Leonardo's mural of Our Lord's Last Supper is hidden by scaffolding, but Beatrice is happy to see that the face of Jesus is revealed. She has always taken comfort in

Jesus' face, and has sometimes of late, when visiting Bianca Giovanna's tomb, poked her head into the refectory to gaze upon it. Eyes cast downward, palm open, Jesus is utterly serene as He announces the fact of the betrayal. He wears simple robes of scarlet and blue, the Sforza colors, a subtle tribute by the Magistro to the reigning family. His tilted head is positioned in the center of a window behind Him, so that He is framed by the bright light outside. The Magistro long ago abandoned halos in religious painting, as Isabella pointed out to her sister, but to signal Jesus' divinity, the Magistro surrounds Him in divine light that comes from a natural source. Beatrice cannot help but think that the Magistro has intentionally given Jesus this halo of sorts. The eye of the viewer is naturally drawn to the Christ in the center, and beyond, out of the window, where the landscape has an endless horizon that seems to extend the very wall of the refectory into eternity. It is as if the Magistro is making a contrast between the finite nature of the event taking place in the picture's scenario, and the eternal nature that is Jesus' essence. Beatrice lets her gaze melt into that of the Lord. If Jesus could be so serene at the hour of His betrayal by someone He loved and trusted, then so can she. It is as if Our Lord is telling her to be brave in the face of this fresh pain. Look past this present drama, He seems to say, for it is temporal, *whereas the love I promise you is eternal.*

She will report to her husband that the Magistro is nearly finished with this great opus. She and Ludovico have visited the dining hall from time to time to gauge the Magistro's progress—or lack of it. The first time, they arrived with Leonardo's apprentices and his equipment, watching the prior's astonished face as lumber for ladders and scaffolds, lengths of ropes, hoists and pulleys were brought into the room under his nose. These materials were followed by bowls of eggs for mixing the tempera, great jars of oil, ceramic pots full of pigments of every hue of every color, stones of lapis lazuli and the mortars to pound them into a powder for mixing the color blue, and dozens of palettes and brushes.

"But all of this in our dining hall?" the prior had asked. "Montorfano did not bring nearly this much!"

"You cannot expect the Magistro to cover a thirty-foot expanse of wall with just a smidgeon of paint," Ludovico answered, as the apprentices and hired laborers carried in easels so that the mural might be copied and studied even as the Magistro painted it. They set up long worktables on which were spread his hundreds of studies for the various parts of the mural—heads, profiles, faces, feet, hands, noses, robes, drapery, plates, cups, even different sorts of foods, all sketched in red and black chalk. Soon the room was overtaken and the prior was demanding to know how long his clergy was to be expected to eat their meals with the strong smell of linseed that already permeated the room.

"My dear Father," Ludovico said, "Giotto could paint a mural in ten days. How much behind him could a greater genius like our Leonardo be?

"Besides," Ludovico added. "You are men of God, sworn to make every sacrifice to His glory. What is the sacrifice of dining in clutter compared to the sacrifice that the Savior made upon the cross for all of us?"

The prior could not counter this point and so closed his mouth—for the time being.

The Magistro, wishing to explain his conception for the mural to his patrons, ceremoniously quoted from the Gospel according to Matthew, " 'Now when the evening had come, He sat down with the Twelve. And as they did eat, He said, "Verily I say unto you that one of you shall betray me." And they were exceedingly sorrowful and began to say unto Him, "Lord, is it I?" And He replied, "He that dip his hand with me in the dish, the same shall betray me." '

"The task of an artist is twofold," the Magistro continued. "To portray the person and to portray the person's state of mind. I shall portray each apostle and his state of mind at the moment that the Lord announces that one of them shall betray Him."

Satisfied that the Magistro was sufficiently interested in

pursuing and completing the mural, Ludovico left him alone. He and Beatrice visited the refectory some weeks later to see, to their happy surprise, that the figures were already outlined on the wall in thin black paint. Slowly, in the ensuing months, a great sweep of color began to wash over the wall, and the prior ceased to complain because he could see daily progress. Though he wanted the artist and his team of assistants and their various sloppy materials out of the dining hall, he could also foresee that the Dominicans of Santa Maria delle Grazie were going to be in possession of a great work of art.

But that was two years ago.

Though most of the painting is complete, Judas—Beatrice assumes that it is Judas because the figure is clutching a purse—remains headless. And unlike all other representations of this event, Judas sits on the same side of the table as the others.

"Judas is always portrayed as isolated from the rest, sitting on the opposite side of the table from Our Lord and the Apostles. Why have you seated him on the same side?" Beatrice asks.

"Because, Your Excellency, he would have been," he answers politely, as if all the painters through the ages until himself have simply been wrong. "One must consider the state of mind of the betrayer. He would have done anything to keep his wicked deed secret. He would have tried to look most innocent. He would not have separated himself from the Twelve. It would have aroused suspicion. A drama must be as true to life as possible to convince."

The painting is, in fact, and as promised, a drama. Each of the Twelve is frozen in the moment, the contents of his mind, and his fear that he is the one who will betray the Lord, etched on his expression and in each movement of the body. Beatrice has never seen a painting that so perfectly captures one moment in time. It is as if the Magistro stopped Time itself and preserved it in his mural. The effect is eerie, she thinks, another of Leonardo's mystical tricks, undoubtedly borne out of his inquiries into the inner workings of man's brain and body. She decides to bring the conversation back to a more practical level.

"And why is the head of Judas not yet painted?"

"Because I have yet to find the correct model for him, a face that might embody betrayal itself."

"But a betrayer might have many faces, some of them beautiful or comely or quite handsome." Beatrice feels the words choking her as they exit her mouth. Does the Magistro realize that the duchess has recently been betrayed by two faces, one beautiful and the other handsome? Has he, too, heard the gossip? Does he pity her even as he must patronize her?

"That is true," he says darkly. "Treachery is too often hidden by a sweet or handsome face." He says it not in a condescending way, as if he is responding to court gossip, but as someone who has also been slain by the deceiver behind the beautiful mask. She has never seen him look so vulnerable. His eyebrows cinch together, and she notices the exquisite web of lines shooting from the corners of his eyes like pencil drawings of the sun's rays. A line of worry bisects his forehead, making it look as if his face might split in two if he continued with whatever thought was passing through his brain.

"Why is it that in others' renditions of Our Lord's Last Supper, Judas is isolated, but in yours, it is Jesus who looks so very much alone?"

"Because, Your Excellency, if you had just prophesied that you would soon be betrayed by someone whom you loved and trusted, and if that betrayal were inevitable, which you knew because it had been revealed to you by God, and was therefore beyond question, would you not feel isolated?"

"OUR task together is simple," Leonardo says, guiding Beatrice to the south wall of the refectory, where he is to insert her portrait into Montorfano's mural. The room has no hearth, and the warmth from the burning fire bowls seems to dissipate into the tall ceiling before it can do anyone any good. Beatrice shivers as the Magistro explains. "You will see on the left side of the painting where I have outlined the profile of the duke and your elder son. See how they are kneeling, as if being blessed by the Pope and St. Francis? On the right side of the mural, I will paint you in profile too, Your Excellency, with your younger son at your side, kneeling in the shelter of the Dominican nuns, whom the excellent Montorfano has so interestingly painted into the scene of the Crucifixion of Jesus, some thousand years before."

Was he mocking the other artist? Leonardo kept himself in a host of legal battles by refusing to make these allowances meant to glorify those holding the purse strings in the commissions he accepted. The Montorfano mural, in fact, embodied all of the present-day conventions rejected by the Magistro—a blatantly Italian backdrop to the Crucifixion; angels with many-colored wings flying about; demons perched on the shoulders of the wicked while saints whisper into the ears of the good; the presence of the pope and other clergy; and soldiers and Crusaders on horseback, witnessing the suffering of the Lord. The mural gives an overall effect of sorrow, whereas the Magistro's painting witnesses the climactic moment of a great drama. One can see not only the character but, as Leonardo himself said, each character's state of mind.

"I need only make a sketch of your profile," he says as his assistants bring him sheets of paper of various size and weight. Wordlessly, he rejects each piece of parchment until he finds one to meet his approval. "And I would like to also make a sketch of your hands folded in prayer."

The assistants return to their task of mixing colors, presumably so that Leonardo can later continue to work on the Last Supper. This is what Beatrice will report to Ludovico, anyway. Easels sit about the room, some upon which rest copies of the Last Supper, and some of which are covered with long white muslin cloths, hiding the paintings. One in particular looks ghostly, Beatrice thinks, sitting in the chair the Magistro has brought for her. She cannot take her eyes off of the tall, white form. Its conical top stretches from the crest of the easel as it stands alone like a specter, looking very mysterious, yet at the same time daring its revelation. Isabella always allows that there is no excitement like pulling the drape back on the work of a great artist. If she were here, she would ask the Magistro to reveal his work to her, as if it were the most natural thing to do. But Beatrice is not comfortable asking to see that which the artist has cloaked. If he has covered it, he must have his reasons.

Because Leonardo says he wishes to sketch her hands, Beatrice pulls off her leather gloves, revealing her pale, dry skin. She is twenty-one years old; how is it that the skin on the tops of her hands can look more wrinkled than the unpressed cloth covering the paintings? The room is very cold, colder even than the church where Bianca Giovanna lies, causing Beatrice's skin to shrivel even more.

"Your Excellency, your hands shake. I will have the friar in the kitchen send a bowl of hot broth to warm you," the Magistro says, his eyes full of concern as he leaves her to order the soup.

Beatrice wraps her cloak about her, standing so that she can pace the room to keep warm. She is drawn to the covered painting. She thinks that she will peek under the cloth, perhaps discovering some masterpiece in the making that she will be able to describe later today in a letter to Isabella. Beatrice has already made up her mind that she will invite Isabella to Milan to be with her when her baby is born. As a gift to her sister, she will make certain that Isabella sits for the Magistro—and not in this frigid refectory for a mere sketch, but in a room in the Castello near a warm fire, where drawings will be made for a fine oil painting like the one Leonardo made of Cecilia. Beatrice will not trust this enterprise to Ludovico, who will only carry it out if he can think of something to ask from Isabella in return, but she will appeal to the Magistro herself. How foolish were the competitions between the sisters in the past. Now they are two grown women, both suffering from losses. Giving Isabella the gift of a portrait by the Magistro is the least Beatrice can do for her sister.

The apprentices are busy at their labors. Surely they would

not stop the duchess from peeking at a work in progress. After all, it is undoubtedly her money that is financing whatever work has been done beneath that long white drape. Pretending that she is moving closer to one of the fire bowls to keep warm, she bends over and lifts the drape, revealing the lower right corner of the painting. She can see that the panel is of dark wood, walnut, just like the panel Leonardo used for Cecilia's portrait. She looks up to see if she is being caught in her act of spying—she is not—and then lifts the drape a little more. On the canvas, a golden ribbon, much like the one the Magistro painted into the boughs on the ceiling of her apartments, rests against a crimson velvet robe. Intrigued that she has discovered what is undoubtedly a portrait, Beatrice proceeds with the unveiling, anxious to know who the sitter might be. If the Magistro is taking commissions for portraiture, then he will hardly be able to refuse the duchess when she demands a portrait of her sister.

Slowly she pulls up the drape. Red velvet embossed with gold makes up the bodice of the sitter's gown. The beads of a simple necklace hang below embroidered ribbon lining the neck, exposing creamy skin. The shoulder is curved, the neck, long. The sitter is a woman, and young. The chin is round, the lips full, but set seriously. Raven hair, pulled back into a braid of sorts, hugs a high cheekbone.

Suddenly, the eyes are exposed. They stare slightly to the left, as they have often done in recent times, when Lucrezia Crivelli has been too timid, or too guilty, to meet Beatrice's direct gaze. Lucrezia refuses once more to look right at Beatrice, instead turning her serious—studious, almost—stare at something just off to the side of the portrait. Look at me, Beatrice wants to scream, pains taking over her body. She is sick in the stomach and light in the head all at once, and she doesn't know whether to bend over or drop to the floor. Instead, she grabs onto the easel for support, almost knocking it to the ground. The noise alerts the apprentices.

"I am not well," she says, dropping the drape over the painting and looking at the stone floor of the refectory, not wanting them to see her flushed, disturbed face. One of the young men tries to approach her to offer his arm, but, without looking at him, she rushes past him and out the door.

The trees in the courtyard of the refectory are bare. The sky has turned from blue to gray, and the air seems much colder than just a little while ago. Beatrice sees that her attendants wait for her in two carriages, all huddled together to keep warm, snuggled under thick blankets, and laughing at whatever gossip they are exchanging to keep their minds off of the cold weather. What if they are laughing at her? What if the talk that brings those smiles to their faces is that the naïve little duchess sits for a family portrait by the Magistro to be painted in a solemn pose with her husband and two children glorifying their union and its issue, while she is also sitting right under the nose of Lucrezia Crivelli, who has taken her husband's heart?

She cannot, will not, return to the carriages, only to see her ladies snap their mouths shut, quieting the gossip because its victim has just appeared. She sees the door of the church and knows where she must go—to Bianca Giovanna, whose sweet spirit will listen to her troubles and soothe her.

The church is empty, frigid, and dank. Beatrice falls on the floor next to Bianca's crypt. "We are both alone," she cries into her hands. "The only difference is that your husband would be with you if he could. My husband uses the death of his precious daughter as an excuse to stay away from me while he consoles himself with another woman. Is she so much better than I?" Beatrice pleads to the dead girl, who offers no response. She feels a pulling within her womb, as if the baby has suddenly become too heavy for her body and is pushing to get out. She doubles over, clutching her belly. The child seems to be making himself known to her at this hour of her need. "Does this child mean nothing to him either?"

In just a few years, she has gone from her husband's sweet-

heart, confidante, and partner to his breeding machine. Lucrezia
Crivelli is beautiful, true, but older than Beatrice, and married.
And, Beatrice is sure, no intellectual match for Cecilia or Isabella,
her former rivals. What is she offering to him that he cannot find
in the arms of his wife? Did Ludovico simply tire of Beatrice because he possessed her? Do men automatically tire of a woman
after she gives him the very best she can offer—love, companionship, partnership in his ambitions, children to carry on his name
and fortune? It seems to Beatrice that a woman's love is something to cherish, not toss aside for some new bauble.

And what bauble? Beatrice thinks that Lucrezia looks awful in
the Magistro's portrait—stern, serious, shoulders drawn tight, as
if she is worried over something. As if she has something to hide.
Beatrice is certain that Leonardo, like the rest of the kingdom, is
upset over Ludovico's indiscretion and has rendered Lucrezia
less desirable than she is. The portrait looks to her as if the Magistro sketched in the outline and left the painting to his apprentices, since the face embodies neither the life nor the mystery
nor the beauty nor the animation of the portrait of Cecilia.

But the meaning of Lucrezia's portrait is inevitable. It is an
indication that Ludovico's feelings for her are permanent. She
has replaced Beatrice. Did he not say that he would only ask the
Magistro to paint a woman he loves? Now she has seen the awful
proof that his affections have flowed away from her like water
draining to lower ground. What is she to do?

You have your children, people will whisper to her. She hears
their voices in her head already, anticipating the words that will
come if she dare complain to anyone of her plight. As if that is all
she, or any woman, should want. Beatrice is only one and twenty.
Must she spend the rest of her life cooing over her children and
attending to their needs while her brief romance with her husband fades more and more from memory? It is unthinkable.

*I should have thrown him to Louis of Orleans at Novara and then
cut my own deal with the French.* Why did she help him? What has
been her thanks? *I should have sided with Isabel of Aragon and*

Naples. It would have been a wiser move. Then, perhaps, the young duke would still be alive, and Beatrice and Isabel would be running the kingdom while Gian Galeazzo busied himself with wine and the behinds of young men, and the present Duke of Milan would be dead or in a Neapolitan prison. Could Aragon—gloomy, unhappy Aragon—have been a worse or more deceitful partner than Ludovico?

"Oh unhappy daughter, forgive me for reviewing the faults of your father at your grave." Is she causing the spirit of that girl unintended grief? Yet she is bitter, and Bianca Giovanna, who had witnessed Beatrice's triumphs with Ludovico, would surely understand her sorrow at this latest and most devastating failure.

Beatrice's ladies—mercifully not Crivelli, whom Beatrice could at this moment tear apart like a lion ripping into a rabbit—appear at the rear of the church with cries of how this incessant sorrow and grieving is good neither for the duchess nor for her child. How Bianca Giovanna had been a happy girl and would not wish for her death to cause permanent grief to those she loved. How the chill in the church is sure to settle in Beatrice's very bones and make her give birth to a sickly boy. She feels arms pick her up off the stone floor, dragging her away.

"You're the lucky one," she says to the crypt, surprised at the snake's hiss that emanates from her throat. Has she ever sounded so venomous in all her life? "You died before your husband got tired of you and threw you away."

FROM THE NOTEBOOK OF LEONARDO:
The swan is white without any spot, and sings sweetly as it dies; with this song its life ends.

She has humiliated herself before members of her court. They will take her parting words to the corpse of Bianca Giovanna and spread them throughout the kingdom. Her stature as the wronged wife is now confirmed by her own testimony. Before a fortnight, everyone in Italy will know.

There is little she can do to counter the damage. She might speak to Ludovico, to impress upon him the harm that he is doing not only to her but to the strength and sanctity of their family, and to the whole of the kingdom by extension. But she is in no mood to ask for his attention or his affection or even his loyalty. If he does not realize what he is doing—that removing his love is the death of something beautiful—she does not feel like reminding him.

She feels like forgetting, and that is why she has summoned the singers and the musicians to her ballroom this evening. She has only one month until she enters her confinement, and what with the winter weather, she cannot spend it as she would like, outdoors on her horse, hunting until the sun sets. So she has decided that gaiety will be the order of the evening.

She does not ask her husband to attend the festivities. She hopes that he hears that Beatrice d'Este, despite his betrayal and public humiliation, is hosting a party. Without him. And dancing and singing with beautiful young men late into the evening. Men who find the duchess alluring despite the fact that he does not, despite that she has grown large with child and is no longer the nubile naïf who came to court six years ago.

Perhaps she will emulate the behavior of other women whose husbands take their attentions elsewhere. She looks around the room right now to see who might be a potential lover and is astonished at her choices. Have they all just recently appeared at court, or has she, in her consuming love for Ludovico, been blind to their charms? It seems that with each twist of her head to the tune of the music, she encounters another pair of tempting and hungry eyes falling upon her. She cannot rise from a curtsey without

meeting some man's appreciative gaze and blushing when she
guesses his thoughts. They are all spry, lean, and young compared
to her husband. She cannot know at this moment what is more
beautiful to her, the thick brown curls of her guests from Calabria
and other cities in the south, or the icy Nordic features of their
friends from over the Alps. Some of the knights, guests from Emperor Max's German court, have let their wolf-blue eyes settle for
an uncomfortably long time upon the figure of the duchess as she
dances, and she notices that she enjoys what once might have
sent her into discomfort.

Were these looks of appreciation from other men always
present? How is it that she has not noticed them until now? Do
they admire how she twirls so gracefully when a pregnant belly
might have thrown a less agile woman off balance? Have they seen
her riding the ever-faithful Drago through the meadows outside
the Castello, astonished that so small a woman has such dominion over so large a beast? Have they heard that she can pierce the
heart of a wild boar with a single arrow, dropping him dead at her
feet? Or are they thinking how the attentions of the Duchess of
Milan might advance their own political and military ambitions?
How is she to know? At this moment, she does not even care. She
is enjoying the notion that her heart need not cease to beat because Ludovico has taken his love away.

This last thought opens a new landscape in her heart. Life,
love, lust does not begin and end with her husband. There are
many fields upon which she might sow the seeds of her affections. And with this new thought, she realizes that she is tired of
this stiff bowing and polite turning upon one's toes; these tame
dances that begin and end with reverence paid to one's partner. It
is time for a new kind of dance, something to match the fresh
daring rising up inside her. At once, a strange force rushes
through her veins and seems to empty itself out in the core of her
being. It feels to her as if some wild creature—and she does not
mean her fetus, but another type of spirit—is expanding inside of

her, demanding her to give some outlet to its pulsing energy. Beatrice feels that if she does not let the creature release itself upon the dance floor, it will consume its host. If she moves fast enough, if she whirls and twirls enough to exhaust the demon, then she, Beatrice, will have peace. Though the room is beginning to spin about her, she knows that it is not rest she needs, but to dance this feeling away.

"Who will join me in the *galliard*?" she asks. She learned the dance from the French King Charles, who relished hopping about on his short legs, showing off his knowledge of the intricate steps.

Galeazz sits quietly in a big leather chair, isolated from the other guests. Why has she not thought of him before? Who else should she turn to for comfort at this time but the beautiful man who pledged his life to her six years ago? Have they both not experienced the most excruciating loss? Why should they not find solace in each other's arms? But Galeazz's deep-set brown eyes look upon the duchess not with the sparkle of adventure or the hope of comfort but with profound sadness; he shakes his head ever so slightly, hoping she knows, that she will not demand that he join her in dance, for then, how could he refuse? He does not wish to release his sorrow, not yet. His heart grieves. She can read that upon his face. If he had sprung to his feet and taken up her challenge, she would have been disappointed. No, that would not be her Galeazz at all, but a man who acts in utter self-interest. A man like her husband. And she never wants Galeazz to tarnish himself by acting like Ludovico.

But others, who are visitors at court and cannot know the extent of the duchess's pain over the loss of Bianca Giovanna, followed by the loss of her husband at such a fragile time, quickly leap to answer Beatrice's request.

"A *galliard*!" she calls out to the musicians. The flute players, instruments poised at the lips to answer Beatrice's request, hesitate. They look at the duchess to make certain that they have heard correctly; that a woman grown large with child is demand-

ing that they play a frenetic French jig, and that she fully intends
to lead the dance.

"Play, I say!" she yells at them. She has never, she knows,
sounded more demanding and officious.

The pipe players begin the lively tune, and Beatrice counts to
four before leading the dancers in the opening steps. She remembers each move of this dance that she practiced for hours
with the toad-like Charles, who was so very pleased with the way
that she picked up his footwork. "It is a dance better for a man
than a woman," Charles had said. "That was only true until now,"
Beatrice had answered him.

Right heel up, left heel up. Skip back, two three. Jump right.
Jump left. Right heel up, now left. Early into the dance, she begins
to feel winded, but she can hardly stop now, not when she insisted
upon having this recreation. She will not spoil her own party. She
is surrounded by young men, men of her own age, who are paying
the most vigilant attention to her every move. Right heel up. Now
left. Twist and jump and again. She is exhilarated. She has had no
idea that she could leap so high into the air at this weight. But why
not? Hasn't she always remained active until the last days of her
pregnancies? The midwives have practically had to drag her from
the hunting grounds so that she could lay up in anticipation of the
births. Perhaps this time she would not be confined at all. She
would dance until she went into labor. Dance and host festivities
and choose who would be her lovers after the baby was born and
she was healed. She would deny Ludovico entrance to her bedroom, just as he has shut his door against her. And if he burst in
upon her privacy, he would find her in the embraces of a beautiful man less than half his age.

Maybe it would be the man now jumping in the air alongside
her, with his bright green eyes and straight, light hair the color of
sand. He is lithe and limber, and his every move seems to challenge her to match his great leaps. He smiles at her, showing his
white teeth, and when he turns, his pink tongue licks the corner

of his mouth in an unconscious way. He reminds her of an animal. He is taller than she, and so she must try harder to keep their eyes on the same level when they jump. When the count is correct, when the pipes are at their loudest, Beatrice bends her knees deep and then springs into the air. She looks up at the eyes of her dancing partner, and she can see that he admires the way she is keeping up with him. High in the air, she feels something sharp in her belly, trying to pull her back to the ground. She does not want to descend, not yet. She wishes she could remain like this, feet off the ground, staring into the bright eyes that are looking back at her. But the pain she feels is more real than this fantastic moment, and she gives in to it. She feels her feet hit the ground, but her knees cannot support her. The young man's smile drops as he watches the duchess crash to the floor. She hits her head, but the thud of that impact is completely obscured by the fact that she thinks that someone is stabbing her in the gut with a great lance. She looks up to see Galeazz's face suddenly above hers, pushing the pale young German out of the way, his strong arms stretched out to wrap around her shoulders.

"Why is someone killing me?" she whispers to him as he lifts her from the ground. And then the world goes black.

When she comes to, the lance is still poking her stomach, splitting her in two. She has known childbirth two times but has never felt this kind of unendurable pain. The lance seems to be inside her, rocking back and forth, tearing her guts apart. She is certainly being killed, but why is she dying so slowly?

The world is red. Others are crowded around her, hands, chests, arms, clothes, covered in blood. What is happening? She hears Ludovico's voice crying out, demanding to know what is going on, and then she hears his cries fading down the hall as someone drags him away. Someone is pushing on her stomach, making the pain greater. A woman, perhaps. Beatrice cannot see through the veil of red that clouds her vision. Everything is draped in it, this bold color. She closes her eyes fiercely to try to remove the tint from the world in front of her but when she opens them again, all is still red. She feels as if the woman on top of her is pulling her insides out, pulling her very intestines out of her stomach, like some horrible form of punishment. A disemboweling for a crime that she has not committed.

The woman stops pulling. She has reached the end of Beatrice's entrails, which now lay in her hands. Beatrice tries hard to focus on this bloody flesh, squinting madly to see what her insides look like. Everyone in the room is screaming now. Someone wipes Beatrice's face with a cold cloth.

"Cover her eyes!" the woman holding Beatrice's insides yells out.

The hands quickly press the cloth over Beatrice's eyes, drowning out all sight. But not before she realizes what is being hurried away from her—a marble-white baby, its tiny arms limp, its head fallen backward, dripping in blood.

FROM THE NOTEBOOK OF LEONARDO:
From what seems a small, light thing, there proceeds a great ruin.

To: Your Excellency, the Marchesa of Mantua
From: Cecilia Gallerani, Contessa Bergamini

Your Excellency,

As the sudden circumstance of your most illustrious sister's death prevented you from attending the funeral, I wanted to write to you to let you know that no posthumous honor was withheld that great lady. Though your own grief must be unbearable, I hope that this account of the adoration showered upon the duchess after her death brings some measure of consolation to your wounded heart. I shall try, to the best of my ability and memory, to chronicle the events following the shocking and untimely manner of her demise, and that of her stillborn son.

The duke was and remains inconsolable. He has shut himself in his room, draped the windows in black, and refused anyone, including the little motherless boys, admittance for many days upon end. They say he has shaved his head and wears only black. Those who have been permitted to see him in recent days say that his conversation consists only of the fact that he would much rather have gone to his grave than seen the light of his life predecease him. Your Excellency is aware, I am sure, that the duchess spent many of her last days in tears over the death of Bianca Giovanna, to whom she was deeply attached, and over the indiscreet liaison in which the duke was engaged with Lucrezia Crivelli. Now the duke is struck with remorse and seems to have cut off his relations with that lady. She is, however, pregnant with his child, due in the late spring. Perhaps the duchess found out about the pregnancy. The news could not have helped her own health, weakened by pregnancy and by Bianca's sudden death. I pray that Ludovico finds solace from his guilt. He takes whatever meals he eats standing, fasts two days a week, and spends long hours at the duchess's crypt, begging God to let him speak to her just once more so that he can assure her of his love. He is lost in a cloud of sorrows, his only spoken words, lamentations.

But I get ahead of myself. I mean to tell you of the great honors bestowed upon the young duchess. At the duchess's passing, the women of the court immediately went to work adorning her body. She was lovingly bathed, I am told, not only in the warm waters of the bath, but by the endless streams of her maids' tears. All of Milan might drown in its tears, such was the love of the populace for the duchess. Did you know that our people would rush into the streets to see her drive by in her chariot, delighted to see her smile, her beautiful manner of dressing, and the cheerful way that she conducted herself always, not to mention the extraordinary way that she could make her horses prance? They are saying all over Milan that her death represents the end of happiness itself.

On the day of her funeral, the duchess's hair was combed exactly the way she liked it worn, parted down the middle of the head and pulled back over her high cheekbones and into a long plait. Ribbons of gold and pearl were woven into her long, dark braid. It has never looked so perfectly pretty. She was dressed in the most extravagant of her golden brocade robes, which made her skin seem to glow, though she no longer breathed. Around her neck was placed a long necklace of pearls strung with gold balls, on the end of which is a cross of the heaviest gold from the land of the Turks, inlaid with many jewels. I believe the duchess would have considered it a suitable gift for her to offer Our Lord. Over her body lay a white cloth embroidered with the arms of the House of Sforza. Pink color was pressed into her lips and cheeks so that she had a lovely, lifelike quality, and believe it or not, Your Excellency, despite that her last hours were spent in pain, her lips formed the slightest, most serene smile. I was very grateful to be able to see her this way once more, so that I could not only impress her loveliness into my memory but also share it with you.

Your Excellency, not only the privy council and all the nobles of the city, along with the foreign ambassadors who here represent every nation of Europe, but the entire population of Milan followed the duchess's corpse from the Castello to her resting place at the church of Santa Maria delle Grazie. You have never seen such a solemn and magnificent procession. At sunset, the ambassadors, including those from the Spanish king and the Emperor Max, the duchess's great admirer, lifted the bier and carried it to the gate of the Castello, where all the world waited to catch a final glimpse of their beloved Duchess Beatrice. The duke and all of his relatives, including the two little boys, were gowned entirely in long black robes, wearing black hoods over their heads. The boys, so young and brave, rode in a small chariot. The family was escorted by the priests and nuns of the city, who led the procession carrying great crosses of silver, gold, and ebony. I believe a thousand torches lit the way for the duchess. Her favorite knight, the esteemed Galeazz di Sanseverino, wore shining black armor, a black mask, and a black garter around his arm. His long hair was dyed as dark as a crow's feathers, and he rode the duchess's favorite horse, Drago, the big white stallion that was a gift from your husband. The animal, wearing a saddle laden with silver-and-pearl crosses and sporting a black feathered headpiece, looked bewildered without his mistress. I could swear that his desperate brown eyes were searching the crowd for the duchess. Galeazz carried the duchess's standards while tears streamed down his face to be escorting his second-favorite lady in all the world to his young wife to another early grave. How sorrowful, yet how comforting, to think of those two friends reunited forever, lying side by side.

At every major intersection of the city, the local magistrates would take the duchess's bier from its last bearers and carry it through their quarter. Your Excellency, I can report that her body was handled from the Castello to the crypt only by loving hands. Whenever the magistrates changed guard of her casket, six new pairs of eager and tender hands covered in fine leather against the cold reached out to cradle this young woman whom they so adored. Citizens of every rank and class turned out to pay their respects. Countless numbers of gentlemen and ladies, laborers, merchants and their wives and children all braved the cold January evening to honor her. It seemed to me that the very winds calmed in every quarter out of respect for the duchess, whipping up again as soon as she was passed into another section of the city. Every shop was closed as if it were Christmas day. Even the beggars and prostitutes abandoned their trades during the procession. Many a haggard man in tattered clothing and a woman with too much rouge upon the face was seen in uncharacteristic lament, with no thought to capitalize economically upon the event, as the duchess's body passed through their neighbor-hoods. I have never seen the lowest echelons of society put aside thoughts of the coin and pay such respect.

Finally, long after the sun had set on this short winter's day, the magistrates reached the gates of the Santa Maria delle Grazie, where six ambassadors from other Italian cities received the duchess's bier and carried it into the church, laying her upon the steps of the altar. The church was draped in reams of black silk, which was very dramatic against its stark white marble. A thousand wax tapers lit the church in her honor. The cardinal himself received her and said the whole of the Mass. The duchess's favorite singers, including Cristoforo Romano the sculptor, sang the Requiem in voices that were inspired by the Heavens. Never have you heard such singing, exquisite in its sadness. I tell you, her soul was sent to God by the very voices of angels. After the prayers were made for the Lord to take her soul—though who can doubt Beatrice's position at the side of the Lord?—and the last, though not final, tears were shed, the body was put into a magnificent sarcophagus, supported by great marble lions. And there, under Donato Bramante's newly finished cupola—one that Beatrice herself so admired—she will rest until the marble tomb Ludovico has commissioned from the hunchback artist, Solari, is ready to be laid over her.

Your Excellency, I must not forget to mention that as the funeral party entered the church, I saw none other than the Magistro standing at the gates of Santa Maria delle Grazie. They say he is putting the final touches on his mural of Our Lord's Last Supper. It has taken him these two years to find the proper model for Judas, but word has it that he found and spied on a poor unsuspecting Jew in the section of the city where they live and followed the man until he felt his features indelibly impressed upon his imagination. Then he made a series of sketches from memory and is now painting that hapless man's face upon the wall, forever to be immortalized as history's greatest traitor. You have never seen a sadder expression than the one on the

Magistro's face as he watched the duchess's corpse enter the church. He stood just out of the light of a torch, but I could make out his features, which seemed to carry the weight of the event in progress. Is it not lovely to imagine Beatrice laid to rest so near the Magistro's mural, almost as if she can gaze upon the face of Jesus, an activity which gave her so much pleasure and comfort and consolation in her last days?

Ludovico did commission the Magistro to make a portrait of Lucrezia Crivelli. I tell you this not to be indiscreet but because I am certain that as gossip spreads faster than weeds, and as you trouble yourself to keep abreast of the current works of the great masters, you have already heard this news. I have not yet seen it, but I hear it is not nearly as nice as the one he made of me so many years ago. I like to think that the Magistro approved of me and of my liaison with the duke, since there was no wife at that time to suffer injury from our affections. Perhaps the Magistro, along with the rest of Milan, so disapproved of Ludovico's affair that he allowed his disaffection to creep into the portrait. This might be fanciful thinking, that an artist the caliber of Leonardo would let the human failings of others infiltrate his work, but it is a woman's thinking, nonetheless, and I cannot help but hope that it is at least partially true. I believe that all of us may anticipate a stunning portrait of dear Beatrice on the wall opposite the Last Supper, a final tribute from a devoted court artist to his patron.

Though it has been some weeks since the duchess's death, the duke's demonstrations of grief continue. Hundreds of Masses for her soul are said daily throughout Milan and the rest of Italy. He has set aside his differences with the prior at the Santa Maria delle Grazie and now patronizes that church above all others. I hear that the path between the Treasure Tower and the church sees a daily parade of gold.

All the games and horse races in the foreseeable future are canceled. When I think upon how much Beatrice adored these events, I am not certain that it is right and proper to cease the celebrations, though I know it is out of honor for her memory. I suppose it would be far too painful to see the seat next to the duke empty of the exuberant spirit and the enthusiasm which she lent to every festivity.

Your Excellency, please accept all my condolences and my deepest hope that this missive will alleviate a small portion of your sorrow. I remain, one who will always be grateful for your friendship,

Cecilia Gallerani, Contessa Bergamini

Chapter Nine

XVI * LA TORRE CADENTE
(THE FALLING TOWER)

*Let those who are in high places take warning, and let
them remember that when Fortune sets you on top of her
wheel, she may at any time bring you to the ground. And
then the closer you have been to Heaven, the greater and
the more sudden will be your fall.*

—*A VENETIAN CHRONICLER*

IN THE YEAR 1499; IN THE CITY OF MANTUA

OD is punishing her. That is all there is to it. One would
think that God would tire of heaping death and misfortune upon Isabella, but that does not seem to be the case. She has
been sure that she brought on all the deaths by praying so hard to
God to allow her second child to be a boy. She was disappointed
when the child had turned out to be female, but two months later,
when the infant died, Isabella realized that the death was her spe-

cial brand of punishment, carefully designed by the Lord to take His vengeance upon her arrogance for desiring something different than what He had planned for her. The sudden deaths of Bianca Giovanna and Beatrice followed, further proof of God's retribution. Wrapped in black for so long, gliding like a crow through the palace, with each death extending her period of mourning, Isabella wondered if she would ever wear color again. Beatrice's death had been so shocking that Isabella had needed the reams of black cloth to remind her that her sister was not merely a letter away. Bad fortune comes in groups of three, however, and Isabella was also confident that God had doled out enough misery. But God does not seem to be at all finished with Isabella d'Este; the horrible and sad death of Beatrice was not the end of sorrow but the beginning of the end of everything. For what seems to be racing toward its death now is her marriage.

What has she not done for Francesco? She elevated the House of Gonzaga by entering into it by matrimony. She has attended to him lovingly through his many strange illnesses and fevers. She has governed all of Mantua, down to the smallest detail, to the praise of its councillors, because Francesco has no patience for the minutiae of administration, preferring to spend his time at the stables or on military affairs. She has brought the finest artists of the day to adorn their buildings and churches. She has charmed heads of state who consider her husband too egotistical and not refined enough to dine with them. She defended his honor, even while his closest confidants informed her that he had a growing reputation as a disloyal scoundrel who spewed all his secrets when in his cups. Francesco's exploits as the commander of the army that threw the French out of Italy grew exponentially every time he recounted the tale, annoying anyone who had to listen, but severely angering the Venetians. Why, oh why do men always believe the legends that spring up around their victories? Especially when these legends are concocted by other men merely to preserve or consolidate their own power? Both Ludovico and the Venetians had encouraged the poets of Italy to write great ballads of Francesco's victory over the French. But that was to demonstrate to the people that their benefactors had saved them. Privately, both ruling parties were disappointed in their captain general's performance—Ludovico, because Francesco had failed to annihilate the French entirely, and the Venetians, because after the war Francesco had shown too much mercy upon the French. Francesco, however, ignored the motives behind the poems and ballads sung in his honor and took the words unto his very bosom, mouthing them all over Italy whenever he had too much to drink.

Moreover, since Beatrice's death, Isabella has played peacemaker between Ludovico and Francesco, whose contempt for each other has become more public every day. She had just taken off the mourning clothes a few months earlier, ready for life again, when she received a letter from Ludovico, accusing Francesco of making secret overtures to the French King Charles. "I have incontrovertible evidence in my very hands," Ludovico wrote. "And if not for my love and respect for you, I would turn the traitor over to the Venetians immediately."

Though Ludovico did not betray Francesco, the Venetians found out anyway and fired him as captain general of the army.

Isabella was devastated that her husband was engaged in political intriguing behind her back, and further dismayed that he was directly betraying both Ludovico and the Venetians, his benefactors. "How on earth do you expect us to live?" she had screamed at Francesco. "We will be crushed between these two great powers. You are going to be the death of the Houses of Gonzaga and Este and of Mantua itself!" She tried to mend things with her brother-in-law by sending soothing letters and a steady flow of gifts—fresh fish that he purported to adore from their Mantuan lakes, carp bred in their ponds, artichokes, and flowers. The fish, packed in ice brought down from the mountains, was difficult to ship, but Isabella spared no expense in cultivating Ludovico's continued patronage.

But Ludovico surprised both the marquis and the marchesa by seeing a way to turn Francesco's misfortune with the Venetians to his own benefit.

The French King Charles had died very suddenly after hitting his head on a doorway. Who had taken the throne but Louis of Orleans, Ludovico's sworn enemy. Louis's first announcement as king was that he was going to reconquer Italy for his two sons, making one of them the King of Naples and the other, Duke of Milan. Ludovico took the threat seriously and realigned with Emperor Max. But who would lead the new Milanese-German army? Ludovico had insulted Francesco after the last war, chastising him for allowing Charles to escape. And Francesco had threatened Ludovico in return by having secret dialogues with the French. Now, with the Venetians against Francesco, Ludovico saw his opportunity. He wrote to Isabella, informing her that he wished for Francesco to once again lead the Milanese-German army, and he was coming to Mantua to discuss the details. Oh, and he would be accompanied by *an entourage of one thousand*. Would that be too terribly much trouble for her?

Isabella sent to Ferrara for sumptuous plate of gold upon which to serve Ludovico and his courtiers. She spent far too much money buying a grand supply of his favorite wines—"light white for breakfast; a clear but strong red with his main meal; neither too sweet, if you please, but from the town of Cesolo, if it's not too much trouble, for those are his favorites," his steward had written. Once he arrived, she gave the duke use of her private apartment and moved into lesser quarters. She ordered jousting tournaments, dramatic plays, and tours of the kingdom to entertain him. She demanded that Francesco not only give the duke a tour of the collection of antique armor in the castle but also allow him to select one of their best horses from the Gonzaga stables.

"I hope that our quaint, backward little kingdom pleases you," Isabella said modestly, knowing full well that while Mantua was not the bustling and modern city of Milan, its charms were many.

"Yes, it's lovely, and it distracts from my misery," he said. He had arrived still affecting the outward signs of the bereaved widower, but these emotions, Isabella observed, he wore like clothes. Beneath the ubiquitous black robe and mantle lay the real man, who, to Isabella's impression, had long ago put aside his mourning. Though publicly Ludovico was in the process of making all of Milan a shrine to Beatrice, emblazoning her image and her heralds everywhere in the city, Isabella had heard that once his son by Lucrezia Crivelli was born, he went back to that lady's company, settling on her the estates that he had once settled upon Beatrice. Isabella was outraged by this news until she heard the voice of her mother whisper in her ear that one must always be generous to one's husband's bastards. The estates were undoubtedly for the boy, and there were certainly lands enough so that Beatrice's two sons would not be cheated in their inheritance. Beatrice—generous, forgiving Beatrice—would have wanted the illegitimate child cared for. Isabella had hoped to hear more from Ludovico about her sister's death, but he told her that dialogue about his beloved Beatrice would only sink him back into the dreadful melancholy from which he had so recently emerged. "Every day I visit her in the Santa Maria delle Grazie," he said. "If you would see the exquisite marble tomb Cristoforo Solari has made for her, and the sweetness of her face as she lay at rest, you would weep and weep."

That was all he would say upon the matter of his wife's demise.

Isabella knew that she had to put aside her emotions over Ludovico's betrayal of her sister and concentrate upon healing the rift between her husband and his potential benefactor. Mantua's safety—and an immense salary of forty thousand ducats per year for Francesco's services—was at stake. Knowing how much they needed money at this time, Francesco was playing a game of volley with Ludovico on the matter of his title. His *title*. Francesco was upset that Ludovico was unwilling to unseat Galeazz of his formal title of captain general of the Milanese army. "What are those two words compared with the money we require to run this kingdom?" she asked her husband.

Ludovico was outraged over Francesco's request. Isabella could think of nothing more she could do to soothe the duke's ruffled feathers, so she decided to employ another strategy. She had one final surprise awaiting her brother-in-law in her studiolo.

"I hesitate to allow you into the rooms where I keep my treasures," she said to him. "You're such the fierce collector that you'll try to bargain them away from me."

"I may," he replied. "But I am not going to leave Mantua without viewing the frescoes of Andrea Mantegna and the painting of the scene on Mount Parnassus. I have heard that one of the Muses is particularly lovely."

"I shouldn't let you see anything by Mantegna," she said. "You have too often tried to steal him from my service."

"Yes. But that was in the event that you should ever have succeeded in stealing the Magistro from mine."

"And how is that gentleman, if one might ever call a painter a gentleman?"

"I have him terribly busy, Isabella. He is finishing his exquisite work in the Saletta Negra in the Castello, which I intend to make my permanent quarters, painting twenty-four scenes from Roman history on the walls. The cost of the paint alone, my dear, is astronomical. The entire apartment will be a tribute to your dear sister, for whom I would happily give my own life if she might live again."

But that does not mean that Lucrezia Crivelli won't be spending most of her nights in those very rooms, Isabella wanted to say, hoping that Beatrice's ghost would haunt the very quarters, scaring the lovers from their lovemaking and their slumber.

"And you will be happy to know that we are once again planning to cast the Magistro's horse in bronze. I remember how upset you were when you saw his bronze floating down the river. I've never forgotten your forlorn face. I made up my mind on that day to make it up to you. When the statue is finished and revealed in the piazza, I shall give a grand ceremony for which you will serve as the lady of honor."

There it was again, the charm that had so swayed Isabella when she had first met her brother-in-law. She thought, for one brief moment, that she could fall under his spell once more, even knowing now the extent of his cunning. For just that moment, she was again the young girl wishing that she, and not her sister, were the wife of this great and powerful prince, this lover of art and of all things beautiful. But even Ludovico's considerable charms could not distill the fact that the sister whom Isabella had considered so lucky was now in a cold tomb, her last days spent in sorrow over her husband's blatant infidelity.

"But that is only if you do not betray me by trying to take the Magistro away from me while he is at his duties," Ludovico added.

"I do not have to do that, Your Excellency. I've already managed, by my own wits, to procure a little piece of him for my studiolo."

Knowing that what she was going to show him would shock him, she stood taller and walked with a greater confidence into her private office. Sitting on a gilded easel, resting under a window where the sun might creep in and light its already luminous quality, was Leonardo's portrait of Cecilia Gallerani.

She heard Ludovico's gasp. "Cecilia?"

"Yes. I wrote to her, asking if I might borrow it. I wanted to compare Leonardo's techniques to those of Giovanni Bellini the Venetian, whom I had recently as a visitor to court. She graciously complied."

"And how did the two artists compare?" Ludovico asked, his words coming to him slowly, still trying to recover from the surprise of seeing his early mistress's portrait in his sister-in-law's home.

"Well, both are painters of natural light. Both use the light of the sky reflected behind their human figures to bring a particular luminosity to their subjects. It is such a unique method, and yet I do not know that the two gentlemen know each other. While both men delicately coat layer upon thin layer of paint to achieve their effect, I do believe that in the end, Bellini's figures are gentler, whereas the Magistro is more adept at bringing out the soul of his subject. He certainly achieved that with Cecilia, don't you think?"

Ludovico did not answer her, but stared at Cecilia's portrait as if he had never seen it before. He did not meet Isabella's eyes, though she did not take hers off of him.

"I would like to compare this portrait to the one of Madonna Lucrezia, but I am not as well acquainted with that lady. Perhaps you might facilitate that for me sometime?"

Isabella was pleased to see his shame. Still, he could not look at her. "Perhaps," he said quietly.

She did not move, watching him stare at the portrait of Cecilia as if it were the first time he was seeing it. She spoke to him silently: *This is why you will conclude negotiations with my husband. Because I know all that you did to my sister; I know the schemes that you concocted when I was but a naïve girl come to your extravagant court. I know how your schemes involve me still. And because I know the workings of your busy mind, I also know your shame. I know your inward emotions are far different from your outward actions. I know that you aggrandize my sister's memory to Milan's populace, while you disgrace it all the while with your mistress. I know these things because, like the Magistro, I can see into the soul, and I have seen that yours is black. And yet I do love you, which you also know.*

"As you can see, we are bound together, so let us do each other's bidding in a spirit of peace," she said.

Quietly she took his arm and led him out of her studiolo, convinced that she had concluded her business with him on this visit. Shame would not go terribly far with a man like her brother-in-law, but it could accomplish much in the short term.

By the time Ludovico Sforza left Mantua, Francesco Gonzaga had a three-year contract to head the Milanese-German army.

Isabella had spent a fortune entertaining the duke, in terms of both her emotions and her finances, but it had been worth it. She had secured employment for her politically fickle husband, guaranteeing to Ludovico that Francesco's days of secretly courting either the French or the Venetians were over. Thus she secured not only Francesco's salary but Mantua's security. One would think that Francesco would recognize the part his wife had played in his salvation and reward her with beneficent acts of generosity and gratitude.

But that was not to be. Instead, weeks later, he sent secret word to the doge begging for the return of his old job as captain general of the Venetian army—a direct betrayal of Ludovico and of Isabella, who had thrown her own guarantee of loyalty behind her husband's signature. The doge was not inclined to reinstate Francesco, as his reputation for duplicity had spread. Then Isabella found out that Francesco offered to have her and their daughter sent to Venice as political hostages to vouch for his loyalty. She immediately sent word to Ludovico informing him of Francesco's traitorous actions. Ludovico, after an initial volcanic reaction, calmed down. Isabella, too, put aside her hurt feelings, realizing that anything she did to ruin her own husband would bring her a hollow victory. For what was the wife of a ruined man but ruined too? Once again, she appealed to Ludovico to forgive Francesco. Allowing that he required Francesco's generalship and valued Isabella's alliance (not to mention the memory of her sister, for whom "I would happily give my own life if she might live again"), Ludovico sweetened the offer a little more and, once again, concluded negotiations with the Gonzagas. Francesco would usurp Galeazz's title. Galeazz, a man secure in the renown for his ability and his valor, would have to be satisfied to be called something else.

Isabella waited once more for the warmth and gratitude to flow from her husband, but she received very different news in place of those coveted things.

To: Leonardo the Florentine
From: Ludovico Sforza, Duke of Milan

Dear Magistro,

Enclosed you will find the deed to a house and vineyard just outside the Porta Vercellina, not far from the Santa Maria delle Grazie. I purchased it some years ago from the monks of Saint Victor, and it has always been quite lucrative for me. In addition to the production of a nice wine, the vineyard also generates a good income. The land upon which it rests is fertile and in a good location. Magistro, in my judgment and in the judgment of every expert in our land, you are the master painter of all masters, dead and living. You have been employed by me these eighteen years in manifold works, and in all of these you have shown admirable genius. The time has come for me to execute the promises made over the years. The land, the vineyard, the income from the aforementioned, and the house upon the land I have deeded to you. Though this gift is small, indeed, compared with your talents and your merits, please take it as a sign that, as in the past, you will find me eternally a loyal patron. In the future, when Fortune permits, I will more fully reward your excellent service and singular gifts.

Signed and dated April 26th, in the year 1499, by Ludovico Maria Sforza, your humble benefactor.

Here comes Isabella's husband now, in his spotless armor, his toes slightly out-turned and his gait swaying with self-satisfaction, a little man inflated with his own opinion of himself. She hates him, this man whom she once loved above all; this dandy with whom she has made two children and nine years of a life. Hates him because when he chose to humiliate and betray, he made certain that the right people were present to see it all. He had attended a festival of tournaments at Brescia in honor of Her

Highness the Queen of Cyprus, urging Isabella to remain at home because he was "worried over her health" after she had "fatigued herself entertaining that demanding son of a bitch, Ludovico." Isabella was not particularly exhausted after Ludovico's visit, but the Mantuan treasury certainly was, so rather than incur the expense of having the appropriate wardrobe made for herself and her ladies, she elected to remain at home. She found out, through malicious tongues that could not wait to share the news, that Francesco had had a lady at his side the entire time—a young woman, Teodora, costumed extravagantly as the Lady of the Joust, wearing his colors, and acting as if she were the Marchesa of Mantua. There to witness the infidelity was Galeazz. Noble, beautiful Galeazz, still in mourning for his wife and his lady Beatrice, had entered the contests with forty of his men. All still mourned, keeping their long curls dyed as black as hawks, wearing armor of black and gold, and carrying heralds in honor of Beatrice, black pendants with bright gold griffins. Isabella wondered if Francesco had dared to present his dreadful little whore to Beatrice's glorious knight. Her only consolation was that Galeazz once again took every prize in the tournaments and Francesco, none.

Isabella has had many thoughts about Francesco's infidelity. Her mother believed that all men eventually fell prey to other women and cautioned her daughters to refrain from making too much of a fuss over these affairs. Isabella is a realist, not a romantic dreamer like Beatrice who lived—and perhaps died—for Ludovico's attentions. She thinks that Francesco has always had little assignations. And of course, like all soldiers, she knows that when he is away on a military campaign, he entertains himself with boys. They are less expensive and less trouble than women, she has heard many a military man say. Moreover, they are present in abundance and, also, apparently willing to secure the favor of their superiors by affording access to their young, smooth asses. So it is with men. A woman mustn't grumble over these things. Isabella knows that this kind of sexual release is nothing

more to a man than, say, urinating. The suspected carnal and casual dalliances with females, too, she has not minded, really; she
has always regarded it as a payback for the massive attention she
receives from other men. After all, Francesco has had to contend
with a wife about whom men write poems and songs and sonnets;
who is sought as a model for masters' paintings; who receives the
finest minds of Europe at her court and dialogues with them late
into the evenings long after her husband has gone to bed. Not to
mention the close relations and constant correspondence with
Ludovico, which would be enough to send any husband into fits.
So if Francesco has needed to affirm his own manly charisma in
the arms of ladies and maids, why should she care? He always returns to her bed desirous of her.

But this time, he has allowed another woman to take the place
of his wife at a public event. She wonders if he did this purposely,
to pay her back for her political support of Ludovico, for coercing
her husband to enter into Ludovico's employ. But what should
she have done? Ludovico was their brother-in-law and the most
powerful prince in Italy, by far. He offered them a fortune for
Francesco's services. Isabella was acting in the interest of Francesco, of their family, and of Mantua by negotiating with Ludovico. Francesco had been difficult and had offered resistance
along the way, but he was also delighted with the prestige his title
and salary would bring. Had he resented it so much that he had to
avenge himself in this nasty and public manner?

Isabella sees that her husband is headed for her studiolo,
where he thinks she must be. He swaggers as if he expects to be
greeted by the doting wife he left at home, who will be elated that
her great warrior of a husband has come home to her. In this, and
in many other things, he is mistaken.

She slips quietly into the parlor, where she has placed the
clavichord she finally wrestled from Ludovico. Beatrice had
had it made by Lorenzo of Pavia, who everyone agreed was the
greatest master designer and builder of musical instruments

that Europe has ever produced. Isabella has always coveted the clavichord, writing letter upon letter to Lorenzo asking him to make a duplicate for herself. But the maestro was always too busy with other commissions from more illustrious patrons, such as the Doge of Venice. After Beatrice died, Isabella wrote to Ludovico asking for the piece to be sent to her so that she might have a memory of her sister when she sat down to play. Isabella had already learned to play all the other stringed instruments and was anxious to master this one, which made the most thrilling and somber sounds by pressing upon beautiful ivory and ebony keys. Lorenzo had painted a magnificent scene upon the lid of the instrument of Odysseus addressing King Alcinous and Queen Arete, asking for safe passage to Ithaca. How she would love to have a large fresco of the scene painted on one of the walls of her studiolo. Perhaps she would see if old Mantegna, growing grumpier by the day in his dotage, would accept the commission.

Isabella has not found any music written specifically for this instrument, so she has been composing her own, adapting her favorite sonnets and poems. She hears Francesco's footsteps approach. Striking the keys with vigor, she sings the lament she has been working on, pleased with the way that the melody complements the words of her favorite poet, and that of Beatrice, Petrarch. *And I am one of those whom weeping pleases; it seems I strive to make my eyes produce a family of tears to match the sorrows in my heart.*

She is very grateful that she has practiced her singing all of her life and that she can make her voice affect the appropriate measures of beauty, sorrow, and pain. Not to mention a seething but controlled anger beneath it all. She is nothing if not nuanced in her actions, and singing and playing are no exceptions.

With the hum of the strings still resonating in the air and her fingers still on the keys, she looks up at her husband and says, "Your Excellency." That is all. She has no intention of helping him through his awkward homecoming; no intention of doing what her mother and every other woman she has known has done, which is to affect a false cheeriness to compensate for their husbands' sins. To pretend that the blow of his humiliation is light, that it does not matter so much to her. That she is not hurt. No, let the little beast squirm.

"What is this, Isabella? You have purchased Beatrice's instrument? It must have cost a fortune." She remembers all those years ago when she realized that his protruding eyes would become more froglike as the years went on. Now her prediction has come true. He stands in the doorway with his eyes bulging, looking like cannonballs waiting to be fired her way. He gestures toward her studiolo. "And whom did I find in your studiolo, making a new, extravagant set of doors and carving a giant cameo of your image looking like some Roman empress?"

"Oh yes, after years of my courting him, Cristoforo Romano has finally come to my service. He found Milan very depressing after the duchess died. So many are saying that she died of a broken heart after Ludovico's public infidelity. Do you believe such a thing possible?"

He ignores the question and its implications altogether. "Cristoforo tells me he is going to make a marble bust of you, just like the one he made of Beatrice. Where are we getting the money to pay for these extravagances? Do you know what they are charging these days for a block of stone?"

"Ludovico is paying you a fortune. Surely the person who negotiated the commission for you is entitled to a small gift for herself?"

"I see what you are doing, Isabella. Even though your sister is dead, you are still trying to keep up with the Sforzas. How often do I have to remind you that we do not have Ludovico's money?"

"But we do have his money. A substantial portion of it is being transferred to our treasury right now."

"So you admit it? The money is not yet arrived and you're already spending it on your vanities. I've caught you borrowing again, haven't I?"

"I've told you before, I am much too full of spirit to allow eight or ten percent to come between myself and the things that I desire." This was the philosophy she has always lived by. If Francesco thought she would change her ways now, he was mistaken. Especially after what he has done.

"And what do you desire now? Your sister's things? Things made for you by your sister's artists? Aren't you tired of picking Beatrice's bones?"

She won't fall into his trap. She is the wronged party. He is the sinner. This confrontation must conclude with that fact understood. She parries, quickly delivering the riposte. "I feel secure that my sister would rather her clavichord be in my hands than in the hands of Ludovico's mistress. A woman's wishes should be honored, even in death."

"You persist in straining our finances." His bug eyes narrow into puffy little slits.

"I do. Because this is my comfort, my lord, for the way you have humiliated me before all of Italy. I advise you to stop complaining before I find reasons to comfort myself further. Be done now and be grateful that this is the extent of the damage."

"Why do you let nasty gossips infect your mind with wicked talk?"

"Because what they say is true. I have found myself asking some difficult questions. What good has it done me to be a devoted wife? What thanks have I received for maintaining good relations with Ludovico, after you tried your best to destroy the goodwill between our houses? What reward has my husband given me but to humiliate me in front of friends and allies?"

"Come, Isabella, I have done nothing wrong. You've always had your admirers."

"Admirers are not lovers. Admirers bring honor and al-

liances to the House of Gonzaga. I might attract and cultivate admirers, but you reap the benefits of their attentions too."

"But I am a man, or have you forgotten? What do you expect?"

"I expect that even a man might act with discretion and decency. From now on, I shall do as I please. If you protest, you may
divorce me, explain yourself to our families and allies, *including*
Ludovico, and let your whore run the kingdom. Would that suit
you, my lord?"

She expects him to be angry, repentant, and finally, seduc-
tive. That is how she would predict the sequence of emotions and
actions from her husband, knowing him as she has since she was
but a child. He should make a brilliant defense for himself, acting
falsely accused, followed by a brief moment of pretending to be
terribly hurt by her suggestion, ending with sitting on the bench
beside her, asking her to play something pretty, and then interrupting her song with lingering kisses to her neck. But he does
none of these things. Instead he smiles broadly, so broadly that
the one missing tooth on the right side of his mouth interrupting
his perfect ivory chain is revealed. "I am going to be very happy
when you can no longer throw your close relations with our
brother-in-law in my face."

"Do you anticipate a rift between Ludovico and myself?"

"I anticipate a rift between that scoundrel and the rest of
the world! If you love him so much, you may choose to go down
with him. Maybe you will even choose him over your own
husband."

What is this insane little man squawking about? She knows
that he has long harbored jealously over her relationship with
Ludovico, but she wonders if it has festered so long that it has
eaten his brain.

"Sir, I seem to be missing a crucial piece of information,
since we have just signed an alliance with the Duke of Milan. I am
under the assumption that, as captain general of his army, you
would be fighting on the same side."

"That may no longer be possible."

She waits for him to continue.

"Negotiators for the Doge of Venice and King Louis have been meeting in secret. I do not know who initiated the contact, but I suspect it was the doge, who has long despised Ludovico. Isabella, they've made a secret alliance to attack Ludovico and split the duchy of Milan between themselves. Here is how it will happen: Venice will attack from the east, the French will march from the north, and Ludovico will be crushed between them."

Isabella has never seen Francesco look so pleased. What is he thinking? "But my lord, you are Ludovico's captain general! You must get word to him at once. You must prepare the army."

"Surely you don't suggest that I fight against both France and Venice?"

"But that is what you have agreed to do!" she exclaims, wondering what piece of information she has yet to either hear or apprehend to have all of this make sense.

"Isabella, I am not a man to throw in my lot with a hopeless cause. I have offered my services to King Louis, and he has accepted them." He bows to his wife, as if he is reintroducing himself to her. As if to say, *Dear Lady, Francesco Gonzaga, Marquis of Mantua, captain general of the Italian army, the man you have known since your sixth birthday, the man who put his signature on a treaty next to those of the Duke of Milan and the Emperor of the Holy Roman Empire has miraculously disappeared and has been reborn as a new man, a French loyalist, a servant of King Louis.*

"Last year you made a vow to annihilate the French, and you succeeded, almost to the man! Now you say you are going to support them? And Venice? Did the doge not dismiss you from his service?"

"King Louis has seen my value and has demanded that the doge make peace with me. With us, Isabella, unless you choose to ally yourself with Ludovico."

"Are you mad?" She cannot imagine how her husband has

adjusted himself so quickly to his new loyalties. "Ludovico is our friend, our ally, our brother, and your employer. You have a contract."

"He is also a widower now. Perhaps you can arrange to divorce me and marry him. I believe that is what you always wanted. Not always, not when you were a naïve girl. Not until you saw the things the Duke of Milan was able to give a wife that the mere Marquis of Mantua could not. I am sure that once Ludovico was exposed to your charms, he, too, regretted the thirty days he dallied before sending an ambassador to Ferrara to ask for a bride. The two of you were so very wronged by la Fortuna, Isabella. Perhaps you can rectify it now."

Francesco has always had a smug air, but never more than now. Satisfied with his speech, he turns on his heels and leaves the room.

For once in her life, Isabella cannot fathom what to do. She has spent eight years cultivating the favor of Ludovico; first, because she had been seduced by his charms, but later, because she found that she loved him in spite of his defects. Beyond the initial attraction of lust, past the boundaries of family and political necessity, they have shared a passion for so many things. Moreover, she has given him more than her friendship and loyalty; she gave him her word. And now is she to join her husband and what appears to be the rest of Italy in contributing to his destruction?

She cannot remain in the same house as Francesco, so she goes to visit her father, who is putting on a series of Latin comedies in Ferrara. Duke Ercole is happy to see his daughter, and not surprised at the news that she brings about France and Venice aligning to rid the country of Ludovico. He's heard it all; in fact, he had sent his own ambassadors to the secret meetings at which it was arranged.

"But Father, how can we turn our backs on Ludovico? He's Beatrice's husband, and the father of her two boys, who will be his heirs."

Ercole's expression does not change. "Ludovico has made his own tomb, Isabella. He played all parties against each other for too many years. His ambitions and his hubris are naked for all the world to see. Louis has always laid claim to Milan. His grandmother was a Visconti, what can I say? He has as much right to the duchy as Ludovico."

"But Beatrice—" Isabella begins.

"Beatrice is in her grave. We must act in the interests of the living. The smart people—and we Estes are the smartest of the smart—will wait this out to see who is the victor. Don't let Francesco move on behalf of anyone, not Ludovico, not the French, not the Venetians. Here is what matters: after this is over, after Ludovico Sforza is a forgotten man long turned to dust, the House of Este will still be standing. And the House of Gonzaga too, God willing, if your husband follows my example."

"Father, I will heed your counsel, though it may cost me my heart to betray Ludovico or to sit by while he is attacked." What did she expect from her father, who, as soon as her mother's body was cold, supported the French in their invasion of her native kingdom of Naples?

"Isabella, why do you think I have lived to be an old man? If you want to see your dotage, you will learn from me: in these matters the heart must hide behind the mind's greater powers of reason."

Still, she cannot bear it. She foresees the scenario: Ludovico, with both enemies closing in on him, will write frantic letters and send hard-riding messengers to Mantua, demanding that Francesco move the army to help him. The missives will get more desperate until Ludovico realizes that he has been betrayed. He will assume that the marchesa is in on the betrayal. And he might go to his grave wondering why. Yet what good would it do her to betray her own husband? To reveal his duplicity to Ludovico? What would she do? Flee to Milan, only to be crushed herself? To end her life a fallen woman and disgraced daughter? A mad harridan who couldn't wait for her sister's death so that she could seize her husband?

She hears from one of her correspondents in Venice that the Venetian army has already set march for Milan. As they cross the Adda River, the soldiers are singing, "Now it's Il Moro's turn to dance!" Was anything more satisfying to a human being than the downfall of the mighty? She returns home to Mantua, where she gets word that General Trivulzio, the Italian traitor who left Ludovico's service years ago over his jealousy of Galeazz, is swooping down the Alps with a huge French army upon the castle of Annona, a Milanese stronghold. Galeazz has vowed to hold the northern city of Alessandria, which would cut the French off from Milan. But his soldiers are once again unpaid and half starved and deserting him. His brother, the Count of Caiazzo, a man of war who could more easily than Galeazz allow his heart to hide behind his greater powers of reason, has openly gone over to the French. Men other than Caiazzo who have also dined at Ludovico's table turn on him, riding to meet up with the French army. The predicted letters fly from Milan into Mantua, begging Francesco to move to defend Milan. Isabella herself makes a plea on behalf of her two nephews, who could lose their lives in the fray, until she finds out that Ludovico has sent them off to the German court, along with a substantial sum of his gold and jewels, and is probably going to flee there himself. Ludovico makes a last appeal to his allies, but none responds.

One by one, the people of the small cities of the duchy of Milan, tired of paying Ludovico's heavy taxes and encouraged by their patrons, who are tired of not being able to collect on the loans they made to the duke, open their gates to the French. Louis, Isabella is told, is astonished at the reception he receives as he trots across northern Italy. He attributes it to his good looks, his superior lineage as a Visconti, and to Ludovico's slow drain on his people's resources for his grand projects. Ludovico sends even more letters via messengers whose horses have been ridden so hard that they die in Isabella's courtyard. Francesco gets weary of the letters and rides to Vigevano—where Beatrice and Ludovico had lavishly entertained him—and openly starts to fight at the side of Louis. He is met there by Duke Ercole, who had waited patiently in Ferrara, throwing Ludovico's desperate letters into the hearth until French victory was guaranteed.

Now there is only the small matter of the duke himself, who must surely be trying to flee Milan. She cannot imagine Ludovico putting up a hopeless fight, sword in hand, manning the Castello against the French all by himself. The last time she saw him, he had complained of being afflicted with the gout, which made it nearly impossible for him to mount his horse.

What, she wonders, will happen to her friends in Milan? Cecilia's portrait still hangs in Isabella's studiolo, seemingly asking her that very question. Will the French be kind to those who had been loyal to the duke, or will they do what conquerors always do—seize property, rape women, destroy the symbols of power, execute the loyalists, torture the artists, and pick the treasury dry?

There is nothing that Isabella can do for Ludovico without endangering her family and the city of Mantua. But she can help his friends. She does not consult Francesco, but sends messengers to Milan to spread the word that Isabella d'Este is offering sanctuary to those who were loyal to the Duke and the late Duchess of Milan. In the letters, she urges them to flee the city before the French arrive, wearing the plumage of the conquerors. Flying on hooves that barely touch the dirt, the Mantuan riders are sent off with their missives. Isabella makes certain that the messengers know to stop at the Corte Vecchio, the residence of not only poor, disgraced Isabel of Aragon but of Leonardo the Florentine, to let both parties know that they and their households are welcome and will be treated kindly in Mantua, despite the fact—or perhaps because—the marquis seems to now be so very close to the king of France. She prays that they reach Milan in time for Ludovico to hear that she has tried to help his friends. She knows that he must think that she, too, has deserted him. She has written to his brother Ascanio in Rome declaring that she would like to come to Milan and fight the French herself. Ascanio wrote back, sarcastically suggesting that in Milan, they would prefer to see her husband with his army. Ludovico can only have a low opinion of her now.

Francesco hears that she is offering shelter to the Milanese and he sends her a furious letter. *I am fighting at the side of Louis XII, King of France, and you are giving sanctuary to those he means to capture? Have you lost your mind, woman?* Isabella sends a brief letter in return: *Your Excellency, you deal with the King of France in your way, and I will deal with him in mine. Since you are so very close to him at this moment, you may tell him so yourself. If he does not fear a weak woman, he may come to Mantua and see me on the matter. I do not fear Louis, only the French language, but I can speak it if I must.*

Is this King Louis not just a man like any other? And does her reputation as *la prima donna del mondo*, given to her by poets and courtiers from one end of Europe to the other, not already intrigue him? She knows how to deal with Louis. She assembles her staff and starts to put together a gift—no, not a gift but a presentation—to greet the king when he inevitably reaches Milan. The order is simple: pack up the same things we sent to Ludovico in the spring—the fresh garda and carp, the artichokes and flowers—and to it add a pair of our special falcons and a pair of the marquis's hunting dogs. Have the gifts in their entirety waiting in Ludovico's palace for the arrival of the King of France. Add this note:

> We wish to convey our invitation to His Excellency to come here and visit us. We know that word has reached your ears of us being pro-Sforza. If Your Excellency visits us, he will convince himself that we are true French. We confess, frankly being free of falsehood, that at one time we were very fond of Duke Ludovico, as fond as one can imagine, both for reasons of kinship and because of the affection and honors he showered upon us. But after he began to treat our illustrious consort

badly, our affections began to diminish and we found ourselves
in accord with the aims of His Majesty, the Most Christian
King Louis. Now that he has shown such honors upon our con-
sort, we are indeed a good Frenchwoman. Should Your Excellency choose to accept our invitation to visit, he will find us
clothed in fleurs-de-lis.

> *Your Humble Servant,*
> *Isabella d'Este Gonzaga, Marchesa of Mantua*

Full of lies, but no matter. It would bring about the desired
end—safety for Mantua and for Isabella's Milanese friends.

Still, every cloud has a silver lining, and in her dark moment,
Isabella wonders if Leonardo the Florentine will take her up on
her offer of shelter. Does she dare rekindle that desire? But why
not? As her father said, we must act in the interest of the living,
and she is still very much alive.

Yet she finds that looking at Cecilia's portrait has become unbearable. The portrait freezes that moment in time when Cecilia
was young and lovely, her only care the pleasure of the duke.
None of the young woman's later sorrows can be predicted in her
serene face. Surely she suffered when Beatrice came to court and
removed her from the home and affections of the man she had
known and loved for ten years. Is she, at this moment, packing
whatever her horses can carry and fleeing another cherished
home? When they are all gone, the lot of them erased from memory, the portrait will still stand as a tribute to beauty, intelligence,
and serenity. No one will think of the pain that the sitter endured,
only of her beauty and her good fortune in being immortalized by
the great genius of her day. All of the pain and sorrow will die
with her.

In the end, it will have been the sorrow that was the temporary thing.

*For you, immortality is at the end of a paintbrush. For me, it is at
the end of my husband's cock. I will achieve immortality through the
births of my sons.*

Isabella recalls how shocked she was when Beatrice said those words. It appears now that Beatrice may have been incorrect. Her sons have been whisked off to the court of Emperor Max in frosty Germany, probably pining for their dead mother and the Italian sun. Would they ever be allowed to return to Milan? Which would carry Beatrice on into history: her issue or her images? Would the French smash to pieces the beautiful bust by Cristoforo, along with the marble twin tomb Ludovico had commissioned for himself and his wife? Would the walls of the refectory painted by the great Magistro be whitewashed by the next generation of clergy, wiped away as useless and antiquated by a new generation? Or, more likely, would the French not want reminders of the reign of Ludovico and tear the refectory down, perhaps torturing the friars?

Oh, all of them would end up nothing but specks of Italian dirt, churned together with the rest of their dead countrymen, should la Fortuna be generous and allow them to die on Italian soil; just more creatures who walked the earth and left it. What did it matter anyway? Fortune is having her way with them all: with Isabella, who once believed that Beatrice had been dealt the better hand; and with Beatrice, who could always make the best of any hand dealt to her, amazing knights and ladies with her luck. Now the luck has run out. The city of Milan, which was in its early days of greatness when Leonardo picked up the brush and painted the duke's seventeen-year-old mistress, is about to witness its own end. Everyone who had made it what it was—the Athens of modern Europe—is now running for his life. The great treasures, paid for by the people who finally decided that they no longer wanted to finance the duke's dreams of beauty, would be scattered to the four winds. Like Pericles, whose people got tired of his vast ambitions and found him guilty of theft, Ludovico would pay for his visions of a grand city.

Suddenly Isabella feels very tired, not fatigued in the body but so heavy in the heart that she wants to sink to the ground. She is weary, not just of the present but of the whole of history, how it continues to laboriously repeat itself. How the cast of characters changes but the scenarios remain the same, as if God were some untalented dramatist who could only write one play. She picks up a long black muslin tarp which she had used to block the sunlight from the windows of her studiolo after Beatrice died, for that is what Beatrice's death brought—the end of warmth and light and all that was good. She drapes the cloth over Cecilia's face, letting it fall to the ground, shrouding memories of the innocent past.

To: Isabella d'Este Gonzaga, Marchesa of Mantua
From: Georges d'Amboise, Ambassador to the King of France

Madame,

I humbly beg you to forgive the bad opinion we have held of you. Now that you are a good Frenchwoman, we are your humble servants.

Soon, the much matured face of Cecilia Gallerani, swollen with weight and worry, is standing in Isabella's parlor. She has fled Milan, along with all of Ludovico's other close allies, sneaking away as Louis entered the city. She throws her arms around Isabella, who takes in the stale smell of travel hanging on Cecilia's clothes.

"Forgive me, I am full of gnats and dust," she says. "But thank God for you, Your Excellency. My husband and I were making desperate plans when your messenger arrived. I have brought my two sons with me. The count has gone into hiding. We thought these arrangements best. On the road, soldiers would be less likely to harm the boys if they are traveling with their mother."

Isabella sends Cecilia into her quarters to wash her face and catch her breath. She has known that refugees from Milan would begin to arrive and she has ordered several small palazzos just outside of town to be readied for their guests. This news, plus the opportunity to cleanse the grime of travel from her face and neck, cheers Cecilia, and she settles into Isabella's parlor with a bowl of hot broth and a cup of wine.

"What has happened to our brother-in-law?" Isabella asks, afraid of the answer. Louis has always hated Ludovico. She cannot imagine that his treatment of the duke would be kind.

"He is on the run. As soon as Ludovico heard that the people of his precious Pavia opened their gates to the French, he realized that the citizens of Milan could not be expected to behave any differently."

"Ludovico treated Pavia as one of his personal treasures. After all of his fantastic improvements to that city, why did the people turn on him?"

"Trouble has been brewing. The scholars at the University of Pavia haven't been paid in a year and have been defecting in droves. Taxes kept rising, but nothing improved for the people except Ludovico's buildings and monuments, which doesn't exactly put food in the mouths of the poor."

Isabella feels a wash of shame pass through her body. Her husband, her father, and two of her brothers rode to Pavia to greet Louis. As former friends of Ludovico, they showed the king around his new palace and hunting grounds. A young favorite of Isabella's in their entourage wrote to her to say that the strangest thing in the whole arrangement was that Ludovico's name was never mentioned. "Everyone pretends that the duke has never existed."

"Ludovico finally received word from Emperor Max that he was able to spare reinforcements, and to fortify the Castello until they could arrive. But the duke knew that he could not afford to wait, in the event that Louis reached Milan before the German army. I tried to see him before he left, but I was minutes too late. Oh, everything was in confusion and chaos. He left his treasurer in charge of the Castello and had packed up what he could. I am told that he insisted that his last stop be Beatrice's tomb, where he knelt for hours, crying and begging her forgiveness. You know that he still carries the guilt from the duchess's death. Finally, his men dragged him away, and just in time because Louis was riding in from the south."

Isabella thinks, but does not say, that Ludovico would have enjoyed the demonstration of histrionics at Beatrice's tomb, but he would be careful not to allow it to interfere with his escape.

"You can't imagine what happened next," Cecilia says. "Milan has produced its own Judas. The treasurer to whom Ludovico had entrusted the guardianship of the Castello sent a secret messenger to Louis saying that he would fling open the Castello gates if Louis would cut him a share of the loot. Even the French think the man is disgusting. Imagine Louis's surprise when that grand fortress was surrendered to him without a blow!"

"It seems that there is no end to the number of trusted friends who will betray Ludovico," Isabella says sullenly. "I am almost grateful that God, in His wisdom, took my sister before she had to bear all of this. I hardly understand it. We are aware of Ludovico's defects, but has he deserved this?"

Cecilia leaves the question unanswered. "They say that when Louis entered the Castello, he thought he was entering a fairy tale."

"I thought the same, all those years ago," Isabella says, pushing aside her own memories of riding across the grand moat and into Ludovico's world for the first time. She does not want to cry, not yet.

"The French—those brutish creatures—had never seen rooms of such extravagant size, decorated with our particular Italian grandeur. And the gardens astonished them. The French king has declared it paradise on earth."

"What will become of Ludovico's possessions?" She thinks of all the ancient manuscripts shelved in Pavia, wondering if they have been scattered by the French, who would have no understanding of their real value.

"Here is the story I heard. The teller of the tale swears it is true. The French are desecrating the Castello. They've no idea how to behave. Apparently defecating in one's own hallway is a way of life for their soldiers. And fornicating where they can be seen by others—indeed, in the company of other fornicating couples—does not bother them in the least, but is part of the French national character. The halls of the Castello are dung heaps, Your Excellency; its rooms, the whorehouses of corporals and sergeants."

"What will become of Ludovico's great paintings? His statues from antiquity? His priceless tapestries?"

"Some of it will be preserved, I am sure. The French king does ardently admire our artists. Louis visited the refectory at the Santa Maria delle Grazie and asked his men to investigate moving the entire wall upon which the Magistro's Last Supper is painted to France! I'm grateful that my portrait by him is safe with you, for the king would certainly confiscate it if it had remained in Milan. He's probably going through my rooms, taking whatever he wants, as we speak."

If Louis and his entourage—her father and brothers included—visited the refectory, surely they must have crossed the courtyard to see Beatrice's tomb. How could they have looked at her marble death mask without weeping in front of the French king? How could they have faced the poor duchess, even in death? Isabella hopes that the experience made all of them sick.

"Louis is looking everywhere for the Magistro because he recognizes his genius—as if Ludovico had not done that eighteen years ago."

"And did he remain in Milan?" Isabella asks, hoping to find that Leonardo was one of the refugees headed for her kingdom.

"No. Leonardo packed up his household and fled for the hills of Bergamo, where he intends to conduct some nature experiments, or so he says. He did receive your kind offer of shelter and will undoubtedly come here after he wearies of life in a small hilltop town."

"At least he is safe." Perhaps she will send a messenger to Bergamo to look for Leonardo, repeating her offer. She has already selected a lovely manor home for him on the Po River, with gardens and a view of the water. Old Mantegna will be jealous out of his mind, but what can one do?

"I have a message for you from Isabel of Aragon. She is determined to make peace with Louis. She's going to beg for something for her sons. But if she cannot reach an understanding with him, she's going to come here. Please give her a house that is not within a reasonable distance from where you quarter me! Of course, we all feel compassion for her, but everyone is sick to death of hearing her troubles. She's a beautiful woman, or was. Why doesn't she go get another husband? One that will actually take her to bed?"

"Some women have no sense of how to survive in this world," Isabella offers. "To others, it's an instinct, like an animal's knowledge of how to feed itself. Though it may initially disgust us, we will charm King Louis and clothe ourselves in lilies, until that, too, is no longer in fashion. I had hoped that my sister was one of our kind, but I'm afraid that she gave in to her fragile womanly heart at the end."

"How marvelous she was in her early days. She vacated Ludovico's bed and his heart of me by the force of her will. I admired her all the while. I truly did. And even more so when she magnanimously reached out to me in friendship."

"The poor darling would be in exile now, in Germany, with her sons. I doubt that even my father's new alliance with King Louis could have saved her that. A woman rises and is damned with her husband," Isabella sighs, though she has made a private vow to transcend that fate.

"Your Excellency, I have done a bad thing." Cecilia looks around the room as if to see if anyone is listening. "I have stolen something for you."

"From the Castello?"

"Yes."

"Then you haven't stolen the object, but protected it."

"That is precisely what I thought. I saw this when I tried to see

Ludovico one last time. I simply could not leave it behind for greedy French hands to desecrate."

Cecilia calls for her valet, who, with another man, carries in a bundle, wrapped in layers of cloth. Slowly they unwrap it, carefully handling its heavy contents. Turning it end over end, they reach the final layer of cloth, sitting the bundle on top of a refectory table and letting the muslin fall. Isabella puts her had over her mouth. It is Cristoforo's bust of Beatrice, commissioned by Ludovico before he married her. Her sister's girlish face stares back at her, serene and gentle, tiny curls caressing her chubby, angelic cheeks and the intricate lace that lined her bosom. Isabella can see Beatrice in her dress, excited to pose for the sculptor. She remembers the pains taken that day with Beatrice's difficult mane of hair, how it was twisted, almost torturously, into the tight braid that became Beatrice's signature hairstyle. The image is almost too much for the surviving sister to bear. She embraces Cecilia, hoping that the tears forming in her eyes will be easily controlled. It is guaranteed to be a long week, what with people arriving from Milan. She cannot exhaust herself so early in the day. "You have brought me my sister," Isabella says, her voice catching on a tiny sob.

Isabella's tears are interrupted by the entry of her footman. "Your Excellency, may I announce another visitor?"

"As you wish," the marchesa says, releasing Cecilia.

"Madonna Lucrezia Crivelli, and son, recently of Milan."

Isabella cannot help it; she curses herself for her ways, but there it is. There is nothing she can do about the fact that her first thought is that Lucrezia might have brought with her the painting by the Magistro. Oh, she realizes that she should want to murder the woman for the pain she caused Beatrice, but that is not the idea that crept into her mind. *Forgive me, dear Lord Jesus, for my sins. But I cannot help the order in which ideas occur to me. It is my nature, wicked though it is.*

"I do not recall sending an invitation to Madonna Lucrezia," Isabella says to Cecilia.

"The message we received was that the marchesa would harbor in Mantua all those who had been loyal to the duke."

"I was thinking of sheltering those who had been loyal to my sister, not those in her service who betrayed her."

Could she really turn Lucrezia away? Isabella thinks that she might. It would serve the woman right for sneaking around with Ludovico behind Beatrice's back. *Dear Lord Jesus, forgive us our lack of compassion.*

"Your Excellency, if I might say a few words on behalf of Madonna Lucrezia?"

"I will always hear what you have to say, dear friend."

"The Crivellis are a fine enough family, but hardly of noble birth. I am speaking from experience, Your Excellency. When the Duke of Milan chooses you for his companion, there is little choice in it for the lady. She might express that she is unwilling, but rejecting one of the great princes of Italy is rather challenging for a woman. I imagine that Madonna Lucrezia saw much opportunity in the liaison for her entire family—even for her husband— if she paired with the duke. It is one of the few ways for a woman to elevate the status of her clan. In other words, Your Excellency, I do not believe the liaison was as much a selfish act on the part of Lucrezia as it may appear."

Cecilia is correct, of course. While a princess of Ferrara might be able to control how far she is willing to let her flirtation with a duke proceed, a girl of ordinary birth may not. If she denied her prince, she might cause terrible problems for her family, whereas giving the duke what he wanted would curry favor for all of her loved ones. "Thank you for reminding us that we should not punish another woman for acting in the interests of herself and her family. Is that not what we always do? Regardless of the circumstances of our birth?" She tells her footman to let Madonna Lucrezia into the room.

The little boy looks more like Ludovico than his sons with Beatrice. His mother has had his thin, black baby hair cut in the exact style of Il Moro: long, straight bangs that hang to the brows, and the rest curving around his face and skimming his shoulders.

"How can such a little one possess such hair?" Isabella exclaims, taking the child from his mother, whose eyes are open wide in either astonishment or gratitude or both. She must have expected a less enthusiastic greeting from her lover's wife's sister.

"He is six months old, Your Excellency, and was born with this mane of black hair." Isabella's welcome must have given her confidence because she adds, "The duke once accused me of mating with a horse."

A blush spreads across Lucrezia's face as rapidly as a bad rash. Conscious of her tenuous position at the mercy of her lover's sister-in-law, she smiles awkwardly and turns away from Isabella's disapproving gaze.

Lucrezia's smile drops when she recognizes Beatrice's bust, sitting almost as if in judgment upon the table. A silence falls over the women, and Isabella lets it linger. She hands the baby back to its mother. "Did you believe that you were in danger in Milan, Madonna Lucrezia?"

"King Louis's hatred of Il Moro is well known. I feared for my boy. Yet the duke did not encourage me to flee with him. When I heard that Your Excellency was offering sanctuary, I came immediately. I realize it is awkward. If you wish me to go, I will try to make my way to see relatives at Cremona."

"The duke made no provisions for your safety?" Isabella asks, almost incredulous. It would not be like Ludovico to discard mother and child without a thought for the safety or well-being of either.

"No, he very generously settled upon me estates at Cussago and Saronno. But I'm afraid that those are in the hands of the French now. I have no idea if they will be permanently confiscated."

"What about your husband?"

"He is less than enthusiastic about my welfare since the birth of the duke's son."

An old tale, retold thousands of times in every generation, Isabella thinks. The girl could not have guessed that when she jeopardized her husband's feelings to become intimate with the great prince of Milan, the inheritor of the Houses of Visconti and Sforza, that she was choosing the wrong man. Now, like so many women who took what seemed to be a risk-free gamble, she has been left with no man, only the man's issue. La Fortuna seems to be getting the last laugh on them all.

"Not to worry. I've a small house where you will be comfortable. You may have it all to yourself, depending upon how many appear from Milan in the coming weeks."

Lucrezia bows. "You are the essence of kindness."

"I expect to soon begin negotiations with King Louis for—well, for many things. I will recommend both of you to him, and I will negotiate with his councillors for the return of your estates and your personal property."

Now both of the mistresses of Ludovico bow to the sister of his wife. What a strange world I find myself living in, Isabella thinks. What would Beatrice make of it all? But she remembers Beatrice's passionate campaign for Ludovico's investiture of the title of duke—her sudden shift in loyalty from her beloved Neapolitan grandfather to her husband. Beatrice would have understood everything, even taking in Ludovico's mistress and bastard son. Did Beatrice not do as much herself for Cecilia at one time?

"But our exquisite city!" Lucrezia looks at Isabella as if pleading with her to change events that are well under way.

"The past is gone, my dear," Isabella says, realizing that she sounds more pitiless than the heaviness in her heart would indicate. "All we have is the present, and how we conduct ourselves will determine our futures. My father and brothers and my husband are at this moment in the company of the French king. They have taken him already on a hunting expedition, believe it or not, on Ludovico's lands, where they made sport in the recent past in the company of the duke. I received the letter this very morning. So you see that if the Houses of Gonzaga and Este, two of the most ancient in Italy, have suddenly become French, then you all have the ability to become French. Yes? *Oui? Que pensez-vous du miracle?*"

Lucrezia lightly touches the ivory of the clavichord. "Is this the instrument from the Castello or a copy?"

"It is the very one. It took me more than a year after my sister's death to procure it, but I wanted to have a memento of her. We both love music so much."

"I recall that the duchess could not play it, and was forever inviting musicians to court to play it for her. She took great delight in its sound."

"Did she?"

"Your Excellency, forgive me," Lucrezia says, blushing again. "Of course you know these things."

"My sister loved music and song, though she did not successfully produce either and was constantly demanding to be sung *to* and played *for*. I obliged her throughout our childhoods. Shall we oblige her now?"

Isabella begins to play a melody that all of them would know, one that Beatrice would often request. The two sisters sang it together, usually at the end of an evening, for its lyrics and melody proved rather serious for most parties. Isabella plays one verse and then signals for the others to join in.

How sweetly the three of them sing together. Isabella wonders if the other two have worked as hard as she has to improve their voices. Beatrice never wanted to practice her singing. She liked to chirp along as Isabella played and carried the song. She loved the fun of it. Was there something in mastering the art of singing that is responsible for the three survivors harmonizing like birds who have long shared the same nest, while Beatrice lies in her grave? It seems impossible, yet that idea slides seamlessly into the next, the one that Isabella has turned over and over in her mind for years, but which now calls for fresh examination: What might a marriage between Ludovico and herself—coolheaded and judicious—have produced? Beatrice could enchant Ludovico. She could fuel his ambitions and do his bidding. But she could not control him. Give her credit: Beatrice had been able to represent her husband in matters of diplomacy in a way that her candor and warm nature could cover for his duplicity. But Isabella could have steered him along the path to ever-increasing greatness. Ludovico needed more than a girl with spirit, more than a woman who would do anything to please him. He needed a cool head and a firm hand to help him through the difficult times.

Cecilia's voice rises to take the high note on the last verse while Lucrezia takes the low, coming just under Cecilia's lovely trill and repeating the words in a mournful register. Now all three women have tears in their eyes. Isabella wonders what is motivating the tears of the others. Loss of Ludovico and his patronage? The uncertainty of exile? Sadness at the death of the young duchess, wronged by at least one of them? Or relief that through the seeming misfortune of their lesser births, they have escaped Beatrice's fate? Isabella's tears are for her sister's fate, but also they are new tears over an old question. Would the entire world have been different if Ludovico had not been so damned pleased with Cecilia and had sent off for a wife just a little sooner? It was a bad choice that bespoke of laziness, lust, arrogance, and a lack of respect for political realities. As if all the world would wait upon his personal desires.

There are no small enemies and no small choices. How often had her father drilled that idea into her young head? One must be eternally vigilant in one's thinking. *From what seems a small, light thing, there proceeds a great ruin.* Where has she heard that before? Not from her father, she is sure. But she is sure of its wisdom.

Isabella realizes that in her contemplation, she has dropped out of the singing and rejoins the sweet duet. The three survivors of Ludovico's affection sing their final verse to the one who could not weather his love. Beatrice's young and blameless face looks back at them, passing no judgment. But Isabella doubts that

Ludovico will take that stance. He will blame the French, King Louis, Francesco, the Venetians, her father, even herself. He will blame God, Fortuna, whomever it crosses his mind to abjure. But did he not seal his own fate with his self-indulgence and his foolishness, which had begun long, long ago? And did her sister not design her own demise when she abandoned her senses and decided to love him?

Perhaps la Fortuna is not so fickle after all.

FROM THE NOTEBOOK OF LEONARDO:

Write letter to French commander about protecting property rights to vineyard.

Have the boxes of books ready in the morning for muleteer. (Use some bedding to pack and protect.)

Don't forget to pick up small stove from refectory.

Take sheaths of paper and box of colors belonging to Jean Perréal and do not forget to ask him for his method for drying color and get the recipe for making white salt and colored paper.

Take boxes of seeds, including lily and watermelon.

Send savings to the bank at Monte di Pietà in Florence for safekeeping.

Note to Bramante. Will try to meet him in Rome.

Send Salai with word to Luca Pacioli to be packed and ready in the morning.

The Saletta is unfinished. Bramante's building projects—unfinished. The Castello is a prisoner; the duke's revenues are seized. The duke has lost his state, his possessions, and his liberty. And none of his projects have been completed.

By the time the Magistro arrived in Mantua, Isabella had taken in so many refugees from Milan that she had to scramble to find quarters for him. But she would have thrown her own mother—*God rest her soul, and Lord Jesus forgive me, but you know it's true*—out of her chambers to accommodate so great an artist. She had arranged temporary quarters for him and his travel party, promising him a lovely home either in town or in the countryside if he would remain in her service. But the Magistro had already found a new employer.

"I am on my way to Venice by request of the signory. One of Duke Ludovico's last strategies was to incite the Turks to attack the Venetian frontiers to distract the army. The Turks would do anything to prevent the French from crossing their country again on another Crusade, so they have begun to plague the Venetians with great enthusiasm. I will demonstrate to our friends in Venice how to wipe out the entire barbarian army by flooding the valley they occupy. In addition, the signory has asked to see designs for my inventions to fight the enemy in vessels that sail below the sea's surface."

"How ingenious," Isabella said. "Would you be so kind as to show me the designs? I am most curious."

But the Magistro affected a grave look. Lowering his voice, he answered her. "I cannot, Your Excellency, though nothing would please me more than to indulge your curiosity. I must not divulge these designs because of the evil nature of men, in whose hands it might cause much murder and mayhem on the seabed. As we speak, I have lawyers drawing up contracts in secret. A motto to live by is this: Do not teach anyone, and you alone will excel."

Strange and mysterious man. So he was on his way, with no intention to remain in her service.

"I see that you have made your own plans. But before you leave us, may I remind you of the long and illustrious career Andrea Mantegna has enjoyed under our patronage. We are very stable here at Mantua, not to mention the constancy of rule of my own family at Ferrara. My husband and my father are at this moment entertaining the King of France. You would be protected here, allowed to concentrate on work, and I assure you, without cares of money."

"Only the demands of the Venetian government would allow me to dare to disappoint you, Your Excellency. My strongest desire would be to serve you; however, I have committed to the signory. There is nothing we can do." He said it without sounding as if he was patronizing her, but Isabella was certain that that was precisely what he was doing.

"Do say you will consider the idea. Perhaps when you have finished your service to the Venetians, you will return to us?"

"I am honored by the suggestion. It will be utmost in my mind at all times." He bowed formally, signaling that it was time for him to leave her presence, or rather, signaling that the conversation concerning his employment in Mantua was over. As she looked at the top of his graying head of hair and through to his scalp, she thought that what he had said was incontestably proper but unlikely in the extreme to contain any element of truth. What a perfectly cagey man.

Nevertheless, she would not allow him to get away without sitting for him. She did sense, however, as she had with Leonardo so many years ago, that one must be patient with him. Charming, but no lover of women, he would neither be manipulated nor would he give in to demands. So she waited, housing his small entourage and indulging his requests. His demands were two: he wished to visit the singer Atalante Migliorotti, with whom he originally traveled to Milan before entering Ludovico's service, and he wished to study the frescoes of Andrea Mantegna in the wedding chamber of the Mantuan Castello. Mantegna had painted the walls and ceiling of the chamber in a way that appeared to open the room into the outdoors. The domed ceiling was transformed into a painted sky from which ladies and putti appeared to be looking down into the room from above. The Magistro spent hours in the chamber, studying for a very long time—according to the report Isabella received—the hind of a dog, replete with long tail and saggy testicles. It reminded Isabella of Ludovico's remarking on the fact that Leonardo had spent more time looking at horses' asses than any man in history. Perhaps the Magistro had an ambitious project planned around canines. Or perhaps he was indulging his fascination with anatomy, be it human or bestial.

Isabella waited and waited for Leonardo to suggest a sitting, and finally, on the eve of his departure, he sent a note asking if he might sketch her in her parlor before he left for his military occupations.

When she arrives, he has taken over the room entirely. Her finely carved table is now his workbench, his materials scattered upon cloths next to the bust of her sister. She has not moved it since its arrival, but it causes no reaction in the Magistro that she can discern. Music fills the room. He has employed a duet of flute and lyre players who pluck and blow an airy melody. She feels like a dancer as she takes her seat in the chair that he has repositioned away from the hearth and into a ray of light seeping in from one of the low windows. Without consciously orchestrating her motions, she feels as if her every movement is in time to the music, arranged by some unseen choreographer. She sinks into the chair gracefully, letting her arms fall gently at her sides.

She has worn her best jewelry, which turns out to be a mistake. He asks her—with the utmost deference, of course, but at the same time, makes it known that there is to be no discussion on the matter—to remove the gold necklace of one hundred links, and the large rings adorning her fingers. Her ladies take the jewelry from her, moving like dancers to the rhythms of the stringed instrument.

"Utter simplicity, Your Excellency," he says. "When I paint a woman, I wish to reveal the essence of the woman, not the extravagance of her jewels. The adornments detract."

She wants to issue a hundred commands to him to make sure that she gets the portrait of which she has dreamed for so long. Yet he invites no comments, and she is enjoying the dreamlike quality that the music is creating. Has this not been for so long a dream? Why should the reality not feel as such? Isabella recognizes the boy apprentice whose indifference toward his master she had seen displayed in Leonardo's studio years ago. He is still beautiful, this young man whom Leonardo calls Salai, and still serves the Magistro with an attitude alternating between flamboyance and disdain; disdain to be serving anyone at all, or disdain to be serving the artist, Isabella cannot tell. But Salai, now tall and probably past his twentieth birthday, produces the supplies Leonardo requests—chalk of red and black, pastels of many colors for shading, sheets of paper of different grades and thickness and size—with a flourish that should be reserved for the presentation of great creations of one's own. Salai offers the Magistro's tools with the pomp with which a great chef enters a dining room with his specially prepared delicacies and presents them to a king. The apprentice, too, seems as if he is dancing. The young man's curls are still abundant, unlike the Magistro's, which have begun to thin. Though the artist is still fit, he has affected a slightly hunched posture that Isabella has not seen in the past. His dress has not diminished in style or extravagance. Both men did seem to bother to pack all their finery before fleeing the French, she cannot help but notice. The apprentice is dressed in grades of silvery fabric, with fancy oversized sleeves that keep getting in the way of performing his duties. His every movement threatens to disturb something that he has just carefully placed. The Magistro pays him no mind as he distractedly receives the materials, staring at Isabella as if she were not at all real but some object in nature he is contemplating.

"I have in mind to do a sketch in which the head is in profile with the body in a counter pose turned forward," he says. "As if the body and the face might say two entirely different things. The language of the face expresses itself though the eyes and the smile, but the language of the body has so many more tools."

Isabella wants to talk to him, to discuss the theories behind his art, to hear the contents of the mind that has created such extravagant beauty. But she does not speak to him. It would be like interrupting an expert marksman as he aims his shot, or a poet as he searches for the exact metaphor.

He gently moves her arms, placing them as he would like them to be. "One must always make the figure so that the breast is not turned in the same direction as the head. Let the movements of the head and arms be natural and pleasing, with various twists and turns. The hands folded just so. Yes, I like that. You will see. You will be very pleased with the drawing."

The threat of this endeavor being arrested in this, its nascent stage, startles Isabella out of her dreamy state. "This is just a preliminary sketch, is it not? You will produce the oil before not too long?"

Oh, how horrible it would be to remain a mere chalk drawing, never bursting into the full bloom of an oil. Never to receive the colors, the qualities of dark and light, the shadows, the gradations, the subtleties and translucent beauty that only an oil could offer. She mustn't allow it to happen. But the tales of Leonardo's procrastination, and the creative ways that he frustrated Ludovico for years, falls upon Isabella's memory with a giant thump, which reverberates throughout her entire system. How will she see to it that he completes the oil and not leave her as a mere sketch; she, Isabella d'Este, muse to many, must not be just another study, a mass of scribbles and lines on a thin sheet of paper!

"Oh yes, the painting. Do not worry. It will capture Your Excellency in all her stunning complexity. But these works do take some time, and I ask that Your Excellency be patient."

"Are you certain about the pose, Magistro? A profile?" A profile. So conventional. So very yesteryear in style. The great beauty of his portraits is that he does not paint in profile. It is hard to capture a soul when it is not looking in one's direction.

"But in your case, Your Excellency, I do not think of this as a profile. I think of it as looking ahead, into the future."

He smiles at her in a way that she thinks is not a smile that an artist reserves for his patron, or for one of illustrious birth, but one that—just for an instant—allows her to know that he has, indeed, seen into her soul. He's read it, she thinks, and accurately so. She is one who will always keep her sights set forward.

"Perhaps that is an attribute we share, Maestro. Perhaps that is why the two of us are here, while others, less fortunate, less forward-thinking, have been left to the past."

"An honor, Your Excellency, to share any attributes with you at all."

She can tell that he is pondering whether or not she has given him, or either of them, a compliment.

Lowering his eyes, he picks up the black chalk and hesitates not one second before letting it hit the paper in slow swirls of motion. His face, however, is still and blank, revealing not one clue as to how he feels about either his subject or the likeness of her which he is in the process of creating.

She wants to talk more about a schedule for the painting, but she dare not. The sitting has begun. She is frustrated, trying to remain still and dreamy for Leonardo, for she wishes to be portrayed with an expression of utmost intelligence and serenity. The two are not always complementary qualities present at the same time in the same face, but if anyone can capture the complexity, as he said, it would be the Magistro. But she mustn't spoil it by allowing the more commandeering aspects of herself to be exposed. She must be remembered as a woman of the future, a woman of vision, not the bossy creature he must sometimes think she is.

If only she could sit for him and watch his progress at the same time. With other artists, she has not had this desire. She has always known that if she was not pleased with the results, she could either cajole or threaten them into making changes until she is satisfied. But the Magistro is different. She is all too aware that he will make his sketch and be on his way before she can have a proper word with him. The man is inflexible, even for an artist.

So she sits quietly, feeling the softness of her hands as they lie one upon the other, hoping that she is the embodiment of Serenity itself, when his pronouncement that he is finished startles her out of her reverie. Before she can speak, he is packing it away.

"But, may I not see it?"

"Oh no. Not before I shade it properly. I will spend the next several days doing so. And then I shall be off."

"But what will you work from for the oil?" she asks, hoping that her alarm—her distrust of him to finish the project—cannot be read on her face.

"I intend to make a copy of it to take with me. You shall have my original."

And with that pronouncement, he and his assistant and his musicians are gone.

Three days later, he has the sketch sent to her. She asks of his whereabouts only to learn that he left Mantua at sunrise. Of course. His letter thanks her profusely for her hospitality, promising her delivery of the portrait of herself in oil at an undisclosed date in the future, depending upon the extent to which the Venetians require his services in matters of weaponry and military engineering. But he is gone, escaping her comments on the sketch, absolving himself of any chance of hearing requests for changes, or, worse yet, another sketch entirely. Isabella had stayed awake most of the night preparing herself for the latter, wondering how she would phrase such a request, should she look upon Leonardo's sketch and not be pleased. One would have to be most discreet. Direct, but not demanding. Solicitous and complimentary, yet firm in expressing one's desires. And if all else failed, there was always the promise of money, which generally accomplished miraculous results with artists. A little up front, with much more upon delivery, if one ever hopes to receive the promised piece.

She snatches the sketch, sheathed between two thick pieces
of parchment, from the messenger and spirits it away to her private rooms, feeling her heart pump louder and faster as she puts
the paper down on her desk, revealing it. She is looking into the
future. Her face is in profile, but the rest of her body is forward.
She was not entirely successful in suppressing her more commanding aspects, because she looks, to herself at least, as if she
might be gazing upon some project she commissioned, judging
whether or not it meets with her approval. Perhaps this is what
the Magistro meant to convey, that it is this very project upon
which she is looking. She does appear to be composed within
herself. And intelligent, yes. She appears serene and commanding all at once. The lines of her face, her hair, and her body are
soft, though, not serious and pinched. Even the hard stripes of
her garment have been softened to flatter the curve of her bosom.
She is sure that the cut of her dress was actually lower than it is
drawn. She appears more serene than sexual, that is certain. But
there is nothing unflattering about the piece, though she hopes
that the tiny pocket of fat under her chin does not make it into the
oil. What strikes her most are her hands, folded so simply, with
the index and middle fingers slightly separated; relaxed and natural, yet looking as if she might be holding something inside herself with those hands, which she does not wish to be revealed.

How she would like to speak to him about it, not to demand
the revisions he undoubtedly fled at daybreak to escape, but to
compliment him on the piece, to say that this sketch alone has
fulfilled her dreams. No, she would not say that because if she did,
he would never deliver the promised oil. And that, she must have.

She did not dream that the Magistro would not deliver the
sketch himself, instead entrusting it to a messenger of the court.
In retrospect, however, she should have anticipated the sly move
on his part, considering his reputation for weaseling out of finishing commissions. And in this case, he did not even give her
the opportunity to offer him money, instead sending the sketch
in exchange for her hospitality. She has no hold over him.

Avenues open to her to procure her precious oil spill forth in her mind. If he will not enter her service, she will hound whoever becomes his patron until that person uses the power of the purse string. If he thinks he can escape her by going to Venice he is mistaken because she has, more than once, had the old doge eating out of her palm. But what if he does not remain in Venice and ends up in foreign service? What if he, in his profound desire to find money for his ambitious and slightly fantastic projects, goes into the service of the sultan of the Turks? It would be just like Leonardo to sell the sultan on his magic, and, from what Isabella has heard, just like the sultan to buy it. What would she do then? Play the vixen to a barbarian? What hold might she find over the sultan of a foreign empire? How could she have allowed this to happen? The Magistro has slipped out of her grip like water. She is not happy, yet she feels a slow smile creep across her face. She, Isabella d'Este, Marchesa of Mantua, and daughter of the wiliest man in Italy, has been outwitted, for the moment, by a painter.

Imagine.

Epilogue

XXI * IL MONDO (THE WORLD)

IN THE YEAR 1506;
IN FRENCH-OCCUPIED MILAN

*I*SABELLA wishes to say so much more to her sister, who, lying in the church under cold marble, feels like a long-yearned-for confessor. Finally, here is one to whom Isabella can confide; one who will not take her words, spoken in confidence, and sell them to the highest bidder or the most pressing enemy. She has grown so accustomed to dissembling, especially in the last years. What relief to kneel by Beatrice's still form and pour out her thoughts. Isabella and Beatrice had wasted so many hours in inglorious competition over meaningless things. Now she wishes that Beatrice were at her side, an ally in the hundred private and public wars, both spoken and unspoken, in which she must engage to stay alive. At the rear of the church, she hears the rustle of fabric. Throats begin to clear in muffled coughs. The entourage grows impatient. Is it because is it late? Or because they cannot wait to inform some French official that the marchesa, despite her posture of being a good French loyalist, has lingered too long at the crypt of the dead Sforza duchess? Who in her party would play the Judas? she wonders. At this moment, only the dead can be trusted. She whispers:

Times are dark, my sister. Either Fortuna has ceased to smile upon us, or is demonstrating for us her great irony. The Pope's bastard and many a man's whore, Lucrezia Borgia, has married our brother and rules in Ferrara in the stead of our pious and saintly mother. Her father purchased the title of Duchess of Ferrara with a large dowry and the threat of invasion. Can you imagine the grief of our dear late father, who despised the Spanish pope? At least that corrupt creature is dead, probably from poison. Oh, no one dies anymore of natural causes. But the Borgia witch has enchanted our beloved brother. I will not allow it to stand. You would not believe who else she is taking between her legs besides our brother, and it makes me too sick in the stomach to say the name. The presence of Borgia blood in the court of our parents has in-spired acts of bloodshed and horror, even from members of our own family. Oh, Beatrice, regret not the sorrows you did not live to endure!

And yet, every morning the sun rises, bringing joys with the same randomness as it brings distress. King Louis has been thrice to visit me in my lodgings, where we discuss all manner of subjects. He is not hunched over and ugly like his predecessor, but tall and handsome, and rises gallantly as the ladies enter the room. Tonight I will dance with him in the rooms you built in the Rocchetta, decorated by Bra-mante and the Magistro. Ironic, no? Louis has held jousting tourna-ments in my honor, and guess who has taken all the prizes? Our own Galeazz, who seems to thrive under every master. It is strange, my dar-ling sister. We do not speak of you, or of Ludovico, even as memories of you haunt the very rooms where we eat, sleep, and dance, where we feel at times your spirit watching us in our duplicity. But what might be our choices? Death and dishonor? Exile? Demise? The Gonzagas might have lost Mantua, and our father, Ferrara, over the mention of Sforza. No, the whole cast of characters assembled long ago by Ludovico is still here, reading their dialogue as if from an old play. The words are the same, but the names of the patrons have changed. Oh, it is strange, Beatrice, and not a game you would have enjoyed playing. For when I speak, I hear the hollowness of my own voice mingling with echoes of the past.

Enough now. I must go, or I will never leave you. There is much to do before the ball. Did I mention the rumors of a new portrait by the Magistro? They say that a merchant approached Leonardo in Florence to do a portrait of his wife, just at a time when the Magistro needed to make a quick sum of money. He painted the woman and delivered the commission, but not before making a copy of it for himself. For the last three years, he has carried it with him wherever he goes, changing and improving it until the sitter is no longer the merchant's wife but some other being. Leonardo is very secretive about it all and will not reveal the identity of his model. But I have heard descriptions of the piece, which sound as if it might have been inspired by the drawing he made of me.

Is it possible, Beatrice, that after all our machinations over the Magistro—that after painting all of Ludovico's lovely swans—I would emerge as his especial muse?

Can you hear the muffled complaints and sighs of disapproval from my companions? If their mistress is found to be a traitor to the French king, they will accompany her to the dungeon, or wherever Louis would choose to put me. I cannot spare another minute, or I might pay for it with my kingdom. If you have any truck with the Lord, ask Him to take pity on the living. And be thankful that death has exonerated you from the evil which we must not only witness but in which we must participate.

Isabella kisses both marble cheeks of her sister's death mask, lips lingering for a moment on the cold, smooth roundness. Ludovico's face she cannot look at, for it is too lifelike, and he is still with the living, though he might as well be dead. Here she is, gloating just a little over her sister's crypt, still hoping, all these years later, that she has won the final victory in their race for primacy. But that is the way with human beings. Beatrice has transcended such pettiness, she is sure, and is at this moment forgiving Isabella's pitiful human frailty.

She tries to pull away from the majestic sarcophagus, but it is

difficult to leave, as if in parting from Beatrice, she is leaving behind some essential element of herself that is too cumbersome to
carry with her into the future. She would like to remain longer,
but realizes that time too long spent with the dead is turning her
still-warm flesh cold.

She takes her time leaving the Santa Maria delle Grazie, allowing her entourage to fall in behind her and leading them to the
prior's office, where she asks permission to enter the refectory to
cast one more glance at the Magistro's portrait of Our Lord and
His Apostles. She ignores the subtle groans and sideways glances
of her attendants, who cannot wait to return to the Castello to
dress for Louis's ball. She asks them to remain in the courtyard
while she alone enters the refectory. The air outside is chilly for a
spring day. The sun is almost setting, and the temperature is sure
to drop. That will teach them. It might even rain.

One cannot take in Leonardo's mural in a glance, for it is not
merely a painting of an event but a fully animated production. Yet it
is the resignation in the face of Jesus that captures Isabella's attention in this, her second viewing. She is struck by Jesus' quiet acqui-
escence to His fate, in contrast with the outrage, shock, and denial
registered on the faces of the Apostles. It is as if He is saying—re-
gretfully, but with complete acceptance—that this is the very nature
of man, to betray. And is it not? One thousand five hundred years
after God sent His Son to earth to demonstrate the Godliness of all,
we are still the same—betrayers. Rejecting the hand that would
reach for us from above and pull us up into Grace, into Glory, into
Heaven. "The betrayal of Judas began on a Wednesday." That is
what they said in Milan when all faces turned away from Ludovico
and toward the French king.

Isabella thinks that she has seen that expression of resignation on Leonardo's face. The Magistro painted the face of Jesus
nonchalant at the moment in which He reveals His awareness that
He will be betrayed by one whom He has loved. That same artist
quickly forgot the favors enjoyed under Ludovico and now serves
the King of France. Who can blame him? He, too, was betrayed,

when Ludovico foiled each of Leonardo's ambitious plans—by keeping him busy with ephemera, by withholding his pay, by sending the coveted bronze for the horse for cannon fodder.

The Horse now sits in ruins in the grand piazza at the entrance to the Castello, shot to pieces by zealous French archers out to have some fun. Why it has not yet been removed is a puzzle to Isabella. It lies in bits and pieces, its noble body parts, so lovingly studied by the Magistro, fallen to the ground. The head, legs, and torso lie inert and in shambles—dissected, just the way that it was said that Leonardo cut up human bodies to see what was inside. What must he think when he sees his masterpiece destroyed, crumbling to greater decay with every rain? In years to come, who will care that the French occupied Italy for a brief period of time, for Isabella is certain it will be brief, considering the scope of her country's history. She is not even bothering to learn good French. But Leonardo's beautiful horse, which might have lasted as long as the statues of the ancient masters, will be dust, just like those who brought about its demise.

She is weary of these thoughts, these problems of loyalty and mortality. She turns away from the face of Jesus, only to confront the image of her sister on the wall opposite, painted into Montorfano's mural. Beatrice is in prayer, hands folded ever so delicately, face luminous and composed as she looks upon Our Lord's suffering. The Magistro captured a sadness in Beatrice that Isabella had not observed while her sister was alive. Perhaps it settled upon her at the end, along with her troubles. Beatrice would be pleased to know that, from across the room, Jesus might be gazing upon her for all eternity; two martyrs, her sister and the Christ. Two innocents betrayed.

Enough of the dead. Isabella walks out of the room, leaving the refectory, the church, and the corpse of Beatrice behind and reentering the world of the living where the setting sun has turned the white blossoms of the trees in the courtyard to a deep violet.

"Take us to the Corte Vecchia," she commands the driver of her carriage.

The attendants try once more to stifle their dismay. They did not know that the marchesa was going to take them on an entire tour of the city of Milan, wearing them out and denying them the hours they require to assemble their costumes and toilette for the evening's festivities. All the better, she thinks. The gaggle of beautiful ladies who accompany her everywhere and for which she is known sometimes arrive a bit overdressed. The less time they have to apply rouge to their cheeks and jewels to their hair, the better. For they know that it is their job to support the beauty and appearance of Isabella without exceeding it. Women being what they are, however, a few always try to get away with outshining their mistress.

"Come, ladies, quit your groaning," she sighs. "One must be flexible if one does not want to end one's life upon one cross or another."

She will leave Milan in the morning, she has decided, even if it does not please the French king. She can no longer linger in this city of ghosts. She will invent some excuse that will spirit her away, and it will have to suffice. But there is one mission left to accomplish before she departs—one, in addition to the further bewitching of Louis this evening. And this one will be the more challenging.

The Magistro is once again making his home in the Corte Vecchia, the old ducal palace where Ludovico arranged for him to live so that he could use the courtyard for working on the horse. She does not anticipate seeing him; he is Master of Decoration for Louis's ball, and would be rushing about the Castello rehearsing whatever he plans for the evening's dramatic presentations. All the better, she thinks, for she does not wish to speak with him, only to get a glimpse at the portrait.

No one is at the studio but a servile young boy. He is not even an apprentice, Isabella can tell, but a servant, who is amazed to see such a grand personage appear unannounced and demanding to see the Magistro's portrait of the lady, which he has brought with him from Florence. Thanks to Isabella's spies, she can describe it accurately, so that there is no mistaking it for another, and no way that this poor factotum can deny her request.

The painting sits on a stained easel, covered by a soiled muslin cloth. The boy lifts the cloth, holding it above the face as if he thinks that Isabella is only going to take a quick glance. She waves at the cloth so that he removes it entirely, and then waves again so that he will leave her to her own thoughts as she views the portrait.

The woman is not beautiful at all, but simple, almost peasant-like. Her hair is darker than Isabella's and her features indistinct from thousands of other Italian women who flood the streets and markets of their cities. She is not looking into the future, but glancing a bit to her right, with her hands folded in front of her. She smiles slightly at nothing in particular. The landscape behind her reminds Isabella of the Magistro's strange rocks in which he had placed the Virgin, the angel, the infant Christ, and the baby John the Baptist in the painting at San Francesco Grande. The jagged green mountains behind the sitter almost disappear into an ominous gray-blue sky. A body of water floats behind the subject's head, and a winding path cuts through what appears to be a riverbed. Is the Magistro trying to give the woman a way out, as Galeazz once suggested of the door in the portrait of Cecilia?

The woman wears no jewelry. Her eyebrows are almost non-existent. The hair is netted, the garment, a simple dress of brown velour, with decorative stitching at the bodice and neckline. She is adorned by nothing, only luminescent skin and that odd fracture of a smile, which, combined with the background, gives the portrait a mystical air.

At any rate, it is emphatically not Isabella d'Este. Now she must start over with the Magistro, demanding again that he deliver the promised oil. Six years and a thousand letters to him have passed and still—nothing! Oh, if he thinks he can continue to outwit her he is wrong. She will hound him to the grave to get that picture. His latest letters of apology use the excuse that he has been called into the service of the King of France, a very de-

manding—and not to be supplanted—master. Does this poor
painter have any idea of the sway she has over Louis? The king has
suggested that she come to Paris for the birth of his next child so
that she can be its godmother. Why does the artist spend so much
energy evading his commitment when it would take so much less
time to simply appease her by painting the portrait? She has patiently manipulated every artist she has encountered. Eventually
they succumb, either to her charms or her threats or her money.
The Magistro is not getting any younger; he must be near his fifti-
eth year. Mantegna—dear, sour-spleened, irreplaceable Mantegna, who lies ill and dying in Mantua—was just beginning his
finest works at that age. But Leonardo is different. It would be just
like him to die before she could get what she wanted from him.

She folds her arms across her chest, stepping back and taking
a final look at the Magistro's obsession. True, it can never be con-
strued to be her. And yet she sees elements of the sketch of herself in the portrait. She can't help but notice that the hands are
folded in the very same way, crossing the body as if to hold in
something that must not be revealed. Even the middle and index
fingers are slightly parted, in the exact same manner and distance from each other. The shape of the neckline is the same, replete with the absence of jewels. The smile is a subtle one, lips
together, just as in her portrait. If this subject has been reworked
to be no one in particular, but is reminiscent of Leonardo's drawing of Isabella, then she has in fact been one of the muses of the
Magistro. The drawing of her anticipated this painting—anyone
who bothers to look carefully may confirm it. The hands, the
arms, the soft lines, the roundness of the bosom, the subtle
smile. The drawing of Isabella is present, here in this painting,
with which the Magistro is reportedly obsessed. But what a
strange man he is to take a portrait and rework it until it is not the
subject at all. What is the purpose? She thought that the Magistro's portraits were meant to evoke the soul of the sitter.
Whose soul might he evoke if the sitter is no particular person?

Then it dawns on her while looking into the brown eyes of the woman, which are shifting slightly to the right, as if something has distracted her out of her meditations. With a genius like Leonardo, even a portrait of another is more a reflection of him than it is of his subject. The soul he means to evoke is his own.

GALEAZZ di Sanseverino's suffering has only made him more attractive. The gentle scrim of melancholia that has fallen over his beautiful features gives him an air of mystery, a new layer beyond the qualities of the masculine ideal that previously made him so desirable. Isabella has tried to dance many dances with him because he is the only person in the room whose face displays what she is feeling on this evening and in this room: that the familiarity of the grand parlor is overbearing. The ladies and gentlemen of the court smile, swirling to the music as if this is their first visit to the Castello, and not a place where they have danced and dined under a former patron. Each time the dance partners meet in rendezvous, Isabella clutches Galeazz's arm tightly, holding on to him while smiling at the king, whose eyes she tries to keep locked on hers. All the while she accepts the compliments praising her as *la plus belle dame du bal* and *la femme extraordinaire* and *la femme qui danse à merveille* that whirl around her from the French noblemen dancing in her circle.

At midnight, the king announces that he has a surprise for his guests. The genius, Leonardo the Florentine, has entered his service and has created a magical beast for the pleasure of the court. It will be unveiled on this night in honor of Louis's supremacy over Italy. A black velvet curtain glittering with planetary symbols and celestial designs rises, while giant chandeliers, each with a hundred lit candles, fall gently on chains from the ceiling, lighting the small stage. As the drape rises, a lion—made of metal and larger than life—is revealed. The animal's big green eyes, which seem to be of painted glass, stare at the crowd. The musicians begin to play a tune that Isabella does not recognize, but from the reaction of the French officers must surely be an anthem or military song of sorts. As the trumpeters blare the strident melody, the animal's mouth magically opens, spewing dozens of lilies at the feet of the King of France. Isabella thinks that she sees a thin wire controlling the action, but she is not sure. What causes the flowers to thrust forward, she cannot imagine. The crowd gasps at the miracle of it all—of the flower-spewing lion; of the king who has taken Italy entirely out of the hands of Italians—and then rounds of polite applause accompany the last rush of lilies falling to the ground. Louis walks through the litter and takes a bow. He graciously holds out his arm, introducing the Magistro, who appears wearing a cape that matches the velvet curtain. The artist looks very old, much older than his years. The lines in his face have deepened and his lovely mass of curls is almost entirely gray. His beard is trimmed, but very long. He looks as if he is trying to turn himself into some sort of wizard. The expression on his face reminds her of that of his Jesus—all-knowing and resigned.

Yes, she wants to say to him, this is how we survive. Isabella smiles at Leonardo, feeling her plans to coerce him into making her portrait dissipate. Louis will follow the precise path with the Magistro as Ludovico—fritter away the artist's time and genius in the service of his own glorification and vanities. Here is Leonardo, the visionary, serving the new master just like the rest of them, whores all. If Leonardo must serve Louis with his magical lion and dozens of other designs not of his own choosing, then perhaps with the portrait of the woman, who is no one in particular, he is serving himself alone. And she will let him. Maybe, at some time in the future, she will ask him to make her a nice picture of the Christ when he was young and working with His father as a carpenter, before His face bore the look of resignation after Judas sealed His destiny. She does not have the heart to pursue the artist anymore.

Isabella sees that the king is staring at her, so she dips her chin to the side in a manner that she knows is fetching and flirtatious and stares back. Then she turns away from him as she would from any man, for every woman knows that all men, even kings, are intrigued by a woman who captures their attention and then turns away. She takes hold of Galeazz's sturdy arm.

"Time has not made you less daring, Your Excellency," Galeazz says, eyes falling in admiration on Isabella's deep décolletage. She had been inspired to have the seamstress lower the neckline so that the moons of her nipples were revealed. She had been viewing erotic Greek vases from Crete for purchase in the week prior, which gave her the idea. The women looked so enticing with their bosoms pushed high and their nipples exposed. Timeless! She instructed the seamstress to make the facsimile, revealing the tiny hint of pink, just enough to ignite the imagination.

"My husband has insulted the French king so many times that I must invent new tricks to keep him from seizing Mantua," Isabella replies.

"Indeed, madame, he will wish to seize something else instead," Galeazz replies, the old dance from love of verbal parry returning to his eyes.

Monsieur d'Amboise, the ambassador Isabella has feverishly courted because of his intimacy with the king, swoops into their dance circle, eyes grazing Isabella's cleavage. "When I write my report to the ladies in Paris, all of them will instantly emulate your design," he says.

Isabella feels the dancers pulling back from her and Galeazz, and she looks up to see what has caused them to ripple away, as if a stone has been tossed into water. The king approaches, his hand stretched out to take Isabella's arm from Galeazz. The knight immediately offers the lady to his king, who takes Isabella's hand and kisses it, eyes lingering on her exposed breasts. The king is tall enough so that when he stands, he has a lovely aerial view of Isabella's cleavage, which, she notices, he takes in amply.

"In all of Europe, could there be another woman like you?" the king asks.

Isabella looks at Galeazz before she answers. "There was one, Your Majesty, but I am sad to say, she is no longer with us."

No one speaks, for everyone within earshot knows to whom Isabella refers. Louis's smile does not leave his face. If he has caught Isabella's reference, he does not reveal it. He pulls her arm gently, bringing her closer to him and whispering in her ear, "Tomorrow, in your quarters?"

"*Je vous attendrais*," she whispers in return. The king releases her hand, placing it on the arm of Galeazz. The music begins again, and Galeazz leads Isabella back into the dance. She wonders if he will mention Beatrice; if her cryptic comment to Louis has startled some part of his memory that he can no longer suppress. But he does not. She imagines that as with herself, the memories are stored, to be taken out at some indefinite point in the future—probably old age—when one can relive them without fear of reprisal.

"I must say, Your Excellency, that I have to agree with the king. In my travels, the ladies of Europe greet me with only one question," Galeazz says. " 'What is the famous Isabella, Marchesa of Mantua, wearing these days?' I do wish they would ask for something else, but they do not. D'Amboise is right. Even in the frigid northern kingdoms, the ladies will all be baring their bosoms within a fortnight."

"Oh, it is a burden to be scrutinized so," she replies.

"What will you do then, Isabella, after you have scandalized the world with your latest fashion?"

She stops dancing for a moment. What will she do? She doesn't have to think of it now. She is, after all, a woman perennially looking toward the future, as if with her steady gaze, she is creating it. It is as if her eyes create a clear path in whatever direction she turns them, so that the past is always retreating and the future takes care of itself. "I don't know what I shall do, Galeazz. I suppose I'll just have to invent something new."

La Fortuna and Our Characters

Isabella d'Este survived the political upheaval and wars of her time, the rise and fall of empires, the turbulent days of the early Reformation, and a notorious rivalry with her sister-in-law Lucrezia Borgia to become one of history's most influential patrons and collectors of art. She gave birth to eight children and outlived her husband by many years, befriending popes, emperors, kings, and titans of art like Perugino, Rafael, Bellini, and Titian. She saw the sack of Rome by the army of Emperor Charles V in 1527, during which time she sheltered two thousand of her closest friends in the Palazzo Colonna, negotiating for their safety with both sides. She died in 1539 at the age of sixty-five. Her last words were, "I am a woman who learned to live in a man's world." Leonardo's drawing of Isabella is in the Louvre. He never painted the promised oil. Her beauty and intelligence are most evident, however, in Mantegna's *Venus and Apollo on Mount Parnassus*, also in the Louvre, in which she is depicted as a pregnant muse in the center of the painting.

Ludovico Sforza raised another army from exile and reentered Milan, where the fickle populace, tired of the French, welcomed him. But his brother-in-law, Francesco Gonzaga, again refused to come to his aid with an army, and so Ludovico was captured by the French, betrayed by a Swiss captain for thirty thousand ducats, a number strikingly reminiscent of thirty pieces of silver. Ludovico spent the rest of his life languishing in a French prison, dying there in 1508.

Galeazz di Sanseverino, though loyal to Ludovico until the end, became a favorite of the French kings Louis XII and François I. Louis restored his estates and his fortune, and eventually he rose to become *Grand Ecuyer de France*, the Master of the Horse. He died at sixty-five, a formidable age for a warrior, in the Battle of Pavia, where, ironically, he had spent many happy days with Beatrice and Ludovico. He never remarried.

Beatrice's sons, **Ercole** (aka Maximilian) and **Francesco**, were reared at Innsbruck by their cousin Empress Bianca Maria Sforza. Maximilian was restored as Duke of Milan in 1512, but was ousted in 1515 by King François and made to live out the rest of his life in France, though not imprisoned like his father. Francesco reigned as Duke of Milan from 1530 to 1535. He died as a result of complications from an earlier assassination attempt. His widow, Christina of Denmark, is famous for her response to a later offer of marriage from King Henry VIII: "Unfortunately, I have but one head. If I had two, I would be at His Majesty's service."

After the death of Francesco Sforza, the duchy of Milan became part of the Hapsburg Empire under Charles V, grandson of Emperor Maximilian.

Cecilia Gallerani eventually returned to Milan after Isabella gave her a good recommendation to King Louis as "a lady of rare gifts and charms." Her son by Ludovico, Cesare, became a soldier. He died in 1515. Cecilia had three children with Count Bergamini, who died in 1514, after which Cecilia continued to host a literary salon. Though Italy's poets considered her one of the great muses, her own poetry was never published. Leonardo's portrait of Cecilia, *Lady with an Ermine*, is in the Czartoryski Museum at Kraków, Poland.

Lucrezia Crivelli lived for many years under Isabella's protection at Mantua in the Rocca di Canneto. Her son by Ludovico, Gianpaolo, became the Marquis of Caravaggio and a soldier, serving, for a time, under his half brother, Francesco. Gianpaolo died in 1535, only a few days after his half brother. He had been on his way to request that the emperor invest him with the title of Duke of Milan, being Ludovico's only living son.

Leonardo's portrait of Lucrezia, known as *La Belle Ferronnière*, named for the decorative ribbon on her forehead, as well as *The Virgin of the Rocks*, in which she may have served as Leonardo's model for Mary, are in the Louvre.

Isabel of Aragon continued in her pattern of gloom and bad luck, signing her letters "a woman unique in her disgrace." She, too, spent years living under Isabella's protection in Mantua. Eventually, she returned to Naples, where she died in 1524. A lovely drawing of her by Giovanni Boltraffio serves as the poster for the Ambrosiana Gallery in Milan. The original is too fragile for display.

Though revered throughout Europe, **Leonardo da Vinci** had money troubles that continued to plague him. After his second stay in Florence, he traveled to Rome, where he worked for Giuliano de' Medici, but his health began to fail. In 1516, the French king François I invited the great master to live near his castle at Amboise, giving him a manor house in Cloux. There Leonardo spent his last days reorganizing his notebooks. He died on May 2, 1519, not long after his sixty-seventh birthday. He was never again as productive as during his years at the court of Milan.

Leonardo's portrait of **Beatrice d'Este** on the south wall of the refectory at Santa Maria delle Grazie has disintegrated almost to shadow, but her faint profile is still discernable in Montorfano's mural, nestled in the drapes of the habits of the Dominican nuns, on the wall opposite *The Last Supper*. Cristoforo Romano's lovely bust of Beatrice is in the Louvre, and the stunning marble tomb of Ludovico and Beatrice is now in the Certosa at Pavia.

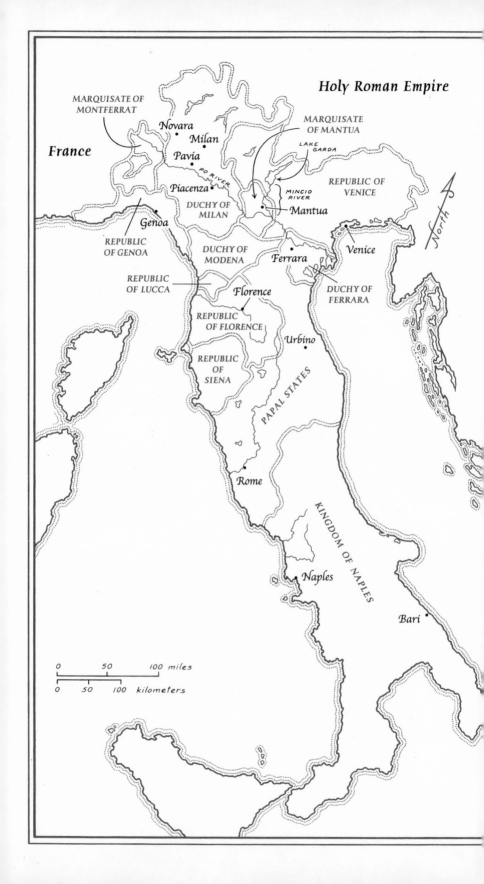